Feline Whispers

Rive Cypher

Published by Bobby Parker, 2024.

This is a work of fiction. Similarities to real people, places, or events are entirely coincidental.

FELINE WHISPERS

First edition. November 19, 2024.

Copyright © 2024 Rive Cypher.

ISBN: 979-8227923639

Written by Rive Cypher.

A wish to the stars

The Thai woman slammed the door and left the place, her feet taking long strides. She refused to cry, she wouldn't let them have the pleasure. In her mind the image repeated itself, her girlfriend and her friend.

-Lisa, love, it's not what it seems!

-There is an explanation for this, Lisa, please let me explain, Tzu and I...

-You... And you...- he pointed at one and then at the other- Go to hell! I don't want to see you again for the rest of my life!

The cold seeped into her skin making her shiver, or was it the result of the helplessness she felt? It hurt, of course it did, not only because of the infidelity but because he had done it expressly with one of her friends. That night he planned to take the big step and finally introduce her to his parents. Lisa was not the traditional kind of girlfriend, at 23 years old she had not introduced them to anyone, she had not even told them that she liked girls. *"I don't have time for relationships ."* It was the answer he usually gave them to evade the question. He did not expect that when he entered his girlfriend's apartment he would find her in a passionate kiss that he knew where it would end. He growled.

-Great, now I have to call my parents and cancel dinner. Luckily I didn't tell them the reason- he huffed, running a hand through his hair.

He continued walking towards his home, he had taken the same route for the last 6 months to see Tzuyu, his girlfriend. Ex-girlfriend. He stopped abruptly

-Damn, I suck at love- she sighed resignedly taking a seat on one of the old park benches. She looked up, the sky was full of stars that looked like little fireflies. Among them she saw the tail of a shooting star. She closed her eyes and made a wish- I want to find my soul mate- she whispered dreamily. Lisa was one of those girls who believed in destiny, magic and happily ever after- but what...?- she opened her eyes upon hearing a noise- Hello? Is anyone there?- but no one answered, instead a second noise resounded. The Thai girl jumped to her feet alertly and looked at the place where that noise came from.

Two benches away from hers was a battered cardboard box turned upside down. The blonde walked over to it and looked around for the cause of the noise and her fear. Nothing. There was no one around.

-Holy shit!- Lisa jumped and climbed onto the bench when she saw the box slide by itself- ok, I must be hallucinating, yeah, because how could a box move s...? Oh my god!- she brought a hand to her chest when she saw it move again- is this witchcraft or must I be dreaming, yeah, when I wake up I'll be home and Tzuyu won't have tricked me- a part of the Thai woman wished that were the case, but the third movement of the box confirmed that it was real- ok, I just have to remove it, right?- she swallowed mentally preparing herself for what she was about to do- ok Lisa, you can do it!- she motivated herself. She knelt on the bench and nervously stretched her hands towards the box- you just have to lift it- she reminded herself. She held the box in both hands and took a big breath, steeling herself. "There's no way back." She quickly lifted the box and closed her eyes in terror, as if there was a jellyfish inside and just looking at it would turn her to stone. *Why so quiet?* She opened one eye to see what it was and smiled when she saw the cause of her dilemma. She let out a laugh as she sat down on the bench and leaned over to get a better look at it. "So you were the cause of this commotion, huh?" She heard a meow and quickly took the little feline in her hands. "You almost scared me to death, my friend." She looked under her belly and wrinkled her nose. "I'm sorry, I didn't know it was a little lady."

The Ragdoll's eyes were slanted and had black lining around the edges that gave the impression that eyeliner had been used, as well as some nice black spots around the eyes.

-You're such an adorable little thing...!- he leaned in when he saw a heart pendant on a delicate chain around her neck.

-Nini...- the blonde read on the pendant and then looked at the cat that remained sitting on her lap- nice name, I'm Lalisa- she caressed the feline's brown fur- you're lost huh? Me too, just in a different way...- she said thoughtfully lowering the caress to the cat's neck who instantly began to purr- I think I'll take you home, it's very cold out here. Then we'll look for your owner- without thinking she took off her jacket forgetting about the cold and wrapped the cat like a taco to keep her warm. Lisa hugged the kitten to her chest suddenly feeling better, for a moment she forgot her disappointment in love. What Lisa didn't know is that that little girl was about to change her life.

Home Sweet Home

The Thai girl's apartment was small but spacious, she had become independent at 17 when she left Thailand and had been living there ever since. It wasn't the best area in Korea but it wasn't bad at all.

-Well Nini, welcome to your new home! ... At least until we find your owners...- he commented while hanging the jacket on the chest.

He left little Nini on the floor and walked into the living room.

- Leo, come here sleepyhead, I want you to meet a cute girl! - he hummed happily at the idea of a possible girlfriend for his furry companion.

She walked past, leaving her keys on the counter that divided the living room from the kitchen and cast a couple of glances at the hallway that led to her room, since the furry one liked to sleep there whenever she went out.

- Leo, come here! - She insisted without any result. Lisa crossed her arms and looked at the kitten that was walking around her- forgive him, he's a bit lazy... Leo, I brought food! - Shortly after, a cat came sleepily to its owner. The one with bangs took the little ragdoll and walked to her cat, a lazy Scottish fold- Nini, this is my dear Leo and... No, Nini, don't leave him! - Lisa quickly pushed the one with whitish fur away when she saw how she lunged at Leo to attack him.

The poor thing bristled up to its tail and fled from the room with its hair standing on end, leaving the blonde surprised at the recent action of the feline that was once again docile in her eyes.

-You mean Nini, you can't attack Leo! - she scolded her holding her in front of her, but smiled when she saw her ears lower in submission and she couldn't continue with her scolding- Well, I forgive you, I guess after being out there alone you must be a little scared- her own stomach growled, Lisa widened her eyes and laughed- You must be as hungry as I am. Come, I'll give you some milk- She walked around the counter and opened the fridge taking out a carton of milk and also a package of sandwich and cheese- This for you... - she placed a bowl of milk in front of the cat and smiled when she saw her drink- wow, for being on the street you eat like a lady

She made her sandwich and walked to the couch, a movie and maybe some ice cream would help her forget her broken heart. However, after an hour and a half of Netflix she understood that neither the ice cream nor the movie would help.

- Stupid Tzuyu! - she blew her nose for the umpteenth time with an absorbent towel, balled it up and took another one to repeat the process. She heard a meow and when she raised her face she saw Nini in front of the sofa looking at her attentively - Six fucking months and he never said anything to me! - she snorted checking her cell phone and then threw it away - and not one fucking call! Not one fucking apology text, as if I hadn't existed! - she sniffed, and turned her attention back to the feline who was still paying attention to her movements - I know what you think, am I pathetic, aren't I? I'm falling apart for a girl who right now must be fucking my slutty friend - she mentioned, as if that animal really understood her - but it was six months, fuck, six fucking months! and it doesn't stop hurting

She lay back on the couch and covered her eyes with one arm. She felt broken and betrayed, she had lived many moments with Tzuyu, before being girlfriends they were friends and that made everything worse.

-History always repeats itself- Lisa whispered, defeated- maybe I should stop trying

She started to sob again. Her relationships always ended that way, her exes used to say that she wasn't very affectionate in her relationships or that she didn't spend enough time with them, and that it was her mistake.

You never have time for me!
You only care about sex Lisa!

You love that stinky cat more than me!
Lalisa Manoban, you're not even listening to me!

These and more were words from girls he once dated and the last one that came to his mind was the one that ended up opening his eyes:

Why don't you ever say you love me Lisa!? I'm sure even if I slept with your best friend in front of your eyes you wouldn't care at all!

That's what Tzuyu had said in their last argument, it had been two weeks since then. That was another one of her mistakes, the Thai girl never said I love you, but that didn't mean she didn't love them. Lisa was very sincere and used to make things clear from the start, although it seemed that in the end her partners ended up forgetting and she was the one who got hurt. The kiss between Sana and Tzuyu came back to her mind, she had never noticed anything strange between them until that night, was it possible that they had already had a romance since then? Although the blonde had the gift of keeping girls away, her time was divided between the dance studio, paying bills and taking care of her cat, even her friends were a priority. *Fuck. Why couldn't she just be a good girlfriend? How hard could it be?* Tears clouded her vision again and before she cried again she felt a weight on her body. She looked ahead noticing the cat looking at her from her chest.

-It's my fault Nini, I always end up pushing everyone away from me- she confessed between sobs. Somehow she always ended up hurting without intending to. She felt the animal's small paw touch her nose and then tilt its head in an adorable way, that gesture made the blonde smile who was enchanted by the feline's grayish gaze- You have beautiful eyes Nini- Lisa caressed her head and in response she purred- I see that someone likes the same ones- I don't know how your owners lost sight of you but I promise that I will take care of you

Jealousy?

-Rosie, I already told you, I'm fine!

-No way, Lisa, I know you. I'll go this afternoon, no buts! Oh, and have dinner ready for me.

Lisa rolled her eyes as she hung up the call. Her friend had been harping on the subject for days; Rose was her best friend and confidant but she still had no intention of talking about her recent breakup. She grabbed her thermos of water and took a sip, after dancing she was really exhausted but she loved the results.

-That was excellent Miss Manoban, as always!

Lisa smiled at her assistant and nodded as she wiped the sweat from her forehead and put her shirt back on.

-Thanks Irene, I like to practice the choreography myself to encourage the kids.

-And it has worked quite well, Miss Manoban, Momo assures that the boys are very excited thanks to their appearances at the rehearsals.

-I'm glad to hear that. And please, I already told you that you can call me Lisa.

The girl's cheeks instantly flushed. Lisa looked at the time and said goodbye to the girl. Being the CEO of her company was a dream. Lili's Dance had been her greatest achievement. Dancing had always been her passion and after moving to Seoul she managed to set up a small dance agency that was slowly bearing fruit.

After buying a few things he decided to head home. If he wanted the food to be ready before Rose arrived, he had to start as soon as possible.

-Oh god, I just hope Nini didn't kill Leo- the idea of leaving them alone worried her. It had been a week since Lisa got the little ragdoll at the park and since then she had to keep them apart to avoid another attack from the feline.

-Maybe it's better with Rose- she said to herself without taking her eyes off the road.

The truth was that during that week he had become fond of the kitten, and without realizing it he had already parked in front of a pet store. The bell rang as he entered. He passed by the toy section and noticed the muzzles

Should I wear one of those?

-Good afternoon, miss, can I help you with something?

-Hello. Well, I think so...- he scratches his neck nervously- You see, I have a new kitten and I thought that maybe a toy would help her relax a little.

-Of course, it was the best choice, I will teach you just what you need!

◇◇🐱◇◇

-Leo, Nini, I'm home!- she closed the door with her foot and with difficulty left the purchases on the counter, letting out a sigh- I'm not going to let myself be influenced by a saleswoman again- she reproached herself seeing all the purchases. After a while she saw a ball of fur run in her direction and smiled- Hey Nini! I wish that lazy Leo would greet me like that- she commented when she saw her rubbing against her leg. The feline had been greeting her in that affectionate way every time she came back from work- or do you already know that all this is for you?

She smiled and left the toys on the floor, having taken care (with the influence of the saleswoman) to add a pet carrier, a food dish and a comb to her purchases.

-I hope you like it, technically I was persuaded to buy all this

The rest of the afternoon was spent preparing food, her friend was the most gluttonous girl she knew.

-I swear, Chae loves everything that is edible- he explained looking at the cat while he put the chicken in the oven- her passion is eating, my father loves it when I bring her home, he never says no to one of her meals.

Lisa's father, Marcos, was one of the best chefs in Thailand, something that the blonde did not inherit by far.

-Shit!- Lisa fanned the charred chicken with her hand while with the other she held the towel that wrapped her body tightly. She had gone to take a shower and in the process had completely forgotten about dinner- Now you know my dark secret Nini, that's why I'm not married yet, my wife would die of hunger or in the worst case, poisoned by one of my dishes- he joked while typing on his cell phone and pressed it to his cheek- luckily there is home delivery service

After a while the Thai girl had already eaten Chinese food and was finishing drying her hair with a towel. The sound of the doorbell indicated the arrival of the Australian girl and she hurried to open the door.

-Hey Lis!

-Hi gorgeous!

The two blondes hugged each other and walked to the couch.

-First things first...

-I know, I know, I'll go get your food- Lisa intervened, standing up with her eyes rolled back.

When she returned she left everything on the table and Rose was quick to start devouring everything in her path, all under the blonde's watchful eye.

-So, how are you?- he asked after swallowing.

-Oh great, my girlfriend cheated on me with one of our friends and maybe there are already plans to get married...! I feel great!

-Lisa, irony is not the key

-And your psychiatric techniques don't help. I hate that you treat me like one of your crazy people.

-To begin with, they are not crazy, they are people with internal conflicts, and secondly- she paused to swallow and continued- what is the point of having a psychologist friend if you can't go to her when you need it?

-I...I don't know how I feel. It hurt me, but more so the fact that it was Sana

-Oh Lis, honey, I...

But she couldn't finish, Rose forced herself to distance herself from her when the feline launched herself at the Australian, leaving scratches and bites.

- Nini, leave her! - Lisa tried to get rid of her without much success, she saw how Leo, who until then was on one of the stools, fled towards the hallway - coward...

-Lisa, take it from me!

-Nini, Rose is a friend, stop!

And with that she got the attention of the animal who immediately stopped attacking the Australian. Nini looked at her from her lap and in an elegant movement she moved to the blonde's lap, who welcomed her happily.

-What the devil...?

-Rosie, this is Nini, my new tenant

Rose looked at the girl and then at the cat without leaving her previous state of shock. Lisa, seeing that her friend did not speak, decided to continue.

-Can he stay at your house?

Both, cat and girl looked at the Thai girl intensely.

-You went crazy, right?

-What's so crazy about you?

-Lisa, that animal just jumped on me and you ask me to take it home with me? That's crazy! - she looked at the cat on her friend's lap - plus it's obvious that she's comfortable with you

Lisa stroked the cat's head and she began to purr contentedly.

-I like you too, furball- the blonde played while still caressing her- but she doesn't get along with Leo- this time she turned to her friend

Rose grimaced at the scratch on her hand and then looked at her friend in confusion.

-Leo doesn't want her at home?
-In fact, I think it's her who rejects him.
-Well, that explains everything.
-What are you talking about?
-She doesn't like it when someone else steals your attention - she explained, distracted by cleaning the remains of blood from the bite on her finger - she's jealous
-Jealous?
-Jealous- she stated confidently- She wants you for herself, and she doesn't plan on sharing you, so I guess poor Leo will have to keep running away.

Lisa looked at the cat sleeping on her lap. How could that cat be so affectionate with her and so aggressive with others? She thought about it for a moment, she didn't want her to go back out on the street. She looked at the charm on her chest and knew what to do.

Nini bad

Nini stretched out on the bed, letting out a cat-like moan. It had been three days since Rose had taken Leo and she was very comfortable. The Thai girl allowed her to sleep with her and she loved it.

She purred, rubbing her little nose on the pillow, soaking in his scent. No doubt that vanilla fragrance was pleasant, although a little strong for the feline's delicate sense of smell, but it was the other one, her natural scent that delighted the animal.

After wallowing a little longer in that exquisite essence, she decided to start her morning.

~What's for dinner?- he jumped out of bed and walked to the living room. The blonde was leaving her food there before leaving for work.

He sniffed around, everything in that apartment smelled like Lisa.

~Why do I need catnip, this is better than catnip!- she inhaled happily and walked to the feeder, where her fish-shaped croquettes and chicken thighs were. Nini wrinkled her nose in disgust- do humans really think we like this ugly stuff? How I miss canaries...

He looked over at the table next to the shelf and spotted a fish tank. His tail danced happily as he left the kibble behind. His eyes focused on that pair of fish.

-What cute and appetizing little fish... Which one of you will be my breakfast?- he purred with pleasure at the idea of trying such a delicacy, his eyes focused on a beautiful and quite appetizing parrotfish, leaving the silver-colored one for later. - Bingo, you will be the lucky one!

◇◇🐱◇◇

-And he asked me out, can you believe it?

-Rose, I don't care what that madman does, he's crazy!- Lisa closed the door behind them.

-Mino is not crazy, Lisa, he just has anxiety problems.

-As you say- The Thai woman threw the keys on the counter as always when she arrived- Nini, I'm here!- she shouted happily while she also left her bag on the counter

-You've become fond of that beast, I hope he has all his vaccinations, my finger got the size of a potato because of him

-Don't exaggerate, it was just a bite... -she was silenced by the Australian's scream- Rose, what did you...? Oh god, no Nini, leave her!!!

The ragdoll bit Rose's leg from top to bottom as if eating an ear of corn.

-Lisa, take that beast away from me!

- Nini darling, come here! - Lisa had crouched down to get the animal's attention - Come on, sweetie, come here! - She clapped her hands a couple of times and smiled as she saw the feline obey her call - Good girl

- Good girl? That animal is crazy!

Lisa made a face and shook her head, hugging Nini in her arms.

-It's not true, it's just that he doesn't like you.

Rose rolled her eyes and limped over to the couch to assess the wound.

-Whatever, as long as that thing is here I won't...- he paused, looking at a specific spot-Lisa, did you change my fish tank?

-What ? Why would I want to do such a thing? I don't even have a spare fish tank- he replied from his room .

Rose approached the fish tank and sure enough, there were no traces of the fish.

-So where are Joohwang and Eunbyul?- he asked, searching through the fish tank with his eyes.

-Well, in the fish tank, Chae- Lisa peeked into the hallway with her phone to her ear- The double cheese and anchovy pizza, or do we change the last bit for mushrooms?

Rose wasn't paying attention. On the floor near the sofa table she saw something orange and next to it another silver one.

He leaned down, taking it in his hands to appraise it and his eyes widened at the sight of what it was. He let out a yelp and strode to the room of the girl with the bangs, who was still on her cell phone asking for his order.

-That animal ate them!

-Excuse me for a second- she moved the phone away, covering the receiver to pay attention to her friend- what thing?

Rose opened the palm of her hand where the fins of her two fish were located.

-Your damn cat ate them!!

Lisa opened her mouth in surprise but then denied it.

-I don't think so, Nini wouldn't do it, she hasn't even touched her food this morning, I think she has an upset stomach.

-Of course he didn't eat the stupid cat food because he already ate my fish!!- Rose whimpered- My babies...that monster ate my babies!

Lisa swallowed, Nini didn't even seem interested in the conversation, she was quite comfortable sleeping face up on the blonde's pillow.

-Ok, anchovies out, mushrooms it will be!

◈◈🐱◈◈

Thai sighed, falling onto her bed.

She had spent the rest of the afternoon comforting her friend over the death of her fish. Who spends their Saturday afternoon like this? *Apparently only me*.

She looked to the left, Nini watched her sadly with her ears drooping.

-The puss in boots trick won't work, what you did was wrong, bad Nini! - The cat tried to get closer, but the blonde stopped her - I'm sorry Nini but you've been bad

Had it been? The Thai woman took her in her arms and left her in the hallway with some difficulty, it broke her heart to see her sad.

That night Nini would have to learn her lesson. She closed the door to her room and went to bed with a strange feeling. Had she made a good decision?

Nini & Chu

Nini hadn't rested that night. What did she do wrong? *Lisa eats fish, why can't I eat it?*

He kept walking in circles, his previous owner kept feeding him fish and he didn't seem angry. *Maybe he bit the squirrel-faced girl too hard?* He growled at the memory of her, why was he always around Lisa?

That night she realized she wouldn't sleep, not if the blonde kept her away from her. *Maybe a walk around the rooftops would help me think.*

The night was cold but she didn't care. Besides thinking, she needed to talk to someone and she only knew one feline who could help her.

He stopped in the alley a few blocks from his current owner's house, the alley led to the back door of a chicken restaurant and he knew that there he would find just the animal he wanted to see.

-Damn cat, if you come back I'll kill you!- Nini bristled at hearing the cook's rough voice, followed by a shoe that almost hit her.

-Humans are crazy...- he whispered coming out of his hiding place

- And you can say that, so much drama for a little chicken

Nini saw a cat of her own breed on some boxes. Her spots were less marked than her own, and her eyes were a dull blue, but the resemblance was still noticeable.

-Hello Chu

-Nice to see you again sister

They both rubbed their noses together, purring.

Nini had missed her sister and was dying to tell her everything that had happened with Lisa.

-Stealing again?

-Hey, I was just testing the quality of that chicken, the meat looked spoiled! - he replied, licking his paws to remove the chicken remains - and where were you?

-Long story

-Well, tell me later, now I have to take this chicken skewer to Coneja

-Don't tell me she already gave birth!?

-5 kittens, luckily they didn't get anything from Mochi or Dudu kills him

-That's what happens to the rabbit for being a cat, how does she dare to leave her house in heat? Poor Mochi just couldn't resist the smell

-Yeah, sure, like he did with Hyuna, right? Mochi is a real bitch, thank god you and I spent the heat at home. By the way, Kai won't stop meowing on the roof, he's getting on my nerves, I told you it wasn't a good idea to mark the tree while you're in heat.

-I was pissing myself! Besides, you know I like Kai...

-Enough to let him get you pregnant?

Nini did not answer, she did not know the answer to that question, however the image of a bunch of blond kittens with honey-colored eyes and a vanilla scent came to her mind.

-Well, I wouldn't mind having a few, although I rule out that possibility, but adoption is always an option.

-Nini, the Kim family would kick you out if you got pregnant by the neighbor's cat, and I think the same would happen if you adopted. Besides, what's the point? I wouldn't want to lose my figure for a couple of babies.

-I know, you prefer to lose her because of the chicken- her sister said ironically, rolling her eyes.

◇◇🐱◇◇

Nini was shocked to see the little kittens feeding on the rabbit, a fluffy Japanese Bobtail. The rabbit, however, was growling in warning for no one to approach her little ones.

-Nini, I'll knock your tail off if you touch one of my babies! Same goes for you, Dudu!

The ebony cat stopped dead, leaving a mouse in front of her. She was a Russian blue and could sometimes be a bit intimidating.

-How ungrateful, I was only bringing you dinner- she snorted disgustedly, wagging her tail disdainfully- you get pregnant and on top of that you mistreat me!

-It was you who wanted me to spend my heat with you, you stupid mustachioed woman!

-And how was I supposed to know you'd stop and have fun with that horrible Persian!?

-You would have done the same thing if you weren't castrated!

They both started to growl and snort.

-Girls, I think we'll visit you later.

Both ragdolls left the tree house where the rabbit had given birth and climbed onto the roof a few houses away.

-Well now tell me everything

Nini snorted, she knew that at any moment her sister would bring up the subject, but how would she take it?

-I... I met someone, I'm living with her and...

-What? A cat? I thought you were more into men, Kai specifically.

-Why did you believe such a thing!?

-Maybe because you meow her name every time you're in heat.

Nini scratched her paw, she hated talking about her changes in attitude when she went into heat, it was something she could not control by instinct.

-Her name is Lisa... And she is so perfect!

-Really? Tell me, don't back down. What's his fur like?

Nini gulped. What was it like?

-Well... He doesn't really have any, just on his head, he's blond and smells so good...

-Holy mother of cats, are you dating a sphynx!? Those things look like Nini rats!

-At least they don't suffer from hairballs- Nini countered, remembering the bitter feeling of constantly spitting out hair.

-Well, how long is your tail?

Female cats usually looked for the cat with the most dominance and for Chu a long tail was a requirement.

- It doesn't really have...

-What!? At least tell me that his fangs and claws are worth it

Nini shifted uncomfortably and denied

-Their claws are very short and their fangs are not sharp.

-By my claws Nini, what kind of freak are you dating!?

-We're not dating, I wish... And she's not a sphynx.

- Worse, she's sick! She must be mangy.

-Choo!

-Well I heard that cod liver oil makes fur grow, we can catch one

-Of course, the one who likes to get into the water the most, you don't even bathe.

-Hey, I took a bath three weeks ago! Besides, what kind of beggar cat are you seeing?

-I never said I was a cat...- he whispered, looking away.

-What? Is she a bitch? Anything but a bitch please!

Nini rolled her eyes.

-She's human Chu, I fell in love with the most beautiful human of all

-Nini...-Chu was about to give her a sermon but the opponent prevented him from doing so.

- I know, don't scold me, I don't know how it happened! I don't even know how I got to that park, the last thing I remember is the sandbox.

- See!? I told you that sand was suspicious! I won't pee there again.

- I don't know Chu, there's something about her that attracts me like no one else, her smell is like a drug to me

Her sister saw her thoughtful, Nini looked excited and didn't want anyone to break her heart.

-Sister, a human would never notice a cat, for them we are just their pets and it is the only affection you will receive from them.

-Nini?

The voice of a male cat followed by a meow made both felines turn around. Nini saw how the huge jet-black Bombay sniffed the air in search of her scent.

-Kai!- Nini ran to meet him, rubbing her head on the animal's neck.

-Nini! Where have you been? I haven't heard from you in days! - He licked the kitten's ear lovingly while purring - You smell strange, were you in heat with another male?

Nini stepped back, it must have been Leo's scent, of course, he was the only cat that had been near her.

-No, my heat doesn't start until the end of the month.

The cat's eyes lit up. Nini knew that the male wanted to be the first to have her and procreate with her, he had told her so more than once on the roof. Although before the ragdoll could not smell the marks that Kai left around her house because she immediately rolled around in it with the need for the male to possess her, but in those last few weeks something in her had changed, there was a scent that managed to drive her even crazier and that was the scent of the blonde human that had been engraved in her mind.

Make a wish

Dreams are just that, dreams, illusions that fade when you wake up... but it is up to each person if they want to make that dream a reality.

Nini returned to the blonde's apartment the next day and was disappointed not to see her there. *Did she notice that I left? That was obvious, the question is, did she care?*

The feline sat by the window, remembering Chu's words
A human would never notice a cat, for them we are just their pets and it is the only affection you will receive from them.

It had hurt her to hear those words, she already knew it but deep down she wanted to believe that there was a tiny chance for her.

~How stupid Nini, how can someone as inferior as you believe that someone as perfect as her would notice you? - she said to herself

Her eyes watered and her chest ached. He shouldn't have fallen in love with her. She was so focused on her sadness that she didn't know when the door opened until she heard his voice.

-No Rose, I've looked everywhere and she's not here! - she sounded upset. She was wearing a giant bra and sports shorts, her face was red and sweaty and she looked tired from her panting. *Had she gone for a run?* - I was hard on her, I shouldn't have taken her out of the room!

The feline's heart raced. It was because of her that Lalisa was in that state, she had noticed her absence and went out to look for her.

The feline stood up and ran towards her, meowing, and that was enough to catch the Thai woman's attention.

-Rosie has already appeared, I'll talk to you later! - he cut off without waiting for an answer and knelt down to reach the feline, lifting her in his arms - Nini, you scared me! When I woke up and didn't see you, I thought you were gone - he hugged her happily, listening to the ragdoll's purrs - I'm sorry about last night, will you forgive me? - he pouted, melting the feline.

~Of course I forgive you!

Lisa laughed as she heard the meows without understanding the true meaning.

- Are you insulting me Nini? - he interpreted in response to the insistent meows

Nini snorted. Seriously, that's what she thought? *How could she prove her wrong?*

The kitten leaned down, still in the blonde's arms, and licked her nose. A gesture that surprised and touched the Thai girl.

-I understand- he whispered, caressing her head gradually- you can sleep with me again

❖❖🐱❖❖

It had been almost two months since her arrival and three weeks since her night out. Nini had noticed that the blonde was a bit distracted during those days, spending less time at home and when she was, she spent hours on her cell phone.

That Saturday morning Lisa was happier than usual. Every now and then she smiled and played with the kitten. On the other hand, the feline was delighted, and after weeks of ignoring her, she was finally paying attention to her again.

Lisa invited the Australian girl to lunch, of course with takeout. She needed to talk to her friend about a topic that was exciting her.

-God Lisa, just tell me…

Both were sitting at the table enjoying lunch. Nini was eating hers next to the refrigerator, the Thai girl had rewarded her with canned tuna and she was more than happy with that.

- Well, do you remember Irene?

-Your assistant? The one who gets her panties wet for you?

The blonde with bangs' cheeks reddened

-Rose, don't say that!

-Oh come on Lisa, you know it's true, the girl is drooling over you

On the floor Nini had stopped eating to pay attention. *Who is Irene and what does she want from Lisa?* Her possessive side was making itself felt as she waited impatiently for an explanation from the girl with bangs.

-Well, we've been talking and hanging out outside of work, you know, to get to know each other.

-So you fucked her

-God no! Rose seriously, stop it

-Lisa, I'm a psychologist, it's an unconscious reaction- she explained, taking another bite of her food and letting out a moan of pleasure as she swallowed.

-Well, we have decided to take a step further and....

-And they will fuck- she finished the sentence with her cheeks full.

-Roseanne Park!- Lisa scolded her- no, we're just going on a date

Rose raised an eyebrow in disbelief.

-Haven't they done that already?

Lisa looked at her with her eyes, making her laugh out loud. Nini, on the other hand, couldn't believe what she was hearing: a date? And that was enough to finally shatter her illusions.

◈◈🐱◈◈

-Hey Nini, here you were- Lisa sat down on the hammock- I thought you had left again

The feline was lying on a stool on the balcony, she didn't even lift her face when she heard the blonde leave and that seemed strange to Lisa.

-What's wrong, are you sick? - he asked, examining her from afar - you're very dull, you're probably thinking about some kitten.

~I think of you- he replied with melancholy

The meow, as always, had been incomprehensible to the blonde, who had drawn her own conclusions.

- So you have a boyfriend...? It's a pity, I would have liked a girlfriend for Leo.

The feline's chest hurt. This is how she sees me, a simple cat.

- Look Nini, the sky is starry, there will surely be shooting stars- said the Thai woman looking at the sky- if you are lucky maybe you can make a wish

Lisa was the kind of girl who could talk to her pet even if she didn't understand it, or at least that's what she thought.

-Look Nini, there goes one, make a wish!

The feline did not hesitate and with her eyes closed she asked for the only thing she longed for.

~I want to be the perfect woman for you...

And once again there was a wish involved, and neither cat nor human were aware of what was about to happen.

Human or feline?

The sun was streaming through the window, hitting her eyes right in the middle, which she hated. She grumbled grumpily. Had she forgotten to close it at night?

Lisa moved, intending to get up, but a weight on her prevented her from doing so. What could it be?

He yawned with his eyes still closed and felt around to find out what it was.

It was warm and had a peculiar but pleasant smell.

-But what...?- her hands felt a soft skin that was not hers. A sound of pleasure from a mouth other than hers made her open her eyes, coming across the scene she least expected.

On top of him was a girl who looked quite comfortable lying on his chest. Her long, unruly-looking brown hair covered her face and half of her back.

The sight of that stranger in her bed sent the Thai woman into a panic. Who was that woman? She let out a scream that woke the girl up, making her jump in fear. In a reflex action she slid to the edge of the bed to protect herself from whatever had caused that scream.

Lisa imitated her, crawling to the headboard, using one of her comfortable pillows as a shield.

-Who are you? And...? Oh my god, why are you naked!?- The Thai girl quickly looked away, what had happened?- Fuck, when did I get drunk!? Why don't I remember taking you to my bed!?

The brunette tilted her head with a slight pout on her lips.

-B-but you carried me and brought me here

Lisa nervously ran her hand through her hair. Why would she do such a thing with a stranger? Okay, she liked sex, but she didn't even remember having sex. *Oh my god, I was raped!*

-No, that can't be, I would remember it!

-I... Can you understand me? - the brunette asked surprised

Lisa looked at her strangely. *Of course she could understand her! She covered her mouth. Oh great, he raped me thinking I was some kind of foreign tourist!*

- Well, I'm not an expert, but I understand Korean pretty well- her eyes went down to the girl's chest and she quickly looked away with a deep blush- I think I'll give you some clothes

-Oh no, I never really liked human clothes.

Lisa widened her eyes in surprise.

-You don't like clothes? What do you wear?

-I don't do it.

The idea of that unusual girl walking around naked disgusted him. Who in their right mind would walk around the streets of Seoul so calmly, just like God brought her into the world? *My God, I slept with a crazy woman!*

-Well, I'm sorry, you'll have to use it here- he walked to his closet and came back with a shirt two sizes bigger than his- this will cover just enough

The Korean made a face of disgust but obeyed, she couldn't help but strongly inhale the blonde's fragrance that had been impregnated on the shirt.

He smiled big and sighed, fixing his eyes on the blonde who had not missed his action.

-You smell delicious...- she whispered smiling.

The Thai girl's cheeks were dyed with carmine

-I... Thanks, I think so- she answered nervously. The girl in her bed looked at her with adoration, her hair was tangled, and seeing that disheveled stranger in her bed and wearing one of her shirts, made her heart beat a thousand times.

On the other hand, the brunette felt strange, much taller than she remembered. She looked at her hands without being able to believe it, she was a human! She smiled when she felt her skin without any hair and then looked at the blonde with pride.

-Lisa, look at me!

The named one swallowed dry

-That's what I do- she whispered embarrassed, she had been looking at the girl's shapely legs long before the brunette gave her permission to do so- wait...- she analyzed the words said by the brunette- how do you know my name?

The girl looked at her confused.

-You told me when we met.

Lisa frowned.

-And how long ago was that?

-Two months?- Nini smiled as she watched the toes of her new feet move.

He tried to stand up and fell face downwards. He let out a groan and then a laugh, all under the confused gaze of the blonde.

Oh my god this girl is crazy! Lisa stood up still under the protection of her pillow.

After a couple of attempts and more falls, the Thai girl came to the conclusion that the girl was either very clumsy or had some kind of retardation, so she understood that she would not hurt her. *My God Lalisa, how low have you fallen! Fucking a retarded girl!?* She covered her face with both hands until a blow on the stairs made her turn around.

-Ouch!- the brunette pouted, rubbing her butt.

-But can you not even walk or what!?- Lisa picked her up and guided her to the kitchen.

-Of course I know, just not on two legs!

"They're legs, not paws..." he corrected her impatiently. He opened the refrigerator and sighed, he didn't normally eat breakfast at home, Irene always made sure to have her coffee and some sandwiches when she got home. He smiled at the thought of his assistant, maybe he would cheer up a bit and kiss her.

-I'm starving, please no more croquettes, they taste horrible!

Lisa ignored the comment. What the hell was he talking about? Croquettes? She finally pulled out a box of milk and cereal.

-Okay, this is the best thing to do- he left both things on the table- take a plate from there, I'll take a couple of spoons and...- he stopped when he saw her sitting happily with the cat's plate in front of her, on the table.

-What are you doing?

-You said to look for a plate

-Yes, a plate for people, not my cat's feeder.

The brunette's cheeks flushed and she looked down shyly. *What's wrong with her now?* Lisa looked at her without understanding until the girl fixed those feline eyes on her again.

-Am I yours?

Lisa almost choked on her coffee. She started coughing frantically.

-W-what?

-You said I was yours!

-I've signed my cat, I don't even know you, and you're already starting to scare me- she turned to her to hand her a spoon but stopped immediately when she saw the brunette putting her mouth in the cereal bowl and licking the milk- What are you doing!?- Lisa pushed her away and with a handkerchief cleaned the remains of milk from her chin- You're not an animal, don't you even use cutlery? My God, you look like a cavewoman!

-Why would a cat need cutlery?

Lisa watched her. The girl was undoubtedly beautiful but terribly scary.

-Who are you?

-I'm Nini, your cat

-No, you're not and let me tell you that...- the dancer finally noticed the pendant on the girl's neck, the heart with the feline's name. That only means that...- Nini?

The shorter one smiled in response.

Crazy thing

Lisa paced around the room, nervously smoothing her bangs. This was crazy. How could it be possible? The feline girl had told her everything she knew, including the wish, which Lisa couldn't quite wrap her head around. Why didn't her wish come true but her cat's did?

- No, no, no, this...- she looked at the brunette on the couch who was watching her intently- this is a dream, yes, I'm dreaming. I'll close my eyes and when I open them everything will be gone- but when she opened them she found the feline eyes a few centimeters away, fixed on her.

-Are you going to kiss me already?

The brunette's question surprised the Thai girl who, in an attempt to escape, tripped over the small table in front of the sofa, falling on her butt.

-Shit!- the Thai girl grimaced in pain as she tried to get up, all under the attention of the shorter girl.

The brunette widened her eyes worriedly when she saw her on the ground.

- Did you fall?

-No, it's just that I like hitting my ass on the floor! - he growled through his teeth.

-Oh...Ok!- Jennie smiled calmly again as if that answer had been enough to know that the Thai girl was fine.

Lisa looked at her in disgust. Seriously, he doesn't understand sarcasm? But she immediately mentally hit herself. Obviously not, Lalisa, he's a cat, he doesn't understand human things.

-Why did you say that?- he paused and continued, noticing the confusion in the feline eyes- About the kiss...- he couldn't help but look away as he said the last thing.

The brunette's eyes sparkled with excitement

-That's what I want. Humans do it and now I'm a human- she explained and tilted her head in confusion- or should I kiss you?

The Thai girl's cheeks flushed, that feline look was starting to make her nervous.

-I-I... It doesn't work like that Nini, you can't just go around kissing people just because they're human- she explained, already standing up, caressing her rear end. She certainly won't be able to sit down for a couple of days- It doesn't work like that...

-I don't want to kiss all humans... I just want to kiss you.

Shit, shit, shit! All of that was being crazy for the taller one. *But then, why is my heart beating as if it were going to come out of my chest?* She swallowed dryly without taking her eyes off the girl in front of her. *Fuck, and why do you not stop looking at her lips? Damn Lalisa Manoban, look away!* With some difficulty she managed to get up to her eyes; She didn't know what was worse, seeing her pretty lips or her penetrating feline gaze.

-No Nini, you can't want something like that, you're a cat and I'm a human.

Nini frowned and shook her head in disagreement. Her cheeks puffed out giving her a childish look. For a moment Lisa wanted to pinch those pretty cheeks. *My god, she's so cute!* She shook her head in denial. *Come on Lisa, focus.*

-It's not true, now I'm a human like you! - She stomped her foot, crossing her arms like a spoiled child in the middle of a tantrum.

"Aww, cuteness!" Lisa smiled. Any fear she felt about that strange madness had disappeared.

Her cell phone started ringing, snapping her out of her trance and she cursed at the name. *Shit, work* . With the whole Nini thing, she forgot that she had to go to the agency.

-H-hey Irene!

The brunette's features tensed upon hearing that name and Lisa swallowed hard upon noticing it. The feline girl's sweet look had disappeared for a truly intimidating one.

-Lisa? Is everything okay?

The little brunette was attentive to the voice on the other end of the line. She was thankful that she had retained her feline hearing, because she certainly wouldn't have been able to hear the phone conversation with a human ear.

-I... Yeah, well, I think so- the Thai girl answered a little distracted, glancing sideways at the brunette who couldn't take her eyes off her- I woke up a little unwell actually, I won't be able to go to the agency today, can you take care of it?

-Anything for you Lisie

- Lisie? - the brunette gritted her teeth. That strange feeling of anger and possession invaded her again.

Lisa noticed the action of the brunette and took a little distance, it seemed that at any moment she would jump on her and not in a loving way.

- Thanks Irene, see you tomorrow at the agency

-You know I'm happy to do it. Don't worry about anything, I'll take good care of your company... Get well soon, Lisie.

When he finished the call, he saw the brunette turn around and disappear down the hallway with long strides.

What happened to him? Lisa didn't understand his reaction.

He heard the door slam and assumed she was in the bedroom. *Well, now I'll have a moment alone* . He took the opportunity to make a call, all without taking his eyes off the hallway in case the feline appeared again. *Would she get angry again?*

She started ringing the bell and prayed that her friend was free enough to answer. She looked at the wall clock, and knew that by the time the Australian woman must be having a consultation.

-Come on Park, answer...- he whispered pleadingly

After a couple of rings the other blonde finally answered.

-Manoban, I hope it's important, Mrs. Sara is in the middle of a crisis...

-Rose, I need you to come as soon as you are free- he blurted out the words quickly without letting her finish.

-Is something wrong Lisa, are you okay?- Rose's voice sounded worried this time

-I need a psychologist, I think I've gone crazy... And I've heard that Roseanne Park is the best at dealing with them.

-Lisa, leave your flattery for later- she was silent for a second and sighed- Give me half an hour, I need to resolve this. I hope it's important.

-Trust me Rosie, it is.

Jennie Kim

Rose and Lisa watched in amazement as the feline girl rested on the Thai girl's lap in a fetal position; she had fallen asleep halfway through the explanation and the girls didn't notice until the end.

-Lisa, this is crazy- Rose looked at the girl on her friend's lap- This doesn't even exist, it's not possible for a cat to suddenly turn into a human by wishing upon a star! A cat shouldn't even have the ability to think, much less wish for something!!!

-I know! Do you think I would have called you if I understood what was going on!?

Both girls kept their debate in whispers so as not to wake the brunette.

After analyzing it for a while, they both resigned themselves to the idea that the brunette was telling the truth. What else could it be?

-So your cat is a woman now...?- thought Rose- a very pretty one by the way, and she will live here too.

Lisa frowned, looking at her reproachfully, had she really just said that her cat was pretty?

-Do you like Nini?

Rose looked at her for a moment and shrugged, stroking her brown hair.

-Why not? She's very pretty though...- he grimaced as his fingers tangled in the girl's wild hair- though she needs a bath and maybe a haircut.

Lisa slapped Rose's hand away, and as if it were a feather, she picked up the brunette princess style.

-It's my cat, and I won't let you near her!

Rose raised an eyebrow questioningly.

-What's wrong Lisa, don't tell me you like your cat?

The Thai woman turned around abruptly, still with the brunette in her arms.

-I promised that I would take care of her until I found her owners and that's what I will do- he clarified with disgust- I'm going to leave her in the room and then we'll continue with this.

Rose watched attentively as her friend walked away with the girl in her arms. Her experience as a psychologist had taught her to read people by their body language, and what her friend had just said led her to one conclusion...

-Oh Lis, that chestnut will be your downfall

◇◇🐱◇◇

The girls had been rambling about the subject, while Rose was preparing dinner Lisa was researching on her phone regarding the subject

-Nothing, there is nothing to talk about this- she growled frustrated leaving the cell phone on the counter

-It's obvious Lisa, how many cats turned into girls have you met?- she asked sarcastically while taking the tray out of the oven- It's not something you see often, but from now on I'll see the stars more, maybe I'll even get my wish of being a millionaire.

-Well, the idea of having 100 dollar bills coming out of your butt is great, although remind me not to touch your money without latex gloves- the Thai girl joked, earning a reproachful look from her friend.

-Very funny

While they were talking they didn't notice the arrival of a third girl with a sleepy expression.

Jennie swayed sleepily as she took a seat on one of the stools and began licking her hand and then rubbing it over her face.

Lisa noticed his presence and raised an eyebrow at his action.

-Hey, what are you doing Nini?

Hearing her name from the Thai girl's voice, the brunette sat up with a small, sleepy smile.

-I... I was cleaning myself up a little.

-Oh... You'd like a bath better.

The brunette wrinkled her nose, and shook her head frantically in disagreement.

-No, I don't like it, that's fine

-You can't go out without taking a bath, Nini, you have to do it- Lisa insisted.

-No, I don't want to!

-Lisa, remember that she was a cat, cats don't like showers- the psychologist explained to her, noticing her friend's displeasure and the chestnut's fear.

Lisa rolled up the sleeves of her shirt and shook her head; she hated being contradicted.

-But now she is human and as a human she must bathe.

-No, no, I'm still a cat!

-When it suits you

-Okay you two, that's enough, you can discuss the shower when I leave, with Lisa's insistence it even seems like you want to share the shower with her.

The girl with bangs blushed, the idea hadn't even crossed her mind, but after her friend's hint she couldn't help but have images of the brunette without a shred of clothing come to her mind, and that thought made her shudder. *Damn Lalisa, what things you think*

-Oh no Lisa, you are not going to think dirty at the table, food is sacred and must be respected! - the Australian scolded her, seeing her friend's sad face.

She began to serve the lasagna on three plates and laughed when her friend came out of her trance, taking her hint.

-Rose!

-Yeah, whatever, deny it if you want- he rolled his eyes- Nini takes one, yeah.... And the lasagna?

Both girls looked from side to side looking for the tray, but there was no trace of it or the chestnut.

-Holy God Lisa, didn't you feed him?

-Of course!

After dinner they sat down on the sofa where the brunette had completely finished the tray of lasagna and was licking her fingers.

-Don't do that- Lisa took his hands to stop him from continuing.

-Are you going to clean them for me?

Lisa opened her mouth but was interrupted by Rose's laughter.

-Oh Lisa, I think he wants you to be the one to lick his fingers.

-Shut up, you pasta!- the Thai girl took a napkin from the table and carefully cleaned the girl's hands.

Nini watched the Thai girl's action curiously. Why didn't she just lick them? However, she didn't dislike that gesture either, her hands touched the Thai girl's and made her feel a pleasant tickle.

-Okay, now they're clean- Lisa cleared her throat nervously and sat down on the couch. They still had to clarify some issues and they hadn't been able to after the brunette fell asleep- Nini, Rose and I need to ask you some questions to understand a little bit, can you help us with that?

The girl nodded.

-Ok Nini, where did you live before Lisa found you?

-With the Kim family, me and my sister are little Ella's pets.

Rose widened her eyes at such information.

-She Kim? The daughter of Kim's businessman?- Rose gave her friend a look- it seems like your cat is a millionaire Lis

-That explains the gold pendant- he thought instinctively that hung around the brunette's neck- and why did you run away?

- I didn't do it, I don't even know how I got to the park, one moment I was at home and then in the dark inside a box

-Why did you make that wish?

Lisa sat back in her seat, that question also intriguing her. Nini thought about it and fixed her eyes on the blonde with bangs, losing herself in them for a moment.

-Who wouldn't want to be perfect for her?

The feline's words were sincere, making Lisa's heart beat frantically, like a derailed locomotive.

-Why would you want such a thing Nini? - the Thai woman asked, curious.

-So that you would love me

- Oh Nini, but I already love you

Nini denied, looking down.

-I don't eat that girl.

Rose widened her eyes understanding the feline's words, however she knew her friend and knew how stubborn she was.

-We were thinking that maybe it would be good to give you another name, you know, a human one.

Nini looked at her with emotion, that idea pleased her.

-I think Jennifer would look good on you.

The brunette tilted her head, not very convinced, Lisa noticed it and decided to give her opinion.

-What do you think about Jennie? And we can continue calling you Nini as a form of affection- the Thai girl smiled big.

-I like it... Jennie- with her eyes shining with excitement

-Kim, Jennie Kim- Rose finished in affirmation- sounds good. How old are you supposed to be now?

-I am two years old

- Cats - Lisa clarified, doing the math - there would be 24 humans... - she widened her eyes - wow, you're a year older than me - she winked at him mischievously

-Oh yeah, Lisa likes older guys, that's a point in your favor- both girls blushed and Rose rolled her eyes- Well whatever, what are you going to do with her?- Rose frowned upon seeing her friend's face- I mean when you're at work Lisa, don't be a slob

-I...

-You can't always be locked in your room forever

-I like it, I like being in his bed all day- Jennie confessed sincerely.

Rose laughed at the brunette's innocence. Lisa, on the other hand, choked on her own saliva.

-Oh Jen, and you haven't seen anything, if you knew Lisa's tactics you would never leave her bed

-Rose!

The blonde was redder than a tomato. On the other hand, the shortest of the three was intrigued. Lisa's tactics?

-I want to meet them, if that means I can stay in your bed.

-No Nini no, you don't need that to sleep there- explained Lusa blushing

- Actually that should change too- both looked at Rose intrigued and she was quick to clarify what she had said- she is no longer a cat, she is now Jennie Kim, a woman like us and I don't think you want to sleep next to her, do you Lisa?

The blonde analyzed those words, sleeping with that cat-eyed girl? As tempting as it sounded, she couldn't mistake the situation. *She's a cat, and you can't feel anything but affection for her.*

-Rose is right, I think you should have your own room.

Animal desire

A week had passed, Jennie had adapted to her new name and the blonde did not seem uncomfortable with her presence, but she still did not like her new room.

She snorted, looking at the ceiling above her bed. This was the guest room, which the blonde had converted into a small studio. There was a bookshelf and a desk, and apart from the sofa bed and the nightstand there was nothing but a plasma TV and a stereo, and to one side there was a full-length mirror.

Why couldn't he sleep with her? He snorted for the fifth time. He was angry to be away from the blonde.

-Stupid Rose and her stupid ideas

He brought the blouse to his nose and inhaled, it was the blonde's and it still gave off her scent. Wearing the Thai girl's clothes was his consolation, at least with her scent he could feel her closer.

A sound at the door made her stop, the smell of vanilla had intensified, that only meant that the blonde was back.

-You can come in Lisa

The door opened revealing the blonde, she had a white harlot that reached her knees. Lisa was thin and much taller than her in her human form, but she had legs that even for that cat were amazing and seeing the Thai girl in that outfit was starting to get hot.

-Hey Nini

-Lisa...- his voice sounded hoarse. Hadn't he drunk enough water already?

The blonde ignored him and made her way into the bedroom. She had been busy that week and hadn't had time for the brunette and for some strange reason she hadn't stopped thinking about her strange tenant.

-This week I've been busy with training at the agency and I didn't even ask you how you're doing in the new room. Have you already adapted?

-Honestly... I hate him- he wrinkled his nose in disgust, making the blonde laugh.

Lisa sat down next to her on the bed and looked around.

-You're right, it's awful, I'm sorry Nini, I used to use it to dance or read, but then all my time was taken up by the agency.

Jennie shrugged it off. Her attention shifted to the taller girl's proximity and back to her fucked up legs. She swallowed hard and shifted in place trying to ease the discomfort in a certain area that was starting to get hotter than it should.

-Okay, that's not what I hate.

-No? So what's bothering you?

-Not being able to sleep on you- she explained without malice, although that comment was not as innocent for the blonde. But she couldn't even speak because the brunette spoke again- As a cat you let me sleep on you, what's the difference now that I'm human?

Lisa swallowed hard. *A lot, the difference is huge.* She thought, trying not to look too much at the part where her shirt had ridden up, revealing her thigh. Lisa's hands itched to touch that perfect skin but her common sense was on alert.

-Well, a lot, before you were my pet and now you are my...

"Am I your wife now?" she asked without understanding, and that sentence turned Lisa into jelly. *God, this cat woman is going to kill me!*

-No, you are not my wife...

- Am I not? - she thought for a moment, increasingly confused - do you not love me anymore because I'm human? - her eyes filled with tears, making her pout

-No! I mean yes! I mean... I mean...- she hit her forehead. *Why are you so damn nervous?* She asked herself, trying to calm down.

Maybe it was because those feline eyes haven't stopped staring at your lips and you're trying hard not to do the same. Her subconscious counterattacked- I love you, that hasn't changed, but we can't sleep together, that would mean something else.

-What thing?

Lisa thought about it for a moment.

-That's what Nini couples do.

-Then be my partner!

The blonde widened her eyes in surprise

-It doesn't work that way Jen...

The chestnut crossed her arms, offended.

- Great! I wasn't good enough as a cat and now I'm not good enough as a woman either?

- It's not that Jennie, it's... You... - but he stopped when he saw the Korean girl leaning in - what are you doing Nini?

-Your smell... Why do you smell so fucking good?

Lisa blushed. And where did she get the swear word from? *I must stop swearing in front of her.*

The brunette crawled torturously slowly towards Lisa, causing the poor Thai girl to go silent with that action.

-Lisa... what does it feel like to be with a woman?

And that was the trigger for the blonde who had two options, jump on him and tear off his clothes or run away like a coward, and she definitely chose the second option.

He jumped to his feet and in a few steps he was already in front of the door.

-I... I-I have to go, I have to take a shower- *a very cold shower Lalisa* - rest Nini

◇◇🐱◇◇

The next day had been the same, while Lisa was preparing breakfast (and by preparing I mean taking them out of the shipping bag), she felt small hands strumming her belly from behind. The blonde jumped in surprise, feeling every fiber of her body sensitive to that touch.

-Jennie, what...?- she tried to turn around but the brunette kept her grip; the Thai girl was trapped between the brunette's arms and pressed against the counter.

-Lisa, you're torturing me...

His voice was hoarse and needy, driving the taller girl crazy, who was dying to let out her wild side. This was pure animal desire. *Oh my god, what's wrong with me!?*

Shit, it's someone else being tortured here. Lisa squeezed her eyes shut. *Fuck, isn't he supposed to be a cat? Why the hell is he acting like a woman?*

-What are you talking about Jen?- he managed to say in a small voice.

-Your smell... I can't stand it...- she purred softly, too close to his lips- I needed...

-I have to go shower!!- Lisa got enough strength to break free from his grip and ran to the bathroom.

And it didn't get any better the next day when he practically greeted her naked in his bed when she got home from work.

-Jennie's here...! Oh shit, Jennie cover yourself!!!- he threw a shirt at her and covered his eyes- Oh my god, what are you doing here like this!?

-Lisa...

The brunette's sobs made her open them again, ignoring the fact that she was still in her underwear.

-Hey, what's up Jen...?

-I don't know what's happening to me, my body burns Lili! It burns when you're near and I don't know the reason!

There are two of us now, my little kitty. Lisa understood her fear, it was new to her although she did not fully understand her drastic change of attitude.

And everything got worse on the fifth and sixth day for poor Rubia, whose self-control was beginning to weaken.

Lisa woke up in the middle of the night when she heard the brunette screaming her name in desperate pleading. Lisa had stumbled to answer her call. She hadn't even gotten into the room when she felt the brunette pull her inside and slam her against the wall roughly.

Lisa gasped at the sight of the girl in such a state, her eyes were dark and dilated and her breathing was accelerated, her hair was more disheveled than usual, and that image had the Thai girl hotter than fucking hell.

-Please Lili, I need you inside me! - she begged in a sob, making the taller girl's skin crawl.

Did her cat really just ask her to make her hers? Lisa, for her part, only thought of the most sensible thing to do: leave the room like the devil himself and, yes, take a long cold shower to get rid of her fever. *This would take a long time.*

Feline heat

The doorbell rang and the blonde was quick to open the door, letting Rose in with a bag of breakfast.

The Australian looked at her friend closely and grimaced.

-You look horrible, you look like a lion and a raccoon mated and you came out as the result- he joked when he saw his friend's disheveled hair and the prominent, dark circles under her eyes- you really need my help and a good coffee- he entered the house and did not stop until he reached the kitchen.

Indeed, Lisa was not in her best days, not to mention that she was swaying in the same place as if she were going to collapse at any moment.

-Are you sure you haven't been bitten by a zombie these days? You look like the living dead, you look disgusting.

Lisa snorted and plopped down on one of the kitchen stools, while Rose took charge of pouring the pulverized beans into the coffee pot.

-You'd be the same if you had three damn days without sleep! - she replied grumpily.

-And why is that? Oh my God, don't tell me you've been fucking Jennie for three days!? Damn, Lisa, you're an animal, you must have crippled her from all that fucking...

-Fuck no! Believe me, you guess wrong.

The sound of the door caught the attention of both girls. The Thai girl stood grumbling at the door and Rose followed closely behind her, waiting.

-Good morning Mr. Chan, what an early riser! - the blonde with bangs sketched her best artificial smile - to what do I owe your visit?

The middle-aged man, however, did not seem at all happy or interested in giving explanations.

-Miss Manoban, the neighbors have continued to complain about your tenant's screams, she doesn't let them sleep.

-Oh well, but why is it my fault that my girl is so hot? - he explained, letting out a giggle to lighten the mood - Don't worry Mr. Chan, we'll be quieter.

"I hope so," the man turned around to walk away down the hallway.

- Happy day to you too! - the blonde shouted sarcastically and slammed the door - damn homophobic old man

He walked over to the couch and collapsed, all under Rose's confused gaze.

-Lalisa Manoban, did you fuck your cat!?

Lisa jumped up

-No way!- he rolled his eyes- But it seems that's what she wants- he left Thai again, I haven't slept in three fucking days because of her screams!

-Screams? Explain yourself.

-She's been very strange.

-How so?

-He's been harassing me all week, but these last three days he won't stop yelling my name and provoking me! - she covered her face, tired. - God, I think I'm going to get pneumonia from having to take so many cold showers!

Rose raised an eyebrow.

-Is he sexually provoking you? I suppose that if you use such a cliché method it is because his provocations have an effect on you- she smiled mischievously when she saw her friend's hot face- Seriously Lis, why don't you just masturbate...?

-No!- the blonde screamed, shocked, without letting her finish- are you crazy?

-Lisa, it's normal. How long have you been without action? As far as I know, you went a whole month without touching Tzuyu before you broke up and since then you haven't been with anyone else.

-It's my fucking cat, Rose!

-She's a damn woman Lisa! She's hot and on top of that she wants you to fuck her. Your situation is extremely acceptable, you're not made of steel Lisa- Rose decided to add something else when she saw her friend's anguish, it was evident that she was having an internal struggle between agreeing to her cat's provocations and rejecting her- I'm not telling you to sleep with Jennie, Lis, but if you must self-satisfy to relax your sexual frustration then do it. Do you think I don't do it? It's extremely liberating!

-Oh my God, Rose, the last thing I want to know right now is how you masturbate!

Lisa sighed overwhelmed with her friend's laughter in the background, she was really about to fall into temptation with that brunette, but her escapes kept her out of the situation.

-How many days do you say it's been like this?

-One week, at first she was just sweet and flirtatious from time to time, but now she's aggressive and practically rips her clothes off when she sees me.

-And what stops you from doing the same?

-Rose!

-Okay, your situation is a little funny.

-I'm glad you find my suffering amusing, my friend- she commented, disgusted.

-Don't be so dramatic- she rolled her eyes when the girl with bangs showed her the middle finger- save it for Jennie, I'm sure in her state she'll be dying to feel it inside her- she thought about it for a moment- but be careful, with those kilometer-long fingers of yours, you're going to leave the poor girl immobile.

He laughed as he heard his friend's growl.

-Fuck, you're insufferable, I don't know how I'm still your friend!

-Because you love me Lis, as simple as that

They both returned to the kitchen and Rose poured two cups of coffee while looking intently at her phone.

The blondes turned around when they saw a brunette with disheveled hair rubbing her eyes in the doorway, that image touched the Thai girl.

-You look like a baby- Rose commented.

Jennie raised her face but her eyes were fixed on Lisa

-Lisa!- she ran up to the Thai girl, hanging on her hips and burying her face in the taller girl's neck.

-Hey, if it's me who came to visit, it's me you should greet as a koala!

-Hello squirrel- he greeted simply without much effort, his attention was on the pretty mole on the Thai girl's neck. Since when are cats attracted to moles? Apparently she is the first and she was dying to feel that little piece of skin against her lips.

Rose made a face and Lisa, even with the brunette on top of her, couldn't help but laugh.

-Shut up Lisa! And why do you call me that?

-Oh, your cheeks are like a squirrel's!

Rose rolled her eyes. During breakfast the brunette behaved just as Lisa had said, she kept looking at her or cuddling up to her.

-Lili, why do you keep ignoring me!?

The Thai girl tried not to shudder at the nickname the Korean girl had given her, because if she paid attention to him she would end up kissing her until she was breathless.

- Jennie, you're literally sitting on my lap.

The psychologist noticed the brunette's actions without stopping paying attention to her cell phone.

-Jennie, how have you been feeling lately?

The aforementioned looked at Rose strangely. What did she mean?

-Brilliant
-I mean, have you been anxious?
-A little...
- Have you felt differently?
-Rose, just tell us what you know- Lisa pressed, impatiently.
-Ok, I think Jennie is in the "estrus" phase right now, and if the internet isn't lying Jen is two days away from entering the "meta-estrus" stage.
-Damn Rose, do you want to talk to me in Spanish?
The named rolled her eyes
-Jennie is presenting her feline heat
Jennie widened her eyes and stood up nervously.
-Kai...
-That?
-We must find Chu!
The two friends exchanged glances and watched Jennie run to her room.
-Who the hell is Chu?

....

Pornographic trauma

-Let me see if I understand, are we going to your house to look for your sister in need?

-Hey, the heat is very strong!

Lisa parked the car in front of the mansion, the Kims were one of the wealthiest families in Seoul.

-If you knew where you live, why didn't you leave? - the Thai woman asked, confused.

Jennie looked at her nervously and looked away at the house.

-Because I wanted to stay with you- she whispered, head down. With that she got out of the car without waiting for an answer.

Jennie circled the house, she knew Chu didn't spend much time there when she was in heat.

In the distance he heard a pitiful meow

-My God, that animal must be getting killed! - Rose had arrived next to Lisa, following closely behind the brunette. The three of them were observing the wall in front of them as if analyzing the situation.

- Ok, and we're just going to stay and watch the wall or....?

Before Lisa could finish, Jennie began to imitate the cat's meow. The feline remained silent as if trying to understand what the brunette was saying.

Everything remained silent for a while, both blondes looked expectantly at the fence with impatience, what were they waiting for?

-On the other side of the fence is the Kim's backyard, there little Ella has a castle similar to a tree house but on the ground and when we are in heat she leaves us there so as not to disturb the house- clarified the brunette.

Shortly afterwards they saw a curious ragdoll peering over the wall. Lisa smiled at the similarity between the cat and the feline

Nini, who must have been her sister. The feline was about to jump from the fence to the tree and slipped as it tried to get down, having miscalculated its movement.

Rose screamed as she felt the weight of the cat and its claws dig into her head.

-Take it away from me!!!

Jennie rushed to remove it, while Wing with bangs looked at her friend checking that she was okay.

-Chu, I'm Jennie- the brunette informed the animal when she noticed his confusion.

- Jennie?

The chestnut shook her head

-I mean Nini!

-Nini! Oh mother cat, what happened to you!? You are horrible! I told you that it was not good to go out with humans

Lisa and Rose watched the girl and the feline meow without understanding what they were saying. That exchange was crazy. When had they gotten into all this?

Rose snorted, bored, and picked up the cat in her arms.

-Ok, it's getting late to watch my soap opera, we have to go!

Chu looked up and observed the girl. *Holy cow, those cheeks!* He reached out a paw to the Australian's face and licked her cheek, causing the girl to look back at him, uncomfortable.

-I'm your cat, darling, do with me whatever you want!

Rose frowned as she watched the cat meow over and over again without taking her paw off her face.

-This is unreal- he said, pushing Chu away from his face- here, another one is hungry- he handed the cat to Lisa and walked away towards the car

◇◇🐱◇◇

In the Thai apartment, Jennie and Chu continued their dialogue and the brunette was in charge of translating for the two blondes.

-So they're both in heat? That explains a lot- Rose looked at her lap, where the cat was happily rolling around- this cat scares me

Rose left after a couple of hours. Jennie and Chu were in the brunette's room; Lisa must have been asleep already but her heat was attacking strongly.

-Fuck Chu, I needed her!- Jennie writhed in the bed in agony, her desire for the blonde tripled with her heat and it was starting to be torture.

-How quickly you changed Kai

-You don't understand, this is much more intense, it burns me! - She ran her hands through her hair in desperation, she wanted to run to the blonde and have her possess her once and for all.

-Hey, I have an idea!- Chu jumped out of bed and climbed onto the desk between gasps- Oh god cat, I need to get in shape

-What you should do is stop eating fried chicken

-Never!

Jennie sat on the stool in front of the desk, waiting for her sister's plan, any idea that would appease her zeal was welcome.

-Let's look it up on the internet, I've seen Ella researching this thing- Chu scratched the laptop trying to open it without success- Damn, it's impossible to access it, it must have a password!

-Just open the lid Chu

-Mmm... abracadabra! Open sesame! Expelliarmus! Bibidi babidi bu!- Chu dropped his head onto the laptop- it's useless, I don't know any more spells, the security is too advanced for me, not even Harry Potter's worked!

Jennie rolled her eyes and opened it effortlessly using her new hands.

-Excellent Nini, I envy your thumbs!- Chu sat in front of the laptop with Jennie behind him- Take those glasses and put them on me!

-Why? You don't need them, your feline vision is more developed than any human's.

-This way I'll look more professional! Now put them on me!

The brunette sighed, her sister was quite a case

-What are we supposed to look for?- he asked, putting the glasses on Chu.

-Leave it to me- he wrinkled his nose- for God's sake, that human is blinder than a mole, no wonder she needs glasses!

The feline's paws began to press keys left and right as she typed into Google. Jennie's eyes widened as she saw what she was typing into the search engine.

How does a human please herself?

-Chu, where do you get that from!?

-I heard the cute girl with adorable cheeks in the kitchen...

-Rose...

-tell Laila

-Lisa!

-That he should pity himself more or he wouldn't relax asexually

Jennie frowned in disgust. Why did Lusa need such a thing when she had her!? She crossed her arms indignantly and growled.

-Lalisa Manoban is a fool!

Chu ignored his sister's complaints and continued his research. He went into a page and smiled when he saw that there were pictures

- Great, they must be moving pictures, you know, like on TV - he clicked on the first one and waited for it to load.

Both the brunette and the feline's eyes widened as they saw a fully naked girl sitting in the middle of a bed with objects around her that both ragdolls were unaware of.

-Ok Nini, pay close attention, you must do everything she does.

20 minutes later...

-God Chu, I don't think I can do any of that!- the brunette watched in amazement as the girl specially used a toy bigger than her hand and complained in the process- and it seems to hurt her!- she covered her eyes in panic

-Nonsense Nini, that's the way humans say it, which she loves- Chu explained without taking his eyes off the screen- Oh my god, I think she's possessed, look how she writhes and arches her back!

Jennie removed a hand from her eyes and quickly covered them again.

-Chu, that's horrible, take it off already!

-But Nini, that's what... Oh feline god, he's sticking his whole fist in! - the cat covered her muzzle with a paw, amazed.

The girl's screams were deafening and they didn't count on a certain Thai woman in shock on the other side of the door. Lisa had gotten up to drink water and on her way back stood motionless in front of the door listening to the moans coming from inside. *Is that Nini?*

He decided he had to intervene when the screams became louder.

-Jennie, what...?- he widened his eyes. In front of his laptop, Jennie and the feline were attentive to the video of a girl without any clothes. His mouth widened. What was his cat doing watching that?

-Lisa?

Hearing his name he took his eyes off the screen, noticing the brunette's feline gaze and frowned at Chu with his glasses.

- Are those my reading glasses? - she asked confused and looked at the screen again - I... I didn't mean to interrupt, I'm leaving now...

The brunette watched the tallest one leave with a deep blush on her cheeks and ears. She would have liked to go after her and curl up in her lap while the blonde stroked her back like the previous days, but she knew that as a human that wish was impossible and that depressed her.

- I give up! Holy crap, I think I've gone to the wrong page, that girl is doing acrobatics with her legs

-Well, if it worked, I lost all desire for it- he made a face of disgust, his desire had completely disappeared- I think it even traumatized me

-How effective! I'll leave you a comment and some stars- the feline began to type, happy to have achieved her goal.

Thanks for the video, after watching it I lost all desire! 🐱

◇ ◇ ◇ ◇ ◇

-Humans think of everything, there are even cat faces!!- she sent the message and both, cat and human, went back to bed ready to sleep.

Sexual tension

The Australian's laughter echoed in the Thai's office, and Lisa was starting to get angry at her friend's attitude.

-Park, if you keep making fun of me, I'll send security to get you out.

Rose wiped away a furtive tear, still smiling. Lisa had called her to talk about what had happened with Jennie and the psychologist had not stopped laughing at what had happened.

-Oh come on Lisa, you know Jackson is one of my favorite patients, his intermittent explosive disorder is under control. I don't think he has the balls to kick me out of your office after his wife got back together with him thanks to me.

Lisa rolled her eyes and sat down in her seat behind the desk and groaned as she heard her friend's laughter again.

-Fuck Rose!

-I'm sorry Lis, it's just that...! Oh god, my stomach!- she held her stomach, unable to stop laughing- Did you really find her watching porn with her cat?

-She's her sister- he corrected- and why would she lie to you? I was traumatized, that cat had my glasses on! It was terrifying.

-I told you that animal was scary, yesterday when I was leaving your house he winked at me- Rose shuddered at the memory- just remembering his hairy and perverted face gives me goosebumps

Lisa nodded and sighed tiredly, massaging her temple.

-I don't know what to do with Jennie's situation, she's very out of control.

-Oh Lisa, the poor thing is trying to release sexual tension and as a human she doesn't know what to do- she took a bite of her hamburger and continued- Why don't you take care of that?

-Are you talking about...?

-Masturbate her? Yes.

-No way

-My god Lisa, you are the most sexual woman I know, if you didn't have a fucking vagina I would say you were a man

-There are girls with penises Rose, besides, how could you think that? She's my cat!

-Physically, Lisa is a woman! What are you afraid of?

-I'm not afraid of anything

-Oh yes, you fear her, you fear that by getting involved with her you also involve your feelings.

-What are you taking about?

-I'm talking about your heart Lisa, you're afraid of falling in love with your cat

Lisa stood up from her seat abruptly. As she was about to answer the door rang and Irene's face appeared in the doorway.

-I'm sorry to interrupt Li... Miss Manoban, one of the partners would like to see you.

-Of course Irene, let him in, Miss Park was already leaving.

Rose stood up, giving her friend a meaningful look before turning and walking out. She had known Lisa since high school and knew how closed off she became after her heart was broken.

He let out a melancholic sigh as he left the building, there had to be a way to make her see things differently.

-Well, I guess I'll have to take care of it on my own- he started the car to his next destination- If Lisa won't help Jennie, I will.

◈◈🐱◈◈

-Good morning, she comes to register.

-Name?

-Jennie kim

-One moment please

After registration, both girls walked to the machines. All under Rose's instructions.

-Well, there are three effective methods for a psychologist, that is me- she pointed to herself- and any human being to release tension and stress of any kind, and they are: The gym, yoga and sex- she named counting on her fingers- but in your case sex is not an option, and it is precisely that sexual tension that we want to release.
-How do you use those three methods?
-Yoga clears my mind of worry, the gym of disgust, and sex... Well let's say that that's a recharge of happiness- she laughed leaving her towel and thermos next to the treadmill- Fine, your job is to get so tired that your only thought will be a bed but to sleep for a century, and this will be your machine- she pointed at the treadmill- that's how hamsters release tension!
Jennie reluctantly climbed onto the machine and stood still. Beside her Rose was already jogging calmly with headphones in each ear. *Was she injured?* The brunette looked at the machine with curiosity. In front of her was a keyboard with buttons and a station for her thermos.
-Maybe I should... - he pressed a button and instantly the tape began to move. The brunette experienced two emotions: fear at the unexpected movement and pride at seeing that he had managed to make it move.
A few seconds later he saw out of the corner of his eye how the Australian turned a button and changed her trot to a faster one.
-I can do it too- Jennie imitated the action using a little more speed, managing to adapt to it with ease.
On the other hand, the blonde had focused so much on her music that she forgot to turn on the brunette's machine.
-Oh Jen I'm sorry, let me go...!- she was speechless when she saw her, the girl was running on that treadmill as if her life depended on it. Her face was soaked and her shorts showed a couple of drops of sweat running down her legs- Fuck, Lisa is going to kill me...- she whispered when she saw that the brunette had not only caught her

attention, but also that of a couple of guys from the gym, who had left their weights to watch her run- Ok Jen, enough!

The blonde's sudden voice made the feline girl lose her concentration and she was startled, managing to miss the sequence of the machine, and being thrown backwards.

-Oh god, Jen! I'm sorry, I'm sorry, I'm sorry!- he ran towards- damn it if Lisa's going to kill me now...!

◇◇🐱◇◇

Rose drove to the blonde's workplace, the brunette's fall had left her with a huge bump on her right eyebrow and in a call from Lisa she had to confess what had happened. Upon finding out, the aforementioned ordered her to take her immediately to her agency, and of course there she would earn a reprimand from the dancer.

-Rose, calm down, it was an accident, it wasn't even your fault.

-Tell that to Lisa, my time has come!

Jennie smiled, she didn't understand what that girl was talking about but she certainly felt great.

-You were right, exercise helps, I feel great.

-That's good, because I feel like I'll die soon at the hands of a certain Thai woman...

Sad reality

Lisa drummed her fingers on the desk in a little nervous tic, while her free hand tried to break the pen between her fingers.

The Australian had called her to inform her about the chestnut's accident and she couldn't help but get angry. What was Jennie doing with Rose? The conversation she had had with the Australian in the morning had not gone well.

-What if she took charge of the matter?- her blood boiled just thinking about Rose relieving Jennie's tension- damn Australian- she whispered grumpily

-Wow, someone's in a bit of a bad mood- the blonde was so deep in her thoughts that she didn't hear the door open- Just to clarify, knock before entering

The Thai girl sat up in her leather seat, watching as the girl placed a cup in front of her and smiled at her.

- I thought you might need a little, I've seen you very exhausted lately.

Lisa nodded gratefully and took the cup, feeling the warmth of the liquid between her hands.

-Nothing a little caffeine can't cure, huh?- he joked, inhaling the aroma and then taking a sip. He sighed- I never tire of thanking you, you're my little lifesaver, I don't know how to repay you for everything you do for me.

The other's cheeks blushed and she gave a shy smile.

-I'll be happy to do it, Lisie, but... - she played with her hair in a nervous manner - you can pay me in one way...

Lisa looked at her with interest. She walked around the table to be closer to the girl, an act that made her assistant even more nervous.

-Do you need a raise? Because if that's the case I can...

-Oh no Lisa, I didn't mean that! - he quickly denied, working up the courage to take her hand - I... I meant... Well, we never had that date we talked about and...

Before he could continue, the door was flung open, revealing a brunette with a radiant smile and feline eyes.

-_Lisa!!

-Jennie, wait!- Rose's voice echoed in the hallway

Jennie's smile disappeared when she saw that the dancer was not alone.

-Lisa?- his eyes traveled from the face of the aforementioned to the intertwined hands of her and the other girl.

Lisa noticed the brunette's gaze and quickly let go of Irene, a gesture that the girl noticed instantly.

-Jennie what...?

-Oh god, I see you're not just fast on the treadmill- Rose panted with a hand on her chest from the chase. She inhaled sharply and blew out a breath- I think I lost all my air

Rose noticed the tension in the room and regretted making such an entrance. Irene looked at her confused by the situation, and Lisa looked at her with hatred.

On the other hand, Jennie didn't even look at her, her eyes were fixed on her feet and Rose knew the reason.

-Jen... Are you...?

-Rose, how dare you take her without telling me!? Don't ever take Jennie without my permission again.

Rose clenched her fists and shook her head.

-You're not her fucking mother Lisa, she's 24 years old, I think she can decide for herself!

-Not while you're under my roof!

-Are you listening to yourself Lalisa!?

Rose was shocked and angry at her friend's possessive attitude.

-I'm not going to repeat it Rose!

-Well, don't do it, it's best for me to go, I can't talk to you like that.

-Maybe it's for the best

Both challenged each other with their eyes, Rose hated arguing with Lisa, but sometimes it was necessary, the Thai girl was very stubborn and never gave in.

He looked away at Jennie and stood in front of her.

-Hey Nini- he whispered sweetly, brushing some of her hair away from her face- are you coming?

-Rose, Jennie is staying with me

-Why don't you let her decide?

-I...

-Stop fighting!- the brunette shouted, tired of the situation. She looked at Rose and smiled- I'll go with you, squirrel.

Rose smiled at the nickname, how had she gone from hating her for biting her and eating her fish, to wanting to protect her from the pain she was feeling at that moment?

Lisa looked at her with a look of abandonment, like a child who has just been left by his mother. She looked down, defeated, and nodded.

- Okay, as you wish, I won't be home early anyway, I've already arranged to meet Irene for dinner.

And that was it, the brunette ran out of the office without looking back.

She heard Rose calling her, and Lisa too, but she didn't want to go back there, not knowing that the Thai girl and that beautiful Korean girl were going to share an evening. And yet she, for some stupid reason, just wanted to be with the blonde who had just broken her heart.

◇◇🐱◇◇

He had run without stopping, without a specific direction, he just wanted to get as far away from that office as possible, as far away from Lisa as possible.

He had stopped in the park near the blonde's house, the same one where he met her and on the same bench where he saw her for the first time.

-I'm a fool- she whispered, wiping the tears from her cheeks- I shouldn't have fallen in love with her...

-That wasn't up to you- she started when she heard the voice behind her.

She saw Rose sit next to her with her gaze on the landscape, Rose happened to be a calm and spiritual person, so she was surprised to see her react like that in front of Lisa.

-But she doesn't feel anything for me

-And how do you know that's not true?

Jennie sighed hurt

-Look at me, my clothes are huge, my nails are broken and my hair is damaged... I'm not as pretty as her, she's so beautiful and I... - he swallowed with difficulty, he felt a lump in his throat - She's perfect. And that girl is too, she's ideal for Lisa

-So you give up?

-What else can I do?

-Fight, fight for what you want

-I'm not good for her Rose

Rose snorted

-Jennie, I'm starting to think you're even more stubborn than Lisa- she rolled her eyes at the girl's refusal- you're beautiful, both inside and out, and if Lisa doesn't see it it's because she's either very blind or very stupid, I'm going with the latter- she paused, thinking about her friend's reasons and sighed- Lisa has suffered a lot, she's already learned to stand on her own. She's not a bad girl, she just has a lot of insecurities, she doesn't usually open up to anyone

-She sees me as her pet
-So let's make her see you as what you are, a beautiful and good-natured woman, which is exactly what I want for her.
-I don't think it's possible.
-Honey, nothing is impossible for Roseanne Park; let's show Lalisa what a great woman Jennie Kim is, and you'll see how she'll drool after you later.

Coffee Cat

-Aa ...

Rose parked the car in front of a very colorful coffee shop; the words Coffee Cat stood out in turquoise letters on the window, with the silhouette of a feline above them.

Rose had promised the brunette that on their next outing they would take her sister, and she couldn't find a better place to take a feline than to a cat cafe.

-I'm in cat paradise!- Chu looked around in fascination. All around the place were cats of different breeds playing with the customers- I feel like I'm in Disneyland for cats!

-Chu, wait, come back!- her sister tried to stop her without success, she liked the place, no doubt, but her mind was still in that office and in the touch of hands between Lisa and that Irene.

-Leave her alone, she looks like a child visiting an amusement park for the first time- Rose laughed as she watched the ragdoll climb a pillar surrounded by rope and her smile faded as she watched her pull a cat to reach the top.

-I won! The place is mine, losers!- exclaimed Chu from the top.

The Australian instead just watched her meow, oblivious to the meaning of her crying.

-How aggressive...- he turned to Jennie, noticing that she was a little distracted- Are you okay? What do you think of the place?

The Korean blinked, snapping out of her thoughts.

-It's incredible, I didn't know there were cafes for cats, in fact we don't like coffee

Rose laughed tenderly and shook her head.

-It's not for the cats, but for the clients. The place is for cat lovers, you can play with them and stuff like that. I usually recommend this kind of places to my patients, it's a good therapeutic method to release stress. Personally, I prefer the aquariums, but Lisa loves this place and... Oh god, I'm sorry!

He apologized as he saw the brunette's smile disappear.

-Don't worry- she replied distractedly- what exactly are we going to do?

Rose smiled and pulled out of her bag a royal blue notebook with a bunch of colored dividers.

-My notebook, I don't leave the house without it, I write everything down here, it's a means of order and balance, I love being balanced with my activities- she explained while turning the pages and stopping on a blank one- well, let's start- she twirled the pen and looked at the brunette- the first thing you need is a bath- she saw how the girl wrinkled her nose, ready to reject it and continued- I'm sorry, you stink and Lisa's method of using wet wipes to clean yourself is not an option, you need a good bath with air fresheners included, it's very relaxing, you'll see

1-Foam bath ☐

-Well, every time we complete something on the list we cross it off, that way we will be able to discard activities and we will know how much we have achieved, okay?

-I think so

During this time they were both lengthening the list, Jennie after a while had relaxed and was drinking a cup of hot milk, while Rose animatedly moaned with pleasure as she gobbled down a piece of her Croissant.

Shortly after they had to leave because of Chu

-That was fun!

-Chu, you started a cat fight and almost left that Scottish Fold hairless! - her sister scolded her in feline language.

The kitty growled in disapproval.

-It's not my fault that they don't know how to defend themselves, that idiot touched my butt!

-It was a blind cat!!
-And what do you know!? It was very suspicious, I think he was just pretending...

While both sisters argued in their dialect, Rose took advantage of the traffic light to quickly scan her cell phone.

○ *Thai Princess* ◈

Rose, where is Jennie???
Why the hell didn't you bring her home!?
Damn it Rose, answer those calls or I swear I'll castrate you!

◈◈

And the list of threats continued.

He put his phone aside and sighed, turning his attention back to the road. *I'll talk to her later*.

Jennie and her sister had stayed at her apartment for the night, the brunette didn't want to go back to Lisa, not after she was at that dinner with Irene.

The Australian had to turn off her phone after ignoring the first 15 calls, the Pretty Savage ringtone was already starting to get on her nerves thanks to the Thai girl's constant ringing.

Mental note, change the ringtone.

◈◈🐱◈◈

-No, I don't want to!
-Come on Jennie, get in the tub!
-No!
- You should do it, it's not that bad!
-No!!
-Fight Nini, fight!- Chu encouraged her from his place eating a nugget

Rose struggled to get the brunette into the bathtub without success, the girl refused to cooperate.

-You know what? As a therapist, I set myself the goal of finding out why cats have this trauma to water, as good as it is- he turned around when he heard the cat's replicating meows- and you better be supporting me or else you'll also be in for a bath!

The feline's eyes widened and in a snap she was out of the bathroom like a soul carried by the devil.

-Coward- Rose rolled her eyes and continued with her work.

His eyes slid over the Korean's nakedness and he held his breath. *Damn, she's hot.* Every one of her curves was feminine and seductive. How could Lisa resist that woman for so long?

-Squirrel, are you okay?

Rose blinked rapidly and shook her head to regain her self-control. *It's just a body Rose.* She bit her lip. *A very sexy and tempting one.* She growled. *Focus.*

-Great...

🐱

On the other side of the city, the Thai woman was debating whether to go to the psychologist's office or let her pride get the better of her.

She shifted uncomfortably in her leather seat. She hadn't been able to sleep all night, thinking of Rose and Jennie together filled her with anger. Why hadn't he stayed with her? Why had he preferred Rose?

-Damn!- she snorted in dismay.

-You look like a panda with those dark circles- Irene burst into her office with two cups of coffee- you look bad Lisie, and I don't plan on finding out why, but something tells me it has to do with that girl

Lisa shifted and sighed heavily, rubbing her eyelids.

-It's a complicated subject Irene, you wouldn't understand it.

-Well, I think it's simpler than you say, but you'll know- he gave her a kiss on the cheek and smiled -by the way, thanks for the outing last night, I had a good time

Lisa forced a smile which she erased as soon as the door closed, leaving her again with her mental monologue.

She had gone out with her assistant that night, just as she had told the brunette, although it was a last minute plan, that date with Irene was not even scheduled, not until she received the call from Rose informing her of the choreographer's accident. Something inside her stirred, causing a strange discomfort that did not resemble cramps caused by indigestion, no, this was different, as if her insides were boiling and twisting in turn. And it was enough to see Jennie with Rose to use her trump card, including poor Irene in the farce. But what did she intend with that?

At the time he had just wanted to upset Jennie, but seeing those feline eyes fill with tears had broken his heart.

-Overcome Manoban, she's just a cat- she told herself in an attempt to erase her from her mind. *But then why did that look of disappointment still hurt me? Why did I feel betrayed when I saw her leave with Rose? Damn it and why am I crying right now?* Deep in her heart she had the answer very clear, although her mind refused to accept it, Lisa was beginning to have feelings for that little Korean girl with a feline look.

◇◇🐱◇◇

Twenty minutes had passed since the girl had left the office. She was still restless and her mind kept torturing her with thoughts of Jennie and Rose. *Shit* . She dialed her intercom and waited.

-Lisa, do you need something?

-Another outing with the best assistant ever, are you free for lunch?

He heard a laugh on the other end.

-I don't know, I'd have to talk to my boss...

-I don't think she'll refuse, as long as you have lunch with her- she joked without much enthusiasm- come by my office when you're done so we can go together

Although Lisa knew it wasn't fair to get Irene's hopes up, she needed to forget that brunette with messy hair who made her heart beat like a schoolgirl in love. *Remember Lalisa, you can't fall in love with your cat.* She told herself before focusing on her work again .

...◈...

New Jennie

Rose held Jennie's hand tightly as the hairdresser washed and untangled the clump of hair. Or was it the other way around?

-God Jen, you're going to break my hand! - he complained with a gesture of pain trying to get away from the grip without success.

-I'm sorry Squirrel, I just don't like water in my hair.

After getting the brunette to bathe, Rose had taken her to the hairdresser, the most tedious thing was that unruly mane that had to be tamed as soon as possible.

The hairdresser sighed in relief when she finally managed to free the last knot.

-Okay, now I can start cutting. Any special cuts?

-Leave it on your shoulders, and moisturize it a little, we want it to look like new. Oh, and it also needs a manicure.

-Count on that

The process was late, that mane was causing a lot of work for the poor hairdresser.

Rose had sat down to wait on a sofa with old magazines, this fact seemed ironic and offensive to her.

-Who leaves magazines from ten years ago? It's like reading that Kristen Stewart and Robert Pattinson are dating when Stewart is currently more lesbian than the word - she rolled her eyes and put the magazine back - for the first time I put myself in my patients' shoes when they have to wait for their appointment. I'm going to ask my secretary to update the magazines monthly, this is degrading

She shifted her leg, her butt hurt, and her crossword puzzle app was already starting to give her a migraine.

-Holy God, how much longer!? I feel like I've been here for a century- she whispered uneasily, while searching through her networks- the internet is overrated

After the hairdressing, the Australian had decided to completely change the Korean's image and she could only achieve this by getting rid of that horrible giant shirt of Lisa's, something that Jennie was not willing to accept.

-Jen, you can wear it, but not to go out. Do you know how offensive that garment is to any fashion connoisseur? That outfit shouldn't even exist.

-Lisa looks good

-Well, you have to admit that anything looks good on that damn Thai girl, especially since it doesn't fit her like a nun's dress- he explained. The girl was so short that the same shirt that looked great on Lisa's thighs covered her knees.

Jennie pouted as a last resort and Rose smiled at her.

-No way Jen, your methods of persuasion don't work with this psychologist, I'm the one playing with minds here, so let's go.

If Rose was losing patience at the hairdresser's, she ended up running out in fashion stores

Jennie didn't accept any outfit, and she hadn't even allowed him to see her in any.

I don't like
Very tight
It's uncomfortable
I don't think it suits me well
He suffocated me!
No...
No.
Nooo!

-Enough, Jennie Kim, if you don't get out of that dressing room right now I'll make sure you don't eat tuna again for the rest of your 9 lives!- he threatened impatiently.

Instantly the curtain of the fitting room opened.

Both Rose and the salesman dropped their chins at the sight of her. The brunette looked incredible in those shorts that accentuated her legs and that matching top that vaguely revealed a bit of her abdomen, and over it, a complementary jacket.

-Jury, after this Lalisa will have to build me a whole altar to bless me- he commented without taking the girl's gaze away.

-Who the hell is Lalisa..?- whispered the seller, enthralled by the curves of the brunette

Rose frowned as she noticed the boy's lascivious glances at Jennie's horn.

-Hey, asshole, they pay you for bringing and carrying clothes, not for ogling the clients.

The boy blinked nervously.

-I...

-Do something useful and go get some tights and matching shoes. Now! - she shouted when she noticed that he was once again becoming enthralled by the Korean girl. Rose rolled her eyes and shook her head as she watched him stumble away - inept

-I'll take it off.

Rose turned around when she heard the girl.

-Yes, because we're taking it, and a couple of other cute things too, and Lisa will take care of the rest.

Jennie looked down shyly at the mention of the blonde with bangs.

-Do you think he'll like it?

-Honey, with those clothes on that body and that face, there is no human being who can resist you- he praised with a half smile- luckily Korean women don't have bushy eyebrows, yours are perfect.

On leaving, Rose decided to leave the shopping in the car and go back to the mall to eat something, she was starving... although she was usually always hungry.

-So much aesthetic preparation made me hungry, what do you think of sushi?

-Sushi?- the brunette asked confused.

-It's raw fish and...

-Yes, sushii!!!- the Korean girl quickly affirmed with excitement.

◇◇🐱◇◇

Once there, the chestnut was delighted with that dish, asking for another portion for the third time.

-Well, someone loves sushi- the blonde smiled watching as the girl devoured it with her hands without any shame.

Jennie looked at her smiling with her cheeks swollen with food and nodded. But her smile faded as she fixed her gaze a few tables away

He swallowed as quickly as he could and stood up.

-Let's go

-What? But they still haven't brought us the bill and...

-Please, let's go- his voice sounded broken and his crystal eyes looked at her pleadingly.

It was enough to turn around to know the reason for her discomfort. At two tables, Lisa and Irene shared a very happy meal, oblivious to the presence of the other two.

-Okay, let's go.

He gestured to a waiter and after paying they got ready to leave.

Instead, at the corner table, Irene was again laughing amusedly. The girl was outgoing and extremely beautiful. At her request, they had gone to eat sushi, although Lisa couldn't stand the taste, so she had decided on ramen.

The girl kept talking about who knows what and the blonde had stopped paying attention to her for quite some time. Her mind was focused on the strange and innocent girl who had once been her cat. What is she doing?

His eyes traveled to a couple of girls who were getting ready to leave the place, he couldn't see their faces, but something about the blonde seemed familiar. It wasn't until he saw his companion turn around that he knew who they were.

- And then I told him...

-Jennie?- he watched both girls quicken their pace without turning around again. His instinct was to go after her but his mind was blocked. Why were Jennie and Rose there?

-Jennie? No, her name is Jin. Lisa, are you listening to me?

Lisa didn't answer. Are they dating? That idea was her trigger, she didn't want Rose near Jennie, she didn't want anyone near the brunette.

Her jealousy got the better of her, and before she knew it she was already leaving the money on the table and standing up ready to follow them.

-Hey, what are you doing? That's a hundred dollar bill, the food didn't cost that much Lis

-We must go.

-But there are still 15 minutes left until the break ends- she commented, surprised, looking at the time on her phone.

-I won't go back to the agency- the Thai woman took out a second hundred-dollar bill and handed it to the girl- here, take the rest of the day, I won't be able to take you, I have to do something important

-What? But... Wait, where are you going!?

-To claim what belongs to me

Plan of love

Two days had passed since what happened with the Thai girl, the blonde had no idea how she had gotten to Rose's house, and early in the morning she left the apartment without the other two girls noticing her.

At that time Jennie had decided to postpone her visit, she did not understand the actions of the humans, but she knew that Lisa was not very happy with her. What had she done wrong?

On the other hand, seeing her with that girl made him angry and sad. He wanted to be the one to take her hand and go out to lunch with her.

-What's wrong Nini? I mean Jennie

-Chu, I miss her- she pouted hugging the pillow

-Well, not me, look, here they give us chicken skewers! - she sighed, smiling - I will marry that woman

-With Lisa!?

-Of course not cat face, with Rose!

Jennie turned around looking at the ceiling, she had never felt this way about any feline, not even Kai. What was so special about that human?

-I would like to know how to make her fall in love with me..

The feline ran to the laptop and looked at her sister with the smile of the laughing cat.

-Move your ass Jendeukie!

The brunette rolled her eyes, but obeyed. This time it wasn't so hard for the kitten to open the laptop. She quickly opened the search engine and her furry little paws began to type.

Steps to make a human female fall in love with you ↖

-They are Chu women, not females

-Here!- he clicked on a page

How to make a girl fall in love with you in 5 simple steps

Chu purred happily, he had found what he was looking for, however the brunette was not so sure, after her past trauma she was wary of that device and its mobile videos.

-I don't know Chu, what if it's not the right page?

-Shut up and memorize the steps, with these tips you will have that woman in the palm of your paw

-I don't know Chu, I'm not that good at those things.

-Well then I'll go with you.

Jennie frowned.

-So that?

-So you don't make a mistake. Besides, she won't notice because she doesn't understand feline language.

Jennie widened her eyes in surprise at her sister's ingenuity.

-You're a genius Chu!

-I know sister, I know. Now let's read a little about it.

◇◇🐱◇◇

-Are you sure you want to go today?

-Yeah

-And why are we supposed to bring your cat?

Chu let out a displeased meow and launched himself into the backseat, growling.

-She's my sister, and...- Jennie thought for a moment- and she doesn't like to stay home alone.

Rose raised an eyebrow, parking in front of the company and looked at the brunette out of the corner of her eye.

-That thing has left me without chicken, I'm almost sure it's happy when I'm not at home- she said ironically, taking off her belt and disconnecting the keys- anyway, let's go get your girl

At the office, Lisa was beginning to suffer from migraines. Being the CEO of her company was exhausting and stressful. When had she stopped dancing and decided to sit behind a desk?

He took an aspirin from the drawer and swallowed it with a little coffee. *When there is a shortage of water, coffee always helps.*

-Hey Manoban, I'm here to get you to pay for my broken nose.

The businesswoman quickly looked up when she recognized her friend's voice. Rose's nose was bandaged, though it didn't look like it had been broken. Had she hit her that hard? Her cheeks flushed with embarrassment as she remembered what had happened. How had she been able to go to Rose's house, force open the door, wait for her return, and attack her?

-Oh yeah! I also have the invoice for my new lock. Damn, couldn't you use the copy of the key under the mat?

Lisa raised an eyebrow.

-I would have used it if you had one there. You don't even have a mat!

Rose thought about it for a moment and said

-Touche, just for that I'll cross that bill off your debt.

-I'm sorry about what happened Rose, I don't know what came over me, I don't even drink excessively!

-Your reason has a name and surname and right now she is detained outside the building for bringing a cat

Lisa widened her eyes and quickly picked up the phone.

-Suga, let the girl in- he ordered the security guard- Yes, the cat can come in too. Thanks- he hung up and let out a sigh, rubbing his eyes wearily- why the hell does he bring his sister?

-I have a divine face, not a fortune teller, how the hell am I supposed to know?

-He's been staying at your apartment, you should know!

-Those two chatter in Morse code, Lisa, I still don't know cat language.

Lisa rolled her eyes. She still had to talk to her friend about what happened, she wanted to know what her current relationship with

Jennie was. Thinking about that gave her a stomach ache. Rose and Jennie? *Never!*

-Why have you come?

Rose shrugged indifferently.

-I wanted to see you...

-And why did you want to see me?

-Not me, she wanted to see you.

The dancer's heart raced. Jennie wanted to see her. Did she miss her? The idea made her excited. After those days without seeing the girl, she was dying to see those feline eyes again. *Control yourself Lisa, you will only see your ...*

His mind went blank when the door opened and he saw the completely renewed brunette enter.

Lisa swallowed hard, that skirt combined with the top left her throat dry. *Cat? Yeah right, what you have in front of you is quite a woman!!* Lisa shook her head, her subconscious was trying to play a dirty trick on her.

-Lisa...

Oh my God, how could a cat have such perfect legs? She held her breath. *Enough, Manoban, stop thinking about it.*

-Nini- she cleared her throat embarrassed, her voice had come out deeper than it should have.

Jennie was different from head to toe, her hair straight and shiny, and that outfit, Chanel? She blinked in surprise. Since when did her damn cat wear Chanel? She looked like a model. What happened to Nini, the girl with the unruly hair, with her giant t-shirts? No doubt at that moment Nini was not there, but Jennie Kim, and she looked extremely sexy.

-Ok Lisa, that's enough, stop messing with Jennie- she took the cat from the brunette's hands and walked towards the exit- I'll go steal food from Hyuna

Lisa made a face

-Of course, aren't you going to eat her instead?

-It doesn't matter, it's sexy and...- Rose let out a cry of pain and threw the cat away- Fuck, it bit me!- she put a finger to her mouth with a pained expression- you know what? Fuck it, I'm going to get my fucking food!

He left the office slamming the door.

Jennie tried to pick up her sister and she bit her angrily

-Chu, don't bite!- he scolded her when he saw the blood on his finger.

The cat hid behind the sofa, snorting grumpily. What was wrong with her?

-Are you OK?

Jennie quickly hid her hands behind her back and nodded a few times.

-I'm fine, great!

-Excellent...

There was a moment of silence and finally Jennie worked up the courage to speak, but it was Lisa who stole her words.

-I... I wanted to know if we can go out... I mean, it's my free time and we can have a drink or...

-Yes! Yes, yes, yes, yes!!!- he looked at the blonde who had wide eyes and cleared his throat- I mean, yes, no problem

-Okay, let me finish a few things and we'll go.

conquering Lisa

1-establish eye contact

    Lisa had decided to go to a Starbucks near the company, luckily it had tables outside since the brunette insisted on staying close to Chu

-Well, it's here- she turned off the car and got out, followed by the Korean- How have you been these days?

-Oh well, Rose took me to yoga classes and bought me clothes!

-I see that...- the blonde whispered, looking closely at the girl's outfit, how could she look so damn good?

-Do you like it?

Lisa's cheeks reddened at the question, just then her gaze traveled down the shorter girl's chest, what was he referring to, her clothes or her breasts?

-W-what!?

-Do you like that girl?

Lisa swallowed in relief, apparently he was not referring to either one.

- Are you talking about Irene? She's my assistant.

-So you don't like it?

-Why do you ask that question? How about you... What is there between you and Rose? - that question sounded like a reproach.

-I love her, she's nice and she lets me sleep on her

Lisa's eyes widened. If she were a pressure cooker, she'd be smoking by now.

"I'm going to kill Rose," he whispered, gritting his teeth.

The waiter took their order and Lisa opted for an iced coffee for herself and a cup of hot chocolate for the chestnut, plus two tuna sandwiches.

While they were eating, each one was immersed in her thoughts, Jennie thinking about how to start the steps to conquer her companion and Lisa cursing Rose for taking advantage of her girl. *My girl? My cat! She* quickly corrected herself.

Chu, calmer, decided it was time to break the ice and let her sister know.

-Let's start. You have to look at her until she looks back at you, that's how humans connect.

Jennie nodded. She fixed her eyes on the Thai girl and stayed like that. She wasn't bad, she had a face worth admiring. She would spend a lifetime looking at that girl and she wouldn't get tired. *She's perfect*.

On the other hand, Lisa shifted uncomfortably, finding it increasingly difficult to swallow her food. She could feel the brunette staring at her intently. It seemed like she wasn't even blinking. *Will she be okay*? She dared to look back at him and instantly regretted it. His face was serious and focused, he seemed to be studying her closely.

-That's it! He's looking at you! Although he seems to hesitate... open your eyes wider, the result will be better that way.

Jennie obeyed, looking at the blonde with wide eyes.

Lisa swallowed dryly

-J-jennie? Are you okay?

His face immediately changed into a wide smile that narrowed his feline eyes.

-Wonderful!

2-find an excuse to interact

-Bring up a topic of conversation!

-I don't know how!- he whispered back with his gaze forward.

Lisa still had some time before she had to go back to the office, so she decided to take a quick stroll through the park, the meal was terrifying with Jennie's psychopathic gaze on her, and in the end Chu had stolen half of her sandwich.

-Ok, you're going to tell him everything I tell you, okay? Here we go...

Jennie's cheeks reddened as she listened to her sister, this action did not go unnoticed by the blonde who totally ignored the cat's meows and focused on Jennie

-Are you okay? You're very red...

-I... You look very good Lisa! - she expressed as her sister was narrating - You look tastier than a chicken skewer in sweet and sour sauce

-What!?- Now it was Lisa who changed color, but that didn't stop the feline.

-I'm going to scratch you so much that every time you look at my marks you'll remember me...

Lisa cleared her throat nervously and stopped walking with some discomfort.

-I think we should go back, Rose must be waiting for you and I have to get back to work.

3- smile at him

The brunette smiled widely at her sister's request. Was it working? She was feeling stupid in front of Lisa doing such things, but she still obeyed.

-Nini... You're starting to get scared...

4-Give him a compliment

-Now let him know how special he is to you!

Ok, that's easy. He smiled smugly.

-I've never felt so bad about fucking someone like I do with you, not even Kai!

Lisa looked at her in shock until she realized the last thing.

-Kai? Who is...?

-Now!

5- Kiss her

Before Lisa could finish her question, she felt a lick on her lips. She jumped back, she hadn't even noticed the moment when the shorter girl had approached, but for a second she thought she was going to kiss her.

-Jennie, stop it, what the hell is wrong with you!?

-I...

-You're acting crazy! Is that what you do with Rose?

-No!

-And who the hell is Kai!?

-Kai...- she swallowed hard. Had he mentioned Kai?- he is... He was my...

-You know what, you better not say anything, I'm not interested in knowing what you do with Rose or Kai or whoever! - he growled, clenching his hands tightly. The truth was that he did care, more than he wanted to admit and the simple idea of imagining the brunette doing those things with someone else, as strange and terrifying as they were, made his insides boil. - Let's go back to the company, I have things to do.

◇◇🐱◇◇

The way back was sepulchral, neither of them spoke at any time, only Chu's meows could be heard in the back seat, who still did not understand how his plan of conquest had failed.

-I can't believe it, what went wrong? We did the 5 steps! That blog is a farce! I'll sue you! I'll make Kook scratch up your curtains and eat the dog, because you must have an ugly chihuahua! - he growled, turning around in his seat - I knew I couldn't trust humans. Next time, rub yourself and purr, that always works.

Jennie ignored her sister's argument, her mind was on the blonde's words. *You know what, you better not say anything, I'm not interested in knowing what you do with Rose or Kai or whoever!* She looked down and sighed. *She doesn't care what she does...*

Lisa walked into her office in a bad mood, inside Rose jumped up closing her book. *Shit, now I'll have to wait until I get home to see how Christian and Anastasia end up fucking.* Rose lamented putting the 50 Shades of Grey in her bag.

-Lisa, what's going on...?

The blonde slammed her five fingers into his face without flinching, staggering Rose with the sudden act.

-That's because you bitch, you're just like Sana, now get out of my fucking sight right now! - she screamed furiously with her hand burning from the impact.

Rose instead looked at her confused with a hand on her cheek.

-What the fuck is wrong with you now, are you ovulating or what the fuck?- he complained impatiently, the blow had made his nose drip crimson- Damn!- he complained when he saw blood on his hand- Are you going to hit me every time you see me!? I'm not your fucking punching bag!

He turned around and strode out of the office, beginning to lose patience. He found the brunette outside the building and with one pull he dragged her to his car.

-Let's go home, I want you to explain to me what the hell got into that idiot now

Confessions

-But how could you think of that!?

Rose was on the verge of exploding, she was tossing and turning restlessly. Jennie had told her about her outing with Lisa and Chu's plan.

-Chu and I searched and...

-And acting like a crazy stalker was the best option...- she said, disgusted.

Jennie's eyes clouded with tears and Rose regretted it, she was being too hard on the girl. Remember Rose, this whole world is new to her. She told herself mentally as she calmed down.

-He said he didn't care who Rose did those things with, he didn't care...

The Australian sighed, holding her in her arms.

-Calm down Jen, Lisa loves you- he whispered while caressing her back- but that plan... My God, at first glance it sounds terrible, even more so if you don't know how to execute it.

-But Chu said...

-Rule number one, don't ask a cat for advice on human things- he heard the ragdoll snort and stuck his tongue out at her resentfully- you shut up, I'm still mad at you and... No Chu no, leave Leo alone!- he exclaimed when he saw the cat biting the poor feline- Holy God, between you and her you're going to kill the poor thing!

Jennie rolled her eyes in disagreement.

-Don't believe it, he loves to play the victim.

-Whatever- Rose walked over to a shelf of books and set it on the table in front of the brunette- I don't know how you know how to read, but that's progress, you'll just have to memorize this

Jennie looked confused

-Ka-ka... Kamasutra...

Rose widened her eyes and stared at the book, quickly taking it.

-Oh fuck, wrong book!- he went back and picked up the right one this time- this is very similar to the last one, but not as intense

-Sex education for teenagers?- she read the title, confused.

-I'm a sexologist too and this kind of thing is necessary, you have a lot of sexual desire for Lisa and you don't even know your human body. What would you do if you saw Lisa naked!?

Jennie blinked thoughtfully and then licked her lips, cuddly, surprising the blonde.

-Oh my God, you're a bitch!

Jennie looked at her offended

-I'm not a dog, I'm a cat

-Well, whatever, you need to explore yourself and then you can do it with her. On the other hand, you also need...- he stood up and took some CD cases and threw them on the table as well- these, you should watch a lot of movies, learn how humans interact with each other and how they fall in love. It's not that complicated- he thought for a moment- you also have to put your sensuality to work, but for the rest everything will be fine.

-I don't think I can do it Squirrel, it's too complicated!

Rose looked at her for a second and nodded.

-And you must learn how to put on makeup. Makeup and posture, that's the essential thing, Lisa likes them very feminine so let's get started.

Jennie started with makeup, doing it over and over again with the constant complaint of the blonde

Outline your lips well Jen

Don't get off your ass, we want you to look more like a woman, not like a fucking clown.

Be careful, you'll poke your eye out with the eyeliner!

Holy mother Jennie, that's too much blushing!

On the other hand, the posture class was calmer, except that at the end the psychologist noticed the cheating.

-Jennie, what's the point of carrying the book on your head if you're holding it with your hands?- He asked with his eyes rolled back.

Finally they both decided to watch a movie, and while Rose thought of a romantic one like the bodyguard, Jennie opted for a very different one.

-Are you serious Jennie? How will you learn to fall in love and be a woman if you watch the Aristocats!?- he told her, getting up from the sofa

-Oh come on squirrel, just a little while, and look how handsome O'Malley is!

Rose rolled her eyes

-If your first choice wasn't Duchess you're screwed, remember that Lisa doesn't have a penis but a vagina- she explained, ironically looking at the screen.

Jennie shrugged indifferently.

-Just because I like Lisa doesn't mean I like all cats or women, I just find her attractive.

Rose jumped and went to the kitchen, leaving the brunette immersed in her caricature.

- God, I feel like a nanny taking care of kids. Now I'm a fucking babysitter! - She uncorked a bottle of wine. She sighed wearily, taking a glass from the shelf - I have enough to do being a psychologist without having to be a babysitter when I get home too - She took a sip and sighed in relief - nothing a little liquor can't calm down, psychologists definitely end up being fucking drunks.

After a while he went into the living room and found the brunette asleep, curled up on the couch.

-Look at you, so innocent- he left his seventh glass on the table and leaned in front of the brunette- so beautiful- he moved a lock of hair from her face- and you came to fall in love with my friend- he sighed sadly- the worst thing is that she also has feelings for you... Just like me...

The blonde sat up when she saw the brunette move. Jennie half opened her eyes and smiled sweetly when she saw the Australian standing in front of her.

-Hey Jenjen, are we going to bed?

The girl nodded, rubbing her eyes and standing up.

-Squirrel- he called her, catching the attention of his opponent.

-Tell me, jen?

Jennie ran up to the blonde and hugged her lovingly, making the Australian shudder.

-Thanks for everything you do for me, Unnie

Rose sighed in disappointment, that affectionate nickname shattered any hope.

-Jennie, what do I have to do so that you see me the way you see Lisa?

-What are you talking about?

-What does Lisa have that I don't? If you give me a chance, I promise to make you happy.

Rose's glasses had gotten too high, just like Lisa's had the previous night. It was her way of letting out her anger and saying things she didn't dare say when she was sober . *You're betraying Lisa.* Her subconscious was saying, but her heart was saying something very different . *You like that feline girl and you're going to lose her if you don't take a chance.*

Jennie looked at her with melancholy and hugged her again. She was a cat, yes, but she understood more things than Rose and Lisa believed, and she knew perfectly well what the Australian was referring to.

-I'm sorry Rose, it's Lisa who has my heart, and I have eyes for no one but her. - I wipe a furtive tear from the girl's chubby cheeks - to me you're like a sister.

Rose accepted her reality, nothing she does for that feline girl will make her feelings for Lisa change. Since I noticed how Lisa looked at you, I promised myself to give up on you and now that I know you will never reciprocate my feelings, I will keep the promise.

-Let's go to sleep Jen, tomorrow will be a long day...

Who the hell is Kim Jisoo?

Lisa had woken up early in the morning, she hadn't slept well that night thinking about the brunette, why did she behave that way?

She groaned in her bed, covering herself with her pillow. *That cat turned your world upside down, Manoban.* She told herself. She turned to the right, trying to fall asleep again, but a snore prevented her from doing so.

He remained silent, still without opening his eyes. Could it have been her? No, the sound repeated itself. When he opened his eyes he found himself in a sort of deja vu, a girl on the left side of his bed, sleeping completely naked; her tangled hair covered her face, and from her slightly open mouth hung a thin thread of saliva that began to soak the pillow.

Lisa's scream resonated loudly, but the effect was not the same as the past with Jennie, this time the girl threw a precise punch without opening her eyes, hitting the Thai girl right on the chin and making her fall off the bed.

-Shit!- she rubbed the bruised spot, standing up. Who was that?- Hey...- she tapped her shoulder without success.- Hey you, wake up.- she shook her shoulder without any response. The girl was still snoring, oblivious to the blonde's calls. Lisa frowned and began to shake her roughly.- Wake up... fuck!

The black-haired girl had thrown a kick, hitting the south side. Lisa's eyes watered from the pain. *Thank God I don't have a penis, otherwise this idiot would have broken it!*

The girl stretched out with sounds of pleasure and Lisa looked at her in surprise, the girl had a good body and was certainly pretty, although she didn't feel the same way as with Jennie.

-By my claws, I think I slept crookedly! - she yawned, sitting up in bed - next time turn down the heat, I don't like it this hot - she tried to stand up but her legs gave way, falling on her butt and letting out a cry of pain - Mother feline, I think I'm crippled!

Lisa approached hesitantly, watching the girl whimper on the floor.

-Are you OK?

The black-haired girl looked at her with hatred and snorted.

-Okay? Do you think I'm okay? My ass hurts and my legs feel like jelly! I'm crippled, and you ask if I'm okay!? Damn human

-Okay, let me help you and...

-No, don't help me, that's what I have legs for! - he tried to stand up and in the process he fell again. He looked at Lisa with a pout and then finished her off with a look - What are you waiting for, help me!

Lisa rolled her eyes and picked her up, the girl was quite heavy for her size

-What the fuck did you eat, rocks!?

-Dah obviously not, I ate raw chicken!

The Thai girl looked at her in surprise.

-Are you crazy? What kind of person are you!?

-Pick me up! - she ordered like a tantrum-ridden child.

-Did I just say you're heavy and you're planning on me carrying you!?

10 minutes later...

-Fuck, my back...- Lisa stretched in pain. Carrying her to the kitchen wasn't the best idea- can you please put your shirt on?

-Never! I hate clothes, they're uncomfortable!

The blonde was amazed, it was like seeing a hateful version of her Nini who had just become a woman.

-Who are you?

The girl thought about it carefully and finally answered.

-Kim Jisoo

-Jisoo?

-Jisoo.

-Who the hell are you and...?

The doorbell rang and the Thai girl's eyes almost popped out of their sockets, whoever it was couldn't stand the disheveled, naked girl in her apartment.

But the brunette didn't think the same and in a quick movement she was already running towards the door. The last thing Lisa saw was her ass disappear into the living room.

- Wasn't I supposed to not be able to walk? - she reproached disgusted when she saw her run, and then remembered the door - Shit! - she ran to the living room and froze when she saw Jisoo with the door open, receiving the visit.

-There's no Pampriya living here, dammit! Shu, go away! - she tried to scare him away with a wave of her hand, but the boy remained petrified - Stupid human, are you also deaf?

Lisa finally saw who it was and sighed in relief, running to the entrance and pushing the girl aside to prevent anyone passing by in the hallway from seeing her naked.

-Bambam!- he finally greeted the boy.

-Priya, did I come at a bad time?

-Just come in- she pulled him inside and closed the door- I have no fucking idea who this girl is and...- she heard a crash in the kitchen and ran to find out what it was- but what...?

The girl was sitting on top of the refrigerator, with the freezer door open, eating pieces of raw salmon.

-Holy God, that girl is a savage!- exclaimed Bambam, seeing the mess in the kitchen- at least tell me she is hot in bed

-Bamban!

-Calm down Lis, I already told you that I came out of the closet a long time ago.

Lisa turned to the upset girl, not even Jennie had caused her so much trouble the first few days of her change.

-Kim Jisoo get down from there right now!- he threatened with a tic in his foot

The girl nibbled on another piece of salmon and shook her head.

-You don't send me, you stupid human!

- Get down from there or...!- Lisa looked from one side to the other- or I'll wet you!- she took a glass of water and gave it to the girl, who jumped, falling from above- Oh god, I'm so sorry! Are you okay?

-Do you want me to flatten out!? Holy sardine, I can't feel my buttocks anymore! At this rate I'll be flatter than you.

-Okay, now! Why don't you put some clothes on and...?

-Never!- Jisoo tried to run, hitting her head against the wall- Shit... - She looked at both Thais and frowned -I said, never!!!- She ran down the hall and disappeared into the blonde's room

-What kind of crazy women are you sleeping with now, Pampriya?

-Stop saying that, I...- the sound of her phone interrupted her, making her roll her eyes before answering- Hello?

-Lisa I...

-Rose, didn't I make it clear to you that I didn't want to talk to you anymore!?

-Yes, I still have a swollen cheek to prove it.

-And the same thing will happen to the other one if... Bambam!

The boy had snatched the phone from the dancer

-Rosie, my little pasta!

-Bambam is that you!? Oh god, what are you doing here in Korea!?

-Vacation ...

-You don't know how much I want to...!

-Human, bring me some chicken! I want chicken skewers!- Jisoo's voice silenced Rose, who had clearly heard the interruption.

Lisa rolled her eyes and took the remains of the salmon for the black-haired girl and headed to the room.

- Fine, I'll give it to you if you get dressed.

-Never!!!

"Who is that?" the Australian on the other end of the line asked.

Bamban clicked his tongue, his gaze on the hallway.

-A friend of Lisa, Kim Jisoo I think her name is...

There was a minute of silence and finally Rose spoke.

-Who the hell is Kim Jisoo!?

Betrayal or Loyalty?

On the way to Rose's house everything was silent, Jennie looked out the window thoughtfully and the psychologist decided to give her her space

Upon arriving, the blonde parked the car and glanced at the girl who was still immersed in her thoughts.

-Jen, do you want to talk about this?

-No, it's okay squirrel, now it's clear to me... Lisa doesn't like me.

-Hey, look at me- he ordered sweetly, catching the attention of those feline eyes, leaving the minor breathless. *Fuck Lisa, how can you resist this woman?* - Tomorrow we're going to make Manoban's panties wet just by looking at you.

Jennie widened her eyes

-Is he going to pee!?

-What? God no! - Rose burst out laughing - I must lend you one of my sexology books so you can learn a little about human anatomy

Rose remembered the brunette's action in the restaurant and dared to mention the subject, it was impossible for her psychoanalytic side not to intervene in the matter.

-Do you think he saw you?

-I don't know, that's what it seemed to me...

-Maybe she didn't recognize you, knowing Lisa she would have followed us and I would be dead right now- she joked with a grain of truth. She knew her friend very well and she knew how impulsive she could be.

-Why would Lisa act like that?

Rose shrugged and smiled.

-She doesn't even know it herself

They both got out of the car and entered the building, at least the psychologist had managed to calm the feline girl who was now happily nibbling on a chocolate cookie.

-So you're a chocolate fan, huh? - the blonde played as she opened the door, laughing - I should give it to you more often - she was surprised when the door opened slightly without even turning the key - but what...?

Rose only had time to turn on the light when a sharp blow landed on her nose, knocking her off balance.

Jennie screamed in shock and went over to help the girl on the ground.

-Squirrel, are you okay!?

Rose looked at the hand holding her nose and the Korean screamed when she saw it covered in blood.

-Calm down Jen, I'm...- but she couldn't even finish. A pair of hands pulled her to her feet roughly, holding her firmly by the blouse. Rose was shocked when she saw the face of her attacker.
-Lisa?

The aforementioned slammed her against the wall roughly, her eyes were bloodshot, she was angry, and the Australian noticed that instantly.

-What's going on between you and Jennie?

-That?

-Damn, I saw them at the restaurant!

-Lisa, try to calm down, you're twisting things and...

Lisa slammed her against the wall again

-Shut up, I'm not one of your damn patients!

-Lisa, Lisa leave her, stop it!!

But the dancer did not obey. Her eyes filled with tears as she looked at her friend.

-No Rose, you can't betray me too!

The aforementioned felt a pang of pain at seeing her friend so vulnerable. From the smell she emanated, she knew she had been drinking, and that only meant that she was more affected by the brunette than she let on.

-Jen, can you make the bed? Lisa needs to sleep and...

-Shit, Rose, answer me! - Lisa was starting to get rougher and Jennie's eyes were filled with fear, which the Australian girl didn't like too much.

Oh Lisa, you're screwing up. Rose looked at the brunette and gave her a smile to calm her down and nodded.

-Go, I'll be fine.

The girl didn't protest and ran to do what Rose had ordered her to do.

Only then did the Australian, in a quick movement, immobilize the one with bangs on the ground.

-Come on Lis, we took that taekwondo course together, so don't come here and pretend to be Jackie Chan now- she answered calmly while her friend was foraging beneath her.- I don't want to steal Jennie from you, Lisa, I'm just trying to help you and help her.

-Don't lie, you like her, I know it and you kiss her!

Rose rolled her eyes

-Don't exaggerate Lisa, I've never kissed her, except on the cheek.

-But you wish!

Rose shrugged.

-Maybe...

-I'll kill you!!!

-I knew you liked her! You're jealous and... Lisa? - the Thai girl had fallen asleep, the alcohol in her system had done its thing- you're stubborn Lalisa Manoban- she patted her cheek and shook her head- I would never be with my best friend's girl. I'd rather give up on Jen than lose your friendship

He stood up and looked at her, so helpless sleeping there that he couldn't get angry even though his nose was still running.

The truth was that Jennie had not only won the heart of the Thai girl, but also that of the Australian girl, however Rose was willing to ignore that feeling as long as her friend was happy.

He grabbed a blanket and a pillow and returned to the living room, finding the dancer in the same position.
-You have to sleep on the floor for breaking my nose.

Catfight

Rose was uneasy, the day before she had doubts. *Kim Jisoo? Lisa's friend?* She frowned, she didn't know any of Lisa's friends with that name. She remembered Lisa's voice in the distance ◊*I'll give it to you if you get dressed* ◊ Was she naked?

-I hope you didn't do anything stupid Lalisa Manoban- she whispered thoughtfully.

He snorted, rubbing his eyes as he headed to the kitchen.

-Good morning squirrel!- Jennie was in the kitchen with her face and hair covered in flour while she served some pancakes on the plate- I made breakfast!

Rose smiled, the brunette had insisted that she wanted to learn how to cook as a human.

Why the urgency?

Because I don't think Lisa likes raw fish, mice or canaries.

Remembering that erased her smile. After her embarrassing night of drinking, Rose had spoken to her when she woke up, even with her hangover alive; as a psychologist she always advised facing problems and she also put that technique into practice, and luckily for her, the brunette did not change her treatment of her.

He thought about Jisoo again. Would it be convenient to talk to Jennie? She must know the truth.

-Hey Jen...- she began, leaning on the counter, attentive to the girl who was imperfectly cutting fruit- what do you think if Lisa was with another girl?

The chestnut reflexively stuck the table knife into the chopping board and turned around with menacing eyes.

-What Lisa is what!?

Rose swallowed hard and shook her head. *Bad idea, Rose.*

Mental note: don't make Jennie angry around sharp objects

However, he had already touched on the subject, and leaving it halfway would only make her angrier.

-It's just a guess Jen, you know... in case Lisa was with a girl who... I don't know... Named Kim Jisoo maybe, and who right now must be walking around her apartment naked and...

She fell down when she saw the brunette's murderous gaze. Jennie as a woman was very intimidating, and at that moment Rose was more than scared with the Korean's withering expression. *Who would tell me to speak?*

-Rose, take me to Lisa right now.

-But...

-Now!

◇◇🐱◇◇

- So if you're going to make one...

- Pee?

-Yes, you have to do it in the bathroom, not in the fucking cat litter box!

Lisa still didn't know who the hell that girl was, she was strange, much more than Jennie. Another cat? *No, please!* This one was more clumsy than Jennie was, more primitive, so to speak, and it drove the Thai girl crazy.

Jisoo clicked her tongue and shook her head.

-Litter boxes are for pissing and pooping, period- He concluded the subject closed- Now feed me, I'm starving!

Lisa looked at her reproachfully with her hands on her hips.

-You ate all the salmon last night, and in the morning you devoured the raw chicken, and you're still hungry!?, you are...!

At that moment the doorbell rang insistently, leaving the blonde speechless. Who could it be?

- Fuck, I'm coming! - she complained at the person's insistence - If you burn the fucking doorbell, I'll...! - but she was speechless when she saw who it was - Jennie? What the...?

The brunette didn't let her finish, she pushed her aside and entered the apartment with authority. Her eyes were dilated and dark and her gaze was menacing and she kept looking from one side to the other.

He began to sniff the air and growled helplessly.

-Where do you have it!?- he asked more like an order

-What thing?

-Where the hell do you have that woman?

-I...

-God Jennie calm down, it's just a misunderstanding...!- but Rose couldn't continue

-Leisaaa, get your flat ass here, I'm dying to talk and I want you to rub my belly!

Rose's eyes widened as she heard the female voice coming from the blonde's room, but it was Jennie who sprang into action.

Both friends saw the brunette run and kick open the door, then enter the room.

-He's going to kill her! - Rose warned, panting and sweating.

-And what happened to you?- he asked when he saw her so exhausted and with red cheeks.

-Jennie jumped out of the car like a bullet, furious, she didn't even wait for the elevator. I followed her up the fucking stairs. Why the hell did you have to live on the eighth floor!?

-But what the hell is happening, I don't understand why...!?

The screams of the black-haired girl alerted both girls

-Long story, let's stop it before it takes her head off

The two of them ran to the room.

Jennie had the girl on the ground, beneath her, holding her hands tightly. The black-haired girl had scratches from the brunette and both had their hair disheveled, looking at each other with hatred.

Jennie didn't attack, she just watched, furious, as the girl below her growled and showed her teeth as a threat.

-But what...?- the Thai woman stopped dead.

Jennie looked at Lisa. She was seething with anger and the Thai woman feared for her life for a moment.

-Lalisa Manoban, explain to me what this woman is doing in your room with one of your fucking shirts!!!

Lisa swallowed hard at the girl's furtive glance.

-I don't know who she is, two days ago I woke up with her naked in my bed and...

The brunette's eyebrows rose, tightening her grip on the brunette's wrists who let out a moan of pain. She tried to speak but in a quick movement the brunette shoved one of Lisa's sock into her mouth.

-You don't talk!- he warned her and looked back at Lisa. Then he looked at Rise- Squirrel, hold this woman for me.

The named one widened her eyes

-What me what!?

-Come and hold it for me!

Rose jumped up to the two girls and adopted Jennie's position.

Her cheeks blushed as she saw the mischievous smile of the girl beneath her, still with the sock in her mouth.

On the other hand, Jennie was quick to stand in front of the Thai girl, who backed away nervously.

- Lalisa Manoban, you're an idiot! - Jennie growled, getting closer to the blonde with bangs - First Rose! - she hit her in the chest - then Irene! - another blow - and now you're trading me for another cat too! - two blows and her tears were already running down her cheeks

Lisa blinked in confusion.

- A cat? I don't know who she is!

-Oh god, are all the cats going to wake up naked and human in Lisa's bed now? How envious...

The Thai girl looked at her friend with hatred
-You're not helping Rose
-Well, now that we know that Leisa attracts female felines, what are we going to do?
-It's Lisa, and how did you escape...? Rose! - Jennie growled as she watched the brunette eating cat kibble on Lisa's bed and Rose distracted, sitting on a pillow

The poor Australian looked at the pillow and then at the black-haired girl, over and over again without understanding what had happened.
-As...?
-I'm a very flexible cat- she winked flirtatiously.
"Who are you?" Jennie asked. There was something familiar in the way the girl spoke.
-You hurt me Jendeukie, it offends me that you don't recognize your own sister

There was a minute of silence while everyone absorbed the black-haired girl's words.
-Chu!?- the three exclaimed in unison with their eyes wide open.
-From the ears to the tail- he looked at his anatomy and clicked his tongue in annoyance- well, from head to toe. What scrawny bodies... and my legs are crooked!!!

And that made things even more complicated. What was Chu's role in all this mess?

◈◈◈

Feline Blood

They all calmed down after knowing that the unknown girl was actually Chu, but not before Jennie hit the blonde a little more.

-But why are you hitting me!?
-For sleeping with my sister naked!
-I didn't even know that Chu...!
-Jisoo!- The black-haired girl corrected.
-Jisoo was here!- Lisa completed in self-defense
-You still saw her naked!

The four girls were in the living room having breakfast with chicken skewers (at the request of the black-haired girl), and only one seemed to be enjoying it.

-These skewers taste heavenly!- she licked the palm of her hand and purred, shifting her gaze to the Thai girl's plate- Laisa, are you going to eat that?- Jisoo tried to steal the untouched chicken from the blonde with bangs' plate, but a grunt, followed by a slap made her stop- Aush, Jennie!- she complained, rubbing her hand.

-It's Lisa, and if you touch her food I'll bite your fingers off! - he warned her in a threatening tone. He turned to look at the aforementioned and smiled, narrowing his feline eyes tenderly. - Eat Lili.

Meanwhile, Lisa and Rose were still waiting. The poor Thai girl was terrified by Jennie's bipolar changes, and the psychologist was starting to get worried about Jisoo's lascivious glances.

- Lisa, I strictly forbid you to have cats in your apartment! - the Australian ordered, crossing her arms in indignation.

Lisa looked at her sideways, her expression confused.
-Why's that?
-Why? Are you still asking, Manoban!? It seems that when cats see you, they start making wishes on the fucking stars!!!

They all turned to the black-haired girl who began to laugh out loud at the Australian's words.

-And what are you laughing at!?- Rose growled indignantly.

-I didn't ask for anything from anyone, and even less for Laisa

-Lisa!- Jennie and Lalisa corrected in unison

- Same. I was a happy cat, and now I'm this abomination! - she exclaimed, pointing at her body.

"Not so abominable, my dear," Rose whispered, playing with a lock of hair as she scanned the feline girl's body with her gaze.

-Rose!- Lisa scolded her when she noticed her change in attitude.

-What? Do you really think you're the only one who can ogle his cat?

-Oh my god, did you hear how bad that sounded!? We sound like zoophiles!- Lisa covered her face in embarrassment.

-And you look like a fucking zoophobe now, relax, it's not like we see them as desirable in their old feline bodies, that would be sick.

-Well, I want to be a cat again, I want my tail and my ears and my claws—Jisoo continued complaining, sucking on her bones- besides, with this body I won't be able to spy on the squirrel while he bathes.

-It's reasonable that you want... wait what!?- Rose widened her eyes upon catching the brunette's words- depraved!- she covered her breasts with both hands, scandalized

-She can't even see them, Rose, she doesn't have x-rays either- Lisa rolled her eyes- Plus she's seen them before, so...

-Lalisa, shut up!

The aforementioned laughed amused at seeing her friend's cheeks turn red, and how she clumsily covered her body with the leftover tablecloth.

-Chu...

-Kim Jisoo!

Jennie rolled her eyes

-Ok, Kim Jisoo, what I don't understand is, if you didn't make a wish, then how come you're human?

Both Lisa and Rose looked at Jisoo waiting for an answer, they had the same doubt as the brunette.

The brunette thought about it for a bit and raised an eyebrow, confusing the other three.

-That?

-You don't think I'll reveal my secret, do you?

Jennie frowned, she was starting to lose patience with her sister.

- Secret? Just say it Chu!

-Jisoo!- the black-haired girl corrected her- and I won't do it, not without getting something in return

-And what do you want?

Jisoo's eyes lit up and she didn't have to think about it too much. She pointed at Rose instantly, causing the poor girl to choke while drinking water, and spit everything out sideways.

"Damn it, Rose!" Lisa growled, wiping the water away searchingly.

However, the Australian was still upset by the black-haired girl's insinuation.

-Me!?

Jennie wrinkled her nose

-Do you love Rose?- he repeated without understanding.

-I want to stay at your house, Lisa is very uncomforting

The chestnut gritted her teeth in disgust.

-Lalisa doesn't have to please you! - he growled through his teeth, clenching his fists.

-J-jennie you're t-you're...

-Shut up Lisa!- ordered the brunette displaced, clenching her fists even tighter.

-Oh, you seem submissive Laisa, everyone tells you to shut up- Jisoo laughed amusedly making her sister angrier

-It's Lisa! Her name is Li...!
-God Jennie, you're going to bite my hand! - the Thai girl exclaimed with a grimace of pain.

Only then did the brunette notice Lisa's wrist firmly held by her hand. When had she held her?

-Lili, I am!- he quickly let go of her with regret

"Calm down, it's nothing," she replied with crystal-clear eyes, rubbing her sore hand.

-Ok Jisoo, you can stay in my apartment- Rose said noticing the excitement in the feline- now tell us

-Umm...I also want yours and his food- he added, pointing at the half-eaten plate and the one that was untouched.

Rose widened her eyes and sighed, giving up, her chicken was delicious

-Blackmailing cat- he pouted as he watched the girl nibble on his food

-Ok, so what?- Lisa asked impatiently.

Jisoo chewed, savored, swallowed, and finally spoke.

-It's delicious!

-Enough Chu, tell us how the hell you are human!- her sister exploded, slamming her fist on the table.

-I don't know!- he finally confessed- the last thing I remember is biting Rose and then you!- he frowned- then I left when Rose confessed to you how she felt!

-What?- Lisa looked at her confused.

-And how did you end up with Lisa?- Jennie asked.

Jisoo shrugged, dismissing it.

-I didn't know where else to go. I went in through the emergency stairs and lay down on the bed, that's all I remember.

Rose analyzed the brunette's words, trying to make sense of it all. Her expression changed at a crazy idea and she looked at Jennie as if that was the solution.

-Jennie had bitten me once while still in her feline form and nothing happened... That means...

-That Chu bit Jennie...- Lisa widened her eyes, understanding the direction of her friend's thoughts.

-I don't understand...

-Jennie, it was your blood that transformed Jisoo- Rose explained slowly- You asked to be human and for some reason your blood can do it now too

Jenlisa-Chaesoo

After getting organized, the girls decided that Jennie would stay with Lisa and the black-haired girl with Rose, which was proving complicated for both humans.

-I swear Lisa, he wants to rape me!!- Rose dropped onto the couch- and he spends all his time naked, he just doesn't want to wear clothes! Can you imagine the look on my mother's face when she saw her!?

Flashback

-Jisoo, don't open the... Mom!- he stopped dead when he saw his mother's horrified face next to a naked brunette who was smiling from ear to ear.

-Your mom came to visit you, we have to celebrate with chicken skewers! - he exclaimed happily, running into the room.

-Mom, this is not what it seems...

-Isn't it!? A woman just ran naked into your room without any shame, explain to me what dignifies this then Park Chaeyong!

Rose swallowed with difficulty, not even her years as a psychologist prepared her for something like that.

-She... I... Is she a friend?

-Squirrel, can you scratch my belly so I can sleep!?- Jisoo shouted from the room, making the poor Australian girl pale.

I swear, I'm dead . She turned nervously to see her mother who was waiting for an explanation with her arms akimbo.

-Chaeyong, I want the truth

-I...

-The truth...

End of flashback

-Fuck Lisa stop laughing!

The blonde with bangs was writhing on her couch. It was her revenge for all the times the Australian had laughed at her, and she was really enjoying it.

-It's a fact, my friend, you've officially come out of the closet. Welcome to the gay world without barriers- Lisa joked, amused.

Rose puffed out her cheeks in disgust.

-I should have told my mom that I liked girls in a different way, she almost had a heart attack!

-Why didn't you tell him the truth?

-Oh right, I was going to say "hey mom, that girl is actually a perverted cat! And guess what? She's the sister of Lisa's cat, who happens to also be human because of a fucking wish upon a star"!

-Of course, and that's why you preferred to tell your mother that you were curious about your sexuality.

-As a psychologist it is reasonable, so I can better understand my patients with that kind of insecurities.

-Great, and then you'll get high to help the addicts, how nice! - Lisa said ironically with a sly smile.

-Don't make fun of me!

-Relax, I'm not doing it, it's just that it's hard for a mother to find out that way that her daughter, Roseanne Park, a renowned psychologist is also a fucking closet lesbian, that's epic- she laughed again at her friend's misfortune- this, my friend, is Karma taking its toll on you for laughing at me

Rose narrowed her eyes, looking at her reproachfully.

-Has this week with Jennie gone better for you than for me?

The Thai girl's smile disappeared as she recalled her week. Had it gone any better?

Flashback

The blonde had just arrived from the agency. She was really exhausted. She left everything on the counter and walked up to her room, as always, took off her work clothes and fell on the bed in nothing but her black underwear.

-Damn, work is going to kill me...- she complained, still with her eyes closed. Dancing didn't exhaust her as much as being behind that desk all day.

She sighed in relief as she felt small, delicate hands on her shoulders massaging carefully, and only then did she remember that the brunette had become her tenant again.

-Wow Nini, I didn't know you gave massages so well- she sighed delighted at the touch of the brunette

-You're very tense, Lili- he whispered in a deep voice, climbing onto her abdomen and massaging her shoulders again- Let me relieve your tension...

Lisa gasped as she felt the brunette's hips so exposed against her half-naked skin and her whole body bristled as she heard a slight moan from the girl.

The Thai woman's eyes opened slowly, sleepily, and she gasped again at the sight.

Jennie was in a sexy black lace baby doll that matched her own outfit. She couldn't help but moan at the feel of it and the truth was that having Jennie in that outfit pressing her hips so close to hers turned her on a hundredfold.

Her breathing was heavy and she could tell the brunette was feeling the same way. Was she in heat again?

-Jennie, this is not... This... - another moan from the brunette resonated when Lisa tried to move her, and in response to her reluctance to stop, she created a perfect friction that drove them both delirious.

-Lili... That... Feels good

Lisa didn't know when the brunette's hips took on a life of their own, but she couldn't take her eyes off that sensual back and forth motion that was starting to wet her panties. *Fuck, control yourself Lisa! It's your cat! It's...!*

-Shit Jennie...- she gasped when the brunette licked between her breasts following her instinct

-Lili... I want to feel like a woman

Oh shit!

End of flashback

-And you almost had an orgasm with that request- Rose laughed when she saw how red her friend was up to her ears- Oh my god Lisa, that girl is pure fire, I imagine you fucked her all night!

Lisa widened her eyes, she was ashamed of having revealed her story, remembering the way she let herself go made her even more ashamed

-No, I... As I could, I ran to the bathroom and locked myself there until she fell asleep.

The Australian rolled her eyes

-What a coward, that baby doll was ready for you to tear it apart, and maybe the southern part of the kitten too

-Rose!- her cheeks were burning and her friend didn't help the situation- Espers, did you know about the baby doll?

-Of course Lisa, I went with her to buy it

Lisa frowned.

-Are you...!

-Before you hit me again, she was the one who asked for it, she wanted something to seduce you and... I gave it to her.

-God Rose, I don't understand, how can a cat wish and act like that? She says things as if she were a normal human!

-Lisa, you have to understand once and for all that Nini and Jennie are opposite beings. That girl is a woman and she is going to try to relieve her desire as such, only with the intensity of a feline. Do you understand what I mean? - Rose paused and when she saw that her friend did not answer, she decided to continue - Jennie is dying for you to fuck her and if you don't do it, she will look for someone else to do it. So far she is acting like a human, but when she is in heat, it will be the inner feline who will act.

-Does that mean that as a cat she will look for any male to mount her?

-That means Lisa, if you don't get your act together you're going to lose her.

Feline Anecdotes

-Just think about it Jen, you could convert all the cats in the world! We would make a fortune!

-Are you crazy Chu? Do you want me to run out of blood? - he snorted in disagreement - I don't think such a thing is possible, it's better to keep it a secret

Both sisters had decided to take a walk around the area, one of the advantages of being cats is that they had a good sense of direction and could return without any problem.

-I miss Dudu and the bunny- Jisoo pouted- and their kittens, the brats must be big

- Me too... You know, we should stop by and say hi.

- Are you serious!?

-Yes, also...- he checked his pocket and smiled- Lisa gave me this

Jennie showed her sister a couple of bills

-Oh yes, humans buy with that paper!

-Yes, we can bring you some tuna or...

-Chicken skewers!

-I was going to say meat- he rolled his eyes- Jisoo, can't you say anything else other than chicken skewers?

The black-haired girl thought about it for a moment.

-Mmm chicken wings? I know! Nuggets!!!

-What an obsession you have with chicken

-I'm sorry Jendeukie, chicken is heaven to me!

The brunette rolled her eyes and they continued walking, her sister was beyond repair.

After buying two kilos of salmon and eating a couple on the way Jisoo decided to change the subject

-How did it go with Laisa?

-Lisa- he corrected. He looked at his sister and sighed- I don't know Chu...

-Jisoo!

-She always moves away when I try to get close, but a few nights ago...

Flashback

Jennie was already ready for bed, she was pleased to be back in the Thai woman's apartment, everything smelled of vanilla and that delighted her.

She sniffed the blouse and smiled, Lisa still let her wear her shirts even though she had bought her a ton of clothes in her size, but nothing was better than sleeping in one of the blonde's huge shirts with her natural smell, it was almost as if the Thai girl was hugging her all night.

-Lisa..- she closed her eyes between sighs, she couldn't erase from her mind the previous night, how her skin shuddered when she felt the warmth of the blonde's hand beneath her. How she longed to feel those hands run over her body at will. She sighed melancholy. Just remembering it made her crotch burn with desire- why don't you take me already!- she growled desperately, her vocabulary had changed quite a bit the time she stayed with Rose. The sweet psychologist lost her patience when she went many hours without eating and cursed at everything, something that the feline was quick to copy- Lili...- she remembered again how good it felt to rub against her, a torturous relief that only managed to make her want more. She let out a sigh when her hand instinctively groped her shorts and gasped at the pleasant sensation- why can't it be you...?- she sobbed eagerly, making a little more friction. I didn't know what he was doing with his hand, but it was certainly nice.

She was about to go for more when two knocks on the door made her stop, her heart was beating wildly, was it real?

-Lisa?

-Hey Nini- the Thai girl came in timidly, playing with her fingers in a sign of nervousness- I don't want to bother you, I just... I can't sleep and...

-You're not bothering me Lili- he smiled happily, having her there was a dream come true. He made room on the sofa bed and patted the side- Come

Lisa obeyed. His body was longer than hers and she noticed that she even vaguely stuck out of the bed, which was neither very wide nor very long. That was a point in her favor, being narrow she could be closer to the blonde.

Lisa turned around, looking at her for a long time, and finally positioned herself on her side, leaning on her elbow.

-I like having you back Nini, I missed you so much- he whispered sweetly

The dim light prevented the shorter girl's intense blush from being noticed. *Can she hear my heartbeat?* Her heart seemed to jump with joy at the Thai girl's words.

-I missed you too

Lisa's smile faded at a new thought.

-You said you were sleeping on Rose, do you miss it?

-I miss sleeping on you

Jennie could hear the girl swallowing hard, she seemed unsure of her next action.

-Then you can do it now

The Thai girl didn't wait for an answer. She gently took the brunette by the waist, positioning her almost on top of her. Jennie laid her head on her chest and shyly hugged her, feeling the warmth and essence of the blonde. She sighed with pleasure. Sleeping like this was fucking heaven.

-Your heart beats very fast- the Korean mentioned, listening to the beats very close to her left ear.

-That's because he's happy.
-Because?
-For you...
End of flashback
-Holy cat that just gave birth, did they fuck!?
-Of course not Jisoo! Just... We slept like that, after that day we slept like that- he smiled thinking about it- God Chu, Lisa is perfect, I think I...!
-No! Don't say it, it will make everything more difficult, remember, she sees you only as a cat

Jennie snorted melancholically
-Well then I guess you did achieve something with Rose.
-Oh little sister, you have no idea...!
Flashback
-Jisoo, do you want more fried chicken?

The Australian's voice sounded sensual and tempting, teasing the feline girl. Rose leaned over the table where she was waiting for her third serving of chicken.

-You know I'll always say yes to chicken.

Rose bit her lower lip and coquettishly climbed onto the table, crawling torturously slow, all under the attentive gaze of the black-haired girl.

-Just the chicken? I have a couple of breasts, if you fancy it- with that she released the first button of her blouse, followed by the second and the third, leaving a provocative red bra in Jisoo's sight- what do you say?

The Korean girl gaped at the opening the blonde opened for her.
-I say I've got an appetite!

Rose laughed flirtatiously and threw herself at the brunette, causing them both to fall to the floor, ready to begin their feast.

-Bon appetit- the blonde whispered in her ear, with a seductive voice managing to drive her opponent crazy.

End of flashback
-You fucked Rose!?

Jennie's mouth was open and her eyes were wide with shock. She never imagined that her sister would get to first base so quickly with Rose.

The black-haired girl laughed and shook her head.

-No way, it was just a dream- she shrugged- but at least I achieved more when I was asleep than you did when you were awake

Jennie glared at her, her sister was too much of an idiot sometimes

-You better shut up and hurry up, I want to see how the girls are doing.

◈◈◈

Dudu, the protector

Jennie and Jisoo arrived at the tree house, the bunny had had her little ones away from humans. The tree house was in a small park with little traffic, which was good for her and her kittens.

-Jennie, if I go up there I'll kill myself!

-I don't think that little house can hold our weight Chu...

Both girls looked up at the house from below, not very convinced about going up. It was old and the wood must have been rotten and brittle. As cats it would not have been a problem to climb up, but after Jisoo fell while climbing the third plank, they had decided to look for another way.

-Rabbit, Duduuu!!!- Jisoo shouted at the top of her lungs - Come out, damn rabbit, I know you can hear me!!!

-Jisoo stop, you're going to alert the neighborhood

-We're in a park, I can do whatever I want here- Jisoo clarified, looking up again- Hey Rabbit, you better...! Aush! What the...!?

The black-haired girl looked down and screamed in pain. The Russian blue fought her foot mercilessly, making Jisoo jump and shake her injured foot in an attempt to free herself from her claws and teeth.

-Jennie, do something!!!

-Dudu, stop it, let her go! - she exclaimed, surprised by her friend's ferocity. The cat growled while continuing to bite the brunette's ankle. - Dudu, it's me, Nini!!!

-Nini?- he snorted when the brunette took advantage of his carelessness to get away - damn humans, get out of here!

She growled again in warning, she wouldn't hesitate to attack again. Why was she so angry? Jennie didn't understand her friend's attitude. Dudu was always rude, although she never attacked humans.

-Dudu, what happened to you!?- Jennie worried when she saw her limping.

He tried to get closer but the cat swatted and growled.

-Get away!

The cat continued to meow and growl in defiance, she was not going to allow the girls to climb the tree.

-Dudu, I'm Nini and this is Chu, we're your friends!

The cat seemed to be wondering about his words, but quickly denied it.

-Human nonsense

-Is it true, damn tofu, what the hell is wrong with you!?

The cat froze

-Chu!?- only Jisoo called her that way- are they really...?

-Yes Dudu, it's us

-Oh my goodness, can you really understand me!?

-Yes Dudu, I already told you, we are cats

Dudu approached Jennie and sniffed her. She immediately snorted and backed away.

-You smell different

-It's a long story Dudu, but you have to believe us- begged Jennie- look, we brought them food!- she left the bags near the cat and walked away.

Dudu put his snout in the bag, and when he saw that it was true, he began to eat hastily.

-God, you look like a damn animal swallowing, leave something for the rabbit!

The cat walked away, licking her paws.

-Sorry girls, I haven't eaten in days.

- Did something happen to your owners? - Jennie asked, noticing that the feline was indeed quite thin.

-I haven't seen them for two weeks.

-Fuck, don't tell me they fired you!

-Not that I know of.
-Dudu, tell us what's happening

The cat looked at them for a moment. She looked exhausted and in pain, and both sisters began to worry.

-A few days ago some humans climbed up to the tree house...- he began to narrate- maybe the babies were crying a lot, I don't know, I had gone hunting and when I came back I found them inside

-Oh Dudu, did they...?

-I did what I could. I attacked them, but one of them kicked me and I was knocked unconscious, and when I woke up...- the Russian blue began to sound choppy, as if she was going to cry at any moment- they had taken them, they took three, the Rabbit only managed to hide the two smallest ones, but she couldn't do the same for the others- finally the feline began to cry. Jennie was surprised, it was the first time she saw Dudu so defenseless and broken- it was my fault, if I hadn't left them alone... Or if I hadn't fainted...

- Dudu, you couldn't have done anything else, you did what you could.

Jennie stroked the feline's back in a comforting manner, while she continued to cry.

-Where is rabbit?

Dudu sat up when he heard his name and looked towards the little house.

-She's upstairs, I haven't had the courage to talk to her after... That. I only go up when I know she's sleeping and I leave her some prey, but sometimes she doesn't even eat it.

-Dudu, you're being very hard on yourself, you should talk about what happened, maybe those kittens aren't genetically yours but you raised them by your side, you're also their mother and what happened affects you too- the brunette explained sweetly.

Jisoo looked up and sighed.

-We must take them with us.

-That?

-Dudu is injured and dehydrated, I imagine that Rabbit must be the same. It is no longer safe here for Nini.

-Chu, the girls have already done a lot for us and...

-Jennie, they are our friends, I am not going to leave them to their fate.

Jennie nodded and looked at Dudu.

- Have him come down and bring the little ones, on the way we will explain everything to them and...

The chestnut fell when she heard her sister scream, turning around she widened her eyes when she saw the cause of her pain.

-Holy mother of cats, get that beast off me Jennie!!!

-Kai?- the feline scratched the brunette angrily, although Jennie knew that he couldn't do too much damage with his claws, his owners cut them every week so that he wouldn't scratch the furniture- Kai, stop it, it's me Nini!

-Nini?- Hearing that name was enough to capture all of her attention. Jisoo instead growled in pain, moving away from the feline.

-Why does everyone attack me and no one does anything to you!?- she complained, but the brunette was focused on the Bombay who approached her cautiously, sniffing the air in search of her scent.

-Don't be afraid Kai, we won't hurt you

-Nini, is that really you?

-It's me, Nini! - Jennie tried to touch him but he backed away

-You smell like a human

-It's because he is, you piece of...

-Chu!- Jennie scolded her.

-Wait, that's Chu?- he looked at them confused- but what do you...?

-Long story

-Your smell...- the cat sniffed again and growled- is not just one

- That?
-You have two different smells, and I've smelled it before.

Jennie thought about it. Leo's scent? How was that possible? She never touched the feline.

-I...

-Look at you, you're a stinking human and you're marked by someone else, you lied to me Nini!

-Kai.. This is...

She wanted to approach him, but he again turned away from her with contempt.

-Don't touch me, human, go with your people! - the feline turned around and ran away.

-Kai!!- the brunette sobbed in pain, Kai was still an important part of her, but Lisa was her whole world- I'm sorry Kai...

Hairy Family

Lovesick Girls was playing on the radio at full volume while the blonde was cleaning. Lisa loved cleaning with Blackpink playing in the background, they were her favorite group.

While humming, she swayed her hips to the rhythm of the music. She was so absorbed in cleaning the display case that she didn't notice the arrival of the brunette.

-Lisa!

The named one jumped, dropping one of the ornaments to the ground. Her eyes widened at the sight of the shattered vessel.

-Fuck, it was a gift from my grandmother!- he lamented with his gaze on the object- The only thing I brought from Thailand- he frowned and turned to the brunette who was next to Jisoo with a box in her hands, then he looked at the closed door and walked there in a couple of strides- But how did they get in if the door has the bolt!?

Jisoo snorted, rolling her eyes.

-The emergency staircase- he clarified as if it were the most obvious thing in the world- Seriously, Cripple, why do you have a human brain if you don't make it work?

-Jisoo!- Jennie scolded her, she hated that she always picked on the blonde. She turned to the girl with bangs and raised an eyebrow, blushing when she noticed her outfit- You're...

Lisa followed the brunette's gaze and blushed twice as much when she noticed her own clothing, a top and a pair of panties. *Fuck, this only happens to me!* She grabbed the first thing she found to cover her half-naked body, earning a laugh from the brunette.

-God Lila cat, I know you're thin, but that feather duster doesn't even cover half of it! - he mocked, looking more closely at the body the girl was trying so clumsily to cover - nice curves, I think I like human anatomy now

Jennie glared at her and elbowed her in the ribs, making her sister moan in pain.

-It's Lisa! -he corrected her- And don't talk about her body like that!

Lisa looked at the box in the brunette's hands and was surprised to hear a meow.

-Jennie, what is it?

-Lisa, they need your help- the feline-eyed girl cut her off, pleading.

The brunette left the box on the floor and Lisa then saw two cats with two kittens. Her eyes widened and she shook her head.

-Jennie, I can't take in all the cats that need a home.

-Please Lisa, they are our friends

The Thai woman hesitated for a minute. She looked at the adult cats and sighed. She really couldn't. She was about to refuse when she met the pleading gaze of the brunette, those feline eyes aroused things in her that had been dormant for years. How could she refuse that look?

He rolled his eyes and shook his head.

-I can't say no if you look at me with those little eyes- he smiled big and was surprised to see the brunette blush, who quickly began to play with her fingers- Look at you, you look beautiful blushing!

That only made the reddish color more intense.

-Ok Romea, that's enough, can you stay or not?- Jisoo interrupted, impatient.

Lisa arched an eyebrow petulantly.

-And since when do you start reading Shakespeare?

-What's wrong with you Luisa, I'm a learned cat!

They both looked at each other for a moment and then burst out laughing in conspiracy. Lisa and Jisoo getting along? That was new.

The Thai girl knelt in front of the box and Jennie imitated her action.

-Look at that, that one over there looks like daddy! - he pointed at the little grey kitten that was lazily sucking on the whitish feline.

The chestnut laughed and moved Lisa's finger to point to the orange kitten who was entertainingly biting the blue Russian's tail.

-That one looks like dad

Lisa looked at the felines in confusion, the Russian blue was dark and the Japanese bobtail was white, and then she analyzed the two kittens

-Ummh no, that one looks like Russian blue

Jennie laughed and shook her head at the blonde's confusion.

-That's not the father, he's not even a male.

Lisa tilted her head in disbelief.

-Is it the Bobtail?

-Nor Lisa, both are females

Lisa made a perfect O with her lips in surprise.

-Careful Jendeukie, it seems that Alisa doesn't know about cats- she laughed amused.

-Shut up Chu!- he turned to Lisa and smiled- She's a rabbit- he pointed at the bobtail, who was alert because of the proximity of the humans- she's the babies' mother. And this is Dudu- he pointed at the cat beside him, who was growling grumpily- She's his mate

Lisa widened her eyes in surprise.

- Are you serious? - he looked at both cats again - who would have thought there were also homosexual cats - he smiled at the felines and laughed - well, females are always a good choice - he winked at the brunette and got up from the floor - fine, they can sleep in Leo's bed, or on the sofa bed, after all you don't need it anymore - he blushed as he remembered the nights they had been sleeping together - well... - he cleared his throat nervously - you noticed that one of them was hurt, right?

On the other hand, Jennie was enthralled by the blonde's profile, by how her bangs covered her eyebrows, by the sparkle in her eyes from the excitement, by the tender way she wrinkled her nose when she laughed and by those luscious, full lips. *She is perfect*.

-Jennie?

-God, Lisa, make me kittens...- she whispered without thinking, still bewitched by the Thai girl's features.

Lisa looked at her in surprise, her cheeks burning. Had she heard wrong?

-Oh Jen, you look like a cat in heat, stop hitting on Manobal and focus on Dudu!

Lisa growled

- Also with my last name? It's Manoban!

Jisoo shrugged indifferently.

-Sorry, I don't speak Thai.

-I'm speaking to you in Korean!

◇🐱◇

Finally Lisa helped Jennie splint the feline's leg with some paddles and gauze.

-Okay, it's not the best, but it works pretty well- he commented, appreciating the bandage- When I get off work I'll buy her one, or we can take her to the vet to make sure it's not broken.

The brunette shook her head as she saw her growl from Leo's bed.

-She doesn't get along well with humans, her owner wasn't too affectionate... he only had her to keep the mice away from home

-So he didn't get much love...- said Lisa melancholy- that's very sad... but I'll take care of changing that!

◇◇◇

I want kittens with Lisa!

While Lisa was at work, the brunette took the opportunity to move the kittens and her friends to the guest room. Dudu remained haughty, while the rabbit began to gain confidence.

-I still can't believe it's you Nini, that story is... Very strange, I would give all my designer clothes to walk on two legs!

The Bobtail posed for cat clothing covers, the Ims were the most eccentric in the neighborhood and all their pets, including the hamster, wore fashionable outfits.

Dudu snorted, limping over to the water trough.

-That's nonsense, Rabbit, look at them, they have no fur or tail!

The white-haired girl let out a reproachful meow.

-Well, it's not like mine is very long...- she wagged her little tail to emphasize what she had said.

-What I don't understand is what do you have with that woman?- continued Dudu, ignoring his female's complaint.

-I?

-No, Puss in Boots! Of course you!

-No problem...

-Aha, yesterday you asked her for kits and you looked at her like an idiot, and now you say that nothing is wrong? I don't believe you- he purred maliciously, returning to the bed and sitting on the feline girl's lap- I think she is the reason why you look like a human

Rabbit covered her snout with both front paws in shock at the discovery of the grayish cat.

-Nini, are you in love with that woman!?

-I....

-And what happens with Kai?- added Dudu

At that moment the door opened, saving her from that awkward interrogation. Her friends knew of her feelings for the black-haired feline, but she couldn't help but think that with Lisa everything was more intense, and she knew that her friends wouldn't understand how a cat could have fallen in love with her human.

-Nini, I'm home now!

The brunette smiled when she heard the Thai girl's greeting. She loved that the blonde took the time to inform her of her arrival.

-That idiot face explains everything- Dudu growled

The door of the room opened, revealing the Thai woman with a small bag of dried meat and another one whose contents could not be deciphered.

-Hey Jen!

-Lili...-he whispered in a sigh

-Look, I brought you this!- he offered her the bag and laughed- Rose says that Jisoo loves those things and that maybe soon she will make her forget about chicken

-Jisoo, forget about chicken? You'll have to erase your mind first before Chu stops eating chicken.

Lisa shrugged her shoulders

-You can always use hypnosis, that's what psychologists do, right? - Lisa looked at the little ones and smiled - I bought some toys and other things, you know... For the kittens, Leo loved those things

-It wasn't necessary Lili, but thank you- she looked at the kittens and then at the blonde- would you like to hold them?

Lisa heard Dudu's growl of disagreement and shook her head.

-I don't think she wants to

-Well, Rabbit doesn't mind, she knows you're helping them- she looked at the Russian blue and clicked her tongue- don't pay attention to Dudu, she's a bitter woman

-I think she's more of an overprotective mother- Lisa stood next to Jennie and accepted her offer- well, let's meet those furballs

Jennie smiled and took the gray fur one

-This is Namjoon- she handed him the kitten and smiled when it bit her nose- he likes you

-That or he thinks I'm delicious- Lisa joked, letting out a giggle.

-You are...- the brunette whispered almost inaudibly and bit her lower lip. That body was a monument and must have tasted exquisite. *What nonsense Jennie! How could humans have taste!?* But her female instinct led her to imagine herself running her tongue over the slender figure of the tallest girl .

A growl brought her out of her thoughts, Dudu looked at her curiously, it was obvious that she suspected something

Jennie cleared her throat and took the other

-And this little one is Solar

Lisa also took it and rubbed her nose with one and then the other, giving it little kisses on the belly and making little sounds to get its attention.

Cat god, I want this woman as the mother of my kittens! Jennie melted just watching her interact with the kitties, she was so sweet and delicate.

-I really like cats, especially when they are this small- said the blonde, sitting on the floor to play better with the felines.

Jennie's eyes lit up at that information. *She would be a great mom!*

He sat down near her, still watching her hands move from one side to the other to entertain the little ones.

-Oh really? And how many kittens would you like to have? - he asked casually.

-Oh, so many of them, I'd fill a whole house if I could! - Lisa joked between giggles.

Jennie on the other hand widened her eyes blushing

-So many!? I... Wouldn't you settle for four or six?

Lisa wrinkled her nose

-No way, there are very few of them.

Jennie brushed a strand of hair from her face. Few? *Of course, since you're not the one giving birth...!* She swallowed hard, imagining Lisa surrounded by her babies made her heart beat faster.

-And do you like any species in particular? - he asked nervously.

Lisa looked at her with a half smile and nodded.

-Ragdolls are beautiful

And Jennie almost screamed with happiness. *Oh my God, oh my God!* Her excitement was at a thousand, and without realizing it she had thrown herself at Lisa, kissing every part of her face with care, invaded by happiness.

When she calmed down her eyes widened. Her face was very close to the blonde's, so much so that their noses were touching. She had never seen Lisa's eyes so close. *Honey*. That was her color. Her gaze lowered to the blonde's full lips and out of inertia she moistened her lips.

Lisa on the other hand was in shock, she could feel Jennie's breath on her lips and that only encouraged her to do one thing. *Kiss her*. She was dying to discover what those delicate lips tasted like. She watched and the brunette came closer but didn't kiss her, instead she delicately passed her tongue along the contour of her lips and Lisa felt like dying with that sensual lick.

The sound of the Thai girl's cell phone was what brought them out of their ecstasy. Lisa carefully pushed the brunette away, without breaking eye contact. What she really wanted was to melt into her lips and never stop kissing her.

-I... I have to answer Nini- she whispered without much enthusiasm

Jennir nodded, pulling away with difficulty and grimacing when she no longer felt the warmth of Lisa's body against hers.

-I'm going to take a bath and prepare dinner, okay? I'll see you later...

But before she parted completely, Lisa gathered her courage and gave him a kiss on the cheek. It wasn't where she wanted to kiss him, but it was a good start.

-That was... intense- the rabbit said after the blonde left the room.

-So, will you answer my question?
Jennie, looking at the door, replied:
-Yes Dudu, I'm madly in love with that human

Possessive Cat

After a week, Dudu had already gained more confidence with the blonde, and was beginning to walk better.

Jennie, for her part, was feeling more and more anxious. Lisa's proximity made her shudder and she couldn't stop thinking about her for a second. *I must be sick, that's what it is.*

-Mommy, what's wrong with Aunt Nini?

-Idiocy Nam, that's what it has

-Dudu, don't say that to the child! - the rabbit scolded her and turned to see her little one - Aunt, there's nothing honey, go play with your sister

When the kittens were distracted Dudu decided to start the interrogation

-Well?, spits out the hairball, what's wrong with you?

The chestnut snorted

- I don't know Dudu, I think I'm sick, I don't have much of an appetite and every time Li... - she stopped before saying the blonde's name - and lately I feel something strange in my stomach - she wasn't going to reveal what was happening in the presence of the Thai girl or just by imagining her.

The gray-haired feline made a sound of disgust.

-If the Thai girl had a penis she would say that you are pregnant

Jennie smiled at the thought. *Pregnant with Lisa?* Her smile automatically appeared on her lips. How could she avoid it? It was a dream.

-Oh, you might have Ascaris, those things are fucking itchy asses!

-I don't have parasites, Rabbit! - Jennie interrupted her, uncomfortable with the comment.

- Are you sure? Those two symptoms are common.

Jennie sat on the couch and hugged her pillow with a pronounced pout.

-Let me guess... you miss her?- Dudu said with his eyes rolled back.

-Too much with too much!

-Jennie left this morning, she should be back soon, don't be dramatic.

Both felines had to put up with their friend's bipolarity. When Lisa was there, she smiled more than she should and almost cried when the blonde had to go out.

-They don't understand! I don't like being without her!

-That's called love- purred the white-haired girl, touched.

-That's called stupidity - snorted the second feline.

-Dudu!- reproached the Rabbit

-It's true, with that idiotic attitude you're going to push her further away.

Jennie snorted. It was true that she sometimes went overboard, but how could she avoid it? That was how Lisa made her feel.

I smile at the memory. Lisa was a sweetheart to Nam and Solar, and that only made the brunette want to procreate with her even more intensely. But she remembered a point against her that put her on the back burner.

He cleared his throat and swallowed hard.

-Rabbit... Does it hurt a lot?

The named looked at her confused

-Do you have parasites? Not at all, you just feel a connection in your body...

-God, I didn't mean that!

The feline thought about it for a moment.

-Are you talking about fucking a cat?

Jennie widened her eyes in horror.

-Fuck no! Why should that matter to me?

-Ah, you talk about fucking a cat! Well, it is a pleasant sensation... Although Dudu's tongue is a little rough, but quite deli...

-Stop, Rabbit, stop! I wasn't talking about that either- Jennie's cheeks were bright red and she had become extremely nervous- I-I meant giving birth

-Aah...! Does it hurt? Like hell! - exclaimed the cat, remembering the sensation - it's the most horrible and painful thing ever! Giving birth to 5 babies? I almost lost my vagina!

Jennie looked terrified. Did it hurt that much? Good God, Lisa will have to settle for eight at most!

-Do you really want kittens with that woman? - the feline was interested.

-God, rabbit, I would give you thousands of kittens if you asked me!

The front door opened and Jennie smiled as she saw Lisa walk in with Rose and Jisoo.

-I already told you Jisoo, you can't eat people's birds! - the Australian girl was scolding her, upset.

-How was I supposed to know that parrot belonged to that man? I didn't see his name anywhere.

-It was on his fucking shoulder!

-So what? Those feathered ones also perch on the branches and that doesn't mean they belong to the tree, right!?- he shrugged- humans make too much noise...- he smiled when he saw his sister- Hello Kitty- he joked- Where are my little furry devils?

-Aunt Chicken!!

Jisoo snorted and looked at everyone reproachfully.

-Who told you to call me Chicken!?- she asked offended and narrowed her eyes when she saw Lisa laughing- Was it you, Cripple!?

-Sweet revenge- Lisa winked at him and smiled amusedly.

Jisoo rolled her eyes and looked back at the minions who were nibbling on her shoes.

-Aunt Jichu, you divine, you guess! I threw out my first hairball!

-How wonderful! I remember that the first one I spit out almost made me choke because it was so big... - she sighed melancholically - such good memories...

Rose looked at her with a grimace and rolled her eyes.

- Well, that's not so surprising, yesterday I ate a whole grasshopper! And I caught it all by myself!

-Good job boy! Next time let it be a mouse, and if it's for Aunt Chu a juicy chicken, without feathers please...

-And we're back with the chicken...- Rose brought a hand to her face, giving up.

◇🐱◇

The four girls were on the sofa watching a movie. Rabbit had gone with her little ones to feed them while Dudu was wandering around the living room.

-Poor me Leo, he'll think I don't love him anymore...- Lisa commented with a nostalgic pout.

-Lisa, Leo was officially adopted by me, there is no more room for more cats in this apartment- informed the Australian

Jennie widened her eyes and shook her head, that would ruin her plans.

-Of course, there is still room, maybe for about eight...- he added quickly.

- Cats!? - Rose exclaimed, scandalized.

-kittens- the Korean corrected- Ragdolls in their entirety- her cheeks reddened and she looked down in shame

Jisoo noticed her sister's change and hit Lisa with an empty Coca-Cola can.

-Ouch! And what was that for!?

-For getting my sister pregnant!

-What me what!?- Lisa's eyes almost popped out of her face

-Jisoo, don't be silly, a woman cannot procreate with another, it's impossible- the psychologist explained slowly.

Lisa didn't say anything and continued rubbing her bump, indignant. She glanced at Dudu next to her on the couch and smiled, it was the closest she had been to the feline and she was thrilled by his closeness.

-Hello, beauty- Lisa greeted her affectionately, catching the Russian blue's attention- are you walking better now?

The feline tried to get away, but the blonde placed her hand on her back and began to caress her, all under the watchful eye of Jennie, who had stopped watching the movie as soon as she noticed the blonde's exchange of affection.

-Oh, you like this?- Lisa smiled as she watched the cat relax- how about here...?- she began to caress her chin, earning the first purrs from the feline. That action made Jennie light up like a torch and not with desire.

-I think that's enough Lisa...- he asked her trying to control his disgust

-Wait Nini, I think I'm winning!

Jennie and Jisoo's eyes widened as they watched the actions of their friend who had never allowed any human to lay a hand on her.

Dudu noticed the brunette's scrutiny and decided to investigate the subject further. He lovingly began to photograph himself in Lisa's hand and then climbed onto her lap.

-You're right Jennie, this human is perfect, and what hands... she sure knows how to touch- he purred as he felt the Thai girl's caresses on his back.

And that was the trigger for the Korean

- Get off my legs Lisa or I'll rip your tail off! - he threatened angrily, gritting his teeth.

Dudu looked at her with interest and smiled like a laughing cat.

- Why? We are friends, you can share it with me from time to time and...

-Lalisa Manoban is mine! - Jennie growled and in a quick and abrupt movement she pulled the Thai girl into the hallway, disappearing into her room.

Rose and Jisoo looked intrigued at the hallway, surprised by the brunette's reaction.

-What just happened?

-Manoban is a bitch and my sister is a fucking possessive- he commented nonchalantly- Don't be surprised if she comes back with a couple of scratches on her back

-Jennie is not like that...

-Everyone knows you can't mess with another cat's stuff, and Lisa is marked

In the room, Jennie slammed her roughly against the wall. She was angry about the scene in the living room, and her friend's attitude. Since when was Dudu so mushy with Lisa? She had to resolve it as soon as possible.

-Jennie what...? Fuck No, Nini I have my perfume! - Lisa complained when the Korean sprayed her fragrance. She wrinkled her nose - and I don't like wearing Chanel

Jennie closed the space between them, just enough for one to breathe the other's warm breath. Was she going to kiss her? But instead, the brunette began to rub her face on the taller girl's chest and neck, leaving the Thai girl confused and breathless as she shuddered at the Korean girl's touch.

- You have my scent, Lisa, and as long as it is like that, no woman or cat should come near you. You belong to me!

◇◇◇

Jennie vs Irene

-From here I get your Chanel No5 smell, why such a drastic change Manoban?

-Our Lisa has gotten too cocky, now she smells of luxury, soon we will see her in a Ferrari

The Thai girl rolled her eyes, Rose not helping matters. Momo was the dance teacher for their agency and the boys wanted to see their CEO in action. Lisa loved dancing and didn't mind taking a couple of hours to do it for her students.

After laughing at her boss, Momo approached the boys to start the class.

-Ok guys, so that later you don't say that Miss Manoban doesn't care about you.

The boys clapped and cheered happily when they saw the Thai girl enter. Lisa waved as she sat down with the psychologist. She had to wait for Momo's class to end before giving her demonstration, and at the same time evaluate the boys' progress in the choreographies for the nationals.

-Hi, I hope I'm not late- Irene made her way through the seats and gave the blonde with bangs a kiss on the cheek, a gesture that was not very pleasing to the Australian.

-Hello Miss Bae, it's also a pleasure to see you again.

Irene looked in Rose's direction and nodded, turning her attention back to Lisa.

-In five days there will be the opening event, how do you feel?

-Moved

Lisa's company was at its peak. Although the Thai agency was quite well known in Korea, it had taken a step further and would soon take her to her home country, Thailand. And she was looking forward to it. Lisa wanted to see her family again and in five days she would be able to do so.

-I imagine so... Here- he handed her two cards- this is your plane ticket and another one for a guest

Lisa took them. She had forgotten that detail. On that occasion Rose would not travel with her as usual when she left the country. She had work matters and had decided to invite the brunette instead, however she still had doubts, Nini could act inappropriately in public, the brunette had not yet been surrounded by so many people and even less in a strange country, what if something happened to her?

-Have you decided who you're going to take? - her assistant asked, taking her out of her thoughts.

-I'm on it...

After the rehearsal Lisa took over the dance floor, cracking a few jokes to warm up. The students admired her for her talent but also appreciated her for her charisma, the Thai girl was the kind of bubbly girl who had no problem interacting in front of a crowd.

-Well, I'm going to try something simple but powerful, I hope you like it- he made a signal to Momo and she immediately pressed play on the stereo.

Every movement was seductive, Lisa simply let herself be carried away by the music. That was her talent, her body overflowed with eroticism without the greatest effort. Her hips adapted to each movement in a natural way and her facial expressions were a complement to her sensuality.

As she moved she couldn't help but think of the brunette. What would it be like to have those feline eyes on her while she did those dance moves? *Jennie*. Her mind visualized her in the crowd, enjoying the sway of her hips, her ups and downs and the slight touches on her body. She was dancing for her even if it was only an imagination in her mind.

She was so absorbed in her mind that she didn't notice the moment the music stopped until she heard the applause. She blinked, regaining her position and smiled in pleasure at the sight of a handful of jaws dropped in admiration and amazement, other gazes showing a desire that she was already used to provoking.

-Holy God, I think I had a couple of orgasms watching you Lis- Rose handed her a towel, still surprised- the beginning was hot, but halfway through the dance it was orgasmic, what the hell was that, who were you thinking of?

In Jennie

-Can't I dance sexy without having to think about someone?

-No, now tell me what are you hiding Manoban or...

-Wow Lisie, that was amazing!

-I'm sure her panties got wet- the Australian muttered.

-Excuse me, did you say something?

-I was leaving- Rose lied with a mocking smile- Lisa, I'll wait for you in your office

The blonde nodded and looked back at the brunette who was smiling widely at her.

-You are too sensual when dancing

-Just dancing?- the Thai girl teased.

-Always

Lisa was about to respond when she heard whistles coming from the students.

Irene looked into the distance in amazement and asked:

-Who is she?

-Who are you talking about...- his eyes widened as he saw who was causing all the commotion- Jennie?

The brunette entered the room, looking cautiously around her as if she was looking for something in particular. She was wearing a long-sleeved top and jeans that beautifully accentuated her shapely legs. *I must be dreaming.*

-She is... My... tenant

Irene looked at her from head to toe in frustration.

-She?- he looked at her doubtfully and cleared his throat- Is that all or...?

She couldn't finish, the brunette had already visualized the blonde, but her attention was on Irene

Jennie had gone on her own to see the Thai girl, she had memorized the way the last time she was there and it was not difficult to find it.

-Lili!- he hugged Lisa. He smiled big when he felt the Thai girl's hands cling to his waist- I missed you...- he whispered that last thing near her ear in a tone loud enough for his assistant to hear it too, and he wasn't wrong.

She heard a cough and glanced at the girl who was glaring at her. Lisa noticed it too, sitting up nervously at the third girl's gaze.

-Oh Nini, this is Irene, she is my assistant...

-I'm a friend of Lisa, a very good friend...

Jen 0 - Ire 1

Jennie's jaw tightened as she took the hint from her opponent. While she already knew that she had ulterior motives with Lisa and that made her furious, however, two could play the same game, and that is what she intended to do.

-Nice to meet you, I'm also very close to Lili- she looked at the blonde with bangs with tenderness and smiled- We are good bedmates

Irene frowned and clenched her fists.

Jen 1 - Ire 1

Lisa watched the exchange rather uncomfortably. She could see how the girls glared at each other and spat out each word with malice.

-You wouldn't be the first one she shares a bed with...- added Irene, downplaying it in an attempt to provoke the brunette.

But Jennie had another ace up her sleeve, and she was quick to use it.

-In fact, I've been the only one for two weeks- she looked at Lisa and pouted- I regret scratching you last night, I got carried away

Jen 2- Ire 1

Although that comment was true, he did not specify that the scratch had been on his arm, nor that he had gotten it when he was frightened by thunder, but he did not intend to tell those details to the assistant.

- See you later, Miss Manoban - the black-haired girl said goodbye with a sour face.

-Wait, Irene!

-I better go- the brunette said when she saw Lisa holding her assistant back.

-Jennie!

The Korean girl didn't stop. She walked down the hall taking strides to get away as quickly as possible. She was angry, she really wanted to surprise Lisa by visiting her at work.

-But he already has a good relationship...- she growled between her teeth without stopping, until she felt some hands lift her by her waist and pull her into a nearby door.

Her first impulse was to scream for help, or just scream, but that idea disappeared when she saw her captor.

-What's wrong Lisa, have you finished talking to your dear assistant?- he asked reproachfully.

Lisa raised an eyebrow with a half smile, she simply liked the Korean's attitude.

-Are you jealous Nini?

Jennie looked at her with latent fury and answered, directly and without mincing words:

-Yes, I am. I hate it when people touch my stuff.

-And what is your thing?- Lisa asked with difficulty.

-You...

Lisa forcefully urged her to wash, mounting her with a quick movement. She didn't care about anything anymore, she couldn't deny how much she wanted the brunette and those words from the shorter one had managed to turn her on.

-Jennie Kim, if there is one person here who belongs to someone, it is you- he spoke with authority and a deep voice that made the Korean girl melt- you are mine, and I will prove it to you.

Jennue moaned in anticipation, but before the blonde could act, the toilet lever in one of the stalls clicked, forcing Lisa to step away and Jennie to step off the cold marble.

With a sly smile, Rose walked to the faucet, washing her hands slowly, without looking at either of them. She applied soap to her hands and after rinsing them she said:

-A piece of advice Manoban, if you're going to fuck in a public bathroom first make sure there's no one else there- he dried his hands and left the place without saying anything else, leaving the girls nervous and with latent desire, but the moment had passed and the Thai girl cursed when she saw a new person enter. Without a doubt she had missed the opportunity again.

Walk to the Zoo

Lisa woke up better than ever, it was Saturday and she could do whatever she wanted.

She looked to her side and smiled as she felt an arm tighten around her. She liked waking up like that, with the Korean girl around her waist and sighing, deep in sleep. The day before she had been on the verge of kissing her, and not only that, she had wanted to melt into her body and explore every corner of her skin, all of that there, in the small bathroom of her agency, which would have happened if it weren't for her friend's intervention.

-What's happening to me with you Nini?- she sighed. The need to have that feline girl near her 24 hours a day was starting to become sickly for Lisa. Although, she had never had that urgency in any of her previous relationships, except with...

-Fuck- he carefully moved away from the brunette so as not to wake her up and went into the shower. He liked to think while taking a shower, it totally relaxed him and at that moment he needed it.

Why is Jennie so different to me? She thought about the reasons, it was true that she had a weakness for brunettes, especially if they were shorter than her, Tzuyu was, Sorn, even Yeonwoo, but Jennie was different. Her exes let themselves be done to the whim of the blonde, Jennie on the other hand was dominant and also let herself be dominated, and she loved both, but above all her sweetness, how could someone be so innocent and at the same time so sensual?

He snorted and stepped out of the shower, water droplets running down his back but he didn't care. He grabbed one of his shirts and put it on with a cheeky bra.

He turned towards the bed and smiled at how cute the brunette looked hugging his pillow. He analyzed the time he had known her and was surprised to discover that it had been 3 and a half months since that girl with feline eyes had appeared in his life and had changed it completely.

She thought about how little Jennie had gone out in that time and felt guilty, even Rose had done more for the brunette than she had done for herself. *But where can I take her?*

She walked to the kitchen and began to prepare breakfast. In those two weeks since the chestnut returned, she had had to learn a couple of simple dishes and decided to prepare the one she was best at: Waffles.

While adding the ingredients into a bowl he heard a yawn and smiled.

Jennie had just gotten up and hated feeling the cold in bed, which meant that the blonde had already gotten up. After getting ready and changing her shirt for one of the blonde's, she inhaled it before leaving. She heard movement in the kitchen and walked there with some laziness.

-Good morning Nini

Jennie smiled at the affectionate tone of the Thai girl.

-Good morning Lili- without thinking twice he stood behind her and hugged her, leaving a tender kiss on her shoulder before taking a seat at the table

-You know, I was thinking that we've known each other for a while and we haven't hung out much.

Jennie looked at her in surprise.

-Are you asking me out?

-No!- Lisa's cheeks blushed

-No?- Jennie asked, confused.

-I mean... God, why is it so hard to talk to you!? - she covered her face with both hands, embarrassed. Her nerves were on edge whenever she was near the Korean girl- yes, I want to go out with you- she continued- I was thinking that Rose and Jisoo could go too and that way your sister could get to know the area a little bit too-she explained as she poured the mixture into the waffle maker and walked over to the shelf in search of two cups- Sure, that's if you want...

She offered him a cup of hot milk and poured herself some coffee.

-I want anything that allows me to spend more time with you....

◇🐱◇

-For God's sake Jisoo, get down from the fucking tree!

Rose grunted, displeased, trying for the fifth time to get the brunette to come down without much success.

-No! That flea wants to eat me! - he pointed at the dog that was barking continuously in his direction.

Rose looked at the dog and frowned, about to lose her patience.

-It's a damn Chinese crested, the poor hairless rat is more afraid of you than you are of it!

-Hey!- complained the owner next to her

-I'm sorry ma'am- he returned his gaze to the tree- get down from there, dammit!

Jisoo shook her head with a pout, tightening her grip on the trunk.

-I'm scared, that thing is very ugly!

-But it's just a dog without much hair!

-I was talking about the owner!

The woman opened her mouth in offence and dragged her dog away, grumbling.

-Come down, damn it!!!

-But what are you shouting at the sky so much?- Lisa and Jennie made their entrance. They had agreed to meet at the zoo and were delayed while they bought snacks.

Rose looked at her with hatred

-Do you really think I'm stupid enough to talk to the sky? - he growled -God, give me patience! - He raised his arms in prayer and looked up.

-Well, you just did- he rolled his eyes- what's happening, why...? Oh shit look, there's Jisoo!

-How clever Manoban...- the Australian woman said ironically, rolling her eyes- the idiot climbed up the tree when she saw a damn dog and now she doesn't want to come down. I've tried everything and nothing!

Lisa thought about it for a moment and nodded.

-Hey Jisoo, I have chicken skewers!

The brunette fixed her attention on the blonde with bangs

-Did you say chicken skewers!?

In the blink of an eye the feline girl was standing in front of the blonde, waiting for her snack. Rose growled in disgust and began to pace.

After that the girls went to the animal area. Jennie was impressed with the pandas, while Jisoo argued because one of the monkeys patted her butt.

-I swear, he hit me! I'm sure I have a mark! Wait, see if...- he made a move to pull down his pants but the psychologist stopped him instantly.

- Are you crazy!? How are you going to take your pants down here!? - she scolded her, frustrated - and it was your fault, you got too close to the cage

-Oh, of course, and I did it because I love having my butt groped by monkeys, right? How was I supposed to know!

On the other hand, Lisa decided to go on her own with Jennie, since Rose and Jisoo argued excessively.

-Oh, look Lili!- he pointed at the aviary with excitement.

-Oh yeah, they have hummingbirds there, come on, let's go.

Both of them entered the place. Inside they were given a dropper with sugar water and guided to the area chosen by the Thai woman.

-This is to feed them, it is a simulation of nectar- he took one of the flower hats and put it on the chestnut's head- this is another method

They both enjoyed themselves among the hummingbirds. Jennie looked like a little girl on her first time at an amusement park, everything seemed new and fascinating to her and Lisa loved to see her enthusiasm.

-Lili look!- she stood still when she noticed one of the little birds coming closer than expected.

-That's it Hetn, now wait for him to come closer and...! No Jennie, no, don't eat him!

Late, the chestnut had already eaten the feathered one

◈🐱◈

-This was exciting, remind me not to have children...- Lisa commented exhausted.

"I think I've gotten old taking care of that pair," the Australian complained.

"I can't believe he ate the poor hummingbird," the Thai woman pouted pitifully.

-I can't believe Jisoo thought peacocks were a flock of giant chickens!- she exclaimed in horror- I swear I almost saw her sharpening knives ready to sink her teeth into them! She's an animal!

Both blondes were resting on a park bench. After being expelled from the zoo because Chu was eating the Koi fish in the pond

-Are you ready for the trip? - asked the psychologist, rubbing her feet.

-I've already packed my bags- he said- I'm just missing a few things.

-You're really not going to take her?

Lisa sighed. She had finally decided not to travel with the brunette. Those days she would have to stay with Rose, as well as the four kittens.

-I think you should take her.

-You've seen how they acted today at the zoo, Jennie is unpredictable.

-She was a Lisa cat, it's her hunting instinct, understand her

-I do Rosie, but I can't risk the event going wrong because of an interruption on your part.

-I think you're actually terrified that you might overstep your boundaries with her- Rose knew she was right when she saw that her friend didn't contradict her- Lisa, she's a woman, look at her as such and if something has to happen then let it happen, you can't avoid her forever, either you stop it or you let yourself go, it's up to you...

Damn psychologist and her damn persuasion techniques. Lisa was between a rock and a hard place. The worst thing is that she is right.

I always fly with you

They had arrived at the airport around 5pm, and their flight didn't leave until 6pm.

-Come on Nini, hurry up!- looking back every five seconds

-I'm trying to do that, Lili, but the wheels get stuck! - the brunette complained with a pout, trying to keep up with the blonde.

Yes, Lisa had finally decided to take the brunette, and Jennie was more than happy to spend extra time with her. Even if it meant getting on a plane.

-Okay, let me carry her- the Thai girl took the girl's luggage and gave her the bag where she carried her essential things in exchange. The suitcases were not that heavy since the blonde did not like to carry but rather bring things. She would have focused mainly on the outfit they would wear at the event, the rest could be bought while in Thailand.

- Why don't we pack in one suitcase? We're not carrying much.

-Because I want to bring almost everything, and we wouldn't have room if we brought too many clothes, or if we only brought a briefcase - explained the Thai girl, looking at the brunette's passport. She had to talk to Hanbin, an old suitor of hers, to speed up the paperwork. Without the passport she couldn't take the brunette. Hanbin, despite knowing Lisa's sexual orientation, never stopped pursuing her and the blonde took the opportunity to use that to her advantage.

◯ ***Pasta*** ◈

Was the kiss with Han yummy? 🤢🤢🤢

◈ ◈

The message made her grunt in disgust. Well, yes, she had to kiss him in exchange for the favor. While the boy felt like he was in space during the kiss, she plummeted. *Kissing a man...? Disgust . Yes .*

◈**Thai Princess**◯

That kiss reminded me of one of the reasons why I became a lesbian 🙈😨

PS: I was about to disinfect my mouth with chlorine or some other corrosive component 🔶🔶

○ **Pasta** 🔶
I know, I know, the male mouth is a disgusting cavity 😒
Happy travels! 🔶🔶
Note: Don't tire Jen out too much 🔶😌
🔶🔶

Lisa rolled her eyes and put her phone away. The Australian girl hadn't stopped bothering her about it these days. But of course, that idea had been going around in her head. *What if it really happens that Jennie and I...* ? Her heart raced at the idea of having the brunette and why not? She was single. She *'s your damn cat!* Her conscience growled, trying to make her see reason. *She WAS my cat, now she's my sexy tenant* . She corrected herself to keep her spirits up. And what's going on with Kai? Her mind attacked again making her doubt. That made her stop dead, the brunette had mentioned that name a couple of times, and Jisoo was also bothering her with the same thing. *Is he her partner?* She hadn't thought about the possibility that the brunette already had someone else. *She wouldn't flirt with me if she had a boyfriend... or would she?*

-Lili?

She turned to the Korean girl with a worried expression and all her insecurity vanished. Could that girl really fool her? She didn't know, but at that moment those feline eyes screamed no, and she believed them.

-Come on Nini, let's eat something before boarding the plane- he took Jennie's hand confidently and guided her towards the cafeteria.

🔶🐱🔶

On the plane Jennie was restless. They hadn't even taken off yet and her heart was already about to jump out of her chest. *Oh God, I'm going to die here!* She pressed her nails hard into her seat, waiting for the inevitable.

One of Lis5s's hands held hers firmly and gave it a gentle squeeze to comfort her.

-Hey, calm down, it's not as bad as it seems.

- Aren't we going to die?

Lisa laughed amused at the girl's ideas and shook her head.

-If that were the case I would never have asked you to come with me.

Fasten your seatbelts and stay seated, the flight to Bangkok is about to take off.

The flight attendant's voice resonated through the cabin speakers, alerting them to takeoff.

Jennie pouted and tightened her grip on the Thai girl.

-It will be entertaining, you'll see.

-Of course, for you who will see me scared- the brunette complained- how come it doesn't scare you?

Lisa shrugged, dismissing it.

-I used to, but I always travel for agency stuff and I'm used to it- she looked into the Korean girl's scared feline eyes and smiled- unlike you, I didn't have someone so sexy to take my hand the first time, so feel lucky- the blonde joked, caressing her hand with her thumb- just try not to think too much

But it was impossible. With the first movement the brunette began to scream as if her life depended on it. Her ears felt as if they were underwater and her viscera contracted as the plane took off.

Shortly after, only a pleasant tickling sensation remained.

-NinI, calm down, it's over

The blonde was embarrassed. Throughout the entire takeoff, the brunette had not stopped screaming at the top of her lungs, earning prickly and disgusted glances from the other passengers.

He ignored the complaints of the other passengers and focused on the brunette next to him who remained with her eyes closed, expectant.

-How did it feel?

The chestnut slowly opened her eyes and looked at her, still feeling raw.

-That was... incredible! - she exclaimed euphorically, like a little girl who had just ridden a roller coaster for the first time - Let's do it again!

Lisa laughed and shook her head.

-We'll do it again on the plane back home- he promised- So you liked the feeling of flying?

The brunette thought about it for a moment and shrugged her shoulders, indifferently.

-I've felt it before...- he replied as if it were no big deal.

The Thai girl looked at her, confused.

-What? Have you flown before?

Jennie smiled widely and nodded with a sparkle in her eye.

-It's the feeling I get when I have you near me. I feel like I'm flying when I'm next to you...

And those words managed to melt the blonde. Lisa smiled heartily and held her close to her chest as if in that simple way she could convey to her everything she was feeling at that moment.

-Me too Nini, me too...- he whispered so low it was almost inaudible. But he had admitted it, he had strong feelings for his little feline girl, and it was just a matter of time before those feelings came out.

FELINE WHISPERS

Heat in Bangkok

Jennie was absorbed in what she saw. From the side of the Tuk-tuk she could see the vibrant streets of Bangkok. Thai pedestrians coming in and out of shops, monuments and temples. Everything had a mystical and enchanting air that had her trapped all the way to the hotel.

-Welcome to my country, Nini- the blonde whispered excitedly in the Korean's ear.
 -This is...! Wow...! It's beautiful Lisa!
 -Not as much as you..- Lisa whispered unconsciously without realizing that the brunette had heard her clearly and that her face had taken on a nice reddish tone because of the comment. The Thai girl cleared her throat- Bangkok is known as *Krung Thep,* the city of angels
 -That makes sense...
 -Oh really? And why is that?
 -Well yes, because you are one
 Now it was Lisa who was blushing. *Are you serious Lalisa? You look like a fucking hormonal brat, focus!* It was incredible how easily both of them blushed or had their heartbeats quicken with a simple word from the other. Lisa was beginning to like that warmth in her chest that only the Korean girl could give her, and she didn't want to stop feeling it.
 -It's here- they both got out of the vehicle and entered the hotel.
 Irene had taken it upon herself to make a reservation at the Mandarin Oriental, one of the best hotels in Thailand. After all, as CEO of the agency, she could indulge herself.

They approached reception and Lisa began to engage in a conversation in Thai with the person in charge.

-Good evening, ladies, do you have a reservation?

-Three days ago, in the name of Lalisa Manoban

-One second please- the girl asked, searching through her laptop- Miss Manoban, Deluxe Premium room, is that correct?

He nodded

-It is

The woman looked at the brunette who turned her head from side to side with an excited girl's smile. Lisa noticed the receptionist's curious look and quickly explained.

-It's my...- he cleared his throat a little- partner... yes, we've come on vacation- he explained with a blush on his cheeks. Luckily the brunette didn't understand a word.

-Oh, I see! - He took out a set of keys and handed them to her politely - enjoy your stay, ladies.

Lisa bowed and took the brunette by the hand to follow the bellboy.

The room was spacious and comfortable, with a bamboo sofa and a mini sitting area to hang out. The carpets were inspired by nature, giving a jungle-oriental look, with furniture with a Thai touch that gave a unique feeling to the place, resort style with views of the river and the city.

Lisa handed the tip to the bellboy and closed the door to inspect the place. Although she earned enough to live in that kind of luxurious suite, she was more of a humble and homely type, but from time to time she allowed herself her luxuries.

-Well Nini, we will spend the rest of the night and tomorrow here, then we will have to go to the opening of the agency.

Jennie nodded in understanding and continued to observe the place.

They both approached the small balcony and the brunette held her breath. From there the city shone magically before her eyes, giving a dreamlike view.

-That one over there - the blonde pointed towards the horizon - is the Chao Phraya River and over there...

-Lili, I don't want to wake up ever- the brunette whispered, smiling- being here with you is...

-Hey Jen- the Thai girl cut her off- this isn't a dream, it's real. You and I are, and we're living this moment together- Lisa hugged her from behind on impulse. She could smell her scent and it was simply exquisite.

Jennie turned around, standing a short distance from the other girl. Her gaze traveled from Lisa's eyes to her mouth, eagerly. Those lips were her downfall. In Rose's movies she had seen the exchange of kisses between humans, very different from the affectionate licks of felines, and she was curious to try that.

She timidly placed her arms on the blonde's shoulders and leaned down to be at the height of the taller one. The Thai girl's breath hitting her lips made her shiver and filled her with anxiety.

-Jen, this is not...

-Lili, please... Kiss me

That request was full of pleading and agony, the poor girl trembled with anxiety to feel the highest once and for all and Lisa decided that it was time to put aside her fears and let herself go. «*Lisa, she is a woman, she watches it that way, and if something has to happen then let it happen. You can't avoid her forever, either you stop it completely or you let yourself go, it's up to you*» . That had been her friend's advice and she would take her word for it.

She slowly brushed her lips against the brunette's, listening to her sigh at the subtle caress. It was like caressing velvet, so soft and delicate. Lisa's hands adjusted themselves to her small waist with care, caressing the sides and making the smaller girl shudder with the slight friction, which was already starting to make her lose her belt.

Jennie was enjoying it, no doubt, but she needed more, more of Lisa, more of her body. She needed all of her.

The Thai girl's senses were distorted when she felt the brunette bit her lip and teased her. That sensual and intimate gesture had managed to turn her on.

-Oh Lisa!- Jennie gasped in amazement as she felt herself being lifted off the floor and pushed onto the bed without any consideration. She was enraptured, lost in the moment, and had no intention of stopping.

Her breathing hitched as she took in the blonde's features. Lisa's gaze was dark with lust and her chest rose and fell insistently. The Korean let out a moan of need, squeezing her legs tightly together to ease her pain and moaned louder as she felt the blonde climb on top of her, and with one leg separate her thighs.

-Li.... Li-sa...- it was hard for him to speak, this was better than in his dreams and he only desperately wanted one thing-Take me

And Lisa was more than willing to do so, if her cell phone hadn't interrupted the scene with a tone that she was already beginning to remember by heart.

-Jen, I have to take care of this- the blonde informed with labored breathing. The brunette didn't answer, she continued caressing the Thai girl's back, making her sigh with pure pleasure. But the phone insisted- hey Jennie, I have to get up

It was then that Jennie opened her eyes and groaned, uncoiling her legs from the blonde's waist with difficulty and groaning as she watched her walk away. *Damn device* . She groaned in disgust, standing up. *She had been so close... again.*

-Hey, hello Irene

Jennie's eyes widened, shocked and furious.

-Lisie, I wanted to know how...

But he couldn't hear anything else. In the blink of an eye, Jennie had snatched the cell phone from his hands and thrown it out the window in a rage.

-Fuck, what have you done Jenni...!?

-Don't you dare leave me again to go talk to someone else, Lalisa Manoban! - he growled, glaring at her and pointing a finger at her before turning around and striding into the bathroom.

Lisa watched her slam the door in panic and gulped. She ran to the balcony and looked out into the garden desperately for her phone. *God, Jennie is terrifying.*

Taking out the claws

-There is Lisa, but how could you think of that?

Her friend's voice was mocking and funny. She had taken advantage of the fact that the brunette was still sleeping to walk around the hotel and talk to the Australian. She spent almost an hour looking for her cell phone in the garden and luckily found it near the pool.

-Rose, you're not helping. If you had seen her, she would have wanted to kill me!

-God Lisa, I want to kill you!! How could you leave her hanging to talk to Irene? - the psychologist scolded her - it's the stupidest thing you've ever done, that girl was ready for you to fuck her!

-Fuck Rose, I know!- she shouted exasperatedly and regretted it when she saw a couple of tourists looking at her strangely- I'm sorry- she apologized and continued on her way to reception- it's work stuff Rose- she continued her conversation- I had to take care of him and...

-It was 1am Manoban! What the hell did Irene want to talk to you about that she couldn't tell you first thing today?

Lisa returned to her suit when Rose had finally stopped scolding her. Had she really done anything wrong? If the psychologist was angry with her it was because she had really screwed up with Jennie.

He thought about the brunette's lips, how soft and appetizing they were and how she let out soft moans with each of his touches.

Take me.

That simple phrase had lit her like a torch.

-I'm an idiot...

She banged her head against the door and groaned. *You screwed up Manoban* . She sighed before turning the handle, and as she opened the door one of his sneakers hit her forehead, making her stagger.

-What the...!?

-Where was Lalisa!?

Lisa rubbed the bruise with wide eyes, Jennie with one of her shirts and disheveled hair looked at her with a psychotic expression. *And now what did I do?*

-I... aush!- he screamed when the second sports car hit his crotch- can you stop throwing...!

This time she threw a pillow, indignantly. The last thing she wanted was to hear the Thai woman

-Shut up Lisa, you lied to me, you said I was just your assistant!- her eyes filled with tears

Lisa's heart broke when she saw the little Korean girl in that state. She closed the door and walked towards her cautiously.

-Hey Nini..- he knelt down in front of the Korean girl. The girl was on the edge of the bed with small sobs - Jen...

-Leave me Lisa...

-Jennie, nothing is happening between Irene and me.

- Stop lying to me!

-But Jen, I'm telling you the...- a couple of sounds at the door made her stop. *Now what?* -Give me a second Nini- she stood up and walked to the door- What the...?

-Hello Lisie!

The blonde suffered when she saw the brunette in front of the door with a cappuccino in her hand and a radiant smile.

-Irene?

-I brought you a...

And it was enough to hear that name for the chestnut to throw itself at him like a rabid animal.

-Get away from Lisa!

-But what...!?- Irene widened her eyes when she saw the furious brunette on top of her and her expression tensed when she recognized her- You!?

And this time it was Irene who threw the first punch. Lisa watched in surprise as the two girls rolled around on the floor, pulling each other's hair and cursing. Lisa could only think of one thing.

Meanwhile in Korea the Australian was cursing, even under the sheets.

- Who the hell is calling at this hour? He felt around on the table next to the bed and unlocked the call without even seeing who it was from.

-Who the hell is he and why is he calling me at this hour!?- she groaned sleepily

-Rose I need your help, I...

-Lalisa Manoban, there are three things that I cannot forgive even my best friend for and they are: being interrupted in the middle of an orgasm, having my food taken away, or being called just when I am about to fuck Selena Gomez!

-What the fuck Rose! Selena Gomez!? I think Ice Cream affected your hormones.

-What the hell do you want so early Lisa, or did you just call to make fun of my song!?

-But if it's 9 o'clock here, in Korea it's like 11 o'clock

-Lalisa!- Jennie and Irene growled in unison.

The aforementioned jumped in fright and put a hand to her chest.

"What was that?" Rose asked between yawns.

-Irene and Jennie!

-What the fuck! You're having a threesome without me!? And to top it off you just made them cum at the same time... wait a minute... How disgusting Lisa, you're calling me while you have your fingers inside...!

-Rose, of course not! For God's sake, what makes you think I'm doing such a thing!?

-I just heard them moan your name, don't lie to me, Manoban!

-No, you just heard them growl my name. I'm going to die!

-Lisa, hang up the damn phone!

-Hello? Lisa?- but only the end of the call tone. Rose snorted and threw the phone on the pillow- Damn ruler- she turned in bed to go back to sleep but something under the sheets caught her attention

-Hey babe...

Rose screamed to the heavens. The last thing she expected was to find Jisoo under the sheets without any clothes on.

-Jisooooo!!!

◇😺◇

-What the hell, they're behaving like animals!!

-She started it!!- they shouted at the same time, pointing at each other with resentment.

-I don't care who started it!- Lisa growled with an ice pack on her jaw. In her attempt to separate them she received a punch from one of the two and that was the only thing that managed to stop the fight. She let out a moan of pain and both of them became alert, ready to help her -Stop, don't even move!- she made them stop in their tracks- this blow- she pointed to her jaw- was both of their faults, so I don't need help from either of them!

-But Lili...- Jennie pouted

-No Lili!

-I'm sorry Lisie, I got carried away by my anger and...- Irene smoothed her hair tangled by the argument- I arrived this morning and I wanted to see you... I mean, see how you had arrived.

-Yeah, sure, just for that...- the brunette grumbled.

-Jennie!

- Since you didn't answer me last night, I got a little worried.

-How attentive...- continued the feline-eyed one with irony

- And on the way to the hotel I bought a coffee and thought maybe you could use some. Like at work...

-Very considerate of you, do you get paid overtime for seducing your boss?

-Jennie, stop!

The named one stood up angrily and approached the blonde with indignation.

-I'm sorry, I'm sorry to be a nuisance to you, don't bother me anymore!- he warned haughtily, taking the ice pack from her hands- and this goes here- he pressed roughly on the Thai girl's bruise, making her moan in pain- and just so you know, cats are good at scratching, not throwing punches.

With that she stormed out of the room, making it very clear who had hit her. She didn't plan on staying there listening to that idiot Irene or she would end up jumping on him again. *You still don't know what I'm like, you idiot.* She cursed at the memory of the assistant.

-And you get ready Manoban, tonight you will have eyes for no one but me. Today you will meet Jennie Kim- He stated threateningly as he walked away from the room. That night promised revenge, but also lust and Jennie was ready to have a little of both.

◈ ◈ ◈

My sensual feline

The event had gone off without a hitch. Lisa had fulfilled another of her dreams. Her initial idea was to set up Lili Dance in Thailand, but due to lack of funds she was forced to start in Korea, and after 4 years she was finally in Thailand.

-Gosh Lisa, the opening was amazing, it's a huge success!

Lisa smiled, Seulgi was one of her friends from Thailand, along with Bambam and Mintty. Seeing her again made her very happy.

- Nice to see you Seoul!

-Bambam hasn't stopped talking to us about your agency since he came back from Korea. We were eager to see your achievements- added a girl with a cap behind her.

-Mint!

-Hello again Pokpak

Both Thai women hugged each other

-Aren't you going to introduce us to that hottie?- Seulgi mentioned.

Lisa turned to her left. Jennie looked stunning that night. She had been stealing glances all night long, and at the opening party she seemed to be going the same way. That red dress looked amazing on her, although Lisa was really dying to take it off. *Relax your hormones Manoban* . She took a sip of her drink and sighed.

-It's Jennie Kim and...

- I was talking about the black-haired girl

Lisa looked back at Irene, the girl was not looking bad either in that tight maroon dress

-Oh come on Seu, have you already set your sights on her?- Mintty rolled her eyes- I think Jennie Kim is hotter, have you seen those big eyes? She looks like a kitten

Lisa glared at her friends. Each one was carefully assessing the two girls who had been pulling each other's hair over her hours ago, and were partly the cause of the horrible bruise on her chin.

-By the way, that thing on your chin looks horrible, what happened to you? Did you get involved with a married woman again?

-Those two- he pointed at Jennie and then at Irene- are the ones responsible for my bruise.

-Aush and grrr!- Mint joked without stopping to look at the girls- I'm sorry but they are very sexy beasts. I would gladly let them beat me.

- Since when did Mintty become a masochist? - Lisa said ironically, uncomfortable, and took another sip of her drink.

-Hey look at that, Suga seems to get into action with one of your girls

Lisa turned around and her blood boiled at the sight. Sugar was chatting animatedly with the brunette and she seemed to like her company.

Lisa squeezed the glass so hard that for a moment she thought it would break. *Damn* . Although, she remembered Suga, and also what a womanizer he was and Jennie seemed to be another of his prey.

-That idiot doesn't get tired?

-Oh come on Lisa, you already know him. Don't be surprised if he goes after your assistant later. That's how he is.

-Well then I'll have to clarify a couple of things- Lisa grumpily without stopping looking at them

-What things?

-Nobody touches what's mine- he drank the rest of the drink and left it on the bar with a couple of bills- I'll treat you.

Jennie, on the other hand, seemed to be having a good time. The drink that she found disgusting and bitter finally eased her discomfort. She had not approached the Thai girl since what happened with Irene at the hotel. The blonde had tried to get close to her without success. Jennie, with her feline instincts and her excellent sense of smell, could sense her even from a distance, and would flee when Lisa was too close to her perimeter.

-So Jennie Kin, do you have a boyfriend? - the white-haired man was interested.

-No

-I didn't believe it, how come a girl as pretty as you don't have a boyfriend?

-The fact that she doesn't have a boyfriend doesn't mean she's alone.

The voice behind them made them both turn around. The Thai woman's eyes seemed to spit fire, and her fists were tightly clenched.

-Lisa? What...?

-Go find another prey Suga, Jennie is mine

Both Jennie and the boy's eyes widened in surprise.

- I didn't know she...

-Now you know, so go away.

The boy looked at her reproachfully but finally obeyed.

-Lisa, what are we...?- the blonde didn't let her speak. She pulled her to a secluded area, a hallway that led to the bathrooms and didn't hesitate to let her in. -What are we...?

The brunette gasped as Lisa roughly pinned her to the door, taking both of her hands and pinning them above her head with one hand, while the other possessively held the Korean's waist. That dominant action turned the brunette into jelly.

-What were you doing flirting with that idiot Suga!?- the Thai girl asked angrily. Her expressions were rough, without being completely rude with the shorter one.

-I didn't... I wasn't flirting...- she answered without taking her eyes off that mole on his neck, the desire to surround it with her tongue and bite it had her receptive. Of course, with that tight black dress, it wasn't the only area she was dying to try- Not with him...- She whispered that last part.

The truth was that she had been trying to get his attention all night. There was one thing that female cats knew how to do, and that was how to seduce their male for mating, and that was her ace up her sleeve.

Lisa tensed, tightening her grip and shook her head, she was seething with jealousy and couldn't control herself, no more

-I hate how all those assholes gave you lascivious looks, they kept eating you with their eyes- he brought his face closer to the point where their noses touched- I hate that they look at you

-I don't want them to look at me- she whispered with her heart racing and desire on the surface. That subtle caress of Lisa's thumb on her waist tortured her- I just want you to look at me

Jennie ended the space between them with a needy kiss. Both devoured each other with hunger and lust, as if there was no tomorrow. Lisa released her hip and lowered her hand to the feline's thighs without breaking the kiss, making her moan on her lips.

-Lili..- he sighed with pleasure. The sensation was torturous, it burned- it hurts...- he could feel his crotch throbbing with desire and it was really painful and desperate. He needed to relieve his discomfort- please I... Ahh!

The blonde pressed her leg right in the needed area, causing the brunette to moan, and that sweet sound was music to her ears.

-Is this where you want me Nini?- he whispered, biting the egg of her ear and pressing again, earning a new moan of affirmation- then ask me for it Jen

-I... Oh Lisa!- the blonde created an exquisite friction with her thigh that was beginning to drive her crazy- I need you Lili, please!

Lisa released her hands and squeezed her hips to produce more pressure. Another moan. The Thai girl's lips devoured the delicate skin of the Korean girl's neck, while the latter scratched her back in desperation. She needed more and the layer of clothing was already starting to get in the way.

Jennie also got excited. Guided by instinct, her hands traveled to the back zipper of the Thai girl's dress and when she was about to lower it, the handle turned, followed by two knocks.

-Shit...

Both girls stood still, exchanging glances. Their lips were swollen, their hair disheveled, and their cheeks were undoubtedly flushed, and their labored breathing gave an idea of what was happening within those four walls.

The door slammed again and Lisa cursed under her breath.

- Just a second! - he turned around to wash and refresh his face - Nini, settle down a bit! - he whispered, fixing his bangs and helping the brunette a little. They weren't perfect but they were definitely more presentable - that will do - however he didn't expect it to be Irene's face that he would find on the other side of the door - Hey...!

-Lisie what...! Jennie?- he saw the brunette appear, who immediately became alert.

The black-haired girl looked at one and then at the other, trying to understand the situation.

-Oh, I was helping Jennie with the closure of the dress!- explained the blonde when she saw the confused face of her assistant.

Yes, to take it down . The brunette thought with a frown. Why did he have to give her explanations?

- Really? Allow me- without waiting he put his hand in the side of the brunette. Right where the zipper was and lowered it a little to check - Umm how curious, it seems that it is fine now

His tone was hesitant, and Lisa was beginning to feel her palms sweating coldly.

-Yes, well, it's that I... Well, I... You see, it's that I had already solved it.

FELINE WHISPERS

-I noticed...- Irene looked at her for a minute more and shrugged her shoulders- I really need the bathroom, so if you don't mind I...

-Oh yeah, go ahead, it's all yours! - Lisa stepped outside, followed by the brunette who was steaming from her ears.

Irene looked at her one last time and smiled.

-Congratulations on today Lisie, you did it- without further ado he closed the door, leaving the blonde nervous about what had just happened.

-Shit, that was close...- the Thai girl sighed in relief - Nini, I...

She felt the Korean's entire palm land on her cheek, causing a loud snap that made her tilt her head. She brought a hand to the painful area and looked at the feline without understanding.

Jennie's eyes were crystal clear but full of fury.

-Don't touch me again if you're ashamed to do so!

-Nini that's not it...

But he didn't let her finish. Before he could react, the brunette was already in front of Suga, whispering in his ear. He looked in Lisa's direction and then nodded, taking her hand and leaving the place. All under the blonde's gaze. Her cheek burned like hell, but it was her heart that was suffering the most seeing her little feline leave in the hands of another.

Now you lost it Lalisa

The call home

That morning was really awkward, during breakfast neither of them spoke. Lisa couldn't even eat a bite and Jennie just stared at her food. The night before the Thai girl didn't leave until the restaurant closed. She didn't even know how she got back to the hotel, she only remembers that when she woke up the brunette was sleeping on the couch.

He put his coffee cup down on the table and looked at her. Her face was unreadable, as if she had created a wall between them. *Serves you right for being an idiot.* He scolded himself, shifting in his seat, thinking of a way to break the ice.

-Is breakfast good?

-Quite.

Ok, that was an idiotic question Lisa, think of something better.

-How did you spend last night?

Jennie raised an eyebrow and dropped her cutlery abruptly. *Very well, Manoban, there's war coming*. She swallowed hard. She was already familiar with that exchange of glances.

- Are you talking about when we ignored each other all night or that moment when you left me aside for Irene... again? Oh, I know, maybe when each of us went back on our own and I had to ask for a key at the reception desk to get in! - she joked about everything, trying to stay calm.

Confirmed, I'm an idiot. She cursed herself for asking those questions. Her idea of dialogue wasn't working. The brunette was on the defensive and that way nothing she said was going to be better.

"Why didn't you sleep in bed last night?" he finally asked. That did interest him.

Jennie took a sip of her milk and shrugged without giving it much thought.

-You were disgusting, I thought you needed it more than me.

-And why didn't you sleep there too?

-Because I don't want to be close to you so you can deny it later- she said that with a hint of resentment. The truth was that she had been hurt by the Thai girl's attitude that night, she even hoped that she would go after her when she saw her leaving with Suga. She wanted her to stop them, she wanted her to act similarly to when she saw them talking. But that didn't happen and that was what made her the angriest.

Lisa nodded silently, giving up. She took another sip of her coffee and listened to her phone ring. They both turned to the bed, where her purse and her coat from the night were.

Jennie snorted and stabbed the table knife into her last piece of salmon, indignantly.

-It's great, I don't know the work activities of an assistant but Irene is very helpful, isn't she? - he said sarcastically, looking away.

Lisa ignored the comment and walked over to the bed. Her lips formed a wide smile when she saw the screen and Jennie bit her tongue at the blonde's expression. Her eyes were shining and her happiness could be seen. She felt a pang in her chest. Was he really that happy to hear from her?

The blonde did not wait any longer and unlocked the call under the watchful feline gaze, who sharpened her hearing so as not to miss the conversation.

-For God's sake Lalisa Pampriya Manoban, you've been in Bangkok for two days and you haven't even deigned to send me a message!?

-It's nice to hear from you too, mom.

Jennie's eyes widened. "Mom?" Her possessive instincts eased, allowing herself to breathe again.

-Pampriya, I haven't heard from you in 7 years. The first thing you should have done when you set foot in Thailand is tell me! If it wasn't for Mina...

-Mom, please don't exaggerate, I'm going at Christmas.

-The last time was two years ago Lalisa, that's a lot for a mother!

-Sorry, the agency takes up a lot of my time- he apologized - How's dad?

There was silence on the line.

-If you want to know, come home. I'm offended that you paid for a hotel in your own home!!!

Lisa smiled. Paying for her stay in Bangkok was like a cardinal sin for her parents, after all it was their home country. She looked at the table and noticed the brunette's intriguing gaze. She had forgotten for a moment that Jennie was still there. And instantly a light bulb went off above her head. *I got it* . She felt satisfied, refocusing on her call.

-Okay, mom, I'll go visit them. But I'll bring company - she heard her mother's happy cry through the phone and rolled her eyes - Mom, don't overdo it. You look like a teenager about to see her favorite idol

-Nonsense darling, I'm your mother, and I'm your biggest fan! I'll make your favorite food! - a crash and falling pots were heard, followed by a curse - Marcos, come cook!! Mina clean Lisa's room!!! My little Panpriya is coming to every room!

Lisa smiled wistfully and ended the call. With her excitement she assumed that her mother had left the phone behind to take action.

He looked at Jennie who was patiently waiting for an explanation.

-We have to pack, Nini, we're going home.

The named function frown confused

- Are we going back to Korea?

-Oh no, we're going back to where I grew up, and I want you to be a part of it.

The brunette's insides turned over and she held back from smiling like an idiot. She was still mad at her. You can't fall for it again just because she looks at you with those beautiful eyes and smiles at you in that sweet way that makes you want to kiss her.

And finally she smiled big and nodded. Apparently she had completely forgotten her anger with the minor, and was at that moment folding and packing her things excitedly into her briefcase, ready to meet

the family of the Thai girl who made her heart beat.

And how can I be angry with the person who takes my breath away and makes my heart race with a simple look? Easy, I couldn't.

◈◈◈

Mama Manoban

-What if they don't like me?

-Jen, you're adorable, who couldn't love you?

Lisa glanced at her out of the corner of her eye and noticed the blush on her cheeks. She loved doing that kind of thing to her. She turned her attention back to the Uber window. Everything about the ride made her feel at home. She used to pass those same streets every day on her way to school.

- Oh, look there! - she pointed to a quaint cafe, nicknamed *the Buddha* - I used to go there with my friends after school... before the place was smaller of course

Jennie looked at her doubtfully and raised an eyebrow, somewhat displeased.

-Friends?

Lisa laughed at his reproachful tone and shook her head, amused.

-I'm not a bitch either, Nini. Just because I like girls doesn't mean I like them all.

After a while they had arrived at the Manoban home. Lisa paid for the uber and hurried to get the luggage. She was touched and excited to see her old home again after years . *The only one* .

-Welcome to the Manoban house- he grimaced at the extensions to the facade and the extra floor- well, with some improvements

- Wasn't it always like this?

-No way, before it only had one floor and three rooms, it was humble but cozy.

Jennue looked at the house and thought of her home with the Kim family, a huge mansion for just three people; they had to bring in two ragdolls to fill the void of little Ella, although that didn't quite fill the void of the house.

-I would have liked to know her as she looked before- she mentioned thoughtfully.

Lisa smiled and was about to respond when the entrance opened, and a heart-rending, joy-filled scream made them turn around in fear.

-Oh my God! Marcos is here! Come quickly! - the woman ran towards the girls and squeezed Lisa in her arms - Holy God, you are taller than the statue of the great Buddha! - she gave her a couple of cloying kisses, and scanned her in more detail - and very thin... - she put her hands on her sides and scrutinized her with her gaze - Lalisa Manoban, are you not eating!?

-Mom, yes I do, just...

-You don't even cook! When are you going to give me grandchildren!?

Lisa blushed, not understanding the change of topic.

-Mom, that's not the point, I...

-Of course she's coming, I'm getting old and you still haven't given me...! Oh...!- her eyes focused on Jennie who smiled amused by the Thai girls' exchange. Of course she wasn't understanding even half of what they were talking about since she was Siamese (or Thai)- Who do we have here now?- she looked at Lisa reproachfully- And your manners, young lady?

The Thai girl rolled her eyes

-Mother, this is Jennie... A friend- he said the last thing in Thai so as not to make the brunette angry.

-Hello darling, come here so we can appreciate you better! - Jennie shyly took a couple of steps and blushed under the scrutiny of the older girl. Those eyes were similar to Lisa's, which managed to make her even more nervous - but what a beautiful girl, I had hips like that when I was young and I drove your father crazy every time I strutted! - she winked at Lisa in conspiracy

-Mother!

-And those eyes, they look like a feline's

"I am!" Jennie exclaimed, happy that the woman had noticed. "I'm Lisa's cat!"

-Jennie!- the blonde widened her eyes

The woman laughed and looked at her mischievously.

- Oh honey, I don't want to know about your nicknames in bed- he patted her on the back and motioned to his daughter- let's go inside, your father seems to be deafer the older he gets

The three women entered the house and headed for the living room. Lisa was happy to be back. Every picture frame, the old fireplace, the small shrine of Phra Achana, and Grandma's pretty sofas with flowers brought back memories of her childhood. Everything was in a different order, but they still looked just as she remembered.

-I'm going to get them a snack, they look scrawny!

Jennie nodded and walked over to the photo rack. She smiled widely at one particular photograph, and couldn't help but pick it up to take a closer look.

Lisa must have been about five or six years old in that photo. She loved the fact that the Thai girl still had the same sweet smile.

-I see that you liked cats even back then- he joked without stopping to look at the photo where the girl was carrying a furry kitten.

-Oh Jennie, wait, I'll look for the album, I have one of Lisa's with her little bottom on it! - Lisa's mother exclaimed happily, leaving the tray on the table and hurrying down the hall.

-Mom! - the Thai woman tried to stop her without success.

-Give up unnie, there's no stopping her. I'm planning on burning that damn album out of shame.

Lisa smiled as she watched the girl leaning against the door. Her sister was huge and had bangs similar to hers.

-Mina, how you've grown!

-Well you beat me, giraffe- her sister mocked giving her a big hug. Mina was two years younger than Lisa, and despite not having seen each other in a couple of years, they kept in touch by phone calls and videos- hey, you must be Jennie cat, how are you?

Her sister was aware of what was happening to Jennie, although she did not really believe that a feline could change so drastically overnight.

-Hi Mina- he paused, looking from one to the other- do all Thai girls have bangs?

Both sisters laughed and the youngest one shook her head.

-God no, only the sexy and stylish ones- he joked smugly- and copycats like her- he pointed at Lisa with a nod

-Of course, it wasn't the other way around?

After a while of talking, Jennie met Lisa's father and if she thought Lisa was quite tall, that man looked like the Lotte World Tower (the tallest skyscraper in Korea).

The conversation at dinner was lively. The Manobans were pleasant and had that vibrant spark that Lisa possessed. They knew how to make people feel at home.

-Jennie, darling, do you want some more?- asked the woman with the ladle in her hand.

The brunette's eyes widened. It was her third plate and she was about to burst. Everything was exquisite. There was still leftover potato stew on the table, the substantial gamjatang and the pakkapoa that was almost finished by the dancer.

-Have some more tempura, you look hungry.

-Mother, what you see is that she is choking, she is green from so much food.

-Lalisa, don't contradict me and finish your bowl. Use chopsticks, I didn't raise you as an animal!

The Thai girl rolled her eyes and complied.

-Well, since when do you two go out together?- asked her father, taking a sip of his tea.

-What!?- the Thai girl almost spits out her food

-They're a couple, right?

-No!- Jennie glared at her, making her doubt her answer- I mean, we are something, I mean...

-Well, I like her, unlike Tzuyu, that girl was very submissive- her mother claimed, serving a little more to her daughter's plate- Jennie looks like she'll give you a good lesson, she reminds me of me!

-Oh sure mom, so you prefer me to be the submissive?

-Who is Tzuyu?- the Korean intervened with interest.

-An ex of Lisa, I actually thought she would be the one you were bringing- her sister stated, saying the last thing to the dancer- It's just that Mintty told me about the two of you...- Mina stopped when she saw her sister's panicked look and the brunette's frown- about your date at the opening and I assumed she was talking about Jennie- she quickly corrected herself.

- Well, I like Jennie.- said her mother- She reminds me of Yiren

There was a brief silence. Mina looked at Lisa, who simply lost her gaze on her plate. Jennie didn't understand the change in atmosphere, but because of the girl's melancholic attitude she decided not to ask.

- Excuse me, I'll take the luggage to the room- the Thai woman bowed and left.

Jennie watched her disappear down the stairs, confused. Who was Yiren, and why did she affect Lisa so much?

A bikini for a cat

The morning was sunny, smelling of salt water and sunscreen. Jennie smiled, she had never been to the beach before and found it truly magical, despite her feline phobia of water.

There were colorful tents and umbrellas with nice sun loungers underneath. The tourists were indistinguishable from the Thais in the water, but no one seemed to care.

Lisa's father had decided to enjoy the arrival of his eldest daughter in Pattaya, a spectacular tourist beach an hour from Bangkok. There they rented a beach house overlooking the sea and Mina was quick to come up with an outing with the girls.

-Hey Jennie, aren't you going into the water? - Mina came out of the water soaked, with a tiny bikini that covered just enough.

-I... I don't like water, and I don't even have a swimsuit- answered the Korean girl, playing in the sand with a stick.

-Oh, who comes to the beach without a bathing suit? Look, even Lisa came prepared.

The brunette looked where the Thai girl was pointing and her jaw dropped. The blonde was coming out of the water like a damn Baywatch Barbie girl. Why was she watching it in slow motion? Because every step of the dancer was art for the Korean. Her slow movements, her skin oozing, and the sensuality of how she pushed her wet bangs away from her face. Jennie felt a current from her crotch to her belly, forcing her to close her legs tightly. But the heat in her South zone became fire when she saw her out of the water. *Oh, cat god!* The Thai girl's breasts looked desirable in that pretty red bikini, and she felt her mouth water when she saw her toned abdomen, and each one of her chocolates. Jennie bit her lip eagerly, she was dying to scratch that area. Her gaze lowered a little more and she almost collapsed when she saw her perfect V-shaped entrance, which was lost in the bottom of the bikini.

-Thailand calling Jennie!- Mina snapped in front of the brunette snapping her out of her trance - Fuck, I know my little sister is hot but don't drool

Jennie wiped her mouth in confusion and Mina laughed.

-I spoke from another mouth

-So how many mouths do humans have? - the brown-haired girl wanted to know with interest.

-Women were gifted by two, one more pleasurable than the other- he growled with one eye and looked at his sister- look, it seems that Lisa Unnie will soon get into action

-Lisa what...?- Jennie clenched her fists as she watched two girls and a boy approach the Thai girl flirtatiously.

-Wait, your clothes are wet!

-She's wet anyway...- the Korean whispered, squeezing her legs together.

-That?

Jennie was about to answer but noticed one of the girls leaning towards Lisa. *That's not for her* .

-Jen, what are you doing? Where are you going?

Lisa on the other hand was starting to feel uncomfortable with the conversation, the flirtatious attitude of the two girls and the lascivious glances of the brown-haired boy were annoying.

One of the girls, the redhead, started playing with one of Lisa's little pictures, making her nervous.

-You're pretty sexy, how about you and I...?

-Get your damn hands off of him!

Lisa was shocked to see the brunette, Jennie was walking towards her in only her underwear. *Fuck* . That body was definitely that of a goddess. The sway of her hips was hellish . *What would it be like to have that rocking on her?* She shook her head. *No Lisa, don't think about that now* .

The brunette had her arms crossed. No one was going to touch her Lisa while she was there.

The red-haired girl looked Jennie up and down, confused by her appearance and her recent interruption.

-And you are..?

-Jennie Kim, and Lalisa Manoban belongs to me

Lisa's legs went limp at the brunette's possessive tone. *Who is she and what did she do with me, Nini?*

-I don't see anything that says it's yours- the girl replied looking at Lisa

Jennie raised an eyebrow and smiled.

-Relax, I can prove it- in seconds the brunette was already in front of Lisa pulling her neck and melting into an aggressive kiss

The dancer felt like she was in heaven. Heaven? In fucking hell! She was burning alive and that Korean girl with a stunning body was Lucifer himself with a vagina. She gasped when the brunette pulled on her lower lip and finished by licking it gently to relieve her discomfort.

That sensation was pleasurable. Lisa's taste was simply exquisite. Jennie sighed, and looked at the girl who clenched her fists in disgust. She smiled. Out of the corner of her eye she could see the other two looking at her with hatred and she loved it. Why? She didn't even know, but as a feline she loved to mark her territory and Lisa belonged to her since she kissed her.

-Is that clear or should I give another example? - Jennie challenged, staring at the redhead.

-Another example! - Mina exclaimed from a short distance, taking a sip of her Coca Cola.

The Thai girl blushed. Her sister had caught the whole scene. Mina was standing next to her with a mocking smile. Mina liked Jennie for her sister, and was ready to ship them.

-Little sister, it seems that you are soaked.

-Shut up Mina, I'm not that thing.

-No? But you just came out of the sea- he pretended innocence and laughed- you can say what you want Pokpak, but that girl... where did she go?

The two looked from one side to the other in search of the chestnut and a scream made them turn towards the sea.

Both Thai girls widened their eyes; in the water, the girl who was flirting with Lisa minutes before was at that moment struggling to come to the surface to breathe, while the furious feline-eyed girl sank her again and again to the bottom.

-Lisa- he dipped his head- It's...- again- Mine!- and this time he left her in the water for longer.

-Oh shit!- Mina exclaimed running into the water

-No Jen, let her go, you're going to kill her! - Lisa ordered, following her sister closely.

The sisters struggled to free the brunette from her victim, but Jennie was immersed in her work. *Nobody messes with Jennie Kim*

Sleeping Beauty

-Hey girls! How did it go at the...? Oh my God, what happened to you!?

Lisa and Mina had scratches on their arms and faces. They had both struggled to free the poor girl, but Jennie had refused to free her and in return they had ended up the same or worse than the victim.

"Jennie is a beast when it comes to Lisa," Mina explained, stirring her disheveled bangs.

"I thought they would come back later," Chitthip said.

-No way, we took advantage of leaving while they were performing CPR on the girl. May her soul rest in peace...- added Mina while crossing herself

-He died!?- Jennie exclaimed terrified.

-No!- Lisa quickly replied.

-After swallowing half the ocean? - Mina continued, shrugging her shoulders - who knows, it's a miracle if she's still alive.

Lisa watched the brunette silently climb the stairs. She stared reproachfully at her sister.

- Did you see what you did? - he growled, plopping down on the couch.

-I'm sorry, sister, I only told the truth. Don't worry, it will pass.

Lisa snorted, covering her face with both hands. *Will it go away?* She looked at the stairs and shook her head .

-I'll go see if he's okay.

There were three rooms upstairs, her parents', Mina's and Lisa's. The latter had been assigned to Jennie as well, even though Lisa wasn't entirely sure about the decision. *Nonsense Lisa, if they're a couple they can share a room, as long as they let us sleep...* That had been her mother's response to her refusal, and Lisa had no choice but to accept.

-Nini, are you okay?- Lisa closed the door behind her and took a few steps forward. With difficulty she made out the brunette in the darkness. The girl was sitting on the bed with her gaze on the floor- hey Jen...- she sat down next to her and observed her. She looked sad and dull, and she noticed a couple of tears in the corner of her eyes- Jennie...?

-Why Lisa? Why should I love you? It hurts... It hurts so much!

-Jen, I...

-I know it's not the same for you. I'm just your cat...- she added in a small voice. She sounded broken and hurt.

-You are more than my cat Jen, and that is what worries me

The brunette watched her attentively. Her feline eyes were crystal clear and she threatened to start crying. The Thai girl hated seeing her like that.

-I know, I'm your tenant too...- she made a face- Whatever that means...

Lisa shook her head. She moved a little closer and brushed the older girl's hair away with her fingers.

-You are the most beautiful woman I have ever seen. And God Jen, you don't know how much I want you.

Jennie frowned and shook her head in disgust, standing up. How dare he say that to her?

- You don't have to lie to me to make me feel better Lisa. I know where I belong. I'm clear about what I am and what I'll always be in your eyes- she turned towards the door ready to leave the room. She couldn't stay there, not with the blonde so close- I'll go with Mina and...- Jennie felt Lisa's hand grab hers without warning. She turned around surprised, her eyes traveling from the hand that held hers to those honey-colored eyes that bewitched her- Lisa?

-I don't want you to go with my sister- he pulled her hand, holding her close to his body and making the little girl gasp- stay with me, Jennie

The blonde's proximity and her scent were like a sedative to her. She couldn't think clearly, she couldn't move from the spot. Her body seemed to want one thing and it was right in front of her, screaming at her not to leave.

-Always- the Korean whispered in response before joining their lips by inertia. She felt like an electrifying current ran through her from the tips of her fingers and ascended to the point where their lips touched each other -Lisa...

On the other hand, the blonde's hands slid up and down the sides of the shorter one, causing an endless number of new sensations to the Korean.

Jennie sighed with satisfaction, those caresses were beginning to provoke other types of reactions in her, some more intense.

-Jen...

But she couldn't finish. The brunette had already brought out her animal side. She roughly pushed the taller girl to the edge of the bed, making her fall on it.

-You're not leaving this time- She warned, and before Lisa could react, Jennie was already on her lap- this is in my way...

The Thai girl moaned as she watched her take off her shirt. That body was simply spectacular.

-I want to feel you Lili- he purred in her ear- I want to be yours

The movement of her hips created an exquisite friction that was driving the Thai girl crazy.

-God Jen, don't stop... that feels so fucking good

He heard the feline laugh flirtatiously. Was that really his Nini? *No, this one is quite a woman.*

-Yes?- he whispered seductively- Then you'll like this more

-What are you going to...? Oh shit!

Jennie's hand shamelessly entered the taller girl's denim shorts, making her let out a perfect moan when her small, delicate hand touched that little button of pleasure.

-And we're just getting started....
-Fuck, Jennie...
-Lisa...
-Yes, touch right there!
-Lisa...
-Shit... Yes, yes, yes!
-Lisa.
-Jennie!
-Lisa!

The blonde's eyes widened. She looked from side to side, alarmed and gasping. Her breathing was rapid, and she felt her heart between her legs.

She expected the first thing she would see would be that pair of feline eyes, but instead, it was her sister's, who looked at her mischievously, stifling a laugh.

-But what...?

-Oh yeah, Jennie there, don't stop!- he mocked between laughs- Fuck Lisa, were you really dreaming about Jennie? No wait, that's obvious. Were you really fucking Jennie while she was asleep??

He laughed again. Lisa sat up immediately, disoriented. When had she fallen asleep?

-And Jennie?- he ignored his sister's questions. He needed to know about the girl.

-She went for a walk on the beach, she was a little melancholy. She saw you asleep on the couch and didn't want to wake you up.

Lisa jumped up and started looking for her shoes.

-Why didn't you do it?

The minor shrugged and clicked her tongue.

-I'm your sister, not your babysitter. I'm not watching your every move, little sister.

Lisa put on her jacket, looking contemptuously at her little sister.

-And why didn't you follow her? Something bad could happen to her!

- Because I'm not a fucking bodyguard either, Lisa. Relax, you're paranoid. Jennie just went for a walk by the sea.

Lisa thought about it. *A walk along the seaside?* She grabbed her keys and hurried out the door.

-If mom asks...

-I know, I'll tell him you went to harass Jennie

Lisa looked at her with all her eyes and walked away. She didn't trust the brunette's approach and had a bad feeling about it. *I hope I'm wrong* . Everyone knows how bad cats get along with water and especially that they can't swim...

Starry night

The wind ruffled her hair. She could hear the sound of the waves coming and going on the shore and it calmed her. She rubbed her arms to warm them up a bit, the cold seeping into her bones. She had decided to take a walk alone to clear her mind, she hated her feelings for Lisa, especially not being reciprocated.

He looked at the sky. A multitude of stars adorned the firmament, giving life to so much darkness.

-Lisa... what else should I change for you?- he whispered, begging for an answer he knew wouldn't come, or so he thought.

-You don't have to change anything for me.

She was startled by the voice behind her and was surprised to see the blonde standing there, looking at her with a worried expression.

-Lisa? What are you doing here?

The named shrugged and walked towards her with her gaze on the sea.

-It's a nice night to take a walk... -he looked at her and smiled- or to sit on the sand to talk... can I?- he pointed to the spot next to her

Jennie nodded, still confused. Lisa looked calm and beautiful. *No, she's always beautiful* . She looked at her profile, and sighed. It was a work of art and she knew very little about it.

-Jen, I don't want you to belittle yourself- the Thai girl continued. She turned her face, staring into the feline eyes, and Jennie felt herself dying from the intensity of her gaze- You are perfect just the way you are, Jennie. You don't have to change for anyone, much less for me- she sighed and shook her head- I have this feeling of well-being when I'm with you that... I don't want to stop feeling like this- she looked at her again- like I was at home...

-Lisa, from the beginning that's how I felt, you are my home

Lisa laughed sweetly, smoothing her bangs.

-If I hadn't known your feline appearance, I would say that you are a very poetic woman, how can you say such things so spontaneously? - he wrinkled his face in displeasure at an idea - or is it another one of Judío's pages?

Jennie widened her eyes and quickly shook her head.

-No! I...- she fiddled with her fingers in a nervous manner, and that seemed to Lisa the most adorable thing of all- I'm just expressing what you make me feel...

Lisa smiled and looked at the sky, letting out a sigh. She felt touched by the sincere way the Korean girl expressed her feelings. Tzuyu was never like that and Yerin...

-Look there, the sky is starry...

The chestnut tilted her head and looked closely at the wide blackish mantle, confused.

-He failed to see the crack...

-Fissure?- Lisa asked without understanding.

-Yes, the crack... you said the sky was starry, but I couldn't see where...

The blonde let out a huge laugh, so much so that her cheeks turned red.

Jennie looked at her in surprise. She had never seen her laugh like that. Her laugh was strange, at least she didn't remember any other human laughing like that. *From now on it will be my favorite sound*. She smiled tenderly, trying to memorize every sound the Thai girl made. She wanted to caress her cheek and feel the softness on it, but instead she let herself be carried away by the impulse and ended up giving her a kiss on the cheek.

Lisa widened her eyes and brought a hand to the kissed spot. That action was completely unexpected for her and pleasantly fascinating.

-I'm sorry Lisa, I...- but she stopped when she felt the Thai girl imitate her reaction, being the one who kissed her cheek this time

Lisa smiled widely as she noticed the shorter girl's blush.

-Now we are even- he looked at the sky once more- tonight reminds me a lot of the day I met you... it was a starry night, similar to this one and with the same full moon

-It's not the same- Jennie said, detailing it.

The blonde looked at her sideways, expectant of her recent words.

-No?

-No, this moon is from Thailand, that one was from Korea

Lisa smiled sweetly

-Jen, it doesn't matter if we're in Korea, Thailand or Japan, the moon will always be the same.

-Always?

-Yes, always- The Thai woman thought for a moment and continued- if at some point we take different paths, it will be enough to see the moon to feel close to you

-Why would you want such a thing?

Lisa looked into that pair of feline eyes. They looked so shy and unsure. Had she created all that distrust in Nini? She had to correct it.

-Let me prove it- he leaned towards her, placing his hand on the other's cheek without breaking eye contact, and then joined his mouth with Jennie's. Slowly, savoring inch by inch those soft velvet lips. He sighed in the middle of the kiss, enjoying the sensation. Both seemed to fit each other, as if they had been designed for each other.

Jennie had to keep her eyes closed for a little longer. That kiss was very different, it was full of feelings, it was delicate and slow as if her lips were made of glass and any movement could break them.

She looked at the blonde. Lisa had a finger on her lips and a wide smile lighting up her face. *She smiled. She liked kissing me ...* That fact filled her with pride. Lalisa Manoban liked kissing me! It was incredible and she was afraid she was dreaming. Was it real?

-I don't want to wake up ever again - he whispered, brushing his lips against Lisa's in a subtle caress.

-So let's stay in this moment and live it forever, because I don't want to wake up either- Lisa whispered in complicity with her eyes closed, enjoying the closeness of the older girl, the smell of her hair and the warmth she gave off.

-I love you Lili

The aforementioned smiled without opening her eyes and took his lips again, this time a shorter kiss than the previous one, but just as full of emotions.

-And I love you, Nini.

Feeling you

Jennie and Lisa were still in bed, after a while under the stars they returned to the house to rest. The brunette was happier than ever. In her mind only the blonde's words appeared over and over again. *And I love you Nini* . She smiled big and opened her eyes. Her smile widened even more (if that was possible). Her feline eyes narrowed completely, giving her a childlike appearance.

There she was, in Lisa's arms like the nights before in her apartment. In all her feline life she had never felt attracted to another cat, but this human had changed everything about her, she wanted her, she wanted her to be the one to make her feel

She snuggled further into Lisa, her face hidden in the taller girl's neck. Her scent again. *Why does she smell so good? She inhaled* sharply, enjoying the girl's natural fragrance. Her heat was soon to return and she was afraid she would act crazy (again). *But how could she avoid it? She's so hot...*

She bit her lip, looking at that mole on her neck and shuddered. The calmness with which the Thai girl breathed and the way her lips remained moist and half-open while she slept had the feline out of orbit.

Jennie ventured to roll her lips over that small, but appetizing mole. The temptation was greater than her sanity and boy was it worth it when she heard a sound of pleasure from the blonde. She felt her southern part contract with need at that sound and dared to repeat the process. This time it was her tongue that decided to play, calmly and with enjoyment she circled the small mole.

Her body was burning more and more, and her sanity wavered when she heard a moan from Lisa. With agility she climbed completely on top of the blonde without stopping the kisses that had spread along her neck. Her tongue and teeth fought to dominate and explore that area of the blonde.

On the other hand, Lisa began to stir. She felt a warm weight on her, a comfortable and comforting one, but also a dampness in her panties and a tickling on her neck. Was she still dreaming? Because that sensation was simply pleasurable.

Her eyes slowly opened in search of the cause of this sensation, and she almost let out a moan at the sight. Jennie on top of her with her eyes closed and rocking on her hips in a torturously slow manner.

-Mmm Lisa...

Holy shit, she was masturbating on top of her! Lisa's heart was pumping fast, as was her wet center. And fuck, who doesn't get turned on by having Jennie Kim herself rubbing her vagina on them? *This is heaven!* The Thai girl cautiously dared to rest her hands on the sides of the brunette. Fuck her rational sense and the constant thought that the girl on top of her was a feline. She's more of a woman than anyone she'd ever fucked.

"Fuck," he whispered as he watched her curl in response to his hold and nearly had an orgasm as he watched her moan and sigh with need.

-Lisa... I need you- she murmured, enraptured by the sensations.

Jennie still didn't realize that the blonde had woken up a while ago. She was so immersed in her pleasure that they had even forgotten where she was. Lisa, on the other hand, had all her senses focused on the Korean, who was biting her lip to contain moans, and gasping when her back and forth motion achieved an exquisite touch.

Lisa couldn't bear the image any longer. She rolled her over onto the bed, leaving the feline-eyed girl under her.

The brunette reacted still panting, but she couldn't do anything but let out a squeal when Lisa's mouth launched itself at her neck, kissing it hungrily and needily. Lisa's tongue made a journey from her neck to her collarbone and went up to repeat the process with need.

-Mmm, Lili...

The kisses were getting lower and lower, and Jennie's shirt started to get in the way. *Damn shirt* . He made a move to take it off, but to his amazement, the brunette, immersed in her feline need, ripped it down to her belly, leaving her rounded breasts exposed.

Lisa found the scene extremely erotic. Her mouth watered at the sight of that pair of pink buds.

-Please Lisa...- the Korean begged desperately

And she was not one to refuse. His mouth was quick to please the girl, making her squeal eagerly when his lips wrapped around one of her nipples while his hand caressed the opposite breast.

The brunette was curling in pleasure and panting, while Lisa focused on her breasts. It was a completely different and delicious sensation. She felt a warmth from the tips of her nipples to her needy clit and it only made her want more of the girl beneath her.

Jennie's hips came to life, rocking in search of the blonde's touch, and when they both touched each other's intimacy, a unified moan filled the room. Fuck her parents, she wasn't going to limit herself with that woman under her.

She continued her kisses down the brunette's abdomen and stopped at her belly. She saw the shorter girl look at her reproachfully when she stopped kissing her and she loved it. Jennie's eyes were shadowed with excitement and her hair looked like a lion's suitcase, she supposed she must look the same since the brunette kept burying her fingers in her hair.

-Oh holy cats, Lisa!!!

The blonde smiled at that expression while still nibbling on her belly, while her hands hurried to pull down the brunette's shorts, all without taking their eyes off the girl's expressions. And boy, that was fucking heaven. She growled like an animal in heat when she saw that body under her completely naked, that woman was simply a goddess.

-God Jen...

-Don't stop now Lisa, don't even think about it!

Lisa smiled sideways and settled between his legs.

-Don't worry Jen, I don't plan on doing it.

Lisa delighted in the sight, the center of the shorter one was soaked and ready to receive her. She took a first lick, making the brunette scream, followed by a second and third. Her taste was simply delicious and she wasn't willing to stop.

-Aah, Lisa...! Yeah, just like that...! Oh shit, yeah!

Lisa wondered how the Korean had learned to swear like that, but with that eager voice it certainly sounded fucking good.

His fingers marked a rhythm on the feline's clitoris, while his tongue played and pressed on her center. The brunette twisted and rocked her hips more insistently, without stopping squeezing her breasts.

-Come on Jen, roll for me- Lisa whispered without leaving her place between the Korean's legs

-Yessisi...! Aaaah...! Lili, I'm going to... Oh shit, Lisa!!!!

And for the first time Jennie felt the release of her desire. Her vision blurred, and her mind went blank, immersed in that intense sensation. She had never felt anything like it. She looked down and shuddered at the sight of Lisa still between her legs, absorbing all of her orgasm and with her burning eyes fixed on her. She felt shaky and light, it had simply been a round trip to heaven.

The taller girl licked her lips as she pulled away from between her legs. Lisa never thought she would become addicted to anything, but she definitely wanted to have that taste in her mouth again.

She crawled mischievously over the brunette until she reached her lips. The girl was flushed from the orgasm and her eyes shone like never before. She looked radiant, even more beautiful than she already was. Yes, Lisa wanted more of that.

-Are you okay?- he asked rubbing his nose with hers

Jennie smiled big, and interlaced her hands around the blonde's neck to bring her closer to her lips.

-That was... wow!- she whispered, not knowing how to define the moment.

-It was- Lisa said giving him a chaste kiss, just as smiling- And it wasn't even half of what I really wanted to do to you

Jennie looked at her mischievously

-Then do it. I'm dying to feel you in every way possible- she clung to the blonde, cutting the small distance between them and kissing her more intensely this time. She couldn't get enough of those lips, and the more she kissed her, the more she wanted from her. Addiction? It was possible, but fuck it, she would become an addict for her, but a fucking happy addict as long as she could have more of Lisa.

Discovered

Lisa was happy. They had both gone down to breakfast after their little romp. They had kissed so much that their lips were burning from use, but she loved it, and they would have continued if her mother hadn't called them to breakfast.

-Good morning...- the Thai woman greeted in a soft voice

Mina and her father were already at the table, while her mother added a couple of pancakes to another plate.

- Excellent day, you'll say- sang her mother, placing two plates down- take a seat, girls

Jennie looked at Lisa and she nodded with a small smile. That exchange did not go unnoticed by Mina.

-And how did you sleep last night?

Lisa looked away from the brunette to trust her sister. That mischievous smile told her that she knew something, and that managed to make her nervous.

-Well, normal...

-Min, honey, the correct question is, how did you wake up? - corrected Chitthip in complicity with his youngest daughter.

Shit . Lisa's cheeks flushed and she gasped a few times in a failed attempt to respond. What could she say without sounding guilty? She remembered everything that had happened and couldn't help but smile.

-From that idiotic face you made, I imagine it was very good- added Mina amused, bringing a piece of pancake to her mouth- and who ate whom?

Lisa spat out her coffee, shocked and embarrassed between coughs.

-Lalisa manoban, that's rude! - her mother scolded her.

-Didn't you hear what he insinuated!?

-Come on, daughter, we've all heard your screams. It's not that bad.

-Mother!

"I thought Jen was being tortured," her mother added, picking at a piece of her food.

-Torturing?- the confused brunette intervened.

-Yes, didn't Lisa torture you this morning? - Mini asked her with double meaning, trying to contain her laughter.

Jennie opened her eyes and shook her head repeatedly.

-Oh no, Lisa made me feel really good this morning

The blonde almost had a heart attack. Seriously, Jennie didn't understand her sister's bad intentions? *Damn*.

Mina laughed as she chewed, earning a spoonful from her mother in reprimand.

-I can imagine that, and how does Lisa eat it?- he asked, rubbing the place where he had hit her.

-Mina!- Lisa and her mother scolded her in unison

-God, daughter, those things are not talked about at the table! - she scolded her, serving more coffee to Marcos - but as if it were nothing... Did you wash your hands well before...?

-Mother, that's enough! - Lisa's cheeks were redder than the word. But that didn't stop her mother.

-Lisa, it's necessary. Do you know how many bacteria are lodged in the hands? I don't want my daughter to have diseases in her vagina....

-Ok, that's it!- Lisa cut her off, turning to see her father for help- Dad, aren't you going to say anything?

The man looked up from the newspaper and shrugged.

-I'm sorry honey, even I heard them.

-You don't have to interrogate Lili, I think she feels uncomfortable talking about this.

-Finally someone who supports me! Thanks Nini

Mini made a face

-So Lisa didn't eat you?

-No, of course not, how could you think of that! - she replied, scandalized, catching the attention of the three Manobans.

-See!?- asked Lisa, happy with the Korean's support.

-He didn't eat it- the brunette continued and sighed, biting her lip- What he did was lick and bite down there in a spectacular way... Oh, and he also sucked!

Lisa's eyes almost popped out of her head. If they were red before, they were now multi-colored.

-JENNIE!!

Her family burst out laughing at the blonde's childish reaction and her obvious blush. Chitthip loved these changes in his daughter and Marcos was happy just having her around; Mina, on the other hand, loved teasing her older sister more.

-Unnie, so it's true that you eat it well!

-Shut up Mina!

◇◇🐱◇◇

Lisa sat down on one of the sun loungers. Her father had gone with Mina to the pier to fish and all she had to do was say the word Fish and Jennie was happy to join them.

She applied a layer of sunscreen and lowered her glasses. She hadn't taken a break for years. The company took up a lot of her time, she loved dancing but hated that office. She sighed, overwhelmed.

-Is there no sun in Korea? - her mother arrived with a jug of lemonade and a couple of glasses - from that anemic vampire face, I don't think so.

-Yes there are, but not for those who are too busy running a company like me.

-You need to take a break, honey, you're young, you still have a long way to go- he handed her a glass and sat down on the adjoining lounge chair- now tell me, what happened with Tzuyu?

Lisa snorted, she hadn't thought about her since they broke up. Her mother had known her for years since they were friends before they were girlfriends. The girl had arrived as an exchange student in Bangkok and that was how she met her.

-He cheated on me with Sana

- Healthy? Who would have thought... - of course, her mother also knew about the Japanese girl - I never liked Tzuyu, not for you... she was a good girl of course, but she never looked at you in a special way and neither did you - she took a sip of her lemonade - But with Jennie...

-Mom... Jennie and I are not a couple

-Still...

-I...

-Look Lisa, I'm your mother and I know you, and that glow that you lacked with Tzuyu you have with Jennie. You look radiant when you're with her even if it's hard for you to admit it- she looked at her daughter in a maternal way- A mother knows about these things, you like that young woman and you like her

-It's a complicated subject, mother... we are very different.

-And maybe that's a point in your favor. The previous ones have been too similar, Jennie is an enigma for you, you never know what she'll do and you love that, I love it! - he laughed when he saw his daughter's face - don't worry honey, I'm not going to take her love away from you, that girl has her eyes set on you

Lisa sat up, taking off her glasses to look her mother in the eyes.

-What if it doesn't work?

-In life you are willing to succeed or fail Lalisa, I have taught you about that. The important thing is what do you want? If you fail it is because you do not try hard and if even trying your best you do not get it it is because it was not for you... but that young woman, darling, was born to be with you.

Lisa thought about it. Was she really destined to fall in love with her cat?

-I'm afraid...of falling in love with her

-Nothing ventured, nothing gained- Chitthip stood up- Just don't hurt her, that girl doesn't deserve to suffer

Back home

-Mom, hurry up or the plane will leave us!

-Lalisa Manoban, don't pressure me! - he scolded her.

Lisa and Jennie had to go back to Seoul. Their stay in Bangkok had been amazing but it was time to get back to work.

Lisa sighed, looking at her old house for the last time. They had returned from the beach house to gather the rest of their things, and buy a few more things along the way.

-Thank you for everything Mrs. Manoban, I will miss you- Jennie's eyes filled with tears, that woman had been affectionate with her

-Oh honey, and we love you. I hope the next time I see you it's with an engagement ring on your ring finger and a huge belly.

-Mom!- the dancer's cheeks flushed at her mother's insinuation

-Do you want me to come back fat? - Jennie asked, not quite understanding.

The woman laughed amusedly and shook her head.

-Not fat, pregnant

Jennie's cheeks invited the color of Lisa's. Did that woman know about her fantasies with Lisa about having kittens?

-How do you know I want to have kittens with Lisa?

- Kittens? Why do you want...?

-Alright, time to go! Bye, we'll call you when we get back! - Lisa took Jennie by the hand and hurried her to the taxi. She couldn't bring up the subject of her feline life with Chitthip.

The woman watched the taxi drive away with a smile of satisfaction and melancholy on her face.

- Will you be okay? - asked Marcos, caressing her back. He knew how much the absence of her eldest daughter affected his wife.

-I think our Lisa has finally found her yin- she took out the necklace that hung from her neck and looked at the pink teardrop-shaped half- Maybe it's time for them to change owners

-Are you sure she's the right girl?

- Did you see the look on my face when I saw Lisa? - He looked back at the front - She's the one

-What if Lisa doesn't feel the same way about her?

His wife turned sarcastically and denied

- Honey, you don't know your daughter, Lisa will do it in due time.

◇◇🐱◇◇

-Hold on to your suitcase- Lisa carried the heaviest one while her eyes scanned the place, looking for something in particular- Where is that stupid Australian?

"I hope that affectionate nickname is not for me," a voice behind them reproached ironically.

-Squirrel!

Jennie ran into the blonde's arms and Rose didn't hesitate to hold her in her arms.

-Hey Jen, I missed you so much! Did you miss me?

Lisa clenched her fists and teeth at the same time as the two girls exchanged, but decided to remain silent, the airport was not the place to punch the Australian again.

-Of course...!!

-Ok, forget about Jisoo!- the black-haired girl growled offended, excluded- There was even a banner for them! Ungrateful...

Rose glared at her and shook her head.

-Jisoo, that's an advertisement for the KFC we ate at on the way here... the welcome signs have the names of the people you're waiting for.

-Well, better for me, I'll hang this beautiful poster in my room!

Rose rolled her eyes, the raven-haired Korean had been a torture for her those days, especially when she almost ate her neighbor's canary.

-And how was your honeymoon?

-Honeymoon?- Jennie asked confused.

-It wasn't a honeymoon Jisoo, it was a vacation- Lisa explained putting away her passport

-But they fucked, right? That's what couples do on their honeymoon.

-Jisoo!!- Jennie scolded her with blushing cheeks

-And how do you know that? - the Thai woman asked her, curious.

-Rose's movies are very explicit, the other day we saw one where a brunette was putting her fingers in another girl's...

-Damn Jisoo, my movies aren't explicit, what you were curious about was porn!

-Very educational...- Jisoo said thoughtfully.

-And what did you do with those kinds of movies, Chaeyong Park? - Lisa asked her mischievously.

-What's up Lisa, you're not the only one with needs

The girls got into the car. Jennie and Jisoo couldn't stop talking in the backseat. While Jennie told her sister about her experience at the beach, Jisoo told her about all the places she had visited.

-And I went to Arturo's and Wendys... Oh, that one with the chicken with a crown!

"Why are they all chicken restaurants?" Jennie asked with a confused look.

Rose snorted

- Don't ask me, I tried sushi and we almost got kicked out when I tried to eat the fish from the decorative fish tank.

-It's not my fault they looked so tasty! Besides, why do they have fish if they're not going to eat them...?

-It's a decorative fish tank, the fucking word says it, to decorate!!
-What a waste of food. Stupid humans...
Rose and Lisa took care of the suitcases while the other two talked about Dudu and the rabbit. The psychologist had taken care of the feline family, and during that time poor Leo suffered attacks from both felines.
-I swear I'll have to give the poor thing therapy, he doesn't even want to come out from under the bed anymore- Rose commented as she unpacked her luggage- one of these days I'll see him filing a complaint for animal abuse
-My poor Leo...
Lisa opened the door and the first to enter was Jennie, followed by Jisoo, the pair soon disappeared down the hallway, leaving the other two alone in the entrance.
-And tell me, did they do it?
-Do what the...?
-No beating around the bush Manoban, you know what I'm talking about.
Lisa swallowed hard. Jennie had not stopped looking at her mischievously along the way and that did not go unnoticed by the Australian.
-Not too much...
-Not too much? Please, if the whole way Jennie was practically screaming at you with her eyes to fuck her in the backseat of the car
Lisa's cheeks reddened at her friend's words - were they that obvious?
-How do you...?
-Every self-respecting psychologist is a good observer.
-You mean nosy...
-It doesn't matter, the result is the same. Now tell me.
-I...

The Thai girl stopped when she heard a pitiful cry. Rose, on the other hand, snorted in distress when she recognized Jisoo's screams. Lisa came to the rescue, running into the kitchen in a hurry, ready to intervene.

-What's going on, why all the fuss...!? Aush! What the hell!- he rubbed his head when he felt a blow and saw a beer can on the ground- Fuck Jisoo, why are you hitting me?

-Foolish human! You have no food here, I'll starve now!

Rose leaned back on the counter calmly and watched the exchange between her friend and the black-haired girl.

-You only know how to insult with that? It's obvious that there is no food, we were on a trip!

-I'll die of hunger, and it will all be your fault!!

-Jisoo, that's enough, I'll call the delivery man to bring something to eat- the psychologist finally intervened, taking her cell phone with indifference.

- Fine, I won't die!!!!

-But no chicken, today it will be pizza

-I will die!!!!

Rose took a bottle of vodka out of the fridge and grabbed Lisa by the sleeve of her shirt.

- You're coming with me, you're going to tell me everything with alcohol in between.

-Are you going to get me drunk!?

-Fuck no, I'm just going to numb the stupid part of your brain so you can tell me everything without having to beg you.

-So you're going to get me drunk!

-Take it as you want Lis, it is an effective method

-I'm not going to take it Rose, I refuse to talk to you about it while I'm drunk! - Lisa refused with her arms crossed.

-Never say no to a psychologist Lisa

-My name is Lalisa Manoban, you're not going to get any information out of me, and that's my last word!!!!

Alcohol effect

-And we almost did it! If it hadn't been for my mother... Good heavens!

After 5 rounds of vodka both blondes had snuck in and now Lisa was chattering away, telling what had happened. Rose on the other hand was using all her concentration to try to get the liquor into the small glass, spilling more on the table than in the

-Shit!

He pouted at the amount of liquor

-And it was amazing Chaeyong, Jennie tastes divine!- Lisa sighed- and her moans... believe me, she's a goddess!- The Thai girl growled when she saw that her friend was focused on the glass and the bottle- Rose, are you listening to me??

He hit the Australian's shoulder, causing her to spill the vodka on the table again.

The named one grunted in disgust

-I don't know what Jennie's fucking pussy tastes like, look at all the liquor that was spilled!!!- he pointed dramatically at the table- now we have less left!

Lisa thought about it for a moment and smiled.

-You know what, I have a bottle of whiskey in the cabinet, that will do.

Rose looked at her reproachfully, the dancer did not usually drink too much

-Are you an alcoholic, Lalisa Manoban? Because if so... - he looked at her analytically and then spread his arms with a smile - welcome to the club!!!

-Okay, go get the bottle- Lisa ordered, trying to stand up without falling.

-And why should I go!?

-Because you must be a good hostess and take care of your guests properly.
-Oh you're right I... -Rose stopped dead- Wait, this is your house!
-Just go get the fucking bottle Park Chaeyong!
-Damn Thai...

Meanwhile in Lisa's room, Jennie continued to tell her sister about her experience with the blonde with bangs.
-So he stuck his tongue in you?
-Jisoo, don't say it like that!- in her time as a human she had learned to be embarrassed by certain comments, and her sister's vulgar vocabulary managed to make her blush to the extreme- Lisa is incredible, and her tongue is not rough!
-Why the hell does Manoban's tongue have to be rough!?

They both turned around when they saw Rose standing in the doorway with a bottle in one hand and a bag of ruffles in the other.
-I...- Jennie blushed, nervous- Rabbit said that this is how Dudu's tongue felt and I thought...
-I already told you Jen, don't ask a cat for human advice.

Jisoo looked at her carefully and saw the things in her hands
-Are you having a party without us!?
-We're getting drunk without you...- he corrected without giving it too much importance.
-Because?
-Because two cats who have never tasted liquor in their lives wouldn't last a round without getting naked in the...-Rose smiled like the grinch at an idea

- Come to think of it, it's very rude of us to leave them out, especially you Jen...!
-And why not me!?

-Sisi, you too...- she rolled her eyes and turned her attention back to Jennie with a sweeter expression- Do you want to join us?

-Yes! - the two women affirmed in unison.

Lisa growled as she saw the Australian girl return with the sisters. What were they doing there? She looked reproachfully at her friend who winked in response, leaving her more confused than before.

-What kind of party is this??- Jisoo wrinkled her nose, looking at the messy room and some fried foods on the floor- And the fried chicken!?

-Chicken?

-It's not a party without Chicken!

Rose slammed the bottle down on the table and glared at the dark-haired Korean.

-That's it! You're going to learn to eat something else, even if I have to force you to swallow every bite!!!

-Never!!

-I'll let you sleep in the bed if you agree.

-Ok!!

Jennie looked at her sister. Jisoo smiled like an excited child.

-Dominated..

-Shut up Jendeukie, I'm close to my heat!! I have needs!

-I said sleep, not fuck... - the psychologist clarified.

-We'll see...

Rose watched as the first one closed and opened her eyes insistently.

-What are you supposed to do, did something get in your eye?

-Dah, it's a double wink!

-God, you scare me, don't make me change my mind or you'll sleep in the garden!

-Never! It's animal abuse!

Rose sat down at the table and poured each Korean a small glass, which displeased the Thai woman, who quickly sat up on the couch in disapproval.

-What are you doing!?
-Serve them a drink, what else?
-I noticed that, why are you doing it!?
-They are human Lisa
-They've never drunk Roseanne, and... fuck, Jisoo!

-Cough cough! W-what a... bitter... cough water! - he complained between groans, the drink had burned his throat.

- She wanted to kill me!!! - she exclaimed horrified with her eyes watering from the liquor - she regretted that I slept with her and wanted to kill me!
-It's whiskey, not water, and it should taste like that, that's the idea...- Lisa explained, wiping the remains of alcohol off her blouse.
-Humans are crazy, how can they drink that garbage!

1 hour later...

-Humans are geniuses!!!- she hugged the half-empty bottle and gave it a kiss- this is the best!

They had been drinking the whole time, from small sips to steep bottle shots. Jisoo was quick to finish her drink, but Jennie had a hard time, the taste was disgusting and her eyes were watering with each sip, giving her severe coughing fits. On the other hand, the feeling of numbness was incredible, she felt more confident, invincible and also more daring.

-Lili, kiss me like that day..

Lisa laughed, hiding her face in the brunette's neck who was comfortably sitting on her lap. When had she climbed on top of her? She had no idea, but she wasn't complaining.

-Jen, we're not alone, it's not the time to kiss you down there...

Jennie smiled flirtatiously and raised an eyebrow playfully.

-I was referring to the mouth, but that sounds better...

-You pervert! Stop insinuating things and help me turn on the music! - ordered Rose with blurred vision pressing a button insistently.

-Rose, that's the microwave

-No wonder it didn't work!- he walked over to the stereo and this time pressed play on the correct button- Oh yeah, let's dance bitches!

-Cats!- Jisoo and Jennie growled in unison

The music played as the Australian girl swayed lightly. Like Lisa, the psychologist liked dancing, although Lisa was far ahead in terms of movement.

-Hey Chicken come dance!

-I have two left legs...

Rose snorted

-What a chicken..- he turned to Jennie and smiled- come on Jenjen, don't let me down!

Jennie, excited, got up from the blonde's lap, leaving her upset at feeling her absence and seeing her go into her friend's arms.

Lisa's eyes widened as she saw how well the brunette's body was keeping up with the rhythm. She cursed the song and Rose for being the one to feel the Korean's hips.

-Damn Jen, I didn't know cats could move so well- Rose teased, still clinging to her.

The named laughed delightedly and simply continued moving.

Lisa watched from the corner of her eye as Jisoo clenched her fists, glaring at the couple for what? But the older feline's anger increased when Rose slid down her sister's leg.

-Move your flat ass Manoban!

-What about...?- but she couldn't finish, the dark-skinned Korean had grabbed her by the shirt and pushed her next to the other couple.

"I thought he wasn't dancing," Lisa said, trying to get into the rhythm.

-I can learn now

Jennie continued dancing, she had never danced before but she felt as if she had always done so, her body felt light.

-This is... Jisoo!?- Her eyes widened as she saw her sister rubbing herself against the Thai girl, her Thai girl!, trying to keep up with her. But the thing was that keeping up with Lisa was no easy task, the blonde with bangs had been dancing for as long as she could remember, her rhythm flowed like a natural instinct and at that moment, with the alcohol running through her veins, she was unleashing herself.

Even Jisoo seemed to enjoy it. What Jennie didn't notice was how many times the feline stomped on the Thai girl. What!? Her sister seemed comfortable with Lisa and let herself be carried away in her arms. But everything got worse when they exchanged glances.

Why were they looking at each other like that!?

-I'm a little hot!- Jisoo laughed, fanning herself while still looking at Lisa. Her smile faded as she looked at her lips. Good God, now she understood Jennie and her obsession with the Thai girl, those lips tempted her- do you hear that?

-What thing?- Lisa asked confused.

-Your lips are talking, they are asking to be kissed.

He leaned down with the intention of kissing her but someone stopped him. Jennie's hand was quicker, grabbing a handful of her sister's hair and pulling it to make her back off.

-It is true, I hear them too, I will fulfill your request - without further ado he joined his lips with the taller one with ferocity and hunger. That mouth was hers and he was not going to allow anyone else to kiss it. Lalisa Manoban was his from head to toe.

Hangover

-Oh shit...- Rose tried to open her eyes with difficulty, her head felt heavy and she had a strong migraine- Holy God, who the hell hit me last night? I hurt all over...

-Can you turn down your fucking volume!?

She turned around when she heard the whispered growl. That raspy voice she recognized from miles away.

- Lisa? - He opened his eyes to look for her better, but closed them immediately. The dim light at that moment affected him as much as if he were staring at the sun.

He rubbed them and opened them again. He was surprised to see the place where he had slept.

"No wonder my back hurts," she muttered heavily. Lisa's chair wasn't too comfortable, but she had apparently slept better than her friend.

Lisa, unlike her, was on the floor, using her arm as a pillow. Her hair was tangled, but what caught his attention was her half-naked body.

-But what...?- he looked down at his own and his eyes widened when he discovered himself in the same condition as the Thai girl- Manoban!

That scream echoed in the dancer's ears, who almost felt her head explode.

- Oh my God...- she sobbed, holding her head as if it were going to fall off- damn it Rose!

-Lalisa Manoban, explain to me why we are naked in your fucking living room!?

Lisa half opened her eyes in confusion. She looked at her friend's body in her underwear, then at her own. She put her hangover aside and ran to the full-length mirror near the entrance.

-Oh my God, don't tell me to fuck you!?

-I don't....

-Holy shit, this shouldn't be happening to me!

Rose frowned and crossed her arms, offended.

-Hey, it's not the worst thing that could happen to you, my sex is wonderful- she crossed her arms, offended- and why are you the one who fucks me and not the other way around?

Lisa raised an eyebrow, ironic, as if it were the most obvious thing in the world.

-Park, you are more passive than words, your work proves it.

-Don't bring my work into this!

-So what happened?

They both exchanged glances and images began to invade their minds.

Flashback

After the whiskey they had changed to gin and that was the end of her sanity. The Australian was no longer thinking coherently, her actions were deliberate.

-I'm a fucking stripper!- she screamed with difficulty on the table while taking off her blouse- catch it Lisa!!

But the blonde was too busy eating the brunette out. Their mouths were fighting for dominance in the battle and neither was willing to lose.

-Damn it, stop exchanging saliva in my presence! - he growled, getting off the table and falling face first onto the floor in the process - Shit!

She looked up and noticed Jisoo focused on the bottle. The brunette had chosen to drink and keep drinking.

-What the hell are you doing!?- Rose scolded her, standing up with difficulty-share that bottle!

-No!- the Korean woman complained, hugging the liquor possessively- it's mine!

-Drunk cat, give me the fucking bottle, dammit!- he lunged at her to win the bottle

-Let her go!

In the struggle, Rose ended up losing her balance, collapsing on the black-haired girl who ended up on the ground.

-Ouch, my head!

-Fuck, you're so clumsy! Why didn't you hold me properly...?- the psychologist left the word hanging in the air when her eyes met the dark gaze of the cat girl. They were undoubtedly the most expressive eyes she had ever seen- beautiful... - she whispered enraptured.

-I know, all of me is- answered her opponent also in a whisper

Rose stopped herself from slapping her and looked down at her lips.

shit, *they're heart shaped!* Her breathing hitched at the sight, her lips were a bright pink and just the right size. *So kissable.*

-Damn cat

-And now why do you insult me?

- For having such fucking delicious lips. I'm going to regret this for the rest of my life.

-Regret...?

The Australian cut off her speech by attaching her lips to the brunette's. At first Jisoo didn't know what to do, lick? But it was impossible, the girl was literally eating her mouth. She tried to imitate her action without much success, her teeth clashed or her lips didn't match.

-Shit!- Rose moaned as she felt a pain in her lower lip. She ran her tongue over it, discovering the metallic taste of blood- Did you bite me?

-Did you like it? I saw that in a movie!

- Cannibals!? You almost ripped my lip off you piece of animal!!

Jisoo frowned

-That's what practice is for- she roughly grabbed the girl's head and this time it was she who initiated the kiss, stealing the blonde's breath, who felt heaven with that rough touch. How could something so clumsy cause such a thing? -Well?- Jisoo asked, still with her eyes closed, enjoying the tickling sensation on her lips.

-You talk too much, just kiss me!

End of flashback

Both blondes were stunned by the memories. Especially the Australian who still couldn't believe his attitude.

-I can't believe I let that idiot kiss me!

Lisa looked from side to side. Her curiosity was different, she wanted to see the cause of her swollen and sore lips.

-And the girls?

They both looked around the living room and it was Rose who noticed the lump on the couch under a pile of sheets.

-There!- he pointed at the lump and growled, rubbing his neck resentfully. -Why did I sleep without a sheet on the armchair and she slept comfortably on the sofa?

-What the fuck are you complaining about!? Weren't you the one who woke up on the floor without even a fucking pillow!

Lisa walked over to the couch and pulled back the blankets layer by layer until she finally found the brunette's delicate body. She smiled as she saw her curled up, hugging herself. The sight filled her with tenderness and for a moment she wanted Rose to disappear so she could get in there with her and hug her for a long time.

-Now all that's missing is your hateful sister- grumbled the Australian

Lisa came out of her daze, it was true, but apparently Jisoo wasn't in the living room. They went to the kitchen and the bathroom without much success.

-Where the hell did that chicken with legs go?

—Rose, chickens have legs themselves.

-Not the fried chicken

Lisa rolled her eyes and continued on her way to the bedroom, where she soon found her and that image disgusted her.

-Speaking of sleeping comfortably, this one won over the three of us

The black-haired girl was in the Thai woman's huge bed, covered up to her neck with the room in semi-darkness.

-Let there be light! - Rose exclaimed, covering her eyes before opening the window.

The light entering the room made the Korean frown, who quickly groaned, sinking into the blanket.

Lisa searched for the blanket, causing Jisoo to curl up into a ball.

The Australian snorted, disgusted.

-Sleep like a log

-And now we see who drank the last of the bottle- Lisa pointed at the bottle which was held tightly in the feline girl's arms- How are we going to wake her up?

-Leave it to me, I'll take care of Jen.

Lisa nodded and left the room heading for the living room. However, when she got to the sofa she noticed that the brunette was no longer there.

-Where could he have gone?

She looked around confused until she heard a noise coming from the kitchen.

-Nini?

He walked slowly to the entrance and smiled at the sight of the chestnut covered in flour. He couldn't help but laugh at the scene, catching the girl's attention, who quickly stopped what she was doing.

-Lili...-she whispered smiling

-Good morning ghost girl

Jennie looked at her confused. What did she mean?

-Ghost girl?

-Of course, you're covered in flour. Do you bathe like this now?

Jennie wrinkled her nose and shook her head.

-I'm trying to make pancakes in a different way- he explained, taking a crumpled sheet of paper- your mom begged me to make it how you liked it but...

Lisa didn't let her finish, she closed the gap between them and kissed her. At first the brunette didn't respond because she was surprised, Lisa never had those outbursts, but it didn't take long for her to follow her lead.

Meanwhile in the room poor Rose was struggling to wake up Jisoo, who simply refused to wake up.

-Damn, you look like a fucking marmot- he snorted and stood close to her- hey Chicken, wake up already Damn!- he touched her shoulder searching without getting any result- hey you, get up!- he slapped her a couple of times. Nothing. *Rose thinks how can you wake up?* - ok, since you don't want to get up I'll eat the whole chicken

That was music to his ears, and an excellent wake-up call for the Korean.

-Did someone say chick!?

On the other hand, in the kitchen things were getting hotter.

-Jen...- Lisa gasped when the brunette slammed her against the refrigerator- The girls are...

-Shut up Lisa, just kiss me- he ordered, launching himself into her mouth eagerly. And it wasn't just his heat that caused it, the blonde in general managed to awaken his animal side in such a way that it was impossible for him to control the carnal reactions of his body- Ahh, Lisa!

Yes, Jennie was good at seducing, but Lisa was good at dominating and she wasn't going to let the brunette steal her place. In a simple movement she had made her change position, and without any shame she squeezed her ass with desire.

The Korean girl was enjoying it, yes, yes, and how could she not? Lisa knew how to move her tongue and not only in her southern part. Jennie's mouth was delighted with the lascivious movements of the opposite tongue, causing contractions in her sensitive area.

-Lili, let's go...

-I'm here for the one you were crying for!

They both jumped away. The brunette had entered the kitchen unnoticed, catching them red-handed, just as Lisa's hand ventured into the brunette's shorts.

-But what are you two doing!?- Rose asked reluctantly behind Jisoo, noticing the labored breathing of both girls- me struggling to wake up the human chicken...!

-Hey!

-And here you are, fornicating first thing in the morning! - she continued disgusted, crossing her arms.

The blonde with bangs' cheeks turned pink. Wow, without Jisoo's interruption, her fingers would have been deep inside the feline-eyed girl at that moment.

Skin to skin

After breakfast the four of them both went to their respective jobs, and on the way back home Lisa had decided that she would spend time with the Korean girl and what better way to do it than watching a movie? Of course she didn't expect it to be exactly Puss in Boots.

-Are you serious, Nini?

The named shrugged without taking her eyes off the screen.

-It's romantic, the way Cat conquers Kitty..- he sighed with the memory

The blonde rolled her eyes in amusement and grabbed another CD from the pile, getting rid of the one already inside.

- There is nothing more romantic than this movie..- moment while taking it out of the case

-I already saw Titanic with Rose and ended up crying

Lisa Snorted

-The Titanic is a cliché, and Rose cries even watching the Teletubbies. You'll like this one

After a while watching Noah's diary, Jennie settled on Lisa's shoulder, attentive to the drama of the movie, and how the protagonists were getting along together. The way Noah looked at Allie with such fascination left the feline intrigued.

-Lisa...?

-Hmm?

-Have you ever been in love?

Lisa thought a bit about her answer, how to talk about that with Jennie?

-I guess we've all liked someone at some point...

-I'm talking about love, Lisa, have you ever loved someone intensely?

The Thai girl sat up on the couch, the subject was making her tense.

-I... I was once in love, but she... -he swallowed, the memory of Yerin still opening old wounds- She's not here anymore

Jennie watched as the Thai girl's expression changed as she spoke, and a part of her felt pain. Knowing that Lisa had loved and still had feelings for this girl affected her.

He looked at the screen and sighed melancholy.

- I wish someone would love me like Noah loved Allie

Lisa looked at her from the side, thoughtful. Could she give something like that to Jennie?

The brunette turned around, meeting the penetrating gaze of the Thai girl. Those eyes were watching her with such intensity that her heart began to beat rapidly. And at that moment, there was nothing but Lisa.

Little by little, both girls got closer to each other, without breaking eye contact. Lisa's vanilla scent mixed with her Chanel essence, creating a strange but exquisite combination of fragrances, while both girls breathed each other. Their distance was nonexistent. Lisa's lips caressed the Korean's with shyness and sweetness. As soft as the subtle touch of a feather, leaving a pleasant tickle in its wake.

Jennie closed her eyes and sighed as the Thai girl finally got up the courage to kiss her. That warm feeling in her stomach could only be caused by Lalisa.

On the other hand, Lisa was enjoying it. It wasn't like the previous, rough and needy kisses they used to give each other. This one was full of feeling, of silent words and hidden emotions. It was the first kiss that made her feel complete, as if those perfect lips had been designed just for her. *Destiny*.

The way their lips fit

together, like a perfect puzzle, left her breathless, and little by little they began to thirst for more...

The Thai girl in a delicate movement sat the Korean girl on her lap, without breaking the kiss, which was beginning to gain intensity.

Oh my God! Jennie was starting to lose her temper, and all she had to do was feel Lisa's hand squeezing her bottom to bring out the beast inside her.

Lisa frowned as she watched the brunette break the kiss and pull away. Did she dislike her touch?

- I'm sorry Jen, I...

The named placed a finger on the Thai woman's lips and denied, with accelerated breathing.

-Let's go to the room, I want to be yours Lisa...

And this time the Thai girl didn't protest, why would she? Her desire for the brunette was palpable and she was dying to join her.

He carefully picked up the brunette and carried her to the bedroom, princess style, all without breaking eye contact.

Cautiously he placed her on the bed and stood there, staring at her, holding his breath. *Fuck, I have Jennie Kim in my bed.* I'd had her sleeping there a thousand times before, but I knew tonight was going to be different.

Jennie gasped as she felt the blonde's weight on top of her, her body shaking with desire and excitement. She was finally going to be hers! She smiled radiantly and arched as she felt the taller girl's hands slip under her shirt and dangerously ascend to her breasts, all under the blonde's attentive scrutiny.

-Touch me... Please- he begged, seeing the blonde's doubt- I need to feel you Lili, I've wanted to since I met you

Lisa shuddered at his words. She began to grope those two mounds of glory, letting out a groan as she felt the soft skin beneath her hands. *Fuck!* Her body nearly convulsed as she heard a moan from the shorter one.

Jennie curled up happily under the younger girl's body, the sensation that the Thai girl gave her with a simple touch was unique. She purred at the exquisite caress, but she needed more, and she didn't take long to let it be known.

Lisa was surprised when the shorter girl switched roles, leaving her underneath, and eagerly tearing off her blouse. She moaned at the sight of Jennie's perfect backside exposed to her, and before she could touch it, the brunette was already getting rid of her blouse as well and giving her kisses down her neck.

Lisa gasped, her eyes half closed, as the Korean's tongue slid down her jugular and descended to her collarbone with a seduction she didn't know she had.

-God Nini, you do it great...

And be damned when you speak, because instantly the brunette stopped her kisses and also got up from on top of her.

Lisa remained motionless, her breathing accelerated and her eyes closed, regretting the distance from the feline girl.

- Lisa, look at me...- Jennie asked in a whisper

The Thai girl's core tightened in excitement as she took in the sight before her. Jennie was standing over her with each leg on either side of her hips and completely naked. When did she actually get naked?

-Jennie...

-Take me Lisa

And who would refuse such a delicious offer? A very primitive Lalisa went into action, grabbing the brunette roughly and throwing her onto the bed.

Jennie moaned at the younger girl's dominance, and moaned again when Lisa's mouth enveloped one of her nipples. Heaven is an understatement, Lisa was fucking Eden.

-Aaah, Lisa!

The Thai girl's teeth nibbled on that pink spot to suck it shortly after, while her hand pampered the second in a thousand different ways.

-Oh shit, Lili don't stop!- and Jennie started to get more eager and horny as the Thai continued her way to the most needy point of her anatomy. *Holy God, she's going to eat me again!* She shuddered all over in anticipation, she was dying to repeat what had happened between them in Thailand and Lisa's eager look announced to her that it would be so.

Lisa smirked as the brunette spread her legs wider to allow her full access and sighed at the sight of her in all her splendor. Totally exposed to her.

-You're so wet, darling...- she whispered, more than ecstatic.

-I'm sorry Lili

Lisa smiled, sometimes she forgot how innocent the feline was in certain things.

-Well, I won't, in fact I'll take care of drying you off.

-Drying...? Aah, Fuck Lisa!!!!- Jennie curled up like in the exorcist when Lisa's mouth began to devour her clit with desire- Yes, yes, yes...!! Oh Shit, Yes!

Lisa slid her tongue back and forth, leaving no corner untouched. The taste of the chestnut was simply intoxicating.

She was enjoying every action of the Korean girl, how her hand was squeezing her left breast tightly and the other was forcing her to stay between her legs, holding her head firmly. Her moans were becoming more continuous and desperate, while she said a chain of curses that only God knows where she had learned them from.

-Mmm Yes, right there...! Ahh...! Lisa I'm going to... LISA!!!!

The girl moaned the Thai girl's name between convulsions. Her body was experiencing the spasms of orgasm, while Lisa focused on drinking every last drop of her fluids, but she didn't intend to stop there. Her fingers went down to the center of the Korean and she looked at her doubtfully, pressing the place without too much force.

-If you want me to stop...

Jennie glared at her between gasps.

-Manoban, if you stop now I'll kill you!

Lisa settled on top of her and it was Jennie who initiated the kiss. Her breathing was still labored from the recent orgasm, but her desire had only intensified. The Korean gasped as she felt the Thai girl slowly and tortuously enter her, allowing her to adjust to the length of her finger.

-L-Lili...

- Hurts?

Jennie shook her head with her eyes closed, the intrusion felt strange and it also hurt a little, but she didn't plan on telling the other girl.

With that clarification Lisa let the second one in, earning a sound from the brunette, she was so wet and receptive that her fingers had no problem entering.

Lisa left them still as she sprinkled kisses across the girl's face to relax her, and succeeded. Jennie began to fidget, urging her to do the same.

-Do it Lisa, make me feel...

As if on command, the fingers began to come to life, heightening the Korean's sensations. An intense fire built up in her belly and spread throughout her body, as waves of pleasure swept through her belly, making her scream continuously, while Lisa continued to move in and out of her.

Their lips met again and the sensation of silencing her moans in her mouth was a pleasure for the Thai girl who was more than stimulated by the brunette's sensual reactions. Could she come just by looking at her? Without a doubt, she was so wet that she could cum just by hearing one more moan from the brunette.

-Come on Nini, I want you to come for me

And Jennie's body was quick to obey, giving her a second and even more devastating orgasm that made her see stars.

Lisa kissed her again as she slowly pulled her fingers out, watching her exhausted feline recover from the climax she had just experienced. Exhausted, with her eyes closed, covered in a layer of pearly sweat and her lips parted in search of oxygen, it seemed to Lisa that Jennie had never looked as beautiful as she did at that moment.

"That was... amazing," the Korean girl said, her voice hoarse and choppy.

-It was- Lisa whispered with a half smile.

Jennie looked at her lasciviously and bit her lower lip, making the taller girl shudder.

- It's my turn to make you feel

Wake up

To say that that night had been the best of her life was an understatement. After reaching her climax with the brunette, they had continued their marathon all night long. Jennie was tireless. Even after her orgasms, she was still eager. Lisa had been devastated; she couldn't remember ever having had a girl as sexual as the feline. She had lost count of the number of orgasms they had given each other.

She smiled as she felt the shorter girl's body on top of hers without any clothes on. *So beautiful...* She brushed a lock of hair from her face and looked at her. Jennie asleep on top of her after having been hers was the most perfect thing of all. *Mine* . She shuddered as she remembered the Korean's devotion. She had never felt such affinity with any woman. Is she the one? A wide smile appeared on her lips. *After all this time...Jennie*

He placed a kiss on her nose and his smile widened as he watched her wrinkle her nose and smile a little while still asleep. Did he really want to wake up like this every day? *I don't see anything better than that* .

He stood up happier than ever and prepared to start the day. Despite having slept only an hour, he felt his energy renewed as it hadn't happened in years. He looked once more at the girl in bed before leaving the room. *Today will be a good day.*

◇◇🐱◇◇

Jennie stretched out on the bed with her eyes still closed. She let out a moan. Her whole body hurt, especially her southern area. She carefully sat up in bed trying not to hurt herself.

- Did I get into a fight with someone? - Confused, she stood up carefully, her legs feeling tense and fragile. In her time as a feline, she used to escape at night and fight with other cats in the area. But had she done it that night?

He looked to his right and was saddened not to see the Thai girl.

She walked to the bathroom and widened her eyes as she looked at her body in the mirror. Her skin was covered in bruises, especially on her neck and lower abdomen. Her panic was replaced by happiness as she smelled the Thai girl's scent on her own skin, and memories flooded back to her like a waterfall.

- Lisa... - she closed her eyes and sighed. The Thai girl's caresses were etched into her skin. Every part of her body tingled from the touch she received the night before. She caressed her neck, remembering the dancer's kisses, and went down to her sternum where the blonde had focused lovingly for much of the night.

He sighed again. He still couldn't believe that he had actually been with Lisa and it had been wonderful.

-What if it was a dream?- that idea made her doubt. She had had similar dreams where Lisa made her hers, but without a doubt that was the most real.

She looked at her reflection with a grimace. Her lips were swollen from kisses and her hair was disheveled. When had she left Lisa to go fight?

The smell of food made her forget all thoughts. She quickly smoothed her hair and after putting on a Lisa shirt and sniffing it, she ran out of the room and into the kitchen. Jennie didn't notice the weakness in her legs and the numbness in her muscles, and before she could enter the kitchen she tripped, falling off Bruces in the doorway.

-God, that was a scare!- Lisa looked at the ceiling with wide eyes and groaned. The sudden impact had made her jump with the frying pan in her hand and the pancake had slammed into the ceiling- Jen, what happened to you?- she rushed to help the girl who was still complaining on the floor- Are you okay?

Jennie looked at her with a special sparkle in her eyes and smiled enchanted.

- Lisa...- he whispered between sighs and hugged her tightly, causing the blonde to fall to the ground as well- I am now

Lisa pulled away just enough to allow herself to steal a kiss from him. Her heart was racing. What was happening to her? She pulled away just enough and smiled as she saw the feline girl still with her eyes on her.

-Good morning Nini- she whispered, helping her to stand- you'll have to be patient, your breakfast is there- she pointed to the ceiling, amused- sit down while I finish cooking

The chestnut obeyed and complained when she felt the discomfort in her body again.

-Where did I go last night after you...I...After we...?- her cheeks reddened when she saw the Thai girl's mischievous look

-After we made love?

Jennie felt her stomach turn at those words. *Love. Love... Lisa loves me!* That made her smile big and she nodded shyly. That was what making love meant, wasn't it?

-I think I got into a fight with someone last night after... that. My body is sore and covered in bruises.

Lisa blushed and looked down, a little embarrassed.

- I'm so sorry Nini, I'm afraid those marks were my fault.

-Yours?

-I did that to you

Jennie widened her eyes in surprise.

-You hit me?

-God, no!- he cleared his throat- let's say I touched you and kissed you in some places very roughly- his cheeks were burning. The brunette's features changed as if she had suddenly understood what he meant. She had a playful smile on her face and her eyes had suddenly darkened- Do you... does it hurt a lot there?- he made a sign and Jennie quickly denied it.

The Korean woman bit her lower lip, assessing the Thai girl from head to toe. She could remember her naked body and how that pale, perfect skin had pricked at her touch. And her taste...

-You taste so good...- he whispered unconsciously, starting to get excited.

—Jennie!- the tallest one's cheeks were tinted pink at the Korean's unexpected words.

-Lili... I'm so hungry- he whispered pleadingly.

-Breakfast will be ready in a second, just...

- I don't want pancakes

Lisa turned to the feline, attentive.

- No? - he made a face as he opened the fridge - well, I can make you some eggs and bacon... there's also pizza from yesterday... what exactly do you want to eat?

-To you...

The hairs on her neck stood up as she heard the whisper in her ear. The brunette had quietly positioned herself behind her. Her voice had sounded husky and sensual, further unsettling the Thai girl's nerves.

As she turned around, she almost fainted. Jennie had thrown her shirt by the door and she had nothing on underneath, which allowed each of her bruises and her anatomy to be seen, altering the taller woman's breathing.

-Jen...

-Can I have my breakfast, Lili?

Jennie gasped as she saw the desire in the Thai girl as she pressed her against the cold fridge

-I think I've also got an appetite...- he whispered against her lips and then shortly after got into action and lost himself once again in the Korean's skin.

Unexpected visit

Lisa was returning to her monotonous life, work was exhausting her and she had almost no time for anything else. Her head was about to explode. Another aspirin? She had lost count of how many she had taken that day. She sat back in her seat and rubbed the bridge of her nose, at the height of her glasses. She really needed more breaks like the one in Bangkok. Bangkok... she smiled widely as she remembered her family, she had missed them, but her mind focused on her meeting with Jennie.

-Jennie...- he whispered to her, closing his eyes. He had lost count of how many kisses they had given each other since then, how many failed attempts they had had to repeat that day. But the truth was that it was getting harder and harder, the brunette had been in heat for three days and was quite suggestive, and the poor Thai girl was finding it harder and harder to control herself.

- Lalisa Manoban

She was so lost in her thoughts that she didn't notice that her office had been broken into. Her face fell when she saw who it was.

-Tzuyu?

The aforementioned smiled widely and sat down on the chair on the other side of the desk. Her outfit was quite revealing, a skirt that showed off a lot of her thighs and a tie-dyed shirt tied under her breasts, leaving her abdomen exposed. Lisa's eyes roamed over her body like a hungry animal and that satisfied the Korean's ego. And it's not that Lisa was a pervert but her hormones were in turmoil with the constant insinuations of her feline girl and her lack of sex was beginning to show. She didn't feel comfortable having relations with Jennie in heat, it was as if she were going to fuck a drunk girl. (quick note, cats when they are in heat cannot control their "hormones" that is why it is difficult for them to reject the male)

-Hello my love! Do you like it? - he turned around to torture the Taulandeses even more - I chose it for you

Lisa frowned, breaking her spell.

-What do you want Tzuyu?

-Is this how you greet your girl Manoban?

-My girl?- Lisa let out an ironic laugh- you mean Sana's girl

The girl made a face of disgust

- Lisa, let me explain, what happened with Sana was...

—I'm not interested in your explanations.

-Nothing happened!

-I saw them with my fucking eyes, don't come telling me that nothing happened!

-It's not what you think, I love you Lisa!- she slid into the Thai girl's seat- only you...- she whispered in her ear, rolling her nose in the Thai girl's ear and earning a shudder from the blonde- you still like my touch Lisa... you still want me

Her hand tried to sneak into the Thai girl's dress but she stopped her abruptly, removing her hand roughly.

-Tzuyu, you have 5 minutes to leave my office

- Are you running me off?

-No, I'm asking you politely to go to hell- he shrugged- but security can also take care of that.

The Korean girl looked at her and shook her head without accepting the rejection from the Thai girl.

-There's another one, isn't there? Are you fucking someone else!?- she screamed hysterically - You're mine Lalisa, you're not going to fuck anyone else!

-And what if I already do it?- he challenged her, leaning on the desk- you're past Tzuyu, and I'm not turning back.

Tzuyu clenched her fists tightly.

-You're going to regret it Lisa, you and the bitch you're sleeping with!

Lisa leaned back cockily in her seat and swung her chair around with a smug smile.

-For your information, it's not a dog, it's a cat- he pressed a button on the intercom- Irene, ask security to... No, better tell pest control to come to my office, there's a rattlesnake

The Korean girl widened her offended mouth and pointed at her.

-You're going to be mine Lisa, even if it's the last thing I do!

◈◈🐱◈◈

Returning home had only made me think about what had happened, why had Tzuyu returned after so long?

-She's a bitch Lisa, maybe she fell short and now she's going for your money- Rose reported over the speaker

-Her father is a lawyer Rose, I don't think money is the motive

-Well then just miss your rod fingers

Lisa sighed. Parking the car in the garage of her building

-I don't know Rosie, something doesn't add up.

-God Lisa, obviously it doesn't add up, that woman doesn't come back after months just for a fuck. She came back for you and whatever the reason is you shouldn't expect anything good from that. Just don't let your guard down, at any moment she'll play her second card.

She hung up the call and headed inside the building. Talking to Rose always helped her get her problems out. *Damn psychologist*. She hated that her friend treated her like one of her patients, but sometimes it suited her just fine.

-Jen, I'm home! - she exclaimed as always, closing the door behind her. - Nini? - she was surprised when she didn't see the smiling face of the Korean girl appearing in the hallway. -Jennie, where are you? - Nothing in the kitchen. She walked hesitantly down the hallway. Had she fallen asleep? - Maybe she's taking a bath...

But his thoughts were dashed when he poked his head into the room and came across an image he certainly wasn't expecting.

- Lisa...

The brunette was completely naked, arching over the bed, while one of her hands touched one of her pleasure points with need. The Korean had been hot all day. Her heat plus the repressed desire for Lisa had her impatient and she could no longer bear her need. Did finding the Thai girl's underwear have something to do with it? Yes, without a doubt that lace lingerie was the breaking point for her cock and at that moment she was gushing.

-Oh shit!- Lisa gritted her teeth. Was there anything more erotic than that feline writhing in pleasure on the bed while moaning her name?

Without taking her eyes off the exciting scene, the Thai girl stripped off her clothes, one by one. Her core was throbbing with anxiety and her mouth was watering.

-Aah, Lisa!

-God Jen, you're going to drive me crazy

The brunette was startled when she heard the blonde's raspy voice. When had she arrived? But her mind discarded all thoughts and she let out a moan of pleasure when she saw the naked Thai girl in front of her. Could she have an orgasm just by looking at her? She had definitely just had one.

Family dinner? (Chaesoo)

-For the fifth time Chu...

-Jisoo!- the Korean corrected her.

-Get away from the fucking hamster! - the Australian girl burst out impatiently. The whole thing was getting on her nerves and Jisoo was making it even more difficult for her.

She rubbed her temple, worried. Why had her mother had the brilliant idea of inviting them to dinner?

Flashback

-Honey, to show you that we are not against your abnormal things, I want to invite you and your... gee...girlfriend... well, that woman, to dinner this Saturday.

-Mother, first of all homosexuality is completely normal in this day and age, and on the other hand Jisoo...- he turned towards the living room where the brunette was watching a documentary on the laptop. He frowned- give me a second Mother- he covered the receiver and walked to the couch looking at the screen with a grimace- Why the hell are you watching a farm documentary?

The Korean stopped the video and shrugged.

-Since you don't want to feed me, I'll have to do it on my own, and what better than with an infinite supply of chickens!?

Rose rolled her eyes, imagining the brunette with a poultry farm just so she wouldn't stop eating chicken. She put the phone back to her ear and sighed.

-Jisoo and I will be busy on Saturday Mother, we won't be able to...

-But you said that on Saturday you would be lying on the couch all day.

-Shut up Jisoo!

-Park Chaeyong, I want you for dinner on Saturday and if you don't go I'll be forced to go myself, and you know what that means!

Rose swallowed nervously.

-Ok, we'll be there on Saturday

-Perfect! Your sisters will be happy to see you!

End of flashback

This couldn't be worse. He snorted, watching the Korean girl lick her hands under the watchful eyes of her parents on the couch.

-What are you doing?- asked his father surprised.

- Oh, she... she just likes to play! - With a slap he made the brunette stop her action

Jisoo looked at her reproachfully, rubbing her hand.

-Why are you interrupting me in the middle of my bath!?

-My God, he doesn't take a bath!?- exclaimed his horrified mother.

-That's what I did until my daughter brutally attacked me!

-It was just a slap...

-Brutally!!!

The Australian rolled her eyes and let her be. Her patience was minimal with Jisoo, how could she stay calm if every second she was causing her neck to twist like a damn chicken? *Chicken... oh God, all this talk about chicken is affecting my common sense!*

The doorbell rang and Rose sighed in relief at the interruption. How had she thought of taking the feline girl to her parents?

A few steps and some laughter gave him goosebumps, it wasn't hard for him to guess who those three voices belonged to.

-Rosie darling, look who's arrived!

The Australian closed her eyes for a moment and counted to three. As a psychologist, stopping and regaining sanity was necessary for emotional balance. As she turned around, she found three completely familiar faces.

-Sis, how long has it been? - the eldest greeted her with irony, arching an arrogant eyebrow. Vanity was her thing.

-Chae!- the youngest of the three newcomers widened a sweet smile similar to Rose's, making her chubby cheeks narrow her eyes

-Shuhua- he greeted the older one indifferently and turned smiling towards the younger one- Fuck Gayoon, you're huge!

The latter hugged Rose affectionately and giggled.

- I missed you so much Unnie!

While the three sisters did not live in Korea, Shuhua had a good position in Australia and her sisters had settled down there, Rose instead decided to go on her own, staying in Seoul, and two years later her parents did the same.

-And I love you, shorty!- She ruffled her hair and turned to the last one. The girl was focused on typing on her phone, not paying much attention. Rose frowned. She hated it when people ignored their surroundings for a little bit of technology. -Seohyun, I think you can take your nose off your phone for five seconds to say hello to your fucking sister, don't you think?

The named one looked up, narrowing her eyes shrewdly.

- Don't forget, Park Chaeyong, that I'm older than you!

-And look at the example you give me- he said ironically, rolling his eyes.

The girl smiled putting her phone in her coat and walked up to the blonde

-It's always a pleasure to see you oppa

-Of course, because we look alike.

-Exactly, only I am much more beautiful than you.

One of the things the Park sisters had in common was their striking resemblance. They all had similar characteristics, whether it was their Asian eyes or their tender cheeks.

-Holy cat that just gave birth, I'm seeing double! What am I saying, double, quadruple!

They all turned to the sofa where Jisoo was standing, looking at the four Australians, delighted by the kinship.

-And who is that? - the second one asked curiously, looking at the Korean.
-Kim Jisoo, better known as the love of your life!

Jisoo rushed to kiss Seohyun's hand who looked at her perplexed by her action.
- Oh, how pretty!
- Not as much as your darling- he winked at his younger sister, making her blush and turned to look at Shuhua flirtatiously- don't worry, there's a little bit of Chu for you too, darling

Rose frowned at her. Was he really flirting with all of her sisters in front of her? *Slut cat!*
-Who are you supposed to be?- the eldest raised an eyebrow in displeasure, looking Jisoo up and down.
-I already said it, I'm Kim Jisoo. Humans are slow, but you're lucky to be beautiful!
-Jisoo!
- Sorry squirrel, I fell in love with your clones
-They are not my clones, they are my hateful sisters.
-Hey!- Seohyun and Gayoon reproached in unison
-And stop being so flirtatious- Rose finished, ignoring her sisters' complaints.
Clare, the girls' mother, returned beaming at the sisters.
-My three little ones are back, how happy!
-Thanks for excluding me, mother, it's always a pleasure to come home- Rose said ironically, rolling her eyes.

-Oh come on Chae, I see you every day- she looked at the girls and Jisoo who was still attentively observing the newcomers- Oh, have you met Jesoon yet?

-Jisoo- the psychologist corrected

-It's the nov...Novi...ugh! She's with Chaeyong

-What!?- the three of them claimed in unison

-Mother, I already told you no...!

-That's right, we're planning to get married in a few months, aren't we, my love...? Oooh! Why are you stepping on me!?

Rose glared at her.

-Say goodbye to fried chicken forever, Kim Jisoo!

-Noooo!

With the sisters already home, Clare set about preparing dinner while the girls waited in the dining room and learned more about their sister's orientation.

-Who would have thought, the distressed psychologist- her older sister mocked.

-Being a lesbian is not affliction, being on my third divorce, that would be affliction. I also do therapy for divorced women, sister, in case you are interested.

Her sister looked at her and Rose smiled with satisfaction at having achieved her goal. She knew that three consecutive divorces had the eldest more than frustrated.

-So you like girls?- her younger sister continued to question her- I thought that you and Sehon...

- God no! Sehon was a misfit and eventually had to undergo my therapies for virile deficiency.

- That explains why you became a lesbian- Seohyun said ironically, amused.

Once dinner was served, they couldn't even say thank you when the Korean woman had already eaten half of her plate.

-My God, is your girlfriend a beggar? She eats like an animal!

-Dah, because I am… a cat to be more specific.

Shuhua widened her eyes in affront. And Seohyun quickly intervened upon noticing her older sister's attitude.

- And what do you do Jisoo?

The girl thought about it for a minute.

- Well, from time to time I killed rodents at home.

-How disgusting! - exclaimed the eldest of the four with a grimace of disgust.

-I was just thinking about it, I swear!

Rose wanted to be a thousand light years away from that table. The shame she felt at that moment was incomparable. Could it be worse?

-Are you in love with my daughter?

-Head over heels!

-What attracted you?

-Your chest!

Rose's mother began to cough desperately as she choked while drinking juice, and Rose was about to burst.

-Thanks for dinner, we have to go now!

-What? But we haven't even eaten anything yet…!

-I said we have to go now!- the murderous half of the Australian managed to intimidate the Korean who quickly took two quick bites and nodded frantically.

"Looks like someone's sleeping on the couch tonight," Seohyun joked as she watched her sister stride out, the Korean following close behind. Both Shuhua and Gayoon nodded in agreement.

Psychologist Park

-How was your Park family dinner?

-Shut up Lisa, I'm not in the mood for your nonsense- she covered her face with one hand between sighs

The Thai woman let out a laugh, sitting down on the stool in front of the therapeutic couch.

-What irony, the psychologist lying on her own consulting room chair- he mocked when he saw her lying where her patients normally sit- they say that psychologists end up being more conflictive than their patients. What do you say?

-That's a fucking truth. Pass me the fucking bottle and shut up.

The Australian was frustrated with her parents' dinner, it had all been a complete waste of her time. She hadn't been long in calling Lisa, that morning her mind was empty and not even Mrs. Wang's constant laments about the loss of her cat could soothe her.

-Get out of my office immediately, and don't ever talk to me about cats again! - he exploded at the mere mention of the feline.

Lisa burst out laughing as she handed me the bottle.

-How could you throw out your patient like that? What happened to your ethics as Miss Park?

-It went to shit when you decided to show up with a cat turned into a woman. You screwed me Lisa! - he reproached, tilting the bottle

-First, stop drinking during work hours, you look like a fucking alcoholic- he snatched the bottle again making the Australian growl- and second. I remind you that I live with a feline girl... beautiful girl...- he sighed at the memory and smiled- and a family of cats

-Stop, what was that sigh and that idiotic smile?

Lisa's cheeks flushed at being discovered. *Shit* .

- I have not sighed

-I'm drunk, but not blind.

Lisa frowned.

-That doesn't make sense, if you're drunk you don't think clearly.

-I do. So start telling or I'll get information out of Jennie, and you know she'll tell me in great detail.

And that was it. Jennie's innocence prevented her from lying, especially if she didn't see anything wrong with the matter. No, she couldn't let the brunette tell her friend what she had experienced that night in her bed, and in the kitchen when she woke up... and the next night on the couch when she got home from work. Holy crap, and not to mention that morning before going to the Australian's office.

She blushed again

-I...

-You fucked Jennie!

-Lower your voice, Damn, and don't call him that!

-Damn it, and you don't even deny it. Tell me everything!

-I...

-Nono, wait- he stood up unsteadily and forced Lisa to take his place on the couch.

-But what...?

-Ah... wait a second!- he took his glasses, the notebook and bent his leg, heading to his stool and assuming his work posture. He cleared his throat and looked at Lisa intently- now yes. Tell me, Miss Manoban, how was your sexual experience with a cat?

Lisa rolled her eyes. Psychologist Park was back on the scene. She looked at the ceiling and snorted, she hated talking about her stuff.

- Yes, I slept with her and...

-I knew it!- The Thai woman turned to look at her and Rose stood up- Please Manoban, continue

-What the fuck do you want me to say, Rose? We did it and it was... God, it was damn good! - He covered his face and shook his head - This isn't right, Rose, she's my cat

-She's a fucking woman Lalisa! And she must fuck like heaven if she gave you that bruise under your mole and you didn't even bother to cover it up!

Lisa widened her eyes in shock and jumped to her feet.

-What did you do to me?!- he ran to the full-length mirror in the corner and cursed at the noticeable pacifier on his neck- Fuck...- he whispered, trying unsuccessfully to cover it with the collar of his shirt.

- Lisa, don't try to cover it up now, half of Seoul saw your submissive mark on the way here.

- I'm not submissive!

-You may be the one who pins her to the bed with those sticks you have for fingers...

- Rose!

-But she has you under control, and that mark only means one thing.

-What thing?

-That cat won't hesitate to bring out her claws if another girl approaches you. You're screwed Manoban, you belong to her.

Lisa thought about it, belonging to Jennie? The thought made her heart pound, but her common sense refused to budge.

- No. What happened was just...

- A slip, Lalisa? Just say it and I'll slap your fucking mouth off! - Rose growled, clenching the notebook and hitting the Thai girl's head with it.

-Power, why are you hitting me!?

-You idiot! You can't play with Jennie, Lisa, she doesn't deserve it!

Lisa sighed in agreement, she was clear about that.

- Rose, I can't fall in love with her...

-What are you afraid of?

-It's a g...

-If you say it again, I'll hit you.

-What if she turns back into a cat? Have you considered that maybe the wish on that star won't last forever?

Rose looked at her analytically, noticing the fear in her friend's eyes. Indeed, she hadn't thought about that detail.

-It's totally feasible. The chances are high... so why not take advantage of it while it lasts?

- Because that would mean falling in love with her and then losing her.

◇◇◇

Friday morning?

Lisa arrived at her office like every morning, and found it unusual not to find Irene at her post with her typical good morning smile and her morning coffee. She frowned in surprise and continued on to her office. *Maybe she was late* . However, when she reached the door of her office she heard laughter inside.

Upon entering, he was surprised to see Irene sitting on the sofa, and on the armrest, Seulgi half leaning towards her, giving a perfect view of her semi-exposed breasts.

-And then... hey Lisa!

The first, upon hearing the mention of that name, jumped to her feet with red cheeks.

-L-Lisi... Miss Manoban- she quickly corrected herself, smoothing her skirt- I... your friend came to see you and I thought I could wait for you more comfortably in your office.

-I see, and what better way to do it than in the company of my assistant, right? - Lisa said ironically, seriously.

Irene swallowed hard, about to respond, but the second blonde got there first.

-Of course Pokpak, Irene is an excellent company- he winked at the aforementioned while playing with a lock of hair

Irene almost choked at the girl's flirtatious action and looked away nervously.

- Oh, well I... yes, I'm leaving now.

-Irene... my coffee

The girl looked at her hand, where her boss's coffee was indeed still there.

- Oh yes, how clumsy! - He left the coffee on the desk and left the office almost running.

"Nice ass," Seulgi commented as she watched her leave.

-Please stop hitting on my assistant...

- Don't be selfish Lis, you already have Jennie, why do you need Irene?

-Threesomes are always a great option- Mintty made an unannounced entrance

Lisa looked at them confused, what were her friends doing in Korea?

-Before you ask, it was your sister's idea- Mintty clarified, looking around the office.

-Mine?

-Do you have another one?- Mintty rolled her eyes- by the way, Mina is already old enough to...

-If you come near my sister, I'll cut off your fingers!

The girls burst out laughing at the dancer's jealousy. She had always been very protective of her sister.

-And where is it?

-He went with Rose to look for Jennie

Lisa made a confused face, she didn't understand what was happening.

-Did Rose know about this?

-Of course, she came to pick us up at the airport.

-Why am I the last to find out?

-Maybe because you're the only one with the cell phone in airplane mode

-My cell phone is not in sleep mode...- he cleared his throat, putting his phone back in his pocket after checking that it was in fact in sleep mode- what is the visit due to?

- Lalisa manoban, you are the only specimen without plans on a Friday- Seulgi reproached, getting off the couch

-It's barely 8 in the morning- asked the Thai girl with bangs.

-Perfect time to soak up some sun on a nice beach in Seoul

- Beach? No way, I have to work.

-You're the boss, you can do whatever the hell you want. In fact, Irene already took care of that.

-That?

- With my charms and a bit of good eyesight- Seulgi squeezed her breasts playfully- I convinced her to give your people the day off

-What did you do, Que!?- he growled, pressing a button on the intercom- Bae, get to my office right now!

Not even five seconds passed when the girl was already standing in front of her with a pale face and trembling legs. Although Irene had a crush on the Thai girl, she also respected her job and knew that Lalisa could be very strict during working hours.

-Did you want to see me, ma'am...?

-Yes, why...?

-Why don't you go change out of that office outfit for a cute bikini that shows off your body?- Seulgie interrupted her friend, looking flirtatiously at the assistant- and while you're at it, bring some sunscreen. I don't want you to get sunburned, cutie.

The assistant blinked in surprise and didn't know what to answer.

-That?

-We're going to the beach, honey, and he didn't take no for an answer.

◇◇🐱◇◇

They had finally ended up in Haeundae Beach, Busan. Two cars had been enough to transport the girls and two boxes full of liquor.

-What are we supposed to be celebrating?- the CEO asked, not very happy with the exit.

- No way Lalisa Manoban- Rose snorted leaving her things in the sand- does anyone know what the hell is celebrated on March 27th? Because it seems that our friend suffers from temporary amnesia

- Oh my God, yes, happy birthday Lisie! - the assistant hugged her and gave her a kiss on the cheek - I hope that... hey!

FELINE WHISPERS

The feline-eyed Korean pushed Irene aside with a search and smiled sweetly.

- I didn't know it was your birthday today, congratulations! - she rubbed her nose against the Thai girl's, leaving everyone surprised by the action.

- Don't rub his nose, kiss it!

- Jisoo! - her blushing sister scolded her.

The aforementioned had also attended. However, unlike Jennie, Chu had never been to the sea, much less surrounded by so many people, so Rose was attentive to her actions, the last thing she wanted was to walk around there shouting her name.

- It's not a big deal... - Lisa replied, downplaying the date.

-Isn't it a big deal? You don't turn 24 every day Manoban!

-You said the same thing last year Park

-Ha, and I don't see you turning 23 again, do I?

-Shut up, I came to get drunk and see butts, not to listen to you argue over stupid things - Mintty had already taken off her clothes, revealing her swimsuit - let's see which of these little Korean fish bites first - she joked flirtatiously, looking at the girls in the sand

- Oh, fuck..- Seulgi almost gasped as she watched Irene imitate her friend- that body can't be real

- Lisa, you had those attributes of your assistant well hidden- Mintty commented scanning her friend's employee

-I didn't even know...

The three of them looked at Irene in surprise, and the girl was quick to notice their glances.

-Is something wrong? Does it not fit me?- instinctively she covered her breasts in insecurity but Seulgi was quick to deny it frantically.

-Honey, with that body you have nothing to envy Kendall Jenner, what a woman...!

The assistant's cheeks flushed and she looked down

with a shy smile. Her eyes shifted to Lisa, awaiting a comment.

-And what do you say, Lisos? Does it look good on me? - he turned around, making the Thai girl's eyes go down to his butt.

-I..

- Lisa, you better look away if you don't want an Irene at the bottom of the sea- her sister whispered in warning.

-What do you mean...?- but she fell silent when she noticed how Jennie glared at the assistant, ready to jump on me at any moment.

Jisoo instead was paying attention to a couple a short distance away. The guy was applying sunscreen on his girlfriend's back and she seemed more than happy to do so. She saw two jars of cream in the sand and took the one with a sunscreen on it.

-Squirrel, can I give you some?

The Australian took another sip of her beer and nodded, her gaze on the sea.

-Yes, I don't want to complain about my back- he stretched out a towel and threw himself at it without any concern.

Holy *cats!* Jisoo not only had an excellent view of the psychologist's back, but also of her perfect ass in that tiny bikini. *I'm in cat heaven!* She settled back on the towel and began to imitate the boy's action, sliding the cream on with the help of her hands.

Rose let out a sigh as she felt the Korean girl massaging the area of her neck, tense from her long days of consultation.

-You have a good hand for massage- he admitted, enjoying the feline's touch.

-Not just for massage...

-That?

-Nothing!

Jisoo continued to spread the white cream all over the area, delighting in the texture of her skin. She grimaced and ventured to undo the knot of her bikini top.

Rose quickly tensed up

-What the fuck do you think you're doing!?

-It's so I can do it better, the swimsuit doesn't allow me to- Jisoo replied with feigned innocence

The massage had gradually become more naughty on the part of the feline, and the Australian did not seem to mind. How long had it been since she had been touched? It's not that she didn't have suitors, but her analytical side made her think too much and in the end she ended up rejecting all her possible sexual candidates. So her body seemed grateful for the feline's pampering.

Jisoo on the other hand had forgotten that she only had to devote herself to his back. Her eyes were focused on his butt, it was nothing like a cat's. *Maybe like a mandrill*. She thought, however at that moment it seemed to her the sexiest thing ever.

-How sexy...

-What did you say...? Aaaah!!

And there was silence. Rose's moan had been heard perfectly on the beach and more than one person had turned to see what it was about. The spanking that Jisoo had just given her had felt more than good and she had clearly forgotten that they were not alone. *Shit*.

Accomplices

-Ah Jisoo, spank me harder, I'm your submissive!

-Shut up, Mintty!

Her friends had been teasing her the whole time about what had happened, especially Mintty and Mina who were sunbathing next to them, oblivious to what they were both doing until the Australian's moan made them turn around.

-Now I am really traumatized. The worst thing is that I won't be able to look my psychologist in the eyes again because I will remember her moans.

-Mine!

They all laughed again

-Luckily we were at the bar ordering cocadas. And wow, what cocadas...- Seulgi's eyes were fixed on Irene's bra, who, oblivious to her lascivious gaze, smiled naturally at the rest of the girls.

-We see that you are still enjoying those coconuts, Seu- Mintty mocked when she saw her friend's silly face.

-And by the way, does anyone know where the Jenlisas went?

-It's her birthday Min, let Pokpak enjoy her gift- commented Mintty amused referring to Jennie

In a more secluded part of the crowd, Lisa and Jennie were sitting on a blanket, cuddling, watching the sunset. Lisa had taken her when the brunette, in a fit of jealousy, had almost drowned her assistant for swimming with the dancer.

- Lisa...?

-Yeah?

-What are we?

That question made her tense. What were they? They had been very close since then and with the brunette's heat on the surface she had been more intense than usual. Jennie was very erotic but without a doubt her heat turned her into an animal, and poor Lisa was really exhausted. Friends with benefits? Lovers? Girlfriends? How should she label the brunette? Her doubts about her relationship with the feline continued to worry her but it was a fact that she felt strong things for the girl.

-I...

-Until we find them!

Both girls turned around. Mina arrived with Mintty, both of them seemed a little drunk and that made the Thai girl angry.

-Mina Manoban, are you drunk?

-Of course not unnie, it was just two glasses

-Two bottles, you mean- Rose appeared behind her with a sour face- Lalisa, if you're going to fuck at least let us know, we were worried!

-You better listen to him, he's in a foul mood, he even looks like mom - Mina whispered to her sister.

- I heard you!

The day had turned into afternoon and afternoon into night. As the sun set, Haeundae Beach was a different atmosphere. The beach parties were unforgettable. A huge bonfire was lit on the sand and the music soon came to life from two large stereos. Friday nights in Busan? Epic. Jennie and Jisoo were terrified of the fire pois and the fireworks, the music and the explosions of the fireworks hurt their delicate feline eardrums and the flashes of light disoriented them.

-They'll burn!- Jennie exclaimed, impressed by the man who was juggling.

-Typical for arsonists- Rose commented rolling her eyes.

- Not all of them are crazy, Rose- Seulgi contradicted, taking a sip of her drink.

-It's pathological Seulgi, people can't help their psychological disorders. I myself have advised my arsonist patients to express their insane behavior in the art of handling burning torches.

-So you incite them to that

-Indeed, that's better than burning houses and singeing people.

The girls occupied one of the booths away from the event. Irene and Mintty took care of the drinks while Seulgi, Lisa and Rose went crazy in the dance area.

-Hey, aren't you dancing tonight? - Mina sat next to Jennie, noticing her absence. To her left, Jisoo was distracted with the Australian's cell phone, apparently MarioCar was more interesting.

- I don't feel like it...
- Can you tell me what's going on?

Jennie sighed. Her gaze was on the crowd dancing wildly on the makeshift dance floor, especially on Lisa, who swayed her hips with ease.

- Oh, what did my idiot older sister do?

Mina had noticed Jennie's glances. Since what happened in Bangkok she knew that there was more than just attraction between Lisa and her and with what Rose had told her she could conclude what the feline girl must be feeling for her sister.

-I don't know what we are, in Rose's movies the boys ask the girls to be their partner, but Lisa...

-Of course not, Nini- her sister interrupted without taking her eyes off the game- in Rose's movies the protagonists always tear off their clothes

- It's not true Jisoo, the protagonists always kiss!

-No, the girls are always open and the other one fucks her...

-Okok, I think I understand now- Mina intervened rubbing her temple- Good God, what kind of movies does Chaeyong watch...

The youngest of the Thai girls looked towards where her sister was, and frowned upon seeing her dancing next to a completely drunk Rose and Irene, more suggestive than ever. At what point did Bae leave Seulgi aside?

-Women... they are all the same!

-Seulgi, you are also a woman- Mintty rolled her eyes at her friend's comment

-For now!

-What happened to you? Weren't you with Irene?

-Just look at her, she wants to be fucked by Li

But before she could finish her sentence, Mina silenced her by placing a hand over her mouth. Out of the corner of her eye she could see Jennie attentive, waiting for the mere mention of her crush's name to jump on the assistant.

Mina analyzed the situation, Jennie was falling into a state of possession very quickly, her jealousy was extreme. *What if the same thing happened with Lisa?* She smiled at an idea

-I got it. Jen, you need to flirt with someone.

-What?- the brunette looked at Mina confused

-You want Lisa to pay attention to you, right?

-Yeah...

-Then do it.

- I don't know Mina. I don't feel very safe about approaching anyone- she commented nervously. Another thing about felines is that they were distrustful of humans they didn't know, strange smells put them on alert.

- Just choose someone you feel comfortable with, but also someone you can flirt with.

-Flirt?

-Yeah

- I don't want to flirt with anyone...

Seulgi rolled her eyes at the Korean's innocence

-Linda, just imagine it's Lisa, remember, the idea is to make her jealous. Do you want Lisa to show interest? Show her that she's not your priority, and that Jennie Kim can have whoever she wants.

- But Lisa is my priority...

-Fuck, stop it Jennie, Lisa is an idiot!- added Rose who had heard part of the girls' conversation- it's time she had a taste of her own medicine

-Medicine? Is the Cripple really sick?

-It's a saying Jisoo- the Australian clarified rolling her eyes

-So Jen... You want our help?

The three Thai girls and the Australian girl looked expectantly at the brunette waiting for an answer, while Jisoo... well, she was paying attention to other things.

- Jisoo, get down from that tree!

-Never!!!

- When did he climb up there? If he was here a second ago

-The question is... How did he get up there?

Mina, Mintty and Seulgi looked in surprise at the Korean feline on top of a coconut palm tree and below a small, trembling Chihuahua barking with difficulty, standing on two legs.

-Damn, that guy dances better than Seulgi

-Thanks Mintty- the named one said ironically, offended.

-I think the poor guy has a tic.

-That's a nice tick- Mintty looked up. She made a confused face- what's it supposed to do?

- I think he's growling- Mina assumed without understanding the Korean.

Rose rolled her eyes in disgust, the feline knew exactly how to get on her nerves.

-It's just that... She's allergic to dogs.

☢☢☢

Is Chaennie real?

Irene continued to sway her hips, while Lisa seemed immersed in the music, oblivious to her surroundings. What could she do to get her boss's attention? She snorted. In all the time she had been meeting and working for the Thai girl, she had never been able to get as close as she really wanted, and with the brunette in the middle, it was becoming increasingly difficult. *Damn Jennie Kim* . However, she wasn't going to miss the opportunity. With Lisa half drunk, and Jennie out of her reach, it was time to attack.

-Hey Lisie...

The blonde turned around with a smile, still moving.

-Yeah?

-Are you having fun?

-Irene, you know me. I always have fun dancing- he confessed, raising his arms to the rhythm of the music.

- I see that- the Korean girl looked at her boss from head to toe while moving to the rhythm of swalla

His desire for Lisa increased as he watched her dance. The Thai girl's swaying was simply spectacular. Getting wet watching Lalisa Manoban dance? That was a fact.

It's now or never . She encouraged herself to take it a step further. Kiss her? Ravage her and make her hers until she was exhausted? Even the idea of stripping right there for her boss didn't sound so crazy with a few too many drinks.

- Lisa I...

-Excuse me!- a tap on the shoulder caught her attention. She saw her boss's younger sister stand between them and clear her throat a little. -Fuck, is that Adriana Grande!?- she exclaimed, pointing at a fixed point.

-What?- Irene was confused. She looked at the indicated spot and rolled her eyes.

Mina clicked her tongue, shrugging indifferently.

-Ah No, it's just Jen and Chae about to kiss.

-What Jennie and Chaeyong What!?

Lisa's scream was heard over the music, catching the attention of the people around her, but that was far from mattering to the Thai girl.

-Hey Lisa, try not to kill Rose, she has work on Monday!- Mina shouted in warning.

-Lisa is going to kill who!!?- Jisoo jumped alertly, leaving the cell phone to one side.

-Calm down Jisoo, Lisa is just going to stop Jennie and Chae from kissing- explained Mintty at her side

-Ah, I get it... WHAT, JENNIE KISSED WHO?- Jisoo looked at the place where both girls were. Jennie smiled at Rose and she moved a brown lock of hair from her face, with the same smile- Jennie Kim, now I'll kill you!!!

The three girls watched in amazement as the first feline passed Lisa, running straight towards the Chaennies with a murderous expression.

-Oh God, what did we just do...- Mintty whispered covering her mouth

-Peace to the soul of Jennie and Chae. If Lisa doesn't kill them, Jisoo will surely do it.

◈◈🐱◈◈

Jennie looked down. She felt awkward about this kind of interaction with Rose. Her heart was racing with nervousness, and she was still hesitant about the plan.

-Calm down Jen, don't forget, it's just to make Lisa jealous.

Even though that was the initial idea, no, Rose couldn't deny that there was a second, dark intention, but of course the brunette didn't have to know that.

The Australian's eyes traveled to the feline's reddened lips, feeling her cheeks burn. Kiss Jennie? *Come on Roseanne, this is no time to be passive*. Shyness took over her, preventing her from taking control of the situation.

Little by little he approached Jennie, he could perceive the brunette's nerves in her gaze and her actions, it is typical for psychologists to read people's physical behavior.

-Chae, I don't think that...

-Jen, it's just a kiss. Don't think about anything else.

The brunette was startled when she felt the touch of their opposite lips. They felt very different from Lisa's, they were thinner, even the taste was different, as was the way they felt on her own. Lisa was delicate but dominant, Rose was tender and compassionate, Lisa's lips sought to coax, Rose's was simple acceptance. But it was not unpleasant, they were certainly lips she could get used to kissing.

Rose on the other hand couldn't help but sigh. She could finally feel the softness of the brunette on her lips, Jennie had evidently gained experience with so much kissing with Lisa but she allowed the Australian to take control.

Falling in love with Jennie had been a mistake, kissing her was certainly another mistake. The Judas kiss had been her doom, and even more so for the main reason for the kiss. *I love you Jennie Kim, but I must accept that you will never feel the same way about me.* And although that detail hurt her, it was going to help her open her friend's eyes. *Jennie was never mine, and she never will be.*

As they parted, he looked into the brunette's eyes and knew it. Jennie was madly in love, but with Lalisa Manoban

-Hey, don't cry.

The feline eyes were filled with tears. Jennie's broken expression broke the Australian's heart, making her doubt her plan.

- I betrayed Lisa...

-Hey No, this wasn't...

But before she could complete the sentence, a strong blow to her jaw made her fall to the ground, disoriented and in pain.

-What the...?

- Don't you ever kiss Jennie again! - the Thai girl growled, ignoring the pain in her knuckles. Her drunken and angry state didn't let her think sensibly. She turned to Jennie and held her close to her body, surprising the brunette - as for you, understand that you are mine and that only I can kiss you!

She was about to join her lips with the brunette when a tug of her hair pulled her away from her destination, hitting her against a nearby table.

- Jisoo!!!

The black-haired girl was panting with anger, and she looked angrily at the Thai girl who was looking at the blood on her hand. The table had hit her nose.

-That's for hitting Rose!- she turned to Jennie and before her sister could act she slapped her that made her head spin- And that's for kissing Rose! What's wrong with you!? I thought you were my sister! I trusted you!!!

Jennie looked at the blonde with bangs on the floor and when she noticed the blood dripping from her nose, her animal and protective side came back to her, glaring at her sister.

Jisoo spun in place like a top at the brunette's counterattack slap.

- Don't hit Lisa again!

They both glared at each other, challenging each other. Their feline blood drove them wild, and between growls and snorts, both women pounced on each other, starting a catfight.

-Jennie, stop it!- Lisa asked, covering her nose.

- Jisoo, don't hurt Jennie, dammit! - Rose screamed, rubbing the bruise on her cheek. She turned to Lisa noticing the drip of blood from her nose - This is all your fucking fault!

-My fault!? It's your fault!- Lisa clenched her fists tightly- You weren't supposed to kiss Jennie in the first place!!!

-And you weren't supposed to flirt with Irene!

-I was dancing!!!

They both looked at each other reproachfully and finally ended up in the same way as the women, fighting each other in a primitive way in a vain attempt to solve the situation by blows.

-Oush, I'll defend Lisa! Don't let a psychologist hit you!!!

"Mintty, aren't we supposed to be separating them?" Seulgi asked, arching an eyebrow.

- That's it Chae, you almost got her, hit her in the ribs, that's her weak spot!!! Damn it Jen, dig your claws in, show her which cat is boss!

Seulgi and Mintty looked at the youngest in surprise.

-Mina, aren't you supposed to help your sister?

-Bah, he deserves it. I support Jenlisa, but after that kiss I think Chaennie is real

-Am I the only one getting excited watching that quartet fight, or does it happen to you too?

Mina and Mintty looked at Seulgi fanning herself, her lower lip between her teeth.

The youngest of the three Thai girls made a face.

- That only happens to you and your sick mind Seu

- You need a girlfriend - Mintty said amused.

-Or just sex- added Mina, holding back her laughter.

-But what the hell is going on here!?- everyone turned around when they heard the altered voice of Lisa's assistant, who looked at the scene in panic.

-Oh, we're watching the fight from the front row, are you joining us?

-What?- Irene looked at them with a frown, not understanding the blonde's response.

-Who are you going for, Chaennie or Lisoo? - Mintty asked.

-Jenlisa is destroying, Chae is terrible at fighting and Jisoo doesn't even know how to hit... or wait, I think she already learned!- Seulgi smiled big as she saw Chu respond to the attack

- Don't just stand there, damn it, do something, you're going to kill Lisa!! - They all turned ironically to look at the Korean girl who quickly cleared her throat, regaining her composure - I mean, my boss, Lisa, can't go to work like that.

Seulgi's expression changed and no one knew when she climbed onto the makeshift stage and grabbed the microphone without warning.

-Chaeyong Park, if you leave Manoban alive, I will rip your head off myself!- the Thai woman's threat was heard furiously through the speakers.

Yin Yang

- Oh God, everything hurts...

-Shut up Lisa, this is your fault

-Ouch, Mina, and be careful, damn it!

Her sister treated her wounds without much care, as punishment for what happened. After the boxing ring, the Thai trio took charge of separating them. Lisa had bruises all over, and her nose was bleeding, Jennie had earned scratches and slaps from Jisoo, who did receive a little more aggression from her sister. Chaeyong, on the other hand, was the most attacked of the four.

-You asked for it. I don't want to even think about how poor Rose must be.

-She asked for it too!

Mina rolled her eyes and grabbed her bag.

-Here, mom sent this to you.

"What is it?" Lisa inspected the black velvet box her sister had just handed her.

-No idea- she handed her a small key- he ordered me not to open it. You know how it is- Mina put aside the cotton and alcohol and sat down next to her sister- by the way, how are things with Jennie?

Lisa snorted. After what happened, Jennie had gone with Seulgi to the hotel.

-She's mad at me for hitting Rose and...

The phone started ringing, silencing her instantly. As she picked it up, her eyes widened.

-Shit!

-What's going on? Don't tell me Chae wants a rematch.

-It's mom

-Double Shit!- Mina jumped up and tried to arrange everything as best she could, while Lisa arranged the sofa

-Throw that behind the couch!

-Lisa, the soda cans!

They both moved from one side to the other. Their mother was very strict with the mess in the house and those two were anything but tidy.

-Looks good. Now... Triple Shit!!

-Stop saying that Mina!

-Have you seen your face, Lalisa? You look disgusting!

-Fuck!

-Wait, I have an idea, where is your makeup?

Mina brushed her foundation here and there. More blush, layers and layers of foundation and she was ready.

Lisa accepted the call and they both gulped as they saw their mother's glare on the screen.

-Mina and Lalisa Manoban, what was so important that you kept your mother waiting all this...!? Pampriya, what the hell is wrong with you!

Lisa looked at her sister and picked up a hand mirror. Looking at her reflection, she almost screamed in horror.

-Mine!!!

Her face was the most similar to that of a clown, except for the red nose, her sister had put so many layers of foundation and powder on it that it had become whiter than it already was.

-I was practicing makeup

-Mina, you don't like makeup, since when are you interested in it? Are you dating someone!?- she exclaimed surprised- Marcos, your daughter is seeing someone on the sly!

-Mom, it's not true! - the girl's cheeks reddened - Lisa asked me to put makeup on her, she's going on a date with Jennie

-What!?- the named one turned to look at her sister with reproach

- Oh my God, what joy! - she looked sideways and smiled excitedly - Marcos, did you hear? Your daughter is going on a date!

-Woman, I'm sitting next to you, I heard clearly

Lisa looked at her sister with her eyes. She hated that she used her to avoid being the center of attention of her parents and in exchange it was Lisa who had to put up with the lectures.

-I knew you would leave your cowardice behind and say yes to that girl! - added her mother, full of happiness.

-No, I... wait, what?

- I'm sorry honey, you're so slow sometimes. Did Mina give you my present?

-A few minutes ago- said the youngest of the sisters

Lisa took the box again and turned it over in her hand curiously.

-What is it?

- You won't know until you open it

Lisa took the small key and opened the lock. She was surprised to see a part of the yin-yang amulet inside the box. A piece of polished tourmaline in the shape of a teardrop. But what surprised her most was the meaning of the amulet.

-This is... ?

-It was my father's and it passed to your father. Now it belongs to you.

Lisa turned the charm over in her hand. But she still didn't understand. She clearly remembered that amulet, her father always wore it around his neck, but she also remembered that her mother used a similar one.

-If I have the yang...

- Yin and yang are a balance, darling, together they complement and balance each other. I don't think it will be hard for you to guess who has your yin.

The Thai woman clenched the amulet in her fist and sighed.

-Jennie...

◇◇🐱◇◇

Take good care of your yang

Jennie reread the card that came with the pink velvet box without understanding the meaning.

-What is a yang?

-Just open it Jennie, I'm intrigued by that mysterious box- Mintty investigated it, full of curiosity.

-Wait, what if it's a bomb!?- Seu intervened cautiously.

The brunette widened her eyes in fright, ready to throw the box.

- I don't think it's a...

An alarm sound startled the three girls and without waiting Jennie threw the box out the window and ran to hide behind the bed. Both girls looked at the window and then at the brunette, surprised by the action.

-But why did you throw it!?- Mintty exclaimed, pressing a button on her cell phone which turned out to be the cause of the sound- They were just calling me

"I think he likes to throw things out of windows," Seulgi commented, remembering what Lisa had told them about her trip to Bangkok.

-I'll go get the fucking box

After retrieving the box and apologizing to the man who had knocked the object over, Mintty set it down on the table, looking at the brunette who was still hesitant to open it.

-Jen, Chitthip sent it to you, I don't think she's capable of sending a bomb- Mintty tried to calm her down.

-Speak for yourself, a rat sent me!

-It was a hamster and....

- Oh, in that case I'll open it! - Jennie began to open the present, licking her lips. She was not a big fan of rodents, but she was a little hungry. She was confused to see a small rose quartz pendant inside, resembling its opposite half.

- A rock? - he said, looking closely at the gift - in the shape of a fang...

-From a drop, and it's not just a rock, it's an amulet Jen
-And what am I supposed to do with it?
-To start...- Seulgi took the pendant and carefully placed it on the brunette's neck- you must use it
-Because?
-Oh well, I think this will answer your question- Min replied, taking out a paper from inside the box.

Jennie took it with curiosity and soon read the fine handwriting of Lisa's mother.

You and Lisa are the embodiment of the amulet, two opposite poles that tend to attract each other. As different as water and oil, but together they form something spectacular.

-Since when did water and oil make something spectacular?
-Mintty!- Seulgi scolded her.

Jennie delicately caressed the pendant on her neck. Only one part of the letter had captured her full attention. *Lisa has the other half.*

Moving

Elsewhere in Seoul, a Korean feline kept screaming with every touch of alcohol on her fur.

-I want you once and for all, Kim Jisoo!

-Never!

Rose had been trying to heal her wounds with difficulty, the brunette was resisting and the Australian was beginning to lose patience.

- I give up! - he threw the cotton on the ground roughly - You can keep your damn bruises as far as I'm concerned, I don't care. That's what you get for hitting your sister!

- Have you noticed how I am? I barely managed to scratch that little cat!

- I would tell you that that is not the correct expression but cats are as slutty as a promiscuous woman herself.

Jisoo looked offended at the psychologist's comment.

-Are you calling me promiscuous!?- she tilted her head in confusion- what's a whore?

-A person who fucks with many people, without shame. Like you!

- I!?

- Don't act like an idiot, you almost fucked my sisters right under my nose!

-It's not my fault they look like you! You shouldn't have kissed my sister!

-I shouldn't have kissed you either!

Rose was red with anger. She could no longer control her anger with the Korean girl and even more so after the shameless flirting she had with her sisters.

Jisoo clenched her fists tightly and denied.

-Well, I regret it too! - she ran to the room and took out a briefcase. She was hurt by the Australian's rejection and could no longer accept it.

-What the hell are you doing with my suitcase?

-I left!- he said, striding towards the kitchen.

Rose frowned

-Kim Jisoo, get those wings out of your luggage, it's going to stink of fried chicken!

Jisoo ignored the complaint and struggled to stuff the bucket of chicken inside, along with a bottle of ketchup.

-You just lost all this! - she pointed at herself dramatically - Don't come back to me begging for forgiveness! This cat is already gone!

And without waiting for an answer, he left the apartment. Rose didn't have time to react when two knocks on the door announced a visitor. She frowned and turned to look at the two women who had watched the scene from the comfort of the sofa.

-Jisoo?- she asked confused and overwhelmed when she saw the Korean girl in front of her door again.

- It's raining...- he whispered with his eyes downcast

Rose looked out the window. It was indeed pouring rain, and her little knowledge of cats had taught her that they hated rain.

-I see it...

The feline pouted in pain

- Will you take me?

The Australian snorted, taking her keys in indignation and heading for the exit.

-You should know that when you break up with someone you can't ask them for a ride shortly after.

-I know that, but technically you and I are not a couple, so it's valid!

Rose thought about it for a moment and nodded.

-Touche. Come on, before the weather gets worse, do you know where you plan to stay?

-Obviously, what kind of cat do you think I am!?

-For a very careless Kim Jisoo, very careless...

Dudu and rabbit saw the door close and exchanged glances, as if they were thinking the same thing.

-Do you think Jisoo and her...?

- Jisoo is very obvious bunny, she says Rose's name while asleep

-It also says sleeping chicken

-Exactly, and there is nothing that Chu loves more than chicken.

The rabbit widened her eyes in surprise.

- Are you in love with Rose?

- The question is... Is Rose in love with Jisoo?

◊◊🐱◊◊

-I already told you Lisa, it was the only thing I thought about.

-Look at my face Mina, I've washed it three times and still all the makeup hasn't come off, and on top of all that you...!- the doorbell silenced her. She looked at her sister, pointing at her reproachfully. -You're not going to get away with this, shorty.

Lisa walked to the entrance and when she opened it she was surprised to find a more than furious Rose and next to her Jisoo with luggage in hand.

-But what...?

-Well, thanks for the encouragement!

-Hitchhiking- the psychologist corrected her, rolling her eyes.

-Whatever, Limario, make me something to eat

-It was nice to see you Chu...- the dancer said ironically as she watched her pass by.

- Jisoo! - the one already mentioned corrected her, already inside, checking the refrigerator.

Lisa turned towards the entrance where Rose was still in her place. Both looked at each other with suspicion at what had happened. She felt bad when she saw that the Australian was indeed in worse condition than her, her eye was almost black and her lip was split in half.

-Rose I...

-Shut up Lalisa

-Hey Rosita!- Mina appeared just in time to cut the attention between the two friends. The aforementioned gave a smile to the younger Thai girl

- What are you doing here? I thought you'd be at the hotel.

-That's what I was getting at. Can I have a ride too?

-Of course, I hope you don't mind the smell of fried chicken in the car. Someone decided to open a suitcase full of chicken wings in the back seat.

-I was hungry! I didn't know he would turn around!

Rose rolled her eyes. She turned her attention back to the younger girl, who had already gathered her things, ready to leave.

◇◇🐱◇◇

-Be careful, it's behind you!!!

-Jisoo, stop it, it's a movie, they can't hear you!

-Look, he turned around! Do you see Cripple? Yes, he heard me.

Lisa rolled her eyes. Watching horror movies with Jisoo wasn't the best decision, she was definitely not her Nini. She sighed. *What is Jennie doing?*

◇◇🐱◇◇

On the way to the hotel Rose remained silent, attentive to the traffic. Mina looked at the psychologist's bruised profile, compassionate.

-I'm sorry about Lisa

-Mini, Lalisa Manoban is the clumsiest person on the planet, but she's also the best person I know. It's just that from time to time she gets stupid- he shrugged, parking the car and looked at the Thai girl next to him- Lisa is my best friend, and this...- he pointed at his face with an amused grimace- is nothing compared to the beating she gave me months ago.

-Jennie has made her a little aggressive

Rose shook her head in disapproval

-Protective and possessive- he corrected- But that's okay, it means she cares.

They both remained silent for a minute, thinking about those words. They both knew how difficult it was for Lisa to accept something like that.

-Do you think I'll finally get over...?

-Yerin left a very big mark on Lisa, but Jennie is creating an even bigger one... as much as Lalisa Manoban denies it, she is more than hooked on her cat.

- How ironic, my sister is in love with her cat

- But there is something that worries me, Tzuyu's return can't mean anything good.

Ghost?

After a while, Rose had decided to stay with the girls. Jennie insisted that she spend the night there and Seulgi convinced her to do so.

-Truth or dare?

A girls' night out could not be without a little alcohol and dare games to complement it. Each of them had already had their drinks and seemed more active than they had all night. Jennie burst out laughing when she saw Mina's cheeks turn red when her dare was to kiss Mintty and in the end she ended up drinking the remaining drink of all of them.

- Lisa is going to kill us for getting her younger sister drunk- Seu commented upon seeing the younger one.

- Lisa is already going to kill us for getting her girlfriend drunk.

They all turned to Jennie, the girl was laughing and saying things incoherently.

-Ok Park, it's your turn to answer

Rose took a sip of her drink and decided on the truth. Mintty and Seulgi exchanged conspiratorial glances and knowing smiles. There was one question they were dying to find out.

- Do you like Jisoo?

-What!? What kind of question is that!?

 -Come on Rose, that girl is beautiful- Mintty encouraged her.

 -And he doesn't look bad- said Seulgi

 -And it seems that he likes you- Mina concluded.

The Australian girl's cheeks were tinged with red and she could barely breathe. There were few times when she managed to get embarrassed by something and this was one of them. She swallowed nervously and shook her head at her friends' question.

-Of course not! How do you think I can like that chicken with legs!? Jisoo is the most unbearable, hateful, desperate being...!

-And yet you like it- Mintty cut her off.

-Come to think of it, Jisoo is an excellent match- Mina commented thoughtfully- and my sister... well, I don't like incest, but Lalisa is hot- she clicked her tongue- and both of them alone, at this time of night and in a huff...

"What is Mini Lisa implying?" Rose asked her with her eyes half closed.

The Thai girl with bangs shrugged, dismissing it as unimportant. Was the alcohol in the psychologist's system really so much that it clouded her analytical ability to deduce her intentions? Whatever the reason, she didn't plan on wasting it.

-I mean, both humiliated by the Chaennie's hot kiss...- Mina continued- who knows what they must be doing right now

- Jisoo never...- Jennie paused and after exchanging a look with Rose they both stood up heading towards the entrance- Do you have the keys?

- Don't forget your shoes

-Hey, where are you going?

-If Lalisa Manoban touches a single hair of that chicken-eater, you'll lose your sister! - Rose threatened before slamming the door.

-Great Mina, you looked for your sister's funeral- Mintty said sarcastically

- Oh No, now comes the Chaesoo and the Jenlisa

- Wasn't the boxing ring enough? You want those four to disfigure their faces?

-Ireneeee!!!

They both turned towards where the screams came from, where Seulgi, already fueled by alcohol, began to whine about her friend's assistant.

-We have to work on the Seulrene too

- With how insistent Seulgi is on Lisa's assistant, I think it's going to take us a long time to convince poor Irene.

◇◇🐱◇◇

-Leisaaa!

Lisa snorted heavily. She dried her hands and mentally tried to stop herself as she walked out of the bathroom wrapped only in a small but acceptable towel. When she reached the kitchen she frowned, looking at the mess in her kitchen.

-What the hell are you doing...?

-Hey, come here!

Jisoo ran to the radio and turned on the song Ghost, quickly standing next to the counter where there was a mess of naked and poorly compacted dough.

-Manoban, you have to get behind me!

-What? Why?

The first one snorted, punching the mass.

- Didn't you pay attention to the movie? It's romantic!

Lisa rolled her eyes. They had just finished watching "Ghots" and Jisoo seemed to insist on imitating the scene.

- Jisoo, first of all Moly worked with clay not flour, and second... Do you know that they end up fucking afterwards?

Jisoo gave the blonde a look and bit her lip. Why not? *Fuck it*. Her heat wasn't letting her think clearly. One of the things about women is that as long as they aren't "stepped on" by a cat, their heat can come back almost shortly after it's gone, which was happening with Jisoo. Lisa noticed the feline's lascivious gaze on her bare legs and instinctively sought refuge behind the first thing she found.

The Korean rolled her eyes

- That chair doesn't cover you, Manoban. What are you afraid of?

-To you

Jisoo stood in front of her and slapped her, leaving the taller girl confused and with a stinging cheek.

-Wake up Lisa, Jennie is with Rose now, And..! Oooh!!

The blonde had hit him back, full of anger. Not because of the blow, but because of what he had just insinuated.

- It's not true, Jennie is not with that idiot Rose!

Another blow from the feline

-Yeah!

- No

-Yeah!!

Each affirmation and denial was accompanied by a new spanking. Lisa refused to accept the feline's theory, and Jisoo simply continued to take out her anger on the Thai girl's cheek.

-Okay, that's enough! - Lisa stopped the Korean's hand.

-Hey, it was my turn!

-I think we already have enough bruises without making more.

There was a moment of silence. Jisoo stared at the Thai girl and Lisa imitated her action. Why was she looking at her like that?

-What big eyes you have...- whispered Jisoo looking at the Thai girl's honey-colored orbs- and such pale skin...- he caressed her cheek, surprising the Thai girl with his action- has your bangs always looked so good?

- Jisoo, what are you doing? - the Thai girl asked, uncomfortable with the Korean girl's touch on her hair.

The feline ignored the question and lowered her gaze to Lisa's blushing lips.

-So thick... So kissable...

Jisoo's fingers slid up to the Thai girl's bottom lip. She definitely liked the Australian girl's better.

-I think we should kiss...

Lisa widened her eyes, and before she could refuse, Jisoo's lips collided with hers. The Thai girl wrinkled her nose. The feline's lips were greasy from the chicken. She heard a sound in the room but it was impossible for her to separate herself from the Korean girl, who held her firmly.

- Lisa, where...? Lalisa Manoban!

That voice... *Shit* . Lisa pushed Jisoo as best she could. In front of them was Rose with her fists clenched and Jennie about to kill her sister.

-Jen what...?

But it was Rose who silenced her, landing her fist on the Thai girl's left eye.

-I'm going to kill you Lalisa!

-Rose, wait!- the brunette tried to stop her.

But the psychologist turned a deaf ear and climbed on top of the Thai girl, ready to attack again.

-Fuck, they're going to leave me without a sister! - Mina ran into the kitchen with Mintty to separate both girls. Seulgi, on the other hand, was trying not to hit the walls, her state of drunkenness had reached its peak.

-What the fuck!?- Lisa brought a hand to her eye and looked at Rose who was held by Mina and Mintty by each arm- Rose? Why the fuck did you hit me and...?

-Bae, is that you?

Lisa wrinkled her face in confusion, her gaze fixed on the owner of that voice.

-Why does Seulgi talk to the stove as if it were my assistant?

"Who knows, maybe because of how hot she is," Mintty joked, earning a reproachful look from Lisa's younger sister.

-What happened now?- Mintty tried to find out, tired of so much drama.

-He fucked Jisoo!- Rose assured angrily, struggling to free herself from the grip of both Thai girls.

-What!?- even his swollen eye opened wide at the Australian's statement

- Are you serious Lisa, In the kitchen?
- Did you fuck her in the kitchen too!? - Jennie interfered indignantly.

-What do you mean, too?- Rose looked at her curiously.

-Why the hell do you think I should fuck her?

-Look at this mess!- Rose pointed around- Don't deny it Manoban!

-What? Ask Jisoo!

They all turned to look at the Korean girl. Jisoo had a finger on her lips, her eyes closed and a silly smile. Rose, noticing this, was quick to pounce on the dancer again.

-Jen, and you don't think about attacking...? Jennie?

-And now where the hell has she gone now?- Mintty snorted, looking for the aforementioned with her gaze- Seulgi, stop kissing the fridge!

-Remind me to never let her drink- Mina asked, rolling her eyes. Her sister's friends were a mess.

-Irene, why are you giving me the silent treatment? - he whined to the refrigerator.

-Done- Mintty promised when she saw her friend's lack of sanity thanks to the liquor.

Mysterious Girl

Jennie ran as fast as she could in an attempt to flee the scene. The streets of Seoul were dark and deserted.

-Damn Lisa!- she screamed hurt- I hate you!

Gasping, she stopped in a park. Unfortunately, it was the place where she had first seen Lisa. Why did she always end up there when she tried to get away from her? She dropped onto the bench, still sobbing. It didn't matter, no one was going to hear her.

However, he did not count on the fact that his sobs actually reached someone's ears.

-Mom used to say that crying is for cowards.

The voice was delicate, with a sweet tone like the one Rose used when talking to her, but for some reason that voice did not calm her down, but rather the opposite.

She glanced sideways at a young woman sitting next to her on the bench. In her hands was a worn book, which she assumed she had reread countless times.

-I also said that young ladies don't go out at night- a smug smile appeared on her lips giving her an attractive and mysterious air- But here I am, and here you are, and without a doubt we both are... or at least that's what it seems to me- she turned to look at her companion and only then Jennie could glimpse the girl's face. She was beautiful, without a doubt she was, with a notable elegance- why are you here?

-I... - the memory of Lisa kissing her sister made her eyes glaze over.

-What's your name, honey?

-J-Jennie...Kim

-Nice name, tell me one thing Jennie Kim, is it because of someone that you are like this, right?... What happened to him?

Jennie blinked and shook her head.

-N-no, she...

- Oh, a girl. I understand...- he shifted a little and forced a smile- tell me what happened?

Jennie didn't like strangers too much, especially there was something about that human that didn't give her confidence, but she needed to let off steam.

-She kissed my sister

The girl raised an eyebrow with a hint of surprise.

-With your sister? That's not good... and what's her name?

-Lili...- he shook his head and quickly corrected himself- Lalisa... Lalisa Manoban

The girl clenched her fists and looked ahead, nodding a couple of times slowly.

-Lalisa Manoban...- she whispered thoughtfully. She closed her eyes and said- I think you should talk to her, maybe it's a misunderstanding... I can sense that that girl is not of that kind

-Lisa? Oh no! Lili is great, but she's always surrounded by...

- Bitches? - the girl said with a mocking smile.

-And cats too!

The girl laughed amused. She looked at the time on her phone and sighed.

-I think it's time for me to go. It was nice talking to you Jennie Kim- he stood up and cleaned his jeans before starting to leave- and try to make things right with Lisa

- I will erm...

- Yiren Wang

Jennie watched the girl smile widely and walk away.

-Maybe you're right- the feline stood up ready to return to the Thai woman's apartment, in the end it turned out that running into that stranger had been a good idea.

◇◇🐱◇◇

-Fuck
-Shut up Lisa... he'll be back.

-Mina, you didn't see his face

-You don't either Lisa, so don't be so dramatic- Rose rolled her eyes. She was still angry with her friend but her psychologist side made her keep control, even though inside she wanted to hit her again- Jennie is very sensitive, she needs time to assimilate that the stupid girl she likes kissed her sister- she said those words with contained anger

-What? Chaeyong you are an idiot, it was your fucking sister who kissed me!

-Don't insult Jisoo, she's an idiot, she does things without thinking!- Rose defended her.

-Of course, I shouldn't offend her, but you can, right?

-Live with me, I have the right!

-Vivia

-Shut up Jisoo!- Rose growled giving him a furious look

-I'm starving and no one has fed me!- Jisoo complained, throwing herself on the couch dramatically.

-You're not an invalid Kim Jisoo, go and cook something!- Rose ordered

-No way, I don't want my apartment to burn down! - Lisa stopped her, remembering the flour disaster.

As the three of them argued, Mina grabbed her coat and keys ready to leave. Seulgi had been overcome by the alcohol and was now snoring on the couch. Mintty instead noticed her intentions and hurried to follow her.

-Four eyes can search better than two- he assured her with a wink, making the younger girl smile shyly.

There was no need to even respond. A couple of scratches on the door startled them both, while Seulgi woke up upon hearing the scream of the black feline.

-It's the doll. I told you it was real!- Jisoo exclaimed, perched on Lisa, in panic.

-What the hell are you talking about?- Lisa asked without understanding- Get off of me!

-From the doll in the movie!

-Are you serious Lisa, you made her watch Annabelle!?

-Would you rather I watched one of your fucking porn movies?

-I don't...!

-Enough, you two! You're too immature- Mina growled as she walked towards the door- I'll go find Jennie on my own, you can join us when you stop acting like a couple of kids-. As she opened the door, she smiled at the sad face of the Korean girl- Hey Jen!

-Jennie!?- Rose and Lisa asked in unison and then glared at each other.

The girl walked in timidly and stopped in front of Lisa, who immediately lowered her gaze. She was covered in bruises, but she felt bad seeing her Nini depressed because of her.

-I don't...

-Why did you kiss her, Lisa?

-It was Jisoo, I...!

The slap resounded in the room. Leaving everyone in shock. Lisa didn't have time to react when Jennie grabbed her by the neck and pulled her closer with her hands.

-You are mine Manoban, and only I can kiss you!

They all looked surprised as the brunette furiously kissed Lisa and the Thai girl, who, still amazed, tried to follow the kiss as best she could.

-That's it sister-in-law, show her who's boss! - Mina encouraged her amidst cheers

"Aren't you supposed to have argued?" Mintty asked confused.

-Damn, my head... what did I miss?- Seulgi's hoarse voice was heard from the sofa

Mintty and Mina turned to see the third Thai girl with disheveled hair and a sleepy face, the alcohol had clearly left her system.

Truths (Chaesoo)

Rose opened the door to her apartment and threw her bag away without giving it any importance. She was still angry, although she didn't understand the reason. Jisoo closed the door and followed her closely with her luggage in hand. It was enough for the Australian to give her a murderous look for Jisoo to pick up her things and leave with her.

-Let this be the last time you run to Lisa's fucking house when she argues with me Kim Jisoo!!!- the blonde growled, striding towards her room, dodging Dudu on the way, who was looking at her alertly- don't look at me like that, he deserves it!- she entered her room and slammed the door.

Jisoo remained in place. Rose's attitude was unusual, why was she so angry? She pouted and left her briefcase aside.

-And what will you do?

She looked down at the ground, the Russian blue was staring at her waiting for an answer.

-She's angry with me.

- Oh, really? If you hadn't told me, I wouldn't have noticed- he said ironically, walking around her with his tail curled up- What did you do to put her in such a mood?

-Nothing! I kissed Luisa and...

-Who is Luisa?

- You know, Manobal

-What did you do? What!?

They both jumped at the accusing voice of the rabbit, who appeared in the hallway at that very moment.

-God cat, don't get scared like that again!- Dudu snorted throwing himself at Jisoo's feet

-How could you kiss that female Jennie!?

-She kissed my female! I marked the squirrel! She belongs to me!

-So that's why Rose smelled like urine the other day- Dudu commented thoughtfully, wrinkling his snout - how disgusting human urine is

-Honey, ours smells like ammonia.

-Ok, stop talking about urine!- Chu interrupted- The thing is, Jennie kissed Rose first, she kissed her!

-You shouldn't have kissed Lisa

-Come on, bunny, Jennie shouldn't have kissed Rose either- reproached Dudu

-Oh, now it turns out that you defend Lisoo?

-You're on Chaennie's side!

-What!? No! I'm for Jenlisa!!!

Jisoo didn't understand that dialect anymore, lately everyone was addressing them with those strange nicknames. *Although Lisoo doesn't sound bad at all.* She thought about that new nickname, until now she hadn't heard it. She looked towards the hallway and decided to go to the Australian girl while her friends continued to debate which shipp sounded better.

- The Jenlisa is real!

-But Lisoo is better!

-Dudu, do you want to sleep on the roof tonight? - threatened the Japanese bobtail, narrowing her cat eyes.

-You're right, Jenlisa is better!

Jisoo stopped hearing her friends when she reached the hallway. She didn't even knock on the door since she never did. When she entered, she was surprised to see Rose standing by the window.

-Hey squirrel, are you okay?

- I am...

His voice sounded dull and without much spirit, but Jisoo couldn't be sure if it was true since his back was turned.

-Seriously, you're not upset about...?

-Jisoo, leave me alone

The Korean turned a deaf ear and walked up behind her. Rose was a little taller, but that didn't bother her. *I like them big.* She looked at the Australian's long, straight hair and for a moment noticed the irony of the situation. Months ago she had made fun of her sister for falling in love with a human and at that moment there was no feline on earth that could compare to the woman in front of her.

-Squirrel...

-That?

- Can I have a chick?

And that question activated the Australian's anger neurons. Rose turned around abruptly, revealing her true appearance.

-Are you only thinking about that fucking chicken Kim Jisoo!?

Her eyes were red, and tears were running down her chin. Her gaze was broken and I could see how sad she was.

-Rose... are you... crying?- she asked doubtfully and astonished, it was the first time she had seen the psychologist in that condition.

-Of course not, animal, my eyes rinse themselves! - she said ironically between sobs - It's a fucking eye wash!

- Oh, how clever! - Jisoo said in admiration.

Rose glared at her, roughly wiping her tears away with the back of her hand.

-Of course I'm crying Jisoo, you're an idiot!- she ran to the bed and dropped down, covering her face with one of the large pillows.

Jisoo looked at her for a moment. She could clearly hear her crying, but as a feline she still didn't understand human behavior. Why was she crying? Out of anger or pain? She never understood things with the Australian.

-Rose...

-Leave me alone!

-If you're not going to chick me, at least tell me why you're crying!?

Rose let out a growl before standing up. Her eyes were blazing, and Jisoo regretted asking that question.

-Why am I crying!? Because I'm an idiot, that's why!- she exclaimed upset, running a hand through her hair with concern and anger- Of all the women in Korea, of all the women on the fucking planet, I came to fall in love with a fucking cat! And on top of that, she's in love with that idiot Lisa!!!

Jisoo clenched her fists, puffing out her cheeks.

-Are you in love with Nini!?

Rose looked at her quickly at that question.

-That?

-You said that...

-I'm talking about you Kim Jisoo! God, you're such an idiot, and yet I still fucking like you!- she brought a hand to her face- Was Lisa right, I've gone crazy like all my patients!

Jisoo smiled widely, then burst out laughing shortly after.

That made the psychologist angry.

-And on top of everything you make fun of me!? Go to hell, you promiscuous cat!

-First of all, I forgot that the hell she's promiscuous- she shrugged her shoulders without stopping smiling- and of course I'm not in love with Lisa, how do you think!?

-But you kissed her...

-And you, my sister- he replied angrily- I'm not going to lie to you, that lanky girl has great lips, and an abdomen that...

-Kim Jisoo!

-But I'm not interested in Laisa, why would I be interested in another woman when I have you?

Rose's cheeks flushed and her shoulders relaxed at those words. But her psychologist side put her on alert.

-If you're trying to use flirting games to make me fall in love, you're very...!

But Jisoo was faster and her lips were already on the Australian's long before she let her finish. She had been watching movies and researching on the Australian's laptop how to properly kiss a human, so her kisses must have definitely improved.

As Rose parted, she sighed before opening her eyes.

-This is very accurate- he finished the sentence before throwing himself on top of the feline and resuming the kiss.

.
.
.
.
.

. I'm your cat (Chaesoo)

The kisses were becoming more and more necessary. *Where had this badass cat learned to kiss so well?* Between kisses, they both became more rough. Rose almost cried when she saw her shirt torn to shreds on the floor thanks to Jisoo's rudeness.

-What the hell, it was a brand name!

But she remained silent when she saw that Jisoo was in the same condition. She swallowed hard. Her clitoris was beginning to throb, demanding the Korean's raw attention. The rest of the clothes were soon gone, both were excited, and they weren't planning on stopping there. Jisoo tried to carry her, but strength was clearly not her thing and in the process she knocked the Australian down.

-But you can't do anything right!?

- Sorry, Si!?, I'm not in shape!

Rose rubbed her sore elbow and struggled back to her feet.

-Next time just tell me to lie down on the fucking bed- he growled taking a seat in the mentioned place.

Jisoo resumed kissing and relaxed when she noticed that the Australian was letting herself go again.

Jisoo's touch was clumsy and rough, especially when he squeezed her breasts, causing discomfort to the psychologist.

-Fuck, gently! Have you never touched a woman before!?- Rose rolled her eyes at the absurdity of his question- forget what I said

-I don't know what I'm doing, I've never had sex with anyone!

-How vulgar, it's fucking, taking is for animals- Rose looked at the girl on top of her. Jisoo looked nervous, but her gasps and dilated eyes confirmed that she was also excited- Jisoo..- he caressed her cheek sweetly, until now they had never had an affectionate approach, but the moment deserved it- Let me show you and then you try to imitate me, okay?

He rolled her over, placing her on top of the feline. His height made it easy for him to move her. With Jisoo underneath him, he was surprised at how good it felt to have the feline in that position. Jisoo was small, but her body was molded to fit under his perfectly. He sighed. The girl was beautiful.

He leaned down to kiss the Korean girl and at the last minute he changed places, kissing her neck and leaving the feline with her lips on a peak. He smiled when he saw how Jisoo's cheeks turned pink and his kiss descended until it reached between her breasts.

-Nice view- he whispered mischievously

-What!? Are you looking at the scenery while you kiss me?

-Obviously Chu

-Jisoo- the Korean corrected her instantly

-And I can assure you that there is no landscape that excites me more than the one below me- the Australian concluded with sensuality.

Rose shuddered at the first moan from the Korean girl as her mouth captured one of her delicate nipples. It was a thick moan, almost like an animal growl that made her wetter than immediately. *Fuck* . And it wasn't just her dominant cat moan, but also the texture of the feline's breasts in her mouth.

-Holy cats!

-You like it? This is... wait, what d

..? Oh shit!!! Wa-wait... aah, Jisoo!!!

The Korean didn't need any more instructions, her excitement reached its peak with that simple kiss on her nipples, and the strength she didn't have seemed to multiply by ten, since in a simple movement she made the Australian spin under her, and her mouth was already devouring both of the Australian's breasts, masterfully managing to get both nipples into her mouth.

-Mmm, Holy God, you're not a cat! You... oh shit!!!

-You're talking about the past, squirrel. Get on all fours, I'm going to show you how an animal fucks.

Was that Jisoo? He almost came at that thick, commanding voice. He didn't hesitate to obey, adopting the most sexually embarrassing position he knew.

-Jisoo, this is not... ahh!

Jisoo's tongue was already working wonders in the Australian's center, circling her clitoris with agility and then pulling on it with his teeth. Jisoo didn't know what it was like to make love. Her feline instinct was carnal and raw and the only thing on her mind was fucking the psychologist properly.

-Honey, you taste better than chicken and that's a new thing.

-Coming from you it must taste like heaven- Rose joked, biting her lip as she felt Jisoo's tongue in her folds once again- God Jisoo, right there

A spank made Rose collapse, and she screamed with pure pleasure when suddenly the delicate but demanding fingers of the Korean invaded her center.

- Oh, fucking mother!!!

-Who is my cat?

Rose frowned in disgust, still penetrated by the feline, and on all fours as the pose required.

-Don't even dream about it, I'm not going to say... Oh God!!

A moan of need left her throat as Jisoo began to move his fingers in and out in search of silence.

-Who is my cat!?- he asked again, dominant, without stopping penetrating the psychologist.

-ME! Ash... fuck... I'm your damn cat! - the Australian girl let out at full volume between desperate moans - aaahh...!! Mmm yes, exactly... oh my God!!

-And we're just getting started

In the hallway Dudu and the rabbit looked intently towards the room with a confused and terrified expression.

-What are you doing?- asked the rabbit, surprised.

-I think Chu is hitting her for kissing Jennie- the Russian blue explained.

The moans enveloped the whole place while both cats watched in the front row as the other two fucked.

- By the cats, look, Jisoo's paw is almost inside her!

-Rabbit, Chu's human legs are tiny, I'm surprised his fist isn't inside yet...

-Jisoo!!!!

- Oh look, I think it's all in!

Rose had just had her first orgasm, and boy was it explosive, her chest rising and falling wildly, while her vagina was still throbbing from the climax.

-Holy shit, you fuck amazing!- he admitted gasping for air- the best sex of my life!

Jisoo cleaned her fingers, sucking them one by one and finished by licking the entire palm of her hand. For her it was feline sex, but for Rose, who had observed all the protocol, it was the most erotic thing of all.

Without waiting he skillfully turned under the Korean

-Do you know what 69 is? - she asked mischievously, already in that position.

- Why is your face on me....? By all the demonic cats!

Rose slid her tongue along the feline's soaked vagina, earning a few moans from the older girl in return.

"We'll see who's cat is," Rose whispered, licking her lips.

Apparently, both of them seemed to be just warming up. By then Dudu and Rabbit had already drawn conclusions, and it certainly wasn't too bad a punishment that those two were giving each other.

Rabbit swallowed hard. Dudu licked her ear and between purrs whispered to her
-Do you want me to punish you too...?
-Are you going to screw up like Jisoo?
-Honey, I'll put everything in you that you want.
-How wild... that excites me...
-Mom, what are Aunt Jisoo and Rose doing?
Both cats jumped
-Moon, what are you still doing awake!?
Dudu grabbed her by the back with his snout to carry her back to the room.
-There was a lot of noise, I thought they were hurting Miss Rose and...
-No buts, go to bed!
.
.
.
.

. Manoban (Jenlisa)

Lisa left her things in the office, and huffed when she didn't see Irene in her respective place. She really needed her coffee.

After having spent the whole night awake because of her feline, the blonde needed something to keep her awake during work. She sighed as she sat back in her chair, rubbing her eyes. Jennie was insatiable with or without her heat and the poor Thai girl's body was starting to take its toll.

-It's a good thing her fingers are small, otherwise she would have been crippled already- she whispered to herself, feeling the discomfort in her crotch from overuse. She looked at the time. Where could her assistant be?

He stood up and decided to pay a little visit to the dance hall, he hadn't seen the boys dance for days.

When he arrived, he was surprised to not hear any music or see any students dancing. What was happening?

-Hey Wendy- he called to one of the students standing

The girl blushed and came to his call with her head down. That gesture made Lisa smile. She knew that more than one student, male and female, had a crush on her, but she also knew that it was something typical in teenagers.

-Good morning, Miss Manoban!

-Lisa- he corrected sweetly.

- L-lisa- the girl almost melted when she said her name

-What's wrong, why aren't you practicing?

-Well, Miss Momo is a bit... Well, see for yourself.

Wendy pointed to the place where Momo was seen angrily picking up a couple of things from the counter, muttering who knows what.

-Momo, what's wrong?

The girl widened her eyes when she saw her boss.

-Lisa! - he bowed in greeting - we weren't expecting you here today

-Is something wrong?

-I... no. It's just- he snorted- Have you seen who your assistant is hanging out with?

-Irene?- she asked confused- But he hasn't even arrived yet

-Well, I think so, in fact it is right there.

Lisa looked at the indicated spot. Indeed, the Korean girl was on one of the benches, laughing happily accompanied by a Seulgi in tights... tights? She snorted. Since when did Seulgi like to wear tights, and such short ones?

She walked up to both girls, feeling Momo's footsteps closely, who was more than interested in the interaction the Thai girl would have with that pair.

-What the hell are you doing here? - she said authoritatively, crossing her arms.

Irene stood up instantly, but Seulgi gestured for her to calm down.

-Hi Lis. Sorry, it was my fault.

-I already know that, that's why I ask you, what the hell are you doing in my agency distracting my employees?

-Lisie I... excuse me, Miss Manoban- he swallowed hard nervously- I... Seulgi... Well...

-Irene, is she the one you reject me for?- Momo stepped forward, catching the attention of the rest of the girls- Is she the one you like?

Irene blushed as she watched Lisa stare at her. She couldn't just say that she rejected her because of her attraction to her boss.

-I...

-And if that's so, what?- Seulgi stepped forward indignantly- Can't you see me, darling?- She pointed at her body to confirm what she had said.

-Clearly, that's why I don't understand why he saw you.

Seulgi opened her mouth in affront and clenched her fists, ready to fight back.

Lisa rolled her eyes and walked away from the scene, she wasn't going to be the middleman in this absurd jealousy dispute. She had had enough with Chu and the whole jealousy thing.

She returned to her office more tired than before. *Maybe she'll rest for a couple of hours on the couch. At least until Irene returns to her workplace.* However, that was the last thing she was going to do, since when she opened the door a smiling Korean woman looked at her radiantly from her place on the desk.

-Jennie?

-Lili...

Lisa checked the hallway before closing the door, and walked over to her feline. Jennie didn't usually visit her during work hours, let alone first thing in the morning, so her visit was completely unexpected.

-Hi Nini- he smiled happily giving her a kiss on the lips- what are you doing here?

- I was feeling lonely at home - she pouted childishly - and I went shopping.

Lisa smiled proudly, she had been guiding the feline to go to the mall and the supermarket, and especially how to make the purchases if she

-Great Nini! Can I see your first purchase?

- That's why I'm here Lili, I want to know what you think.

The Korean stood up and dropped the coat that had been covering her body until now. Lisa's eyes nearly popped out of their sockets when she saw what the feline was hiding under the coat. Thin, tiny red lingerie was the only thing covering her body, leaving her toned abdomen and shapely legs visible to the Thai girl.

-Jennie...

No matter how many times they made love, Lisa maintained her excitement as if it were the first time she saw that perfect body. And her vagina desperately announced her need to make Jennie hers.

-Lili- the feline cautiously climbed back onto the desk without taking her eyes off the dancer. Lisa in a suit was exciting, and even more so with those tight pants and matching tie- I need you

-Jen, I'm on work hours, I don't think... oh my god!

Jennie was certainly not going to take no for an answer and before Lisa could refuse, she spread her legs, revealing her tiny, soaked thong to the Thai girl.

- I want you inside Lili- he whispered with need, arching against her excitement.

-I thought your heat was over- he whispered approaching the Korean

-Lisa, my animal side is not the only one that desires you- he explained, playing with the Thai girl's tie- I desire you as a woman and as a cat, I desire you in every possible way, and right now I'm dying for you to stop making excuses and fuck me once and for all.

Lisa arched an eyebrow mischievously and stepped away from the Korean, leaving the girl confused.

-I think I've been very good to you, Jennie Kim- he explained as he loosened his tie and removed his buttons one by one with a flirtatious half smile- in return you've been a bad girl, and that's not right.

Jennie widened her eyes and quickly shook her head, afraid that she had disappointed the Thai girl.

- I'm sorry Lili, I didn't...!

But Lisa put a finger on her lips to silence her.

-No more Lili for today. I'm going to punish you for being bad.

-Lili I...

-Manoban- he corrected her while he spread her legs and smiled sideways again- and your punishment starts now

-I... Aaah, Lisa!!! - the Thai girl had descended without preamble to the feline's crotch and all she had to do was move her thong aside a little to start devouring her like never before - oh God Lili...

Hearing the nickname Lisa pulled away making her get off the table, and holding her neck as she moved even further away from her.

-If you call me Lili again I'll fuck you so hard you won't be able to walk for a month. Be obedient Kim and lean on the desk so I can see that cute ass of yours.

Jennie moaned, somewhat disoriented. Lisa had never done it so rudely before. But one detail that drove her crazy was the way the Thai woman held her neck. When felines are going to penetrate a female, they immobilize her right on the neck, which is as exciting for them as stimulating a woman's clitoris.

Jennie obediently turned around, exposing her ass to the dancer. She was aroused and the moisture on her thighs confirmed it. As a feline, she loved animal sex and this pose was the closest to feline mating. What she didn't expect was that Lisa was more than prepared for the occasion.

-You know, it wasn't nice of you to show up like that in my office during work hours- she continued after delighting in the view. She walked over to her purse and opened a shopping bag next to it- I had something interesting planned for tonight Jennie, but since you're here I think it's best to put it to the test.

Jennie heard the Thai woman open a plastic wrapper and arrange something with metal and straps. What the hell was she doing? She tried to turn around, but a hand on her neck prevented her from doing so.

-Quiet, kitty- Lisa whispered in her ear and then sensually licked her earlobe.

Jennie almost melted from the touch, where had her sweet Nini gone? There were only traces of a sexy and dominant Lalisa Manoban and she couldn't deny how much she loved it. With Lisa leaning on her back and holding her neck firmly she was on the verge of collapse.

-Lisaaa!

Jennie's scream could be heard throughout the office, possibly the entire agency. It was totally unexpected for Jennie to feel such penetration in the form of a member. Fingers? Not even close, that thing didn't feel anything like Lalisa's long, perfect fingers.

- Do you like Jen? She's the exact size of my fingers

-Aahh! Since when are your... Mmm... your fingers so long!?- Jennie could feel each thrust of the unknown object hitting her uterus and making her scream- Mmm fuck!

-This, kitty- the Thai girl paused as she squeezed her ass- is a vibrator, attached to a harness and it'll be the closest thing to a penis you'll ever have in your life, because no fucking man is going to be inside you while I exist, much less a woman. Do you understand?

Another powerful thrust and Jennie was already starting to see stars. Was one of them her shooting star? Because she was going to be eternally grateful for him fulfilling her wish.

- Oh God, Lisa! Please don't stop!

- It's Manoban! - he grabbed Jennie's hips tightly and continued to thrust in and out with force. - And it's clear that I don't plan on stopping. - The brunette hadn't managed to cum properly when a second orgasm was taking over her. But that didn't seem to matter to the Thai girl. - Come on Kim, cum for me!

-Fuck! Yeah, just like that...! Aaahh...! They see me... Manoban!!

A third orgasm? Definitely, and Lisa wasn't going to stop until she got her fourth.

-Until you call me Es, good kitty- he gave a mean look and saw the feline arch with pleasure- let's go to the sofa Kim, it's new and I'm dying to try it out

Chanel brand

-I'm better!

-No, I'm better!

-Enough!- both looked at Irene- It's Lalisa, I like Manoban!- admitted the assistant with red cheeks, tired of the two girls' dispute

-Lisa?- Seulgi and Momo asked, surprised and disgusted.

-What the hell is it about Pokpak that attracts all the sexy women!?

- She's beautiful- Irene said with a smile

-And sensual- added a student

-And dominant- Wendy claimed between sighs.

-And it must fuck wonderfully

Seulgi and Momo looked at Irene angrily.

-What? Have you seen his fingers?

And Jennie had seen and felt them well. After six orgasms the feline was exhausted, both sweaty and exhausted. After a final fuck in which they left the dildo aside and dedicated themselves to double penetration, while Lisa masterfully used her fingers, Jennie imitated her as best she could, exploring the Thai girl's interior in the same way. Both looked into each other's eyes and silenced their moans with kisses.

- I love you Lisa

The Thai girl tensed. They had both ended up on the couch, with Jennie on her chest and she caressing her back. That confession from the feline-eyed girl brought her back to the exact moment when everything had changed for her.

Flashback

-But how beautiful my girl is!

A few giggles in the passenger seat

-Lisa Basta, you're driving!- But his smile told her he wasn't very serious.

The girl squeezed the Thai girl's hand, catching her attention.

- I love you Lisa

And for thousandths of a second, Lisa was able to enjoy the moment, just seconds, because soon after everything was chaos.

-Careful!

The last thing he saw was the blinding light of the branch, a horn honking insistently and his girlfriend's scream, and finally the impact that turned everything dark.

End of flashback

-Lili, are you okay?

Lisa blinked out of her thoughts. Jennie looked at her with concern and when she brought a hand to her face she realized that she was crying.

-I... yeah, I'm fine- she got off the couch, drying her tears and began to gather her clothes- It's just that...

Two knocks on the door alerted her.

-Shit!- he grabbed all his clothes scattered on the floor and threw his coat at the Korean girl- Cover yourself, Jen!- he whispered- Come here!

Another touch

-Lisie, can I come in?

Jennie glared at Lisa but the Thai girl ignored her, she couldn't get dressed so quickly, and she wasn't going to let her assistant see them like that during work hours. *Think Lisa, think*

-Jen, hide under the desk, please- she put her hands together in supplication, pouting in a way that convinced the Korean- wait a minute Bae!

He buttoned up his shirt and threw the rest of his clothes in with the feline. He didn't have time to put anything else on.

He sat down at his spot behind the desk and took a breath before allowing his assistant to enter.

-You can come in

The girl entered submissively with a couple of folders and the Thai girl's coffee. The affair in the ballroom left her embarrassed, especially since Lisa had witnessed it.

-Lisie, what happened a little while ago at the...

-Irene- Lisa stopped her with authority- whatever happens between you, Seulgi and Momo is none of my business, but please, resolve your things away from the students.

Lisa tried to maintain her composure even though she was more than uncomfortable and embarrassed. Talking to her assistant practically naked was embarrassing, and even more so having Jennie so close to her intimacy.

-Lisie, I'm sorry about what happened- she apologized, leaving the coffee and papers on the desk and smiling radiantly, leaning over him- To make it up to you, I can invite you to dinner tonight, what do you say?

Lisa smiled uncomfortably, she could feel Jennie's murderous gaze on her waiting for an answer, and on the other hand the hopeful gaze of her assistant. *And now how do I get out of this?*

-Irene, I... Fuck!- Lisa clenched her fists, almost letting out a moan.

-Lisa, are you okay?

-High!

The assistant stopped dead in her tracks, not understanding what was happening to her boss. However, Jennie knew perfectly well what was happening. Lisa swallowed hard. She looked down, and shuddered at the image. Kneeling between her legs, Jennie ran his tender tongue over her folds and from time to time licked her clitoris to heighten the sensations of the Thai girl. She was definitely a fast learner.

Damn feline!

-I'm fine. Oh God... wonderfully- Lisa closed her eyes, gripping the edge of the desk tightly, restraining herself from screaming in front of her assistant.

- Are you sure? You don't seem...

-I said I'm fine!- She stopped her again. Her attempt to close her legs was useless, Jennie had her held tightly and her head stuck to the taller girl's crotch with no intention of moving away- Mmm fuck

-Lisa, was that a moan?- Irene widened her eyes and clasped her legs together to keep from getting carried away by the passion in her mind. Was it possible? She didn't know, but the sound the Thai girl had made had definitely turned her on.

Lisa sat up and shook her head frantically with her cheeks flushed.

-Of course not, Irene! How could you do that!?

The assistant nodded and her eyes widened even more, swallowing with difficulty, while her cheeks turned red.

-L-lisie is that a...?- she pointed timidly towards the couch and Lisa cursed as she realized what she had forgotten.

How the hell could I have forgotten the vibrator!? Embarrassed and excited at the same time, she nods nervously. Clearing her throat to clear her voice

-I... you'll see Bae

-Calm down Lisie, I understand that you must have needs, I do too- he walked over to the dildo and stood in front of the desk again- But if you want, I can help you with that- he slid his hand over the vibrator, from top to bottom, with his gaze fixed on the red-faced Thai girl, and sketched a half smile- if you like, the help can be mutual

Lisa let out a scream making the assistant jump.

-Irene, get out of my office right now!!

And as soon as the girl left the office, Jennie came out of her hiding place, taking her fingers out of the Thai girl's insides.

Listening to the assistant's flirting made her angry and she couldn't think of any other way to stop it than by suddenly penetrating Lisa. The second thing she thought about was coming out of her hiding place, but that would mean killing Irene right there.

-If that woman flirts with you again, I'll kill her, and after that, Lalisa Manoban, you!

Lisa swallowed hard and then smiled earning an angry look from the Korean

-Wipe that smile off your face, I'm serious!

- I'm sorry Nini, I just love seeing you jealous- he pulled her, making the Korean fall into his lap- Did you forget that you marked me with your Chanel perfume?- he reminded her playfully- I'm your property. As long as that fragrance is on my skin, no woman will touch me.

Jennie thought about it for a moment and snorted.

- In that case you should buy me 5 more perfumes, the one I have is half finished.

Lisa pulled her closer to her body, noticing that the girl was only wearing her bra and ventured to slide her tongue down the shorter girl's neck, earning a sigh.

-How about we leave the subject aside and finish what you started?- she whispered flirtatiously.

- I think so...

-Lalisa, what are you doing fucking Jennie during work hours!?

-Fuck Seulgi, close the damn door! - Lisa scolded her, covering Jennie's body as best she could, and her own behind her.

.

.

.

.

. Healthy?

- For God's sake, what happened to that one?

The girls burst out laughing as they watched Rose trudge along with a grimace of discomfort.

-Rose, is everything okay there?

The Australian sat down carefully and grunted.

-Damn, I'm going to kill that idiot Jisoo

-Oh my God, did the chicken girl hit you that hard?- Seulgi mocked amused.

Another laugh. Rose rolled her eyes and took the younger Thai girl's glass. She couldn't handle her friends.

-Hey, that's mine!- Mina complained, puffing out her cheeks.

-You're a minor, and I need it more than you- he took a sip and snorted- Kim Jisoo is an animal

-You knew that very well- Lisa joked, earning a hateful look.

-Do those little fingers hit that hard?

-Seulgi, yours aren't that long, let's say.

-Not all of us can have those big fingers, Manoban!

Lisa looked at her fingers smugly.

-Anyway, Chae, did Jisoo hit you hard last night or why are you walking like that?- Mintty asked mischievously.

-She did, but in the process the idiot threw me to the floor, and in the process made me fall down the stairs!

-But who the fuck fucks near the stairs!?- Lisa criticizes in disapproval

-The one who fucks in the kitchen spoke

-Shut up Mina!

-I wasn't fucking, I was running away from her, she's tireless!- Rose explained grumpily.

They all laughed again

-The Kim sisters are beasts! A few days ago Lisa and Jennie were doing their thing at the agency!

-Seulgi!- Lisa's cheeks reddened

The friends had met at a nearby bar. It was Saturday night. Jennie and Jisoo had stayed at Rose's apartment, while the Australian and the 4 Thai girls went out to celebrate. That night, another Thai had joined the group.

-Let me see if I understand, Lisa's little friend is now Rose's little friend?

-Bambam, you've missed too much, it's a long story

As the friends were talking, the silhouette of a Japanese woman stopped in front of them, silencing them immediately. Mina and Rose immediately looked at Lisa, ready to intervene.

-Hello girls

-Sana, what are you doing here?

-I'm glad to see you too, Rose- the Japanese girl looked at Lisa - Hello Lisa, how have you been?

-After you fucked my girlfriend? Great- the blonde said ironically with disgust- Are you serious? You fuck Tzuyu, and after months you come up to me to ask how I've been? - Lisa I don't expect an answer

- Lisa! - Mintty scolded her when she saw the punch she threw at Sana's nose.

-Fuck you!- the dancer concluded, clenching her fists. She had stopped caring about Tzuyu, but the Japanese girl's betrayal had hurt her even more because she had been her friend- You were my fucking friend, dammit!- she approached her and hit her again- She was my girlfriend!

-Damn, if he keeps this up he's going to figure it out- announced Bambam without interceding.

-Rose, aren't you going to do anything?- Mina asked, after all Rose was the one who best controlled her sister's anger.

-What? Lisa hit me a thousand times, I get to watch her hit someone else!

Mintty rolled her eyes and grabbed Lisa's shoulders to separate the

-I trust you!

- Lisa is enough

The Japanese girl struggled to her feet. Blood was pouring from her mouth, and her nose was not in any better condition. Not to mention that her clothes were ruined as well.

- Lisa I'm sorry, I loved Tzuyu since I saw her at the Institute

-And why the hell didn't you tell me!?- Lisa growled with helpless tears- you should have told me, I would have walked away from her! Instead they preferred to deceive me!

- It just happened, Lisa!

- It just happened, of course... - another blow that made the Japanese girl step back - that too, it just happened - he turned around and prepared to leave the premises, leaving Sana half unconscious on the floor

Her friends were calling out to her behind her back but she was reluctant to go back. She didn't want to see the Japanese girl's face again. *Damn her*. She strode across the parking lot and pulled out her keys, ready to head home, until a voice made her stop.

-Lalisa Manoban. How long...

-G-Dragon?

The boy smiled friendly and walked up to her.

-Hey!

Lisa hugged him in amazement, she hadn't seen the boy for years.

-I haven't seen you since...

-It doesn't matter now Lisa...- the boy looked at a spot between the cars and his face tensed- there will be a party soon and my band will play there, you can go, Sehun will be there, so you can invite Chae

-I don't know if...

-Come on Lisa, for old times' sake. Yiren would have liked it

That name caught Lisa's attention and she didn't think twice.

-Where will they play?

□□□

-Dudu, you have to put your foot on the red one and your hand on the yellow one... No, you're doing it all wrong!

The feline growled and left the place in a bad mood.

-I have 4 legs Chu, I don't know what the hell you mean by feet or hands!

-Cats, look, he's almost done it!

The rabbit tried with difficulty to touch the assigned color with her front paw, moving back as far as she could without moving her back paw from its place.

-Playing twister with two cats was not the best idea

The Kim sisters had stayed at Rose's house with the felines and to kill time they had decided to play.

-Hey, how about we play cards! Whoever loses takes off their clothes!

-Jisoo, we don't have hands

-And we don't wear clothes

-Ok, you know what, I give up, I'm going to get drunk!

Jennie looked reproachfully at her older sister.

-Kim Jisoo, since when do you like getting drunk?

-I don't, that's what Rose always says when she gets mad at me.

-Speaking of which, how are you doing with Rose? - the brunette was interested.

- Oh great!

-Yes, you have my children dressed up! - complained Rabbit, wagging her little tail haughtily.

-And we have days without sleep because of your screams!- Dudu finished disgusted.

-It seems like you're killing her- said Rabbit

-Girls... I think I fell in love with Rose!

They all looked at her with irony.

-If you didn't say it, we wouldn't have noticed- Dudu said sarcastically.

-Well, don't be surprised when I have a mini Jisoo!

-Chu, they are both females- Dudu explained, he knew for sure that it was impossible

-What about the Virgin Cat!? No cat mounted her and yet she had gatisus!

"I think I'll go get some alcohol," said Jennie, overwhelmed by her sister's nonsense.

- I'm going with you Nini!

-Dudu, cats don't drink- explained Rabbit, bewildered.

-Well, I'll be the first.

Yiren

4 years ago...

-Honey, can you turn off the heating please?

- Whatever you ask for, darling

Yiren smiled as she watched Lisa obey and turn around a couple of times to look at her with a sly and suspicious smile.

-That?

The Thai woman shrugged without taking her eyes off the road.

-Can't I see my girl?

- Lisa, we're on the road, you're not going to convince me with your charms.

The named one let out a funny laugh

-Calm down, honey, we're not going to get intimate in the car... - he clicked his tongue and smiled mischievously - although you didn't complain last time when...

-Lisa!- the girl blushed at the memory of the Thai girl- You are insatiable Lalisa Manoban, whoever knows you knows that you don't keep your hands still

-Why leave them still when I can touch all that?- she asked mischievously pointing at her girlfriend's body.

-Lalisa!- she covered her burning face- stop embarrassing me

Lisa laughed again and squeezed the girl's hand. She was happy and had her life planned out for that day. She had been preparing everything for that day for weeks, and everything had to go as planned.

-Yir, what if we get married?

The girl turned to look at her quickly, shocked by the question. Had she heard correctly?

-What?- she asked incredulously.

-You're 19 years old Yerin, you still haven't lost your hearing- he joked with his eyes on the road

-Oh God, Lisa, are you kidding me? Because if so...!
-Honey, I've never been more serious in my life.
The girl let out a scream and quickly recovered, covering her mouth with both hands.
- Manoban, are you proposing to me while driving? You're not very romantic.
-But if original
The girl rolled her eyes in amusement, unable to erase her smile, all under the intense gaze of the Thai girl.
-What are you looking at?
-It's not my fault I have a beautiful girlfriend! Correction, a fiancée...
A few giggles in the passenger seat
-Lisa, stop it, you're driving!- But his smile told her he wasn't very serious.
The girl squeezed the Thai girl's hand, catching her attention. They both looked at each other, connecting instantly.
- I love you Lisa
And for thousandths of a second, the Thai woman was able to enjoy the moment, just seconds because after that everything was chaos.
-Careful!
The last thing he saw was the blinding light, a horn honking insistently and his girlfriend's scream, and shortly after, the impact that turned everything dark.
Her body refused to react, she felt pain running through her everywhere. *What had happened?* Her eyes were heavy and she had a hard time opening them. In the distance she could hear screams and the sirens of an ambulance but she couldn't stand up.
-Yi...Yiren...
When she regained consciousness, she managed to open her eyes. A blinding light dazzled her, forcing her to close them again.

The little she could see was a pair of unfamiliar faces with masks, and the feeling of her face covered with an oxygen mask, and connected to hydration and blood tubes. What was happening?

-Yi...

-Miss, stay calm, everything will be fine.

-Give him more morphine

-He has lost a lot of blood

-How is the other girl?

- I don't think he'll survive.

Lisa tried to ask what they were referring to, she wanted to know about her fiancée, but she was never able to ask the question because I fainted again.

Finally he regained consciousness and everything was clear. His eyes curiously scanned the pale walls of the room. A line with reddish liquid fed his veins from his arm, and his body was covered only with a surgical gown, and over it a blanket.

- Lisa!

Rose stood up from the chair next to the stretcher, making it creak immediately. She looked exhausted, with a couple of shadows under her eyes, she had clearly not gotten any sleep that night. Her face was worried, and from the redness of her eyes it was obvious that she had been crying. But why? Flashes of the accident came back to her mind. The car that came out of nowhere next to her car, the blinding light. The car turning over and the screams.

- Yiren!

-Calm down Lisa, you can't exhaust yourself, the doctor said...

-Rose, where is Yiren?

The Australian lowered her head, looking melancholy. She refused to answer the question, but she couldn't hide the truth from him.

- Lisa, Yiren....

But I don't even need to finish. Lisa shook her head a couple of times, reluctant to hear what her friend would say.

- No, no Rose, tell me it's not true!

- I'm sorry Lisa, they couldn't get him to wake up.

Tears were running down the Thai girl's cheeks. She had stopped feeling the pain of her lessons, because the pain in her heart was greater.

-Is Yiren...?

Rose nodded regretfully, she knew this would destroy her friend.

- Dead, the impact was on her. The doctors could not save her Lisa

.

.

.

.

Back to the past

- Lisa, I thought you didn't know anything about G-drago and his band

-I told you Mintty, I found him yesterday- answered the dancer, dodging people. The place was a house full of university students, which was not a very pleasant environment for Lalisa, who had left that world behind after Yiren's death.

-This place is probably a brotherhood. What the hell is G-Dragon doing giving concerts in this kind of crowd?- Rose pushed a couple to get past them without touching them. She was angrier than usual and still didn't understand why Lisa had accepted that invitation - and what makes that idiot G think that I want to see Sehun?

- I think Sehun wants to see you.

-Who is Shun!?- Jisoo questioned with a disgusted expression, not even pronouncing the name correctly.

Rose looked reproachfully at her friend and snorted.

-Thanks Lisa

The friends had not gone alone, their group of Thais accompanied them, and G-Dragon was no stranger to them, they all knew each other quite well. Jennie and Jisoo had also attended the gig at the request of the eldest feline, getting away from Rose was costing her a lot.

-Jisoo, I already told you he wasn't flirting with me!- Grumpy Rose coming back with a couple of beers

- He called you cutie!

-He calls everyone that, he's a fucking 19-year-old bartender!

-What!? That was a bartender!?

- I give up- Rose rolled her eyes. Asking the feline to accompany her for a drink had not been the best idea, especially when the boy asked her order with a wink and a bit of flirting. The Korean feline had not taken long to pounce on him and leave him with the 5 claws on her right hand tattooed on his face as a reminder.

-You are an animal

On the other hand, the rest were waiting at one of the tables near the stage where the band would perform.

-Hey Manoban!- the boy appeared with an electric guitar on his shoulder and a smile- you came!

-Hello Dragon, we have also come

-Chae, Sehun will be happy to see you- the boy ignored the rest and focused on Lisa again - Come with me, there's someone who wants to see you

-See me?

-Sure, like the old days

Lisa tilted her head in confusion, but stood up, ready to follow the Korean. Rose's hand stopped her and with a hesitant look she shook her head, not liking the idea. But Lisa's curiosity was greater.

-I'll be back in a moment

Rose cursed as he watched her walk away through the crowd with the guitarist.

-That Dragon guy, wasn't he in love with Yiren? - Mina asked curiously.

- She was, she was... - said the psychologist looking towards the place where they had disappeared - but Yiren always had preference with Lisa

-Yiren?

Everyone turned around. They had forgotten that Jennie was also among them. Mina and Rose widened their eyes. Naming Yiren might make her angry. The other two also turned their faces away, ignoring the question, but Bambam was unaware of Jennie's aggressiveness and was quick to respond.

-It was Li's girlfriend... ouch! Rose, did you hit me?

-Who me!? Never! - the Australian replied through gritted teeth.

-I thought it was Tzuyu- Jennie continued questioningly.

-Tzuyu was too, but Yiren was her great love. Hey! Mintty?

-Don't look at me, it wasn't me

-His great love...- Jennie slowly pronounced the word, feeling a lump in her chest.

-Jen, Yiren is part of Lisa's past- Rose explained, trying to calm her down.

-True, but only because of the accident, otherwise Lisa... Aush, Seulgi!?

- Sorry Bam, it was a spasm

As much as the girls tried to secretly silence the Thai, Bambam seemed determined to let it all out.

-Accident, what happened?

-What happened? Yerin died, and the worst thing is that Lalisa was going to propose to her... oooh!!! You too Mina!?

-Jen, wait, where are you going!?- Rose stood up from the table, ready to follow the feline who had already taken off running.

-Rose, stop chasing my sister! - Jisoo, overcome with jealousy, was quick to follow the Australian

-You're a big mouth Bambam

-Me? What did I do?

ㅁㅁㅁ

-Where are we going?- Lisa was confused, they had left the people behind. They were in the back garden of the house. There was hardly anyone there, except for a few couples.

-Be patient Lisa, you'll see.

The boy stopped near the pool and looked at the Thai girl with a smile. Lisa was starting to get worried about the boy's attitude. Why so much mystery?

- The girls must be wondering where I am, I better get back.

-Perfect, but first why don't you take a look at the pool? I think there's a mermaid there.

-Mermaid?- Lisa looked confused and her heart almost stopped for a moment. Her hands were cold and her face paled. A girl in a bikini came out of the water, completely soaked. Lalisa knew that body well although she still couldn't believe what her eyes were seeing.

The girl stopped in front of the pair and squeezed her dripping brown hair with her gaze fixed on the Thai girl.

-Hi love

-Y-yiren?

The girl smiled excitedly, taking a step closer to Lisa, but the latter stepped back in fear, shaking her head several times.

-No, this is not true, you are not here.

- Lisa, honey, it's me

- No! Yiren is dead! - tears began to fall from her eyes

The girl rushed to take his hand, frantically shaking her head, tears also flowing from her eyes.

- It's me Lisa, I'm alive, look at me- she raised the Thai girl's face with her hands so that she could look into her eyes- touch me- she squeezed her hand- feel me...- and finally she joined her lips to Lisa's

And it seemed like time hadn't passed those 4 painful years, but something had changed, the texture of her lips was different, the kiss was different, everything was simply different.

As she pulled away from the kiss, she sleepily opened her eyes, entranced and confused by the encounter. The girl in front of her smiled radiantly and threw herself into her arms.

- I love you Lis, you don't know how much I missed you- he gave her a kiss on the cheek and fixed her bangs as he often used to do- But everything will go back to the way it was. We are together again and nothing will ever separate us again.

Was it a dream? Was the girl he had sworn eternal love to really standing before her again?

-Yiren I...

-Jennie, wait!- Rose shouted from a distance

And the bubble of the past finally burst, returning her to her present. Jennie. When she turned around she saw the brunette watching the scene in pain. Her red eyes and broken expression told her that she had witnessed the entire encounter with Yiren.

-Jennie...- he whispered. But the feline shook her head and ran away while rubbing her eyes to remove the tears that prevented her from seeing the path- Jennie!

She tried to follow her but a hand stopped her. Yiren looked at her with a serious expression and held her hand firmly.

- Lisa, let her go. She will understand that it is me you love. It is time to resume our love.

Lisa looked at the wooden fence the Korean girl had jumped over and nodded. Maybe it was for the best, letting her feline girl go, but was it really what her heart wanted?

-Yiren?- Rose finally arrived at the place, surprised to see the girl, but her surprise turned to disgust when she saw the intertwined hands of both girls.

He frowned looking at Lisa

-Where is Jennie?

Lisa looked down and it was Yiren who dared to respond, without much tact.

-She jumped over the fence there- he pointed to the place with his hand- I think that girl has problems, she is not well

-That's right, unfortunately her problem is called Lalisa Manoban and she ruined her life from the moment she met her - Rose shook her head, disappointed in her friend - I hope you're happy Lalisa Manoban, you finally broke her heart - she said angrily - if something happens to Jennie, it will be your fault - saying that she ran away ready to follow the trail of the brunette

My true love

- Oh Lisa my love, you don't know how happy I am!

The girl hugged the taller girl's arm with possession. Having the Thai girl's warmth again was what she had dreamed of for years.

They had left the house where the party had been held to be together, but Lisa's mind was still full of doubts about the whole accident story, and Jennie's mind was still full of doubts. *Will she be okay?*

Without thinking, his thoughts came out on their own.

-The doctors said they couldn't do anything to save you.

-Oh well, the doctors are very inept, honey, I was transferred to another hospital.

Lisa stopped walking and looked at her doubtfully.

-Another hospital? And why didn't anyone tell me?

-You were unconscious for two days, Lisa.

-And you're technically dead! I only knew that your mother had taken your body. I couldn't even attend your funeral! I didn't hear anything else about you!

- There was no funeral Lisa, I'm here

-Yiren, you show up after 4 years and expect everything to be as if nothing happened?

The girl looked at her confused, why not?

-We were going to get married Lisa, we can do it now!

-You never answered my question! You never said yes! - Lisa ran a hand through her head, the situation was starting to get upset. What was Yiren doing there? And even stranger, how was she alive?

- Lisa, what do you mean?

-Yiren, I don't understand anything, this matter is very absurd.

-There's nothing to understand, darling, I was transferred and...

-And why have you disappeared? I never received a letter or a message from you, you disappeared from my life completely. Do you have any idea how bad I've been through these last 4 years?

-That didn't stop you from fucking Tzuyu...- the Korean girl said reproachfully.

-That?

- Oh come on Lisa, I know about your girlfriends, or was it a secret that there were so many stupid girls behind you? And that weirdo at the party...

The mere mention of the chestnut made his blood boil; he wasn't going to allow anyone, not even Yiren, to talk about his feline like that.

- Don't talk about Jennie like that!

- Oh, so Jennie... she too, Lalisa? You fucked her too!?- his face had become intimidating, but he quickly relaxed his features, smiling again- But it doesn't matter about her anymore, now we are...

- No

- No?

Lisa pulled her hand away with searches, taking distance from the girl

- I cried for you for years Yiren Wang. I lost my heart when I thought you were dead. I always thought that you would be My only great love.

- I am Lis, I am your great love, and you are mine!

Lisa shook her head thoughtfully.

- You're wrong Yiren. If you loved me you would have come back sooner, but you preferred to let me believe that you had died.

-It was the best Lalisa!

- The best for whom!?

-You don't understand!

-But what is it that I am supposed to understand!?- Lisa was starting to lose patience

-If you stayed he would have killed you!
-Who would have killed me!?
-G-Dragon!
-That?

Flashback

- Please Yiren, Lalisa Manoban doesn't deserve you!

-Ji yong stop it, I love Lisa!

- No, you must love me! I am better than her! - he clenched his fists in indignation - if you don't get away from Manoban, he will kill her!

The girl stepped back in some panic.

- You wouldn't be able to..

-Do you want to test me Yiren? I will do anything to have you, even if it means killing someone.

End of flashback

-What?- Lisa continued to take everything in without understanding.

-He planned the whole accident Lisa- the girl cried inconsolably- I had no other choice...

-And you knew?

-I didn't want love!

The Thai woman denied in disbelief

-Wait... you knew he was going to kill me that night and you still didn't tell me?

-No Lalisa, the idea was never to kill you that night. I was the one who was going to disappear.

Flashback

-If I disappear, will you leave her alone?

The boy smiled triumphantly

-Of course, beautiful, here I only care about you.

- Do you promise me she won't get hurt?

- The blow will leave both of you wounded, the idea is that everyone believes that you are dead. This way it will be easier for Manoban to let you go, and you can be happy with me instead.

Yiren wiped her tears and nodded.

-Okay, we'll go see a movie tonight, just do it.

End of flashback

Lisa was in shock, she didn't even recognize the woman in front of her sobbing, broken, or were her tears even fake?

- Not only did you fake your death, but you were also with him this whole time?

- Lisa, I don't...

-Shut up Yiren! I don't want to hear any more lies, damn it! I loved you! Did that not matter to you!?

-I loved you too Lisa, I still love you, I've never stopped loving you!

-And why does he accept it now?

- He realized that I don't love him, Lisa understood! He will let me be with you!

Lisa shook her head. Even though her words were true, something had changed in her. The girl in front of her no longer looked like she used to, she no longer made her sigh like she used to, simply nothing was like it was before.

- I loved you for years Yiren, I'm not going to deny it, and I was devastated when you left. I thought I would never find someone like you again... but I was wrong - he sketched a small melancholic smile - Yes I did find her, even better

-What?- the Korean asked surprised.

Lisa's smile widened even more at the memory of the feline.

-I found someone who makes me smile, who greets me with emotion after a long day of work, who alters each of my senses, who even made my life completely crazy.

-Don't tell me you're talking about that Jennie?

-Nini appeared in my life when I had definitely given up on finding love, believe me Yiren, I tried, I really tried hard to reject this feeling, but I couldn't.- she looked at the sky and sighed - Jennie won me over, in the end I fell in love with my cat

-It must be a joke

-I'm fucking in love with Jennie Kim, Yiren! And I don't mind saying it anymore!- She smiled widely, her heart pounding at the mere mention of the feline. It felt good to admit it. She frowned as she realized where she was- I don't even know what I'm doing here...

- You're not going to leave me like this, Lalisa!

- I'm sorry Yiren, you are my past- he looked up at the sky, a bright star was twinkling overhead- Jennie is my present and my future...

-What? Are you going to leave us for her?

-You ended our relationship the moment you planned your escape with Ji Yong, you were a coward Yiren, you should have told me and yet you didn't. I don't want you back in my life.

- That bitch is not going to take your love away from me Lisa, I will not allow it!

The Thai girl turned around and smiled big.

- She's a cat, Yiren, and she didn't take anything from you, I gave it to her of my own free will.

-Where are you going?- he asked when he saw her running.

- I'm going to find Jennie, I have to tell her that I love her! - she shouted at the top of her lungs without stopping. Her hand tightly held the yang pendant that her parents had given her, the same one that linked her to the feline. Now - I'm coming for you, Nini.

Feline change

Could it hurt more? Or the real question, would it ever stop hurting? Her heart felt like it was breaking, that girl was Yiren, Lisa's love and she had returned. She had no business being there anymore, Lisa undoubtedly preferred Yiren over her. *After all, she never loved me.*

She settled down on the roof and sniffed. Her feline instincts made her feel safer on top of the roof than anywhere else.

-I shouldn't have fallen in love with a human...- she whispered sadly, feeling tears running down her eyes- I should never have become a human

- No, you shouldn't have.

Jennie was startled when she heard the voice accompanied by a mewling sound. In the darkness she didn't notice the jet-black shadow on the tree beside her, but now that she looked closely she could clearly see a pair of yellow spheres shining in the gloom.

-Kai?

The feline in a perfect jump landed on the roof and approached the girl with suspicion, Jennie's scent was that of a human and that caused detachment in him.

-Hello Nini, I see that you are not happy as a human...- he wagged his tail in disgust without stopping to look at her.

The brunette looked down, at some point in her feline life the arrival of the Bombay would have given her a tickle in her stomach and made her purr. But there, on the roof, she felt empty and broken, and not even he could change that.

- No, I'm not, I wish I had never become one - *I wish I had never met her.* She thought melancholy, with the Thai girl engraved in her mind .

-Tell me one thing Nini, do you want to be a cat again?

Jennie looked at him thoughtfully, the feline seemed to be serious.

-Yes, I do want to
-Would you stay with me?
-Yes Kai...

The feline looked at her for a moment and wagged his tail. He had been following her closely.

-Then follow me...

Jennie looked up at the sky. The moon was shining brightly and stars decorated the firmament. A burst of light passed briefly, catching her attention. A shooting star. Maybe it was time to return to her old life. *Goodbye, Lisa*.

ooo

-What do you mean it doesn't appear?

Lisa was pacing back and forth in despair. She had returned to the party and her friends had left. Mina had called her explaining that they were at Rose's house and that there was no sign of Jennie.

- You idiot! God, I should hit you for...! Jisoo, No!!

But the black-haired girl had already gotten ahead of her, landing a fist on the Thai girl's cheek.

-Ouch! It doesn't seem to hurt in the movies!- Jisoo complained, licking her reddened knuckles.

-Fuck...- Lisa screamed at the blow, in pain

-But why do you always end up hitting each other like animals!?- Irene complained running to get some ice

Rose looked reproachfully at Seulgi as the assistant walked away towards the kitchen.

-What is she doing here?

-What? I thought you were having a party!

-Kang Seulgi, we're looking for Jennie! Why the hell would she have a party!?

Irene returned with the ice, causing the pair to fall silent. Rose gave the Thai girl a dirty look, causing her to gulp. The assistant on the other hand walked towards Lisa, ignoring the rest.

-Are you okay Lisie?

The dancer pushed the ice away and denied

-No, we have to find Jennie

-But where could it be...?- asked Mintty

-Girls...

- I already looked in my apartment, but nothing- Lalisa said thoughtfully.

-Umm girls...

-Lisa, don't be an idiot, I was running away from you, your apartment would be the last place I would go- Rose assured with disgust- none of this would have happened if you weren't so...

-Chi..

-Well, think about it, Chaeyong Park, you are the psychologist- declared the indignant Thai woman.

-Chic...

- Psychologist, Manoban, not a detective!

-GIRLS!

-What do you want Seulgi!?- they all shouted at the same time

-My-My...!

-What about you?- Irene wanted to know.

-My...

-Speak at once!- Rose ordered

-Look!

They all turned towards the point the Thai girl was pointing at and both Rose and Lisa widened their eyes when they saw a Jisoo in ragdoll form.

-Is that...?

-Jisoo?- Rose knelt on the ground confused. The feline meowed and growled with her fur ruffled, she was undoubtedly angry.

-Now it's Chu- Lisa corrected, leaning towards the feline- but what happened to her?

- I don't understand, she seems angry.

-Is that what you don't understand, Rose!?- Seulgi exclaimed, upset- I don't understand why the hell Jisoo is a cat!

-Yes, Jisoo is a cat...

-That means Jennie must have transformed too...- Lisa analyzed, worried.

-Can someone explain to me what the hell is going on here!?- Seulgi insisted, almost pulling her hair out.

-Seulgi, Jisoo and Jennie are cats!- Mina explained looking at the feline

-Cats?- Irene asked incredulously.

-That explains a lot of things...- Mintty mentioned

-Now I understand why Jisoo was shaking her nails at the curtains

-And he climbed trees when a dog appeared.

-Oh, and when he threw up that ball of fur!

-Seulgi, that was a rat

The girl widened her eyes, covering her mouth to keep from vomiting.

Rose stroked the feline's fur and she immediately began to purr and rub herself, making the Australian smile.

-How will you fuck? Now, Jisoo will stick her cat tongue in your...?

-Mintty!

Rose looked at the feline who let out a flirtatious growl.

-*That "Grr" was a, I'll stick my tongue in deep, honey.*

-Mina, hanging out with Mintty is doing you harm- Rose scolded her with her cheeks red with embarrassment

-Wait, does that mean that all this time you have been fornicating with animals?- Mintty surprised

- Exciting, isn't it? - Mina ironically rolled her eyes - Anyway, the important thing now is to find Jen, if she has become a cat again it will be difficult to find her.

-It's true, we don't know what Jennie looks like as a cat- Mintty supported

-Nini- Lisa corrected- her name is Nini

-Nini, Jennie... Whatever!

-We can put up wanted signs- everyone turned to Irene who lowered her head, ashamed for intervening- I mean, that's what we did at home when our puppy went missing.

-Excellent idea, that's why I love you!

-That?

-Nothing!

- Maybe it will work. Does anyone have a photo of Jennie as a feline? - Mina asked.

-Me- Lisa was quick to look for the snapshots with the feline, her eyes filled with tears when she saw her former Nini as she knew her.

-Alright, give me that picture- Mintty took the photo and her jacket- Irene, Seulgie and I will go take down those ads and hang them around the area, you three try to find her wherever you think she might be hiding, and you...- she watched Jisoo lick her butt and stand there frozen at being discovered. Mintty wrinkled her nose- You keep doing your thing... very well, let's go!

Don't worry Nini, you'll be back home soon.

What Lisa didn't know was that the feline was already at home, in her old house.

Search

Lisa dropped onto the couch, they had searched the surroundings and there was no trace of the Korean

- This is my fault

"Absolutely," Rose said, placing two cups of coffee on the table.

- You're not helping Rose
- You deserve it Lalisa, I told you not to hurt her, Jennie didn't deserve it- she left a bowl of milk on the floor and found it strange to see Jisoo in her old form- Lisa, if you find her what will you do? I mean, she's a cat and...

-What are you implying Rose? I'm not going to fuck my cat!

-Technically you already did it on more than one occasion- he clicked his tongue when he saw Jisoo focused on his milk. After all, she had done it too- But what are you going to do with what you feel?

Lisa clutched the pendant in her hand, half of the yang she had found in the pillow on the side the feline usually slept on. That only meant Jennie wasn't coming back.

-I'm in love with her Chae- she whispered melancholy

-What are you saying?

-That I love her

-Sorry, I didn't hear well.

- I fucking love her! I love Jennie Kim!
- Do you realize what you're saying? You like a cat?

-Yes Rose, I know, I fell in love with my cat and... Ouch! Why the hell are you hitting me!?

- A slap is what you deserve for being an idiot! Are you just now realizing it? - growled the Australian, giving him another slap - How do you feel about that? - she asked, this time as if she were talking to a patient.

Lisa looked at her in surprise, with a hand on her cheek.

-Right now... sore- she rubbed her affected cheek- Don't use your psychology on me Park- she growled this time rolling her eyes- I want Nini back

-Even if she's a cat?

-It doesn't matter if she's a cat- he said- I just want to have her in my life.

-You're an idiot, you should have gone after her and not been an idiot with Yiren.

-What did you want me to...!? Oooh! Jisoo!

The feline snorted, pulling out her claws. Lisa put her finger in her mouth to remove the blood, the feline had bitten her.

-I think she's also upset about what you did to her sister- Rose said, caressing the feline's ear- With a woman like Jennie, how could you...? Oooh! She bit me!- she exclaimed in surprise- Jisoo, wait!

But the feline did not stop. The ragdoll growled at the window and launched herself dramatically.

-Oh my God!- Rose widened her eyes in fear, covering her mouth with both hands.

-He's not suicidal, he jumped down the emergency stairs.

-No Lisa, my building doesn't have an emergency staircase!

They both ran to the window, alarmed. The feline was clinging to the frame, her fur standing on end. She let out a meow when she saw the Australian and Rose was quick to grab her.

- For God's sake Jisoo, if you're going to throw tantrums at least go out the door! - the psychologist told her walking towards the entrance, followed by the feline - go, and don't scratch the door when you come back, meowing is enough

The feline growled and walked out the door with her tail pointed.

Lisa was amused by the interaction between her friend and the cat and thought about what her new life with her Nini would be like.

Could they understand each other that well? She smiled. Woman or feline, she didn't want to be away from Jennie.

-I want my Nini back

Rose sighed heavily. Her friend had ruined it.

-After this Lisa, I don't think Jennie wants to get back with you.

Lisa pouted and sat down on the couch.

-Can I stay here tonight?

-Ok baby Manoban- the Australian girl said ironically when she saw how vulnerable her friend was becoming- but I'll put some pillows. Every time we sleep together you end up touching my butt.

Lisa looked at her mischievously

- That's because I secretly want to fuck you- Lisa teased, taking off her shirt and throwing it on the couch, ready to follow her friend to the bedroom. But that action didn't go unnoticed by the Australian- what?

Rose watched intently at the six little squares that jutted out exquisitely from the Thai girl's abdomen, which sensually ended in a V. *Since when did that idiot Lalisa have those fucking abs?*

-I'm thinking that I shouldn't spend my time of abstinence with you, you never know when you might sin.

Lisa watched as her friend licked her lips, her gaze on her abdomen, and covered herself with a nearby vase.

-Let's put those pillows right, or you might rape me in the middle of the night.

Rose rolled her eyes

- I wish I was so lucky, Manoban.

◦◦◦

-Chu, did you see something?- asked the rabbit looking from one side to the other.

-Nothing, and your Dudu?

-Girls, the three of us are in the same tree, it's obvious that I haven't seen either.

-Shh- Chu put his paw in the Russian blue's mouth, making her spit in disgust.

-Fuck Chu, I don't want to spit out your hairballs!

-Look there!

They all looked ahead intently. The felines were looking for Nini on their own, but instead they came across something completely different. With Jisoo back as a cat, her feline perception was working again.

- Human eyesight is crap, my night vision was almost useless- commented the ragdoll

"Poor hairless beings," lamented the rabbit.

-Hold on and listen

In the alley a woman in leather was talking angrily to a man in a cap. The girl seemed upset about something.

-No, she didn't accept it! That idiot must disappear!

- Why don't you just walk away from her and be done with it?

- Lisa is my love, I won't let her be with anyone else!

The three women covered their mouths in surprise. Were they talking about the same Lisa?

-Yiren I...

-Ji Yong, do what I ask of you once and for all!- she sighed trying to calm down and smiled- and I promise I will compensate you very well- she whispered near the boy's lips.

To her right, a second young woman watched the scene in silence. They both saw Yiren leave in disgust and only then did the young woman dare to speak.

-I don't understand why you like that idiot, she's unbearable.

- It wasn't always like this

- No, she changed when you took her away from Lisa.

-I'm better than Lisa!

The girl burst out laughing, openly mocking the boy and denied it.

-Nobody is better than Lalisa

-And that's why you betrayed her with Sana?

-Shut up Drago!

- Tzuyu, with Yiren back Lisa will never be yours

-Well, if she's not mine, she'll be no one's- he growled, clenching his fists- I want Lalisa Manoban out of the reach of any woman, especially that Jennie!

-Are you talking about wiping it off the map?

- You said it, whatever it takes

The three women watched them both leave the place, surprised by the conversation. Who were those people and why did they want to hurt Lisa?

-We have to tell Laisa!

- Lisa- corrected Dudu

-But how? You're a cat now, Lisa wouldn't understand you.

-Good grief, it's true!

- Why do you think you turned back into a cat? - Rabbit asked curiously.

-Maybe the humans are right and the wish is over

-We have to find Jennie and ask her for help to save Lisa- explained Dudu, determined. If anyone could help them, it was the brunette.

-Do you think he cares about Lisa after what happened?

- It's Nini, she won't let them hurt Lila

-How are you so sure?

-Because he loves her. And when you love someone you don't let anyone hurt them- his eyes automatically fell on the Rabbit

-Where could it be?

-There is only one place where Nini feline could have gone... The Kim mansion

Felines?

Lisa stretched out on the bed, feeling warm and cozy. Since when was Rose's bed so big? Normally when she stretched out she touched the headboard of the bed, but this time she couldn't even reach the pillow. *She was strange...*

She sat up in bed and looked to her right, shocked at the huge barrier of pillows. Am I dreaming? She looked up, but she couldn't even see the Australian girl. Was the wall they built before going to sleep that big?

He looked around and was alarmed to see his clothes spread out on the bed, including his underwear.

-Roseanne Park, if you abused me while I was sleeping I swear that... !

But a few grunts silenced her. What had that been?

-Rose, are you there?- a new feline growl confused her- Is Chu with you?

He tried to peek out with difficulty. To his surprise, he found it easy to climb over the pillows, apparently his nails had grown long enough to catch on the fabric.

-I feel like I'm climbing the homework mountain, this is pathetic, since when did you become a compulsive pillow hoarder?- she commented without understanding when the wall of pillows had grown so much. -Hey Rose, what..? Rose?- Lisa looked confused at the other side of the bed. There was no trace of her friend, the only thing there was a white and orange American Curl, lying face up on the bed, where had that cat come from?

For some reason he started sniffing around, trying to figure out who the feline was. All he had to do was roll his fluffy tail just a little to alarm the kitty, who jumped up on all fours, snorting and growling.

-Lalisa Manoban, why did you bring another cat? Weren't the ones we already have enough?

Lisa widened her eyes when she saw that the one who had just complained was none other than the American Carl, standing in front of her.

-Rose?

The named one widened her eyes, FULL of panic

- Oh my god, I knew fucking a cat girl would bring consequences! Now I developed feline powers!

-Shit... I must be dreaming.

The Australian knew something about that voice was familiar. But how was that possible?

-Lisa? Lisa is that you?

-Oh my God Rosie, what happened to you?

-Me? Have you seen yourself in the mirror yet?

-You're a cat!- they both said in unison- What!?- they exclaimed at the same time

Both Rose and Lisa jumped out of bed with the intention of reaching the mirror but in the attempt they fell face first to the floor.

-Shit!

-My feet don't work! I can't stand up! - Rose tried to stand on her hairy female legs without success, it was impossible for a cat to maintain balance for long.

-Wait, it's-it's almost there!- Lisa crawled to the Groomer. The big challenge was to get up. -Rose, come here, I'm going to climb on your back.

-What's it to me?!- the Australian woman fell to the ground again.

-Rose, stop trying, you're not going to be able to stand on two feet... I mean legs! - he corrected - help me up!

-You're not getting on my back Manoban!

-Come on!

-Force me!

And Lisa didn't flinch. With the little control over her new body, she leapt at the Australian, tossing her around. Orange, white and grey fur splattered everywhere as meows and growls echoed throughout the room.

-Ouch! Lisa, you killed my ass!

-Of course not, it was your tail, cough-cough! Fluffy!- Rose's fluff coughed.

-But what's going on here?

They both stopped when they heard a loud and dominant female voice at the entrance of the room. What woman had just interrupted their fight?

When they turned around, they were both surprised to see the Russian blue standing at the entrance, wagging her tail from side to side.

-Dudu?

-Honey, no one is home and the kids are asleep, how about you lick my...? Oh!

The second feline stopped at the entrance. Her voice was soft and sweet, unlike the other one.

-Doe?

Lisa and Rose were surprised. Were they really understanding what the felines were saying?

-And who are they?- Dudu asked haughtily.

- I like the Siamese!

Dudu growled in complaint, glaring at Lisa.

- Siamese? - With a little more strength in her paws she managed to reach the mirror, as did Rose, and they both let out a meow of panic.

- That's me...?

- Oh my God, I'm a Siamese twin!

-And I... Holy crap, they cut off my ears! - she turned angrily to see her friend - Did you cut off my ears while I was sleeping!?

-You're an American Corl Rose, don't be dramatic- the Thai girl replied rolling her eyes.

-Did you say Rose?

Lisa and the aforementioned turned around at Dudu's question. The feline was intimidating, they feared that at any moment she would attack them.

-Rose?- he repeated cautiously.

-Yes, it's me! Holy crap, I can't believe I'm talking to a cat... well, technically we were talking to Jennie and Jisoo, and they were cats.

-What happened to them?- the Russian blue was interested.

-We don't even know, we woke up like this this morning- Lisa explained, watching Rose sway on all fours as she walked.

-Did you eat any rotten mice?

-Rabbit, they are human, they don't eat those things.

-Oh, right!

-What was the last thing you did last night?- asked Dudu, attentive.

-After taking out Chu we...

Lisa and Rose looked at each other as if the answer had suddenly come to them.

-Chu bit us last night!

-I bit you many times and nothing happened to you- commented Dudu without understanding.

-Maybe Chu is different...- Rose began using her psychologist methods

- Wait! - Lisa took the Australian's reading glasses with her little finger and placed them on her friend.

-Thanks Lisa- Rose cleared her throat, suddenly feeling professional. She frowned- Gosh, I can't see anything with my glasses.

-Feline vision is a thousand times better than that of humans- explained Dudu- continued

-When Chu bites human Jennie, she also changes. For some reason, when Chu becomes a cat and modern...

- It's stupid Rose

-Think about it Lisa, if a fucking cat bites Jennie she turns into a human

- So if Chu bites a human...?- Lisa analyzed thoughtfully.

-Does it turn into a cat?- added Dudu intrigued.

- This is unusual! - Rose was beginning to lose her sanity. It was all very crazy.

- The point is that now you and I are fucking cats, and with Jennie as a cat...

-Shit

-I don't want to be a damn cat forever!

-Hey!- Dudu and Rabbit growled in unison

-No offense, but I'm not going to be looking for a cat to fuck me! - Rose added alarmed. The idea of going into heat terrified her.

-Ok enough, let's go with the girls, maybe we can think of something- Dudu calmed them down

- Wait, did they find Nini? - Lisa asked hopefully.

-Yes, Chu is with her

-We must go and...

The door of the building opened.

The four felines fell silent and hid. Two hooded men crept stealthily through the living room towards the hallway. Who were they?

-Damn, just what I needed, thieves- Rose complained disgusted

The four followed closely behind the pair. One focused on the bathroom, while the other entered the kitchen. Finally, after checking Rose's office, they entered the bedroom.

- They're not taking anything- Lisa whispered confused.

-What do you want?- Rose asked, not understanding either.

-That smell...- Dudu seemed to suspect one of the hooded men

-It seems that there is no one- whispered one, relaxing his shoulders.

- I don't understand, Tzuyu said Lisa would be here. She wasn't in her apartment either.

-What?- Lisa was surprised, what did Tzuyu have to do with this?

Both friends were petrified when they saw one of the boys take off his mask.

-Sehun?

The young man smiled as he fell onto the Australian's bed.

-God, everything smells like her- he sighed with pleasure and laughed when he came across something- Just look at that, how cute- he took the lace panties from her clothes and brought them to his nose, inhaling the girl's natural scent. He let out a moan- fuck, Rose smells delicious

-Hey, those are mine! - Lisa complained with a snort but was greatly surprised when she saw the second hooded man take off his hood - it can't be...

-Sehun, don't be disgusting, take them if you want, but let's go now

-D-dragon- the Thai woman murmured, still in amazement.

- Tzuyu won't be happy- Sehun announced putting Lisa's panties in his pocket

-I still have to look for that Jennie- he sighed- Yiren is going to kill me when I tell her I didn't find her

They both left the room, and soon after, the apartment. Leaving the two friends in shock. Lisa remained silent, processing the information: why did Tzuyu send them to look for her, and what did Yiren want with Jennie?

-I knew his smell was familiar- Dudu said with distrust

- Oh yeah, the man in the alley

- What are they talking about?

-That man was in the alley yesterday with two girls

-Tzuyu and Yiren- Lisa answered

-I thought that pair couldn't hold each other- Rose said, more than confused.

-Yerin suspected that Tzuyu had feelings for me but she never gave it much importance

-Well, he wasn't wrong- Rose said ironically.

-Dudu, what else do you know?

-Tzuyu wants to kill you- answered the rude Blue

-That?

-Not only that, Yerin wants to make Jennie disappear

-I think at the end of this I'll be the one who needs a psychologist- Rose announced with a slight headache.

-Dudu, take me to Jennie- Lisa ordered decisively.

On the roofs

-Wait! Oh God, I'm going to fall!

-Rose you just have to jump

-That's easy for you to say, Lalisa, with these little legs I'll never reach that roof!

-What are you waiting for? Get going or more cats will arrive in the area! - warned Dudu from the other roof

Finally Rose jumped up and almost screamed proudly at her achievement. But after a dozen houses her poor little feline paws couldn't take any more.

- I give up, this is exhausting!

-Rose, you were a cheerleader in high school

-They never made us jump off roofs in the fucking Lalisa Manoban cheerleading team!

Lisa was radiant. Her feline agility was impeccable, her jumps almost perfect and her mastery on all fours was innate, she looked like a feline from birth.

-My feline name will be Lili- announced Lisa thinking of the nickname that her Nini used to call her.

-What a gay name

-Dudu, yours isn't very serious, let's say.

-Rabbit, don't even talk!

-Well, I'll just be Rose.

-Chae, with that tail and those ears, you look better as a squirrel.

-Shut up Manoban!

-Ok, this apple is missing, we have to hurry up

-There are like a dozen houses, I can't afford any more!

The Russian blue saw Rose panting with exhaustion and knew that at this rate they would never get there.

- Fine. Rabbit, you go with the squirrel, Lili and I will continue on the roof.

-And why is Lalisa still on the roof!?- Rose complained offended.

- Just look at her, she jumps like a flea

Indeed, Lisa was ahead, skilfully leaping from roof to roof. She felt free and agile like she had never felt before. *Being a cat isn't so bad*. She leapt again, euphoric, feeling like her paws were barely touching the ground.

-Hey you!

Lisa stopped instantly, the voice was coming from that house

-Yes, you!

Lisa turned around, she didn't see anyone on the roof.

-Hello?

-On the balcony

Lisa hesitantly walked to the edge and sure enough, a grey cat was looking at her curiously. The feline was nibbling on a plush mouse and quickly changed to a ball of yarn.

-Come on, come here!- ordered the kitten, spinning the yarn between his front legs.

Lisa looked back, Dudu must have been far behind because he still couldn't see her. She decided to obey the feline.

-You are not from this area, Siamese twins are not very common around here.

Lisa saw the average European, wearing a cute shark hat. However, his attitude was strange, reminding her of Seulgi when she was drunk.

- I'm... I'm visiting.

-Oh, how great! - he purred, rubbing himself against the leg of a chair romantically.

-Are you OK?

-Forgive him, he ate too much Catnis

A second feline appeared from inside the house. This one was an orange tabby. The male had a cute bear hat on. Why do they have hats? And unlike the first one, this one seemed to be in his right mind.

- I'm Kook and this is Taeh
-I am Lali... Lili
-Lili? And what brings you here...?
-Hey, you two fools, what are you doing distracting the Siamese?
Both cats looked up at the roof, Dudu had arrived and didn't seem too happy about the interruption.
-Hey Dudu, I'm so glad to see you!
-Cats, they're all the same- snorted the brunette
-We are gay, don't forget it.
-Yeah, that didn't stop you from fucking me that last time, thanks to the cats you didn't impregnate me, you inept- Dudu growled- luckily I'm neutered now
-What Taeh did what!?- exclaimed the rabbit who was watching them from the lower part of the house

Kook gave the feline an intimidating look, apparently he was also unaware of that story.

-You and I will talk about this later.

The common European lowered his ears in submission and lay down on the ground next to his companion.

-Damn, I'm tired, my paws are wet and I think I broke a claw on the roof! Can we continue now? - the squirrel growled next to the Japanese bobtail
-Where are you planning to go?- Kook asked.
- Don't be nosy, Kook, remember that curiosity killed the cat - Dudu said maliciously.
-How grarrious!!
-Taeh- Kook silenced him- Come on, where are you going?
-To the Kim mansion, we're looking for Chu and Nini!
-Doe!

-Mmm... I don't think they're there- commented the Orange tabby
- No?
-Kai will make his mark official- explained the feline
-What brand?- Lili asked.
- Don't you know? Nini accepted him as her male
"What does that mean?" the Thai woman asked, starting to get alarmed.
-It means that he is your partner now

The hairs on the Siamese's back stood up in disgust, and her dominant side was quick to make itself felt.

-Where are they?
- In Kai's backyard, he made a drinking spree to celebrate
-What the hell is a glutton?- asked the confused Australian.
- Oh, it's what humans call a party- explained the rabbit.
-And why that name?
-What do they do at a party except swallow and drink?
-Ok, good point
-Enough, tell me right now where that idiot Kai lives- Lisa growled.
"Why the rush?" the feline wanted to know.
-Jennie Kim is my cat and I won't let any fucking feline take her away from me.
-Late but sure, you had to lose her to realize that you loved her, right idiot? - the squirrel mocked, rolling his eyes.

Both males exchanged confused glances. Who were those two felines and why did they want to prevent Kai from having Nini? However, there was something they did not understand.

-Who the hell is Jennie Kim?
.
.
.

Cat fight

-Holy Cats, this is disgusting!- Jisoo made a face when she saw the menu -Oh God, it's alive! Get that thing away from me!- She jumped onto her sister's back with a disgusted expression, leaving the cat who was carrying the food confused.

-Chu, we are cats, this is what we eat- she commented dully, watching the little rodent escape. As much as seeing her old group made her happy, she still missed her other life and her human. Lisa

- I know, but there's a grill there, you can cook at least, we're not animals either!

-Chu, we are animals

-And she had it in her mouth! Do you know how many bacteria a cat has in its mouth? How do I know it doesn't have rabies? Chu dropped down on the grass in surrender. -I miss Rose, she always gave me chicks... I liked those weird Thai girls, Mini Laisa and...

But she stopped when she saw the tears in her sister's eyes. Although Jennie was trying not to think about Lisa, was that possible?

- I don't understand how Kai's bite turned you back into a feline- he quickly changed the subject to distract his sister.

- What I don't understand is why you also became a cat.

-Maybe because it was you who transformed me. When you become a cat again, I also return to my natural state.

- I'm sorry Chu, I know you liked being human

The feline shrugged, reserving herself on the grass.

- I used to like fried chicken and I do now too. Nothing has changed! - he joked, trying to cheer up his sister without success - Listen Jennie, I don't think this thing with Kai will work...

-Don't call me that again! Jennie disappeared, I'm Nini, I never stopped being one and...!

-Hey, did you hear that?- a Bengali intervened.

-What do you want Jin?

-Cat Fight!- exclaimed another kitty in the distance

All the felines approached the place where the growls and snorts were coming from. The black fur jumped like cotton mops in the air.

-Who's hair is being trimmed? I hope it's that ugly black Persian because...

-Hey, I'm here! - the feline complained.

- Oh no Jihyo, I was talking about another horrible Persian!

The cat growled at Chu before walking away. Nini, on the other hand, was attentive to the dispute. What was happening?

-Lili, that's not Kai!

Lisa stopped attacking, leaving the feline's ear between her fangs and her paw on its neck. She moved away a little and looked at the fearful, hairy animal.

- Aren't you Kai? - she finally asked the feline beneath her.

-Of course not!

Lisa quickly stepped back and looked around. Cats' scents were stronger than humans', and their senses were more sensitive. Their noses picked up scents in a different way, nothing like humans'.

The Siamese sat gracefully and licked her paw delicately, pretending as if nothing had happened.

A little further away, Nini and Chu were trying to find out who had started the fight.

- Can you see anything?

-Are you serious Chu? If you're on my back, you're supposed to be the one who should see

-Oh holy cat!

-That!?

-Mother of all felines, what a beauty!

-What the hell are you watching Chu!?

-There are two new cats in the neighborhood- explained a cat next to Jennie- one of them just gave JB what he deserved for no reason at all

- He deserved it for impregnating my sister- commented a feline purring with pleasure

-What? And what are you doing here?- the brunette wanted to know, still trying to see beyond the pack of cats.

-The Siamese is looking for Kai- explained the same cat

Nini made a confused face. Is it some kind of adventure of Bombay's? *Maybe she's in heat and that's why she came looking for him* . She took her sister off her back and slipped between the cats. She needed to find out who it was.

-Enough Lili, it's not him either!

Nini widened her eyes, the feline mentioned was as big as a male and her fur looked shiny and silky. Cat shampoo? *Possibly* . But it was seeing her eyes, a deep and penetrating blue, that for some reason made her shudder.

-Nini!

The aforementioned jumped in astonishment and backed away when she saw the feline running towards her. Would she hit her? Would she know that she was now with Kai and get even? She arched her back at the same time that her tail fluffed up in a sign of danger.

Lili, seeing the action, stopped her step, sensing the feline's warning.

-Who are you?

-I...

-Fuck Lisa, you're going to kill every black cat in the place! What part of being a Bombay didn't you understand?

Nini ignored the feline that had just arrived, her mind only focused on the name she had pronounced and her entire body shuddered at the mere mention

- Lisa?

- Yes, I'm Lisa, your Lili!

Lisa smiled between purrs as she watched her ragdoll run towards her, but when she realized that her eyes were reflecting anger, she tried to escape from the feline.

The squirrel watched in surprise as Nini threw herself at the Siamese. Both felines rolled on the grass amid a meow of complaint from Lisa and a growl from Nini.

- No Nini, leave her!

-That's Nini, bite his back!

Dudu looked at Chu reproachfully. The feline was making movements with her paws as if she had a punching bag in front of her.

-We are supposed to stop her, not encourage her to continue.

- Oh yes, you're right, but first... - she turned to where her sister remembered the Siamese - Break her tail Nini, they'll show you who's boss!!

Finally Nini stopped. She was on top of the Thai girl. She was angry but the cat's own scent beneath her was turning her on in a carnal way. Why did her body act like this in front of Lalisa Manoban, as a human and as a feline?

-What are you doing here?

-I came for you Jennie, I want you to come home.

- I'm home now- she contradicted- How are you a cat?

-Beautiful cat

-Hyuna!- Nini growled at the intervention of the feline in heat

- Jennie, I'm not leaving without you- Lisa clarified, sitting in front of her.

- It's too late Lisa, I'm already with someone else

-With who?

-With me

Lisa saw a mustard-eyed, jet-black feline approaching from the crowd with an air of grandeur. She frowned as she saw the Bombay stop in front of her.

- Are you Kai? - Lisa looked at the feline with a grimace. He wasn't pretty at all.

-Who are you?- asked the Bombay arrogantly.

- I am Lalisa Manoban, and that feline belongs to me

Kai let out a menacing growl, approaching Nini.

- Don't tell me this is the Lisa you left me for?

-Hey black, she never belonged to you!- Chu exclaimed reluctantly among the furry crowd.

-Now yes, and I won't let...

But Lisa had already pounced on her. Nini's eyes widened as she watched the Thai, now Siamese, biting and scratching the feline. She growled and attacked like a true expert cat, and for some reason Lisa's warrior attitude excited her.

-You're very obvious Nini, it's obvious that you want that Siamese to pass her rough tongue over your...

-Dudu!- under the ragdoll's fur her cheeks had turned deep pink, luckily for her, the hair hid it

-That's Lisa, bite his dick! What do I mean, dick!? Rip off his hairy black balls!

-Chi, which side are you on!?- her sister scolded her.

-Lisa's of course! Have you seen how sexy she is as a cat? It makes you want to... oooh!

-The one who will leave you without a tail will be me, you chicken with legs!

- Are you...?- Jisoo looked at the American Curl without understanding. But only one person spoke to her that way- Rose?

-Isn't it obvious?

Finally, and with much fuss, Kai's owners came to the yard, finishing the feast. The poor feline had ended up with a bitten paw and a scratch on his left eye.

-This won't stay like this, cat- warned the feline in his owner's arms.

"Human," Lisa corrected him with an air of superiority.

Kai was taken inside the house by his owner to heal his wounds, while the 6 felines took refuge in a nearby bush.

-Did you see the bald spot he left?- Chu mocked amusedly.

"I'm still spitting out hair," Lisa complained between coughs.

-Why did you say all that?- Jennie continued, distancing herself from her. She still won't forgive her for what happened.

-Because it's true Jen, I want you back

-What happened to Yiren?- he asked in a bitter tone.

-I always thought Yiren was the love of my life- the Siamese confessed, lowering her ears in a sign of submission- but I was wrong. I didn't love Yiren half as much as I love you- Lisa cut the space with the brunette- I'm in love with Jennie Kim…

- Jennie Kim disappeared- Nini said in disgust. After all, she had become a feline again.

-I know, and I happen to be in love with Nini too- Nini swallowed hard, trying not to throw herself at the Thai girl, but Lisa wasn't willing to leave without her feline- I love you, as Nini or as Jennie… as a cat and as a woman

- Lili…

Lisa used her paw to remove one of the pendants that had formed the amulet from her neck. She grabbed the thread from which the drop of rose quartz hung with her snout and placed it at Nini's paws.

-You are my other half, you complete me

-I'm scared Lisa, I don't want to suffer anymore

-Let me prove to you that it won't be like that.

-I don't know, I...

-Stop rejecting her and kiss her or I will!

-Rabbit!- Dudu growled beside her

Nini smiled and put her nose against the Thai girl's, rubbing it gently, and soon after she left a lick on her cheek.

-But Lisa, how will you turn back into a human? I'm a cat now and I don't think I can...

Lisa put a paw in her mouth to silence her.

-My physical condition doesn't matter, if I'm with you, none of that matters to me.

The feline denied

-But what about your job, and your family...?

-Fuck Nini, he said he doesn't care!!!- Chu exclaimed impatiently

-Ok, this is all great, but I do want to be human again!- Rose shrieked upset- I'm not going to eat rats and cat food, let alone piss in a litter box! Besides, what will happen to my job, my patients!?

-Forget about your job, you have me

Rose looked at Chu who smiled mischievously between Purrs

-I WANT MY LIFE BACK!- the Australian woman shouted, glaring at the feline and pointing at her with a paw- You, you turned me into this monstrosity!

-Hey!- the rest of the kitties exclaimed, offended.

- I'll kill you Kim Jisoo!

Meeting on the rooftops

- I can't believe it's really you

Lili and Nini moved away from the felines as soon as the squirrel jumped on poor Chu. It was a new experience, a date on the rooftops? Lisa had never imagined something so strange in her life, of course the fact that she was a cat already broke all her expectations. But she didn't want to be anywhere else at that moment.

Up there on the roof they had a great view of Seoul. Who would have thought that cats had that kind of view? *Beautiful* .

-This is a dream- whispered the Siamese, enraptured by the sight.

- Yes... you are a dream- whispered Nini between sighs, that Siamese was everything she wanted. She was big and beautiful, with an elegant bearing. How come I hadn't noticed before how attractive Siamese were? *Because I am interested in this Siamese in particular.*

-Did you spend a lot of time on the rooftops?

- Oh no, we were afraid of getting pregnant, Jisoo almost died when Jin was going to ride her

-And what happened?

- She sent a maid, the woman came out in time and threw a slipper at the poor guy, after that we had to take care of him. Although Jisoo always went to the neighbor's house when she was in heat

-Is that where Jin lives?

- No, they have a pet chicken there...

Lisa made a confused face. Could a feline want a chicken to mount her? Chu was very strange.

-She must be very sad without you- for a moment Lisa was saddened by the little girl. She had also been affected when Jennie left her apartment, after all the felines were Ella's.

Nini lowered her ears sadly, she missed the little girl, but she didn't want to be away from her Lili, not again. Her eyes sparkled with an idea

-Come on Lisa, follow me!

They both set off across the rooftops. Lisa didn't know where they were going, but she didn't hesitate to follow Jennie, she trusted her.

On the other hand, the squirrel was more than furious, after her fight with Chu, Dudu had to intervene. And disgusted, she walked away from the place.

-Damn chicken-eating cat!- She snorted angrily, after all it had been Jisoo's fault

-Rose?

The named one growled when she recognized the voice.

-Go away Jisoo or I'll bite your paws!

- Not my little paws!

Seeing the feline innocently hiding her front paws made her shudder, but she tried to act strong.

-What do you want?

-Why did you attack me?

-Why? If you hadn't bitten us back then, I'd still be a happy human with a great salary and beautiful blonde hair! Instead, I'm here like a fucking cat!

-Beautiful cat!- Jisoo corrected, fascinated by the feline version of the girl.

The Australian looked at the feline and for a moment forgot all her anger. How was that possible?

-I'm still mad at you Kim Jisoo!- she lied nervously

-Come on Squirrel, let's make love, not war- she commented flirtatiously.

Rose rolled her eyes

-so many movies affected you

- You didn't think the same about those techniques I learned about how to put my fingers in...

-Kim Jisoo!

-That's what you were telling me last night, kitty, Miaw! he winked, making the American Curl blush.

ooo

Jennie and Lisa finally stopped, and the Thai girl immediately recognized the Kim mansion, after all, they had gone to look for Chu there.

-Your home?- he asked suspiciously. What were they doing there?

-I want you to meet my first love

Lisa didn't have time to speak. She saw the feline climbing the tree and didn't take long to invite her. Her first love? She immediately went on alert, she wouldn't hesitate to attack any cat.

They entered the mansion through the second-floor window and walked through the dimly lit room, which was not very difficult for them, since night vision allowed them to see perfectly.

Lisa noticed a bed and on it a bundle wrapped in sheets

Nini let out a couple of meows and the Siamese backed away when she saw the bundle moving.

-Nini?- a sweet, sleepy voice asked from over the bed. Lisa saw the little girl lean over to turn on the light, revealing a pretty little girl with feline eyes almost as pretty as her human Nini's. -Nini!

The feline immediately climbed onto the bed and began to rub against the minor with affection, she had missed her former owner.

- Oh Nini, where have you been? Where is Chu? - she hugged the feline tightly - why did they leave me? Do they not love me anymore?

Lisa's heart broke as she watched the little girl sob and instinctively she climbed into bed to comfort her as well.

Seeing the feline, she stopped and wiped her tears, amazed.

-And who are you?- she touched the Siamese cat with doubt and Lisa immediately began to purr. She climbed onto the little girl's legs making her smile- how cute! Is she a friend?

Romantic Nini attached herself to Lisa and gave her a lick on her snout, surprising the little girl who understood what was happening.

- Oh, is it...? Is it your girlfriend Nini? - she lowered her melancholic gaze - you left because you're in love... - she whispered - it's okay Nini, I don't mind being alone. At least you'll be happy

The visit with the little girl had been painful, both felines had stayed with her until she finally gave in to sleep, only then were both cats able to leave the room.

"I missed her a lot," Nini confessed with pity. They had gone up to the roof of the mansion

- It's normal Nini, she's your owner
-She's a good girl, her parents don't spend any time with her.
-How can parents not pay attention to their daughter?
- It's just that Ella... well, she's not entirely normal.
-What are you talking about?
-She can't walk Lisa, for her parents, she is a burden

Lisa remembered the little girl and the wheelchair next to the bed, but she didn't find it a burden.

-I think she's a wonderful girl, it's their loss.
- Yes, but she is the one who suffers for it. She is always alone.

Lisa looked up at the sky and nodded.

-From now on, Nini won't be here- The feline looked at her without understanding- we will come every day to see her

The ragdoll's eyes lit up

-Oh really?
- I want her to continue being part of your life, and you of hers.
.
.
.

Mochi on the attack

-Squirrel...?

-Hmm?

-Are you mad at me for biting you?

-Kim Jisoo, why else would I hang you from the tree!?

The American Curl watched the ragdoll from the ground. Hanging the feline with a rope had been a challenge on her small furry body. But she had been a girlscout, and could tie knots and traps in no time.

-How did you do this without thumbs!?

-I can tie knots even with my tongue, darling

-How versatile! You must do amazing things with that tongue.

Jisoo purred flirtatiously.

-Jisoo!

She was hanging by her tail, which made her end up upside down in the tree.

-We should kiss...

-Why should I kiss you?

-Because I'm upside down

-AND?

-I feel like Spiderman, only in this case Catwoman will kiss me!

Rose rolled her eyes, holding back a smile. The feline was quite a case. She was about to respond when a suffocating heat began to invade her spine, sending shockwaves through her pelvic area, causing her to arch her back in an unusual way for her.

-Fuck, what the...? - her southern area felt hot and humid, making the Australian feel strangely uneasy- what the hell is this!

Chu watched as the squirrel began to rub itself on the grass, and to emit some very erotic purrs that undoubtedly began to cause need in her. She knew perfectly well what was happening to her and it was not good at all with her tied up.

-Squirrel, untie me!

But Rose ignored her. She felt doped up. Had she been drugged? But beyond the enchantment, she felt a strong need for...

-Jisoo, take me!- the words came out pleadingly from his snout. He didn't even have time to think about it, his animal instinct demanded it- Now!

The Australian's desperate meows had the poor feline in tears, and that plaintive song was the feline's call to mate. She was inviting Jisoo to fuck her, and she wasn't going to refuse. But tied up, it was impossible for her.

-Mmm, but what a nice little gift... meow!

Jisoo froze upon hearing that purring voice.

-Shit...

From among the bushes appeared a wide-eyed orange Persian, wagging his tail with dominance as he walked toward the American Curl.

-Your scent is...Meow, Exquisite!- he purred, rubbing himself against the tree.

-Mochi, cat face, get away from her! She's my female!

-And miss that? - He pointed with his paw at the feline who was beginning to raise her tail suggestively, giving the male an excellent view of her feline intimacy - very nice.

-Fuck, will you shut up and fuck me already!?

-Grrr, how greedy, meow!

The feline was already ready to possess her when a growl made him stop, at the same time he was hit on the ground.

-You touch her and I'll rip your ears off!

Dudu was standing over the cat in a threatening manner. His hatred for the feline that impregnated his female was such that he could tear its head off right there.

-That's my cat! - exclaimed the rabbit, approaching Dudu with Nini - God cat, how her wild side excites me!

-Don't kill me! You're not going to leave 35 kittens without their father, are you?

-Fuck, have you fucked so many cats?

-What can I tell you... I'm a very helpful guy.

-It's true, even I get pissed off!

-Taeh!- Kook growled next to him with a bad face. He gave the Persian a look of hatred- I'll kill him.

-No, kook, no!!

-That's it kook, break his legs!- Chu yelled from the tree- by the way, what about Lila?

Everyone fell silent, including the two males who were attacking each other, when they heard some pleading meows. But it was Chu who was the first to react.

-Lalisa Manoban!

-Hey, even he pronounced his name correctly!- exclaimed Rabbit surprised.

-With that, who wouldn't do it?- Dudu mentioned ironically.

Both of them watched the scene again. Above Rose was Lisa, biting her back like a dominant male about to penetrate her. Rose's scent not only disturbed the males, but also the dominant cats, and Lisa, in her inexperience as a feline, was more prone to fall into temptation.

-Oh my god, Lalisa, I swear I'm going to kill you when I get over my heat, but right now I need you inside, damn it!

-I'm not going to fuck a bitch...!

-Lalisa!- the growl came this time from the younger ragdoll. Nini was tense with her eyes flashing with anger- consider yourself dead Manoban!

-Nini, this is not what it seems! - Lisa tried to defend herself without much control.

-Oh no, you're just biting the back of your friend's neck wanting to fuck her... Nothing much, huh?

-Doe!

Lisa's eyes widened as she watched the feline run in her direction and only then did she let go of her friend's neck. *Holy crap, Jennie's going to kill me!* She ran as fast as her four legs would allow her.

-Don't you swear, you traitorous cat! - Jisoo shouted instead.

-That's it Nini, control that beast!

-Rabbit, shut up and help me stop her before she kills Lalisa- asked Dudu, running after the felines.

-Meow, where did that Siamese come from!?!- Mochi purred still trapped under Kook- I like them dominant!

-Well then you'll like what I'm going to do to you, because... Aush! Taeh, why are you scratching me?

- Are you going to grab Mochi in front of me!? All cats are the same!

- What? I didn't mean that, I meant...

-Lalisa Manoban, don't leave me like this! - Rose, with her excitement at its peak, ran after the felines, in need of affection.

-Wait pretty kitty, I can give you the love you need!- exclaimed the Persian escaping from the male's grip to chase the Australian in heat- Let's make it eternal!! At least until another cat in heat appears...- he whispered that last thing without stopping running

- Stop, I'm not done with you!!

-Kook, don't even think I'll let you fuck that furball, you can only make me meow!

-That's it Taeh, don't lose sight of your male! - Jisoo encouraged him. Everyone had apparently left, leaving her there, still upside down in the tree - wait a minute... GET ME DOWN FROM HERE!!! - she squealed between meows. But she stopped when she realized that no one came to her call. She pouted, looking towards the place where everyone had gone - don't leave me here alone... - she whispered melancholically.

-Oh no Chu... You're not alone...

-Holy cat that just gave birth, the crybaby!
-What? I'm not even crying. It's me, Hyuna.
Jisoo looked at the feline near the tree and widened her eyes.
-HELP!!!

◈ ◈ 🐱 ◈ ◈

-Oush, Oush, Oush...
-Stop complaining Manobal!
-It wasn't you who was thrown off the roof Jisoo!
-They left me hanging like a prey! Hyuna fell and raped me!
-What are you two complaining so much!? I almost got fucked by a fucking cat, and Lalisa... Wait a minute...- she turned to look at the older ragdoll reproachfully- who the fuck is Hyuna?
-Oh, Hyuna is a crazy cat who harasses Chu
-She's terrifying, she used to sneak in through Ella's window to watch me sleep!
-Hyuna...- Rose clenched her fangs tightly . *I'll take care of that.*

Union under the stars

-You're almost there! Just a little more! Lisa, you're not doing it right, you have to...!

-Shut up Chaeyong, it's not that simple!- the Siamese continued her work, with difficulty putting her paw in the fish tank- wait, I think I've already...

-Lisa!- Rose climbed up when she saw her friend fall into the fish tank- let me help you, don't go... wait, wait!!

But it was too late, Rose tried to grab her friend, but the Siamese in her panic pulled her with her, making the Australian fall into the water with her.

-Lalisa!

-Oh god, we're going to drown! - meowed the desperate Thai, trying to get out of the water.

-If I die in this fucking fish tank I'll kill you!

-Wow, looks like someone needed a bath before the ceremony- Mina's mocking voice sounded from the entrance- Mintty, get a towel!- she shouted as she brought the felines out.

Rose, snorting, climbed onto the couch. Her fur was thicker than Lisa's, so she weighed twice as much.

-Here you go... Aww, Rose, you look adorable!

The aforementioned let out a growl and turned her back on her friend to continue drying herself with her tongue. In those days as felines they had had to adapt to the change, although they could not even try to catch a mouse, much less a canary.

Flashback

-Come on, just eat it!

-Kim Jisoo, I'm not going to eat that thing! Oh god, it's looking at me!- he covered his face with his furry little paws.

"He's dead," Jennie explained, placing a mockingbird in front of Lisa's paws. Her fur fluffed up as she looked at the Siamese and she purred, rubbing her nose against the other's. "I hope you like it, I caught him myself!"

Lisa looked doubtfully at the little feathered creature with some pity. Even though he was dead, what should she do?

-Oh thanks Nini, this looks...- she glanced at the bird and swallowed- delicious...

The ragdoll purred happily and rubbed against the Siamese's neck tenderly.

-Wait a minute, why the fuck do they give Lisa a fat fucking nightingale, while they give me...!? This!

-Hey, don't be ungrateful, it was hard for me to catch it!- Chu complained, lowering his ears in nostalgia.

- Did it cost you to catch a damn cockroach!?- Rose saw the insect and jumped with her hair standing on end - God, it moved a leg!!!

End of flashback

After weeks, Mina and the girls found out about her change and it wasn't easy to assimilate, especially for Seulgi who almost fainted when she saw Jisoo typing on the laptop with reading glasses on the bridge of her little snout.

-Lisa was right, Jisoo is terrifying with those glasses- commented Mintty

-Is that the only thing that scares you? Because I'm terrified of seeing that!

They all turned to where the girl was pointing.

-Look on the bright side, if Chu didn't know how to write, we wouldn't know right now that those two balls of fur are Lisa and Chae- she said naturally while reading what the feline was writing.

They all assimilated what was said.

-What Lisa and Rose what!??

End of flashback

Mina continued drying her sister. She noticed that the feline was a bit anxious and finding her in the fish tank trying to catch Seulgi's fish proved it.

-Everything will be fine unnie

-Well, it would look better if you at least used a bow, look!- Seulgi took out a small cat dress from a bag- Rose will look sexy in this other one- she took out a similar one but shorter- showing off her sexy hairy legs

Both Mina and Mintty burst out laughing as they watched the Australian growl grumpily as she left the room, not without first scratching Seulgi.

-Ouch, what did I do!?

-Girls, what are you waiting for, it's getting late!- Irene's voice echoed in the hallway, as she looked at a tablet- we have to follow the itinerary

-Baby, stop being an assistant for a moment, it's a party!- Seulgi mocked

Irene glared at her and then continued with her schedule.

-Someone has to make sure nothing is forgotten

-Like what?

-Like the cake for example

Seulgi widened her eyes as she realized that she had indeed forgotten the cake in her bakery.

-Shit!

The assistant smiled triumphantly, looking at the feline this time. Finding out that her boss was a cat was strange, but it didn't surprise her as much as it did the Thai women.

-Lisie, if you leave now we'll get there on time.

-How did you take it so well that Lisa was a cat? - Mina asked.

-Well, maybe because I had already gotten over the shock with Jennie and Jisoo- he shrugged- and a cat typing on my tablet is not something you see every day.

-You were lucky, at least he didn't wear glasses with you- Mintty commented amused.

-Ok, enough with the talks -Mina took her sister in her arms- it's time

◈◈🐱◈◈

-Oh god, there are cats all over the place!- exclaimed Chitthip looking around- and what are we supposed to do on the balcony?

-Mom, it's a party. Let's say they are invited.

-Where is Lalisa? You told me that... Oh my god, she wants to attack me! - she announced, upset, seeing a feline stick to her leg.

Mina rolled her eyes and picked up her sister who was trying to give affection to her mother.

-I was just saying hello to you.

-Mina Manoban, get those cats off the roof, their fur is allergic! Look, that animal has rabies!

Mina Mirto towards the snack table, where the feline was happily devouring a piece of the cake

-Mother, this is Chu and that is frosting

Everyone started to take their seats. The idea of doing it on the balcony had been Mintty's, after all they couldn't fit all those cats into Seulgi's apartment. Lisa had wanted it to be in Bangkok, in the presence of her parents, which had been a challenge.

-There, those were the last ones- exclaimed Mintty exhaustedly opening the last cage of cats- remind me to kick Lisa's ass when I'm done, that will be my wedding present

Everyone fell silent as the music started playing. In front of them was a beautiful arch of sunflowers, and just below was Lisa waiting with a white rose in her mouth and her eyes full of tears.

-Aww, look at her, she's happy!- Seulgi exclaimed, touched.

Mina frowned as she noticed her sister was a little uncomfortable.

-Seu, did you remove the thorns from the rose before giving it to her?

The named one covered her mouth thoughtfully

-Oops, I think I forgot that little detail...

On the other hand, the Siamese's nerves were greater than her pain. How long should she endure the thorns sticking into her tongue? *Damn Seulgi, I'll scratch her while she sleeps.* But all her thoughts of revenge vanished when she saw the entrance of the ragdoll. Everything lost importance, her sight was focused on her Nini as she approached her timidly and excitedly in a pretty white tutu. Behind her, Moon carried a pillow with a small box on it on her back, and further back Namjoon was trying to take off his tie and his mother was pulling his ear with her teeth as a reprimand.

-Lili..- the feline sighed when she was close to the Siamese. And Lisa altered all her senses

-Nini- he answered in a whisper

-Alright, let's get started with this!

They both looked ahead confused as they saw who would be in charge of directing the wedding.

-Chu?

-Obviously, who else was going to marry them!?

-Kim Jisoo, come here immediately!- the American curl's growl made her raise her tail and ears in happiness. Hearing Rose always managed to excite her.

-Don't be afraid, darling, there goes your cat!

Lili rolled her eyes, turning her attention back to Jennie. Soon, Joy, the shepherd's cat, took Jisoo's place in front of the couple.

-On this starry night, we will begin the union of these two felines who have decided to unite their souls in sacred matrimony! - the feline began seriously.

While the cat spoke, all the felines remained silent, attentive to Joy's words, something similar to the human guests, although for different reasons.

"What are they supposed to be saying?" Seu whispered curiously.

"I don't know, I don't speak cat language," Mintty replied with a shrug.

-Now you can say your votes

Lisa took a deep breath before speaking. This really made her nervous.

-If you had told me a couple of months ago that my life would end this way, I would have laughed until I cried- he began with irony- but here I am, in my home country, about to give myself to the woman...

-Cat!

-Jisoo!- the Australian scolded her.

-To the cat I love- Lisa corrected- so with the moon as my witness, I, Lalisa Manoban...

-Lili!

-Jisoo, if you keep interrupting, I'll give you a damn bosal!- threatened the squirrel, about to lose patience.

-I promise to love you and take care of you every day of my 9 feline lives until I run out of breath

Nina was fluffy like a cotton ball. This touched her in many ways.

-Nini, it's your turn- Joy brought her out of her trance

- Oh yeah! - Nini looked at the feline and then at the Siamese smiling tenderly at the latter - From the first moment I saw you I knew I didn't want to belong to anyone but you - she looked at the sky and smiled at the wide variety of stars that shone that night - I loved you instantly Lisa, and tonight I thank that star, our star, for having fulfilled my wish, because thanks to it I was able to get you to fall in love with me - she sighed - I love you Lili, every inch of me belongs to you - she lowered her face shyly - I'm sorry you can't be human again

- Jen, I don't have to be human to be happy. You're all I need.

-Oh god, I think I'm going to cry!

-Don't be dramatic, they're just two fucking cats meowing.

-You have no imagination Mintty!

-Shut up you two!- Mina silenced them, smiling as she watched the two felines join their snouts to close the bond.

-My favorite part is coming...- Chu whispered, rubbing his paws anxiously.

Suddenly, in front of all the guests, humans and cats alike, they witnessed how that feline kiss full of feelings was enough to create a flash of light on the threshold. Both Lisa's and Jennie's bodies shone in a halo of golden light that gradually increased in size and changed shape just like the two felines.

-Fuck, is that...?

-That will be her curse, and it will only be broken with a kiss. Then, it will take the form of her true love...- Chu whispered seriously.

Mina frowned, looking at the black-haired girl.

-Jisoo, is that Sheck's?

They all widened their eyes

-Jisoo!- they all shouted in unison when they saw the feline again in her human body.

-That's my name

-You are human!

-Of course I'm not...- but when she looked at her hands she confirmed that it was true- Mother cat, I'm beautiful again!- she looked at the felines who were looking at her with shock- No Chu, Kim Jisoo has become bastards!

-Jisoo, watch that vocabulary!

As she turned around, Jisoo was enthralled by the sight of the Australian

-Squirrel! You're human!

-And you're naked!- Mina announced, covering her eyes, blushing.

-Oh god, Marcos, look, your daughter is naked! Park Chaeyong, put some clothes on right now!

On the other hand, Lisa and Jennie were not usually surprised. Not even in their 9 feline lives had they imagined that they could become human again.

Lisa took her now wife's hand and kissed it

-Lalisa, can you explain to me what's going on here!?

-It's very simple, mother, I fell in love with my cat- he explained, looking into the eyes of the girl with whom he hoped to share the rest of his life, and that girl was none other than Jennie Kim, a cat who wished to be human.

End...?

Epilogue

1 year later...

-Honey, hurry up, Jisoo must be scared!

The Thai girl left the apartment looking ironically at her girlfriend.

-Knowing Jisoo, the doctor must be deaf with her screams.

Jennie smiled, shaking her head, and closed the space between them, standing on her tiptoes and giving her a small but tender kiss that made the taller girl sigh. After becoming human, the girls had returned to Korea, back to their human lives.

The kiss changed from sweet to intense, managing to stir something in the blonde's belly.

-How about we just go back home and...?

-Lili, you haven't gone into heat yet- the Korean girl complained amused. Although they had become human again, both Rose and Lisa had retained a part of their animal attitude.

The Thai woman shrugged as she walked towards the car.

-I don't need to be in heat to want you- he winked at her, remembering that Nini had said something similar to him in the past- let's go

-Yes, or he'll kill me if he realizes I'm not here.

-Oh come on Jen, at a time like that I doubt Jisoo would notice.

Meanwhile in the hospital...

-JENNIEEEE!!!

The screams of the black-haired girl reigned in the hospital corridors, reaching the ears of her friends who waited nervously in the waiting room.

-Poor Jisoo...

-No, poor Jennie, it will be her funeral- Mintty argued.

-Lisa is a wild girl since she became human again, they fuck like rabbits

-I don't fuck like that!- a white-haired girl growled, offended.

-Nayeon, it's just an expression- Mintty clarified, rolling her eyes- and where did Dahyun go?

-Oh, he's with Nam and Moon in the hospital garden. You know how they like to hunt butterflies.

-And eat them by the way

Although, after months Jennie had decided to do the same with Rabbit and Dudu, and she couldn't leave the children behind. Dudu didn't take too long to take up with humans to support his family and although it was a little more difficult for Rabbit, she also adapted perfectly.

Shortly after, a purple-haired girl came in carrying two little ones, accompanied by Lisa and Jennie.

-I met these two at the entrance- Dahyun mentioned with irony

-How is Jisoo doing?

-Since he entered the operating room he has not stopped cursing you.

-He's going to kill me

-Look on the bright side, if Lisa is widowed Irene will have a chance...

-Mintty is that supposed to be the good side!?- Seulgi growled angrily

The named shrugged her shoulders

-For Irene yes

Back in the delivery room...

-Come on honey, push, almost there! - the doctor encouraged her - just a little more, it's not that difficult!

-If it's so easy, why don't you do it!?- Jisoo growled between gasps, the pain was incomparable- Holy crap, I'm going to burst!

-Jisoo, calm down, you have to relax

-Look what you did to my beautiful body!!! I look like a...!- she stopped at the pain of a new contraction- a fucking barrel!!!

Rose rolled her eyes, she knew as a psychologist that Jisoo's attitude was normal in the middle of labor. Artificial insemination had been her idea, however her uterus rejected the donor again and again, unlike Chu who accepted it at the first opportunity.

-You know I wanted to do it, now stop complaining and push for good!

-AAAAAHHH!!!!

After two hours, the brunette had finally managed to get out of her torment. Two hours of cursing and whining, but she had finally succeeded.

-Doctor, how is my sister?- Jennie asked when she saw him leave.

-Excellent, the little ones are under review, but they will be brought to you in a moment- he announced while taking off his gloves, leaving the brunette relieved with the news- your wife's intervention was amazing

-Rose?- Lisa asked joining the conversation

-He threatened to withhold fried chicken from her if she didn't speed up the delivery, and the girls were soon born!

-Wait a second... the girls?- Dahyun asked, remembering that the brunette had mentioned only one

-Oh yeah. They ended up being twins.

Jisoo was taken to a room where they soon brought the two little girls to her.

-Oh Chu, they are beautiful! - Jennie whispered, touched as she saw one little girl being breastfed by her sister and the other in the arms of the Australian who was in tears.

-Roseanne Park crying? Now I've seen it all.

-Shut up Lisa!- he ordered between sobs

-Congratulations Rosie, you are beautiful- Lisa leaned down to look at the little black-haired girl, she was a tiny vision of the Korean

-Hey girls...

They all looked towards the door where Bambam was watching them with a serious expression. They knew why he was there and it was not exactly the feline's birth.

Lisa, Rose, Mintty and Dahyun left the room to receive the message

-Do you have them?

-D-dragon, Sehun and Tzuyu are behind bars. Sana was saved by the skin of her teeth

Lisa looked at Rose and it was the Australian who spoke for her.

-What happened to...?

-She fled, they are still looking for her

Lisa sighed uneasily. When they returned to Korea, they had filed a report of attempted murder and the police were quick to act. However, Yiren was the one who worried her the most.

-We will find her Lisa, Yiren is not going to touch Jennie

-I hope so Bambam, I hope so...

Inside the room, Nini was lovingly holding one of the little girls.

-They remind me of my little ones- Nayeon commented smiling.

-What are their names?- Mina asked.

-This is Jeongyeon, and that one- he pointed to the one sleeping in Jennie's arms with a nod- is Yeri

Jennie looked at the little girl's hand in her arms confused.

-Jisoo, on the bracelet it says Jeongyeon, not Yire

The black-haired girl checked her other little girl's arm

-Oh, you're right!

-Are you serious Chu, you can't identify your own daughters?

-Let me go Nayeon, I'm a first-time mother!

Nini looked back at the little girl and smiled. What would it be like to have a little girl with Lisa?

Soon the girls entered the room, each trying to hide the information they had received. The best was Rose, who, being a psychologist, knew how to handle her emotions well. With everyone except Jisoo

-Kim Jisoo, stop feeding her, you have to burp her!

-As if it were *Coca-Cola*

-Mintty you don't help

-I fed my kittens until they fell asleep.

-Human children shouldn't be like that- continued Rose taking the little girl from Jisoo- you must feed them just enough and burp them or else they will cry

-Ok Mom Rose, I see that someone studied the subject well.

-Whatever, we are a beautiful happy family!

-No Seu, Jisoo and Rose are, Nayeon and Dahyun too, even Lisa and Jennie...- Mintty intervened- on the other hand I change girls like I change panties, and you... Well you're still waiting for Irene to give you the yes, which I don't think will happen.

-Shut up Minty, we're one big happy family, pet included!

-Speaking of pets, what happened to Leo...?

Everyone was surprised when they remembered the feline. How could they have forgotten it?

Meanwhile in Las Vegas...

-That's it mommy, I won!!!

-Another bowl of milk?

-Skim please, Miaw- Leo winked at the cat he was tending and went back to his card game, leaving his owner and that pile of aggressive cats was the best decision

◇◇🐱◇◇

Back home, Lisa brought down the groceries with Jennie's help. The brunette had a craving for sushi, and what half-feline human would say no to fish?

-Lili...

-Yes Jen?- he asked closing the car

-I'm not going to have kittens

-Pets, love? With the memory of Leo, I think I don't want to have any more animals for a while...

-No Lisa, I mean... I want to be the mother of your children.

Lisa widened her eyes in surprise, then smiled at him without taking it too seriously. A kiss on her lips and finally he took her by the hand to lead her into the apartment.

-As many as you want, love. We should even start procreating tonight- he said that last thing mischievously, making the feline-eyed girl shudder.

Across the sidewalk, a silver Mercedes remained parked. Inside, its driver watched intently as the girls exchanged views and gripped the steering wheel tightly as he watched them kiss.

-Jennie Kim, you're going to pay for taking what belongs to me- she took out a lipstick, and after putting some color on her lips she smiled maliciously and started the car- You'll soon be back to me Lalisa Manoban...

.
.
.
.
.